JESSE DANGELO

BLACKBIRDS DANCE

THE SKINNER SAGA PART 2

Encyclopocalypse Publications
www.encyclopocalypse.com

SPECIAL THANKS

Leah Dawn Baker
Shannon Marie Ettaro
Sean Duregger
Paul Deaux
Natasha Holley
Crystal Cook
Adam Monreale

And my lovely wife, Lauren
For putting up with me
You rock

CONTENTS

Foreword — ix
John Durgin

1. Swamp Justice — 1
2. My Soul To Take — 9
3. Copper — 17
4. Scar Tissue — 23
5. A Call For Help — 33
6. A Well Respected Man — 39
7. Sweet Tooth — 51
8. Dynamic Duo — 61
9. The Rez — 71
10. Stickball — 81
11. The Spirit Council — 91
12. Premonition — 103
13. Medicine Bag — 111
14. Witch Hunt — 121
15. Out Of The Bag — 129
16. Rescue Mission — 137
17. Victimology — 143
18. A Call To Arms — 155
19. Tail — 165
20. The Prophecy — 173
21. Stowaway — 181
22. A Crash And A Scream — 189
23. When Shadows Dance — 197
24. Scene Of The Crime — 205
25. Know When To Run — 215
26. Mean Bone — 229

27. High Roller   239
28. Hot Blooded   253
29. Change Of Plans   261
30. Tactile   269
31. The Executioner   279
32. Blood Storm   283
33. Showdown   295
34. Lead The Way   309
35. Batshit   325
36. Moment Of Truth   335
37. Faith   347
38. Airborne   357
Killer Queen   403

About the Author   427
Also by Jesse D'Angelo   429

FOREWORD
"SHIFTING"

JOHN DURGIN

Back when I was a young boy, I wanted to be an artist. I loved comic books, and the idea of drawing scenes was something that fascinated me. As I grew older, I had dreams of going to art school. I practiced shading, learning proportions, and many other techniques needed to master my artistic ability. I carried my Marvel Comics "How to" book everywhere I went, trying to teach myself the techniques pros use. For those that don't draw, let me tell you something: It's HARD. Like an eye on a face being off a quarter of an inch makes the face distorted hard. You can spend countless hours trying to fix that one eye and make it look right, only to realize the whole time it was the nose that was off.

And then I read *IT*, my first foray into adult horror after a childhood of reading Goosebumps. Suddenly, my dreams changed. I wanted to write horror. I wanted to read everything that Stephen King had ever written. I attempted to write some really awful horror movie scripts and short stories in high school, only to discover the ideas were easier than execution. Let me tell you something about writing as well: It's HARD. Anyone can come up with an idea of a story but putting pen to paper and *telling* that whole story, making it compelling, creating tension, etc., that's a beast of a different nature.

Why am I telling you this stuff about myself? Because I want those of you reading this to understand how hard it is to become good at one of those things, let alone both. And becoming great at both? There are not too many people that can claim that. Tolkien drew art and maps for *The Hobbit*. Brom creates all of his own creatures to go along with his epic tales. There are more, but the point is that naming those artist/author combos isn't easy.

Which brings us to Jesse D'Angelo. The first book of Jesse's that I read was *Doomsday Dogs*, an apocalyptic werewolf novella. I instantly found myself loving his blend of humor, horror, and action. After that, I read *Dying Sheep*, a story from the perspective of a serial killer who returns from the dead to go all Jason Vorhees on their asses, and again noticed the perfect blend of many different genres. So how fitting that the *Skinner* series is about shifting, alternating between two different species. Because that is exactly what Jesse did while creating this series, and all of his books for that matter. This beautiful cover you opened to bring you to these words? Jesse drew that. This epic tale of vengeance, full of action, horror, thriller, and many more genres? Jesse wrote it. Let's go back to the point I made earlier about how difficult it is to master one craft. Jesse has done it with two. He has created a world full of characters that are memorable and unique. Villains that are both terrifying and believable. When I read the first book in this series, *Skinner*, I loved how it felt like a mashup of Action/thriller/horror. I couldn't wait to dig into *Blackbirds Dance*. You never know going into a sequel if it's going to be a collection of the greatest hits from book one, or if it will elevate the series to another level. I'm happy to report the latter with a smile on my face. This book is phenomenal. As well as Jesse can write action scenes and mix in the humor throughout, I personally feel this book has some of the most terrifying scenes he has written as well.

Jesse has shown us that he's a bit of a shifter himself, and this book is the accumulation of that. He's an artist that can write, and a writer that can draw. He can make you laugh, get your heart pounding with an intense action scene, then have your jaw drop open as you read the terror unfolding. When the reader is introduced to the Raven Mocker, they will know exactly what I am talking about. It's been a blast following Will Shaw in the Skinner saga, and I'm excited you get to read this amazing follow-up to the spectacular first book.

With beautiful art, smooth as silk prose, and a plot that keeps you reading, I think it's safe to say this is Jesse D'Angelo's best work to date. So turn the page, spend some time on the Cherokee Reservation.

John Durgin
September, 2024

BLACKBIRDS DANCE

THE SKINNER SAGA PART 2

SWAMP JUSTICE

BAYOU LAFOURCHE, *Louisiana*

AMBER EYES TRACKED TWO TARGETS FROM A CLOAK of blackness.

The pair of horrified rednecks stumbled through the bayou at half-past three in the morning, one of them clutching a bloody left shoulder, his bearded face a sweat-soaked portrait of pain and terror. The other man pulled at his friend's shirt, frantically hurrying them through the bog towards their boat.

"Where is it? W-where is it?" gasped the injured one.

"Come on!" his friend shouted and yanked him along.

The eyes followed them. A cat's eyes.

Claws flexed. A black tail lashed. Bundles of wiry muscles shifted beneath a black coat. He was a master of the shadows. Black on black. And these little men were mice. At any moment he could have pounced, but he preferred to toy with his quarry. With silent footsteps, he slowly trailed them as they limped forward.

Up ahead was a light.

Two more figures stood beside a pickup truck, with a large pirogue boat docked nearby. The headlights shone bright as the two men paced and smoked, waiting for their comrades, pistols holstered at their hips and AR15's ready on the tailgate. A scream snapped them to attention.

"Guys! Guys!"

The terrified men tripped through the shadows towards them, panic in their eyes. The two by the pickup grabbed their rifles as their friends collapsed onto the ground before them.

"Jesus, Wyatt! What the hell—"

"Start the engine and go!" the wounded man begged, staggering back up.

"Wait, where are the kids? What happened?"

"They're gone!" the other man said. "It's after us!"

"Get in the boat! Come on!!" the wounded man insisted, limping as fast as he could and jumping onto the large, flat-bottomed swamp skimmer. "It's gonna kill us! We gotta go *now!*"

The shadow listened and laughed to himself.

They didn't have a chance. He watched as the men with guns jolted their aim left and right, clumsily sweeping the area. Civilians. Amateurs.

"What is it?"

"S-some kind of animal!"

"Will you come on already! It's coming!"

"Go go go!"

The first two men started the engine of the pirogue and the giant fan mounted to the aft of the boat roared to life. The second two cursed at the darkness and jumped into their pickup and threw it into gear, confused and frantic, no idea what they were even running from. The driver hit the gas and tore off down the country lane as the boat zoomed down a parallel channel of the bog.

The shadow made his decision.

The fast-twitch muscle fibers in his black haunches launched him through the air. The men in the cab felt a concussive force as a large, heavy blackness crashed into the bed behind them. The pickup lurched and swerved on the dirt road as the driver struggled to hold the wheel.

"Shit! What the fuck was th—"

The passenger window shattered inward at that moment as a massive, black-furred fist punched through. Five sickle-shaped claws wrapped around the man's face and clenched down into the meat of his head. He howled with blind abandon as the creature raked its talons back out the window, tearing streaks of flesh across his face. Hot blood pumped through his fingers as he struggled to hold his face together.

"Aaaagghhh!! Shit!!"

The driver lost control. The pickup shot around the next corner way too fast. Everything went upside down as the vehicle flipped off the side of the road, cartwheeling into the swamp. It crashed and rolled into a muddy field of reeds and sinkholes, glass shattering, steel bending. It began to sink.

The passenger was motionless and covered in blood, his mangled head hanging low. The driver crawled from his shattered window, filthy, bleeding and rattled. He reached into the cab and pulled out his AR, dragging himself several feet away before he commanded his wobbly legs to stand.

He shouldered the rifle and spun each way, surveying the desolate country landscape. Here the frogs and crickets told no secrets. They were all alone out here in the dark. There was not even the light of the moon, only the broken headlights of the truck to illuminate the bayou.

"W-what...the fuck...are you?"

The shadow circled. He released a growl deep and guttural enough for the devil to hear. His sharp teeth gnashed and his mouth watered. He watched the fear in the little man's eyes intensify. He felt the tainted energy radiate from his target, yellow and stained, moldy-white swirls. A bad man, right down to the core.

The black figure launched through the air and landed on the hood of the pickup. The horrified man froze, trembling. Whatever it was, it crouched like a gargoyle, waiting for him to turn around, a reverberating rumble in its throat. Slowly, the man forced himself to look, as if he'd somehow be able to focus, remain calm, and fire.

His eyes searched the darkness and found more darkness. Blackness. A black blot, huge and crouched, sat on the hood of his truck. Eyes like angry gold. The man tried to scream, but the oxygen decided to suck inward instead. He began to lift the rifle with shaking hands.

The black figure bolted off the hood. Claws and teeth blared. Screams of agony and brutal murder filled the night.

. . .

THE PIROGUE ZIPPED ACROSS THE SURFACE OF THE bayou, skipping and throwing sprays of swamp water in its wake. The giant fan blasted them forward in the darkness, and the wounded man dared to release the pressure from his shoulder to take a look. Thick blood oozed through four parallel slashes. He winced and reapplied pressure, sitting and catching his breath as the other man steered the boat.

"There it is!" the driver pointed and aimed the vessel ahead. The shore was fast approaching, a silver Suburban waiting on its banks. He didn't slow, instead choosing to crash the boat onto the mossy bank and skid to a halt inland. "Come on, Ed!"

"I... I can't, Wyatt... I can't..."

"Come on!"

Wyatt yanked his partner up and dragged him off the boat. He ran ahead through the muck, pulling out his car keys. Ed couldn't help but glance left, right, all around. That thing was still out there. Gasping for air, strength diminishing by the second, he lurched forward as Wyatt unlocked the Suburban and jumped in.

"Come on, God damn it!" Wyatt shouted and slammed the door.

He turned the key in the ignition.

The suburban suddenly erupted in a plume of flames, a concussive wave blasting through the air. Hot shrapnel exploded in all directions, blowing Ed off his feet. He landed by the water, his body ravaged and caked in muck, lacerations etched across his face, and shards of steel imbedded in his guts.

Orange flames howled and burned. The odor of burning human flesh and gasoline floated in clouds of smoke. Ed groaned and tried to move, but pain sliced at him from deep inside, forcing him to stop.

He heard an engine. A vehicle, a car. Its low grumble teased from a cloak of darkness. Ed turned his head to the side so he could see the road before him. It was a country lane, just dirt and rocks with rows of bald cypress trees on either side. It stretched out and faded into pure blackness. But then through the black curtain, two lights appeared in the distance. Headlights.

The grumble of a 360 horsepower LT1 350 cubic inch V-8 intensified and the lights grew brighter as the vehicle approached. Gravel and twigs crackled beneath its tires. Orange and yellow flames reflected off its polished-black paint job. A 1970 1/2 Chevy Camaro Z28, the mechanical beast crept into the fire-lit clearing, engine growling like a predator. Ed watched helplessly as the classic muscle car came to a halt. The driver's door opened.

Will Shaw stepped out.

He strolled around to the front of his car, observing the death furnace before him. From Ed's perspective, the tall Indian was a silhouette accented by the fire light. He wore dark slacks and black, steel-toed boots. A black leather jacket accentuated his already broad shoulders and athletic build. Hearing the pained grunts and fidgeting from the wounded man, he casually made his way over.

Ed trembled as Will walked up to him.

"P-please..." Ed begged, "There's something out there! An animal... A-a fucking monster!"

Will did not move or say a word.

"Please! We have to get out of here! *Hnng!* Th-that thing is coming!"

Will did not move or say a word.

"Who the hell are you? Wh-what do you want?"

Will took a step closer and spoke in a smooth Kentucky drawl. "How ya doin', Ed? Those little girls are back with their families now. Thought you might wanna know."

"Oh God, please! I never touched those girls! I-I swear!"

"Nah, you were just fixin' to sell 'em off to the highest bidder."

The man broke down into ugly tears, his blood mixing into the muddy earth.

"Please, mister! I-I'm sorry! I swear! But please, *please!* You gotta get me out of here! That thing is out there! It'll kill us both! It was like, like a panther or something! Oh God, it was a monster!"

Will leaned in. "Hurts real bad, huh? Dying in the mud? Right where you belong." His brown eyes showed no sympathy. His handsome face was rugged, with four days of salt-and-pepper sandpaper on his chin. A smile crept across his lips.

"Oh please, mister! I'll give you anything you want! Anything!"

"Anything? Hmm..." Will scratched his chin. "How about you just give me your best scream?"

"Huh?"

Will's face began to warp. A shimmer ran across his features, the bending of light. Like waves of heat over a paved road on a blistering summer day, the image of Will Shaw began to warp away. The mangled man squirmed and whined, watching helplessly as Will shimmered away from this plane of existence, and in his place, something else stepped in.

It was a towering black mass of muscle. Powerful haunched legs, mighty chest and shoulders, curved claws like crescent moons. Yellow, predatory eyes glared down at the puny prey. Lips parted and a muzzle of long, dripping fangs snarled.

With nothing left to do but die, Ed could not help but to oblige Will's request. He screamed with all the terror in his soul as the black cat finally pounced and began tearing him to pieces.

2

MY SOUL TO TAKE

CHEROKEE RESERVATION, *North Carolina*

THE BABY WAS GETTING FUSSY.

He was only a week old, and it had been a long day. Mamaw and Papaw had come to visit along with the cousins, and everyone wanted baby time. He had been passed around and cooed at, serenaded, cuddled. He'd been fed, had his naps, and enjoyed a delicate luke-warm bath in his special baby tub. All attention was on him, little Benny. At seven pounds-four ounces, with brown eyes and a tuft of fine, black hair on his head, he was the angel Mommy and Daddy had been praying for.

Now his little face crinkled into a grimace and he squirmed in discomfort as his mommy, Maria Tsagasi, paced the nursery, rocking him gently as she hummed soothing tones. Hector Tsagasi leaned in the doorway, smiling proudly at his wife and son. They were a handsome young couple, healthy and fit, each with copper skin and long, jet-black hair.

"There we gooo... Sleepy baaaaby..."

It was working. Benny's eyelids drooped and his flailing slowed. Soon he was asleep, blissfully warm and snug in his mother's embrace. She took her bundle to the crib and eased him in. A stuffed animal monkey lay beside him in case he got lonely and a carousel hung overhead in case he got bored. On the wall behind the crib was a large dreamcatcher, more for decoration than any spiritual superstitions.

Maria gave her son one last tender kiss on the head, then switched on the baby monitor. She crossed to the doorway and Hector slid his hand across her hips, pulling her close. He kissed her cheek and they remained there for another minute, just admiring the miracle they had created.

"I still can't believe he's ours," she whispered.

"Come on. Daddy needs a drink," he said, playfully smacking her butt.

She giggled as he led her out of the room, closing the door behind her but leaving it open a crack. They continued to talk as they moved down the hallway, their voices fading away as they left young Benny on his own. He shifted in his crib, enjoying his baby dreams and the comfortable feeling of being protected and loved.

THERE WAS A STRANGER ON THE REZ THAT NIGHT.

It was a presence, neither male nor female, not physical or spirit. Anyone who saw it would only catch a momentary glimpse, and even then, they would be unable to describe it. They might say they saw a shadow, or simply felt a malevolent chill in the night. That they saw nothing but darkness, yet somehow knew that someone, or something, was there.

It moved down the silent streets in the dead of night. It didn't walk, it didn't creep, and it didn't float... it moved. An intangible, elemental force, it had no name, no home, no soul of its own. But it did have hunger. Moving down the dark streets, it tasted the air and smelled warm, fresh life.

Someone was coming. A man walking his dog.

The presence sucked in its breath and pulled its extremities inward. Tentacles and tails and wings and whatever else this abomination was made of folded up, wrapping around themselves. Forcing its form into another shape like a black octopus, there was no spine or skeleton to restrict it. The black wraith stretched out vertically, grew out an oval knob on top, then a protrusion on each side. Next, two tentacles stretched to meet the ground and more came to fill out the shape.

The man with the dog walked on down the dark road. He saw the dark figure walking across from him. The dog-walker couldn't make out any features, nor could he focus on them in this heavy darkness if he tried. But he raised his hand for a polite wave, and the dark figure across the street replied with a simple nod. The dog growled but its owner tugged at the leash to silence it. They made their way back home and thought nothing more of the stranger walking in the shadows.

The dark presence released its posture and allowed

its crude human disguise to unravel. Tendrils and black viscera spread out like a drop of ink in a glass of water. Stretching to its full size, it continued down the roads and alleyways, tasting the air. Looking for something special.

It passed into a residential area. Small houses and run-down shacks dotted the landscape; not a single light was on inside. A tractor sat out in a field to the left, and two burned-out husks of old cars were rusting in the fields to the right. Some houses were simply trailers while others were nicer and better maintained. None of that mattered to the dark entity. It flicked its tendrils into the neighborhood, letting them graze across mailboxes, picket fences, parked cars.

It glided over to one house, tasted the air, ran its feelers across the walls, sensing the energy inside. The creature lingered there for a moment, then decided no, not this house. On to the next, then the next. It moved across the street and stopped, deciding to look at another house more closely. Black tentacles silently swirled, caressing the walls and windows. It tasted the air, a translucent black tongue flicking in and out. No, not this house. It moved on.

The beast reached a cross street and saw a cul-de-sac up ahead. It plunged forward, looking closely at each abode nestled in the dark pocket of countryside. The air tasted fresh and clean and the being knew it was close. One house had a swing set out front as well as children's toys scattered in the yard. The beast closed in on the house, tasting the air, stroking the walls... no, not this house.

The next house was small and simple, nondescript. A

single sedan was in the driveway. The lights were all off. An energy pulled the black shape forward, something it sensed inside. Its tendrils felt at the walls, that horrible tongue licked the air. Yes, this was it. The entity crept around the house, feeling each surface, scanning as it closed in on what it was looking for. And there it was.

It stopped at a window. The energy was ripe and fresh, clean and pure. This was it. What the dark creature wanted was just beyond one meager pane of glass. With a nightmarish grin, it pressed itself against the window pane, smashing its formless mass against the cool surface. From an outsider's glance, it would appear to be a big mound of black goo just stuck there. But to look closer, something else was happening.

The entity was finding its way in. Through cracks in the wood, between the very atoms in the pane of glass, the blackness slowly pushed through. Smoke and dark tendrils worked between every microscopic gap until after a minute, it began to seep through to the other side. Slowly, like juice pulp through a strainer, it squeezed its way in.

The puddle of black goo on the inside of the window began to spread, and soon, half of the entity's form had passed the threshold, writhing and undulating with the effort. It grunted and hissed, pulling the rest of its noncorporeal form through. After nearly five minutes, the creature slipped the last of its tendrils through without even cracking the window.

Little Benny slept peacefully in his crib.

The dark being drew in a breath, tasting the sweet aroma of innocence. Its ghostly form billowing in the shadows, the foul thing drew itself closer. Its black mouth drooled somewhere within its swirling folds. It peered down on the child resting peacefully, swathed in a sky-blue blanket with printed monkeys and elephants. The child's skin was soft and smooth, his little chest moving with each tranquil breath.

Closer. The darkness moved in, oh so slowly. Tendrils and swirling black membranes stroked the edge of the crib. The baby monitor sat on a table, its red light on, ready to alert the parents for when it's time to change a diaper or sing a sweet lullaby. An acrid smell filled the sanctuary of youth, some nauseating recipe blending battery acid and rotting garbage.

Closer. Benny stirred in his sleep.

The dark creature gripped the crib, leering over the edge. It moved in, its form undulating over the sleeping newborn. Slimy black lips parted to reveal not rows of sharp teeth, but gray, diseased gums. The sinister jaws spread open, forming an O shape, creeping in closer. Closer.

It pushed the carousel away and the device crashed to the floor with a plastic thump. Benny kicked and mewled. He began to fuss and stir, squeaks of infant discontent coming from his pink lips. The black creature came down and found those lips, parted them open, and gave little Benny a kiss.

Then it began to suck.

HECTOR AND MARIA TSAGASI WERE SOUND ASLEEP when the static sounds of a fussy baby came through the speaker. They both groaned and stirred in bed, and the father began to get up, but she touched his arm and stopped him.

"It's okay, I got him," Maria said, kicking her legs off the bed and lurching to her feet. She stretched and stumbled across the bedroom, wearing only panties and one of her husband's oversized t-shirts. Baby sounded hungry. *No, actually, he sounds different,* she thought. It was not his usual clear, sharp cries; it was muffled and sounded like the crib was shaking around.

Maria crossed into the dark hallway, running her fingers through her hair and untangling a knot. The sounds from the nursery stopped, but she kept going to the end of the hall. She reached the baby's door, adorned with cut-outs of cartoon characters, and twisted the knob, pushing her way in.

The young mother stepped into the void of the nursery and felt a cold chill shoot up her spine. The awful smell stung in her nose. There was slight ambient light in the room, but around the crib, all she could see was darkness. Undulating, evil darkness. She drew in a sharp breath and the foul creature suddenly bolted up and away from the crib, shrieking a horrible, high-pitched wail.

It spread out its membranes like great black wings and suddenly launched itself backwards. No time to seep slowly out through the window, the creature instead smashed through the pane, flying out into the night and leaving shards of glass and molding on the ground outside.

The horrified mother ran to the crib and looked inside.

Little Benny lay lifeless, his pink flesh turned gray and shriveled, all the life and spirit drained out of his tiny body. Maria dropped to her knees, trembling, shivering. Tears burned in her eyes and her mouth gaped open, and at first no sound would come out. Then she screamed. And screamed again.

She screamed for the rest of the night.

3

COPPER

GOLDEN MEADOW, *Louisiana*

SHE LAY FULLY DRESSED ATOP THE CHEAP BEDSPREAD in the Southern Breeze Lodge, staring up at the ceiling fan and drumming manicured fingertips on her firm stomach. Red neon light crackled through the blinds, and the only other illumination came from the small TV which had been muted. The bedside clock told her it was 4:15 a.m. She shifted to her side, fidgeted, then flopped again onto her back. Her feet kicked nervously off the side of the bed, her tactical boots still laced on tight. Her gun and badge sat beside her overnight bag on the dresser and her gaze kept flicking over to them as if still in denial that, yes, she really was here doing this.

The pistol was a two-tone Glock 22 .40 caliber, the badge a gold shield awarded by the state of Tennessee to Detective Shenandoah M. Glass. A sworn officer of the

17

law. A respectable, honest, and good person. Then why was it, she wondered, that she could no longer look at herself in the mirror, or at her police ID photo?

Shenandoah shot up in bed, unable to keep still anymore.

She sat there kicking her feet, her mind racing behind crystal-blue eyes. Her hair was a short, dirty-blonde bob, her physique the result of dedicated exercise and strict diet. At 5'5" and with a face like a fairy tale princess, she had something to prove to all the boys in blue. She could hold her own. She could run, fight, shoot, and take care of business. But tonight she was sidelined.

Springing to her feet, she began to pace. She couldn't sleep, eat, shower, or watch TV. Her nerves were wired, her heart pounding. All she could do was wring her hands, grind her teeth, and wait. And pace. She checked her phone again. No new messages. 4:18 a.m. She continued to pace, rubbing her arms at the chill of the room, and trying to ignore the smell of mold.

Headlights in the parking lot swept across the window and she turned at the sound of a familiar mechanical growl. Her heart sped up, listening to the engine being turned off, a car door opening and closing, and footsteps heading her way. She grabbed her gun and ran to the door, peering through the peephole. Breathing a sigh of relief, she stepped back and put the pistol back on the table. She ran her fingers through her hair, trying to quickly make herself look as nice as possible.

The electric lock buzzed and the door opened.

Will came in and smiled at her.

"Hey, Copper," he said.

"Oh my goodness," she said in her chirpy Nashville twang, running to him and wrapping her arms around his neck. "I was getting so worried."

"Ahhhh, it's okay. See, I'm fine."

He pulled her into a deep kiss and she melted into his arms, his strong hands caressing her back. She ran her fingers through his close-cropped black hair, feeling the bristles of his salt n' pepper beard stubble against her face. Will pulled away, smiling at her with those winning dimples and running his thumb across her cheek. He stepped further into the room and pulled off his black leather jacket.

"So how did it... y'know?" she asked.

"It went fine."

"So, did you...?"

"It's done," he said and tossed the jacket onto a chair. "We don't have to worry about those scumbags ever again."

"S-So, what happened? Did you—?"

"The less you know the better, babe." Will swaggered over and wrapped his arms around her as she wilted in disappointment.

"I already know what you do, Will. What you *are*."

"You don't need to know the details of my missions."

"But I could help."

"You do help," he said, giving her reassuring little kisses.

"I don't mean providing intel or cover, baby. I mean I want to get out there and *help*. You can't just keep fighting these bastards on your own."

"First off, you're a single mother and I'm not about to

put you in unnecessary danger. And second, you're an officer of the law, babe. You want to become a vigilante executioner? You want to watch me turn into a monster and tear criminals limb from limb?" He pulled back and looked her in the eyes, his gaze penetrating deep. "The less you know, the better."

She rolled her eyes and made a face at him. "Fine."

He chuckled at her antics and sat down to take his boots off. As he began to untie the laces, Shenandoah noticed five shallow lacerations on the back of his right hand. Her eyes went wide and she immediately tried to examine it.

"*What is this?*"

"It's nothing, baby. Doesn't even hurt."

"Oh, for God's sake," she threw her hands up and slapped them down into her thighs, "come over here into the light." She took him by the wrist and pulled him into the cubby area beside the bathroom where an overhead light shined. "How did this happen?"

"Ummm, what did we just get finished talking about?"

She crossed her arms and glowered at him, tapping her foot.

"Oh, all right!" He gave in and shook his head. "I punched through a car window at one point, okay? It's nothing, really. By this time tomorrow it'll be mostly healed."

Shenandoah went to her travel bag and pulled out a small medical kit. She pulled a chair beside Will and sat down, taking out iodine and bandages. "Well, just let me clean it, okay? Don't want it getting infected."

"Really, it's fine."

"Stop fussing. You're such a baby."

"Look, I was about to take a shower anyway. I should get clean first before you dress a wound, right?"

Her shoulders drooped as she realized he was right.

"Fine... But I'm joining you."

THE SHOWER WAS HOT. HARD PRESSURE. THEIR bodies were pressed together, soapy hands exploring every wet surface. She was smooth and pink. He was hard and bronze. His hands traced her firm breasts and caressed the nipples with his thumbs. Shenandoah threw her head back and moaned, letting the spray of water wash down through her hair. They giggled and soaped each other up, using the shower head to rinse themselves. She checked on his minor wounds and gave them kisses.

They continued to kiss and touch.

Will's arousal was reaching critical mass. He took the initiative of turning off the shower, throwing aside the curtain, and stepping out. In a second, he tossed a towel to Shenandoah in the shower and began drying himself with another. But it was a quick and sloppy drying job, as he dropped his towel after a cursory pass and swept her up into his arms. She hooted in surprise and dropped her towel, laughing and happily allowing Will to carry her off into the bedroom.

He threw her onto the bed.

She giggled and bounced. Watching him with sultry eyes, Shenandoah poised herself up on her elbows. Will looked at her like a cat sizing up a mouse, ready to pounce at any moment. Their naked bodies were toned and still wet. She looked him up and down, admiring his beauty. Then she lay down, happy to let him have his way.

"Come and get it, big boy."

4

―――――――――

SCAR TISSUE

GOLDEN MEADOW, *Louisiana*

BITCH. BETRAYER. MURDERER. KILL HER. RIP OUT HER THROAT. SHE LOCKED THE DOOR. FIRE AND SMOKE. BURNING LUNGS. BITCH.
   JANAE.

WILL LEANED ON THE SINK AND WATCHED THE FLOW of water down the drain. He spat the last of the toothpaste out and rinsed his mouth. Stepping back, he looked at his reflection in the motel room's bathroom mirror. His eyes were tired, his beard stubble coming in thicker than he usually let it grow. It seemed like every day he spotted new gray hairs on his chin. Forty years old. Damn.

He shook his head and turned back to the main bedroom. Early morning light seeped through the edges

23

of the curtains, and Shenandoah was still fast asleep beneath tangled sheets. The room still smelled like sex. Her body was firm and athletic, yet still pink and delicate. He tried to focus on the woman in his bed, but there was still another woman under his skin. Janae.

RIP. TEAR. SHRED FLESH. BLOOD.

SHE WAS ALWAYS THERE, STANDING IN HIS BLIND spot. No matter what he was doing or thinking about, she would be lurking in his mind, poking her head in to remind him. To make sure that he could never forget, to hold him on her leash. She'd ruled over his psyche these last two years. Her eyes, her lips, the touch of her dark ebony skin, the flick of her tongue all over him. Her firm, petite weight on top of him, riding and grinding. The noises she uttered when he made her orgasm again and again.

The cold sting of her betrayal.

Will clenched his jaw and turned to slip into his clothes. He nimbly got dressed, careful not to make a sound. His wallet, keys, and Canik TP9 sidearm went to their appropriate places, and his jacket and boots came last. Zipping up his bag, he saw the glint off the edge of his old dog tags in the pocket. He pulled out the chain and watched the two Army-issued tags dangle. Most vets never took them off. Will stuffed them back into the pocket, not seeing any practical use for them.

He gathered his bag and stood at the foot of the bed

looking down at Shenandoah. She was beautiful, strong, loyal, and he knew she loved him... but he couldn't give her what she needed. Nobody could ever be allowed to get close to him again. People who got close had a habit of either dying or stabbing him in the back. Besides, no matter how wonderful Shenandoah was, or how good she treated him, she could never compete with... her. Janae. No woman could.

BITCH. HATE HER. RIP OUT HER THROAT.

WILL CONTEMPLATED KISSING SHENANDOAH'S forehead before leaving, but didn't want to wake her. She had his number. He quietly went to the door and snuck outside to the chill of the October morning, leaving Louisiana in the rear-view mirror.

CHATTANOOGA, TENNESSEE

WILL SHIFTED INTO THIRD AND BLASTED THE BLACK Camaro down I-75. Crisp wind blew in the open window and through his hair, bringing with it the scents of home. He tapped the steering wheel and worked a strawberry sucker around in his mouth, admiring the beauty of the architecture in the cloudy-gray light. Opting against music this morning, he simply enjoyed the sounds of the city. Cars driving. Birds chirping. Kids playing. A street musician at the base of the Walnut Street bridge strumming an acoustic guitar.

Will's stomach craved a sandwich from the Market Street Deli. And a beer. But there were other stops to make first. He pulled into the parking lot of the Post Office and parked his car, hopping out and smiling politely at passersby. Striding through the glass front doors of the government building, he went to his P.O. box in the far corner and unlocked it with a small key on his ring. The door swung open and he was greeted by a pile of junk mail.

Beside the pile of mail was a cell phone.

Will took out the phone and pressed the power button, turning on the device. As it started up, he flipped through his mail, throwing each piece of junk in the recycling bin. An electronic *chirp* came from his phone and the screen indicated that he had five unread text messages and eight missed calls. He smiled and shook his head. The messages were all from the same person.

- *Hey old fart why you duckin me?*

- *Yoohooooo Will??*

- *We training Thursday or what? Geoff is doing a no-gi class*

- *Omg old man answer your phone!!!*

- *You suck*

CASEY MADISON SHOT IN FOR A DOUBLE-LEG takedown.

Will expertly sprawled and circled around, taking

her back. The Brazilian Jiu-Jitsu class was in full swing, with multiple pairs of opponents rolling on the mats. Everyone wore skin-tight rash guards with a wide variety of colors and designs, shorts, mouth guards, and athletic cups. The sounds of Kendrick Lamar bounced off the walls and fueled the fire for the combatants, each trying to dominate and impose their will.

Casey was fourteen now, five inches taller, and much stronger than when she first met Will. Her hair was pulled into tight braids and her eyes sparkled with playful intensity as she tried to escape Will's submission attempt. He loosened his guard, giving her a chance to escape.

"Tuck your chin and get onto your left hip," Will instructed.

"I-I can't," Casey said.

"You can do it. Twist onto your left hip. Twist, there you go..."

Will allowed her to wrench her way out of his grip and switch positions. She got to her feet with Will on his back, feet up in the air to keep her from passing his guard. Casey tried to get around his feet as he swiveled and swerved and kicked, keeping her at bay. The game continued and they smiled at each other.

"You got nothin', old man!"

"Pssh. Big words for a little girl."

He kicked out her feet and the little warrior fell to the mat with a soft thud. She giggled and pounced right back at him, the battle raging. Will finally locked her into an arm bar and she begrudgingly tapped out. They both fell to the mat to catch their breath as the last seconds of the round ran out and the buzzer rang.

Across the vast gymnasium space, Will and Casey moved from Jiu-Jitsu to striking. They found an area to themselves and worked on punch combination drills.

"One-two, one-two. Let's go," Will said.

Casey hit the pads. "So what's the deal with this new *friend?*"

"Who?"

"You know who. The cop. Pocahontas. Sacagawea."

"Shenandoah," Will chuckled, holding up the mitts. "One-three, one-two."

Casey complied by hitting the pads in the requested combination.

"Well?"

"What about her? She's fine."

Casey's eyes rolled up in her head. "Is she your girl-friend? Is she just a friend? What's the deal?"

"I don't know," Will said. "I rescued her son last year. Three-two, three-one."

Casey continued to hit the pads and circled around him. "I know," she said. "You told me about that. And that she saw you as the jaguar. So she *knows.*"

"Yeah, she knows. Keep your elbows in."

Casey danced around Will, peppering the pads. She could see that she was making him uncomfortable, which amused her even more, so she kept pushing.

"Soooo? Is she your new girlfriend or what?"

"Anybody ever say you're a little pain in the ass?"

"*Well?*"

Will groaned in exasperation and dropped his hands.

"I don't know, okay? Yes, she's my new girlfriend. Happy?"

"Oh, yeah. You sound so passionate."

"Uh huh, and what about you? I don't exactly hear you gushing to me about your love life."

"I'm fourteen."

"So? Are there any boys you like at school?"

"Pssh, I don't have time for boys. Hold up the pads."

Will made a face and held the pads back up for her to hit, assuming a fighting stance again. Casey bounced around, practicing her head movement, then once again peppered the pads with jabs, crosses, and hooks.

"Good," Will encouraged. He glanced at the lobby behind Casey and noticed a slender, attractive black woman enter the training facility. "Now, keep going until the next bell, then we gotta wrap it up for the night."

"Why?"

"Because your mom's here."

Casey sighed and continued to punch.

LaShonda "Bri" Madison sat on one of two benches, watching the action. She had a warm smile and wore a red wig, donning respectful yet cute office attire (Wait, office attire, or is she a nurse?). She admired the men and women rolling on the mats trying to choke each other, and the fighters sparring on their feet. It was an atmosphere of fun, learning, and strength. It was a place for her baby to feel a sense of camaraderie, to make friends, and most importantly, to learn to defend herself.

"You know," Casey said with a smirk, "if things don't work out with Sacagawea, I think my mom likes you."

"Great, thank you."

"Hey, at least now we have an excuse for us to know each other," Casey said, and the bell rang. Everyone sparring stopped to catch their breath, hug, and slap hands. "You're just Will, my friendly MMA coach."

"Yeah, maybe she'd like to watch the next time we sneak out to go hunting."

Casey laughed and gave Will a sweaty hug, bumping her boxing glove against his padded right hand in a show of respect. "Yyyyeah, maybe not just yet."

"Okay," a voice yelled from across the room, "good class, everyone. Fall in. Anybody who wants to stay late and keep training, feel free." The students formed into a circle and one at a time gave a quick bow and hug to the head instructor, then to each other. Everyone was tired and sweaty, but smiling.

Will and Casey finished hugging their classmates, then walked over to Bri in the lobby. She stood up and walked to the edge of the mat to greet them, beaming a bright smile.

"You're looking so good out there, baby," Bri said.

"Thanks, mom. Will is teaching me everything he knows."

Will held his tongue and just smiled.

"Thank you, Will," Bri said with a smile. "Well, c'mon baby. We got to go."

"Oh, can't I train just a little longer?" Casey's eyebrows scrunched together and she bounced with teenage discontent.

"No, we have to get home. You need to do your homework, have dinner," Bri leaned in to smell her daughter, "and take a shower. Sorry, baby."

"Fine," Casey sulked, ambling over to get her gym bag. Most of the other students did the same, collecting their things, slapping hands, and saying goodbyes. A small handful of people remained on the mats to practice, while others hit the showers in the locker rooms.

"She's really doing very well," Will said to Bri as they watched Casey put on her shoes and get ready to leave. "Getting very tough."

"Good," Bri said, nodding. "Thank you for all your help."

"Oh, my pleasure, ma'am."

Casey trotted back over and gave Will a fist bump.

"You taking off?" Casey asked.

"In a little bit," Will answered. "Gonna hit the heavy bag a bit first. Take a shower."

Casey nodded. "See you next week?"

"You know it."

They smiled and said their goodbyes as mother and daughter backed toward the doors, waving at Will and the others. He smiled and watched them go to their car and pull away into the chilly evening. Turning back to the mats, he went over to the heavy bags. After nearly two hours of holding back with a small teenage girl, he felt a deep urge from within to not restrain himself anymore. He stepped up to his favorite heavy bag, strapped on his gloves, and began to pound it. Harder. Harder.

WILL FINISHED HIS WORKOUT AND HIT THE showers. He changed into his clean sweatsuit, feeling invigorated. The other instructors left, and Will was happy to be the one to lock up. With his gym bag slung over his head and shoulder, he went around the gym turning off the lights. He fished out his keys and stepped out the front door into the night. Locking the door and turning to the parking lot, he made for his Camaro. But there was another vehicle off to his left that he at first didn't pay any attention to. It was a champagne-colored Chrysler Pacifica van, and two figures waited in the shadows by the driver's door. One of them stepped forward.

"Hey, boy," the man said.

Will stopped. He knew that voice. "Papaw?"

Through the shadows, Papaw Jimmy approached from across the lot. The other man sat huddled in a wheelchair, his eyes downturned. He had gained so much weight, and his face still bore the long scars left on that fateful night two years ago. He was a shell of his former self, but Will recognized him instantly.

"Jax..."

Jackson Cooper did not make eye contact.

Dumbfounded, Will stood in shock as Jimmy approached him, a somber look on his face. "Boy," Jimmy said in his thick Kentucky drawl, "you sure are a hard man to get ahold of."

5

A CALL FOR HELP

WILL WAS in shock as he stared into his grandfather's face. His heart raced as his eyes ticked from Papaw Jimmy to the man in the wheelchair. He tried to speak, but his mind was pulling in two different directions.

"Papaw... Jax... W-What the... How..."

"It's good to see ya, boy," Jimmy smiled and put his hand on Will's shoulder. "Now, you gonna give an old fart a hug, or what?"

Will let out an exasperated chuckle and pulled Jimmy in close. They hugged good and tight, and Will was amazed at how strong the old bear still was. He pulled away again, his mind spinning, not sure what he wanted to say to who, or in what order. He finally laughed and slapped Jimmy's shoulder.

"It's good to see you, too," Will said. "What's going on?"

"Ahhh," Jimmy grumbled, "got some things to talk about."

"Okay, but... I mean, how did you find me?"

Jimmy pointed his thumb back over his shoulder. "I couldn't. But I did find yer friend here."

"And all but forced me to help him find you," Jackson muttered, eyes still fixed on the ground. "Thought you might be here. You tried calling me enough times from this place, so I figured this would be a good bet..."

"Jax," Will whispered and slowly stepped around Papaw Jimmy, focusing on the shrunken man before him. Jackson's body instantly tensed and he jerked back in his chair. Will stopped walking, not wanting to frighten him.

"So, we good, Jimmy?" Jackson huffed, pulling out his keys and activating the automated driver's door lift. "You don't need me anymore, right? We found Will, so I can leave now. Right? We're good?"

"Yep, we're good," Jimmy said with a sigh.

"Good," Jackson said, hurriedly rolling his chair onto the ramp and activating the hydraulic lift. "You guys have a nice night. It's been lovely, let's do this again sometime."

"Jax, come on, man..." Will began walking again, hands held palms-up. He watched helplessly as Jackson got in and slammed the door. Will closed the distance, putting his hands on the door panel and leaning in to look his old friend in the face. Jackson jumped back in his seat, fear throbbing in his eyes. The scars had changed the landscape of his features , and his once ruddy complexion was now pale after two years of hiding from the sun. A shaggy beard had grown in and he barely bothered with grooming anymore.

"Get away from me, Will."

"Jackson, *please*, man. I... have you been... are you okay? How's Dominic?"

"He's fine, okay? Can you just..."

"Jax..." Will searched for the words. "I-I miss you, man. I just... I can't think of any more ways to say I'm sorry. I really just wish... wish that you'd forgive me, brother. I don't know if that's possible, but..." Will's eyes burned and he fought back the tears. "I just sure wish you could find it in your heart to forgive me."

Jackson's eyebrows crunched together, incredulous. He leaned forward in his seat to look Will directly in the eye.

"Forgive you for what, exactly?" Jackson asked. "Forgive you for sending a demon from Hell to murder my wife in front of me? In front of my *son*? Forgive you for breaking my back, forcing me to use a colostomy bag for the rest of my life and turning me into a fucking freak? Or forgive you for traumatizing and scarring my son for life?" He searched Will's face for an answer but found none.

"You want to know how Dominic is doing, Will? He wakes up screaming every night, and those are the nights he sleeps at all. He doesn't talk, doesn't have friends anymore. He's like a fucking hermit crab, hiding from the world. The child psychiatrist he's seeing tells me about the dreams Dom describes to him, which all involve either him being torn apart by monsters, or his mother being torn apart by monsters, and her bleeding, severed head calling out to him for help... *That's how Dominic is doing, Will!*"

Will deflated and stepped back away from the van.

Jackson started the engine, not wanting Will to see his tears.

"Okay, Jax."

Jackson accelerated off into the night, leaving Will with his head hanging low. Jimmy came up to Will and slapped a supportive hand on his back as they watched the tail lights vanish down the road.

"Come on, boy," Jimmy said. "Take me somewhere with good coffee."

City Cafe in downtown Chattanooga was the place to go. With red and white checker-pattern upholstery, mini juke boxes on every table, and glass cases full of cakes and pies, the 1950's theme was in full swing. Darlene Love sang about her fine, fine boy over the speakers, and the aroma of coffee and bacon drifted in the air. Servers buzzed around the tables like bees on a honeycomb. The main dinner crowd had mostly left, leaving only a few sparse tables where diners were still seated.

Will and Jimmy had a booth in the corner.

Jimmy took a sip of his coffee and winced.

"That's what you call good coffee, huh?"

Will ripped open four packets of brown sugar and dumped them into his coffee along with one mini-creamer. He stirred it up and took a sip. Hot and sweet, just how he liked it. He looked across the table; worry was seeping into the wrinkles around his grandfather's eyes. Will cleared his throat.

"So it's now three babies now?" Will asked.

"All boys," Jimmy nodded. "All on the Cherokee Rez. All in the past two weeks. This last one was three days ago. I found out about it 'cuz I got a call outta the clear blue sky from Pete Littlejohn, askin' me for help." Jimmy took a sip of his coffee and continued. "I ain't talked to ol' Pete in dang near forty years! But he and I were friends way back in the day. And when me and your folks left The Rez, Pete stayed behind. He's the principal chief now. Pete knows about me, about us. Skinners. So when this started happening around The Rez, he reached out to me for help."

Will nodded. "What does he think is causing this?"

"The first victims, the Tsagasi Family, the mother says she saw the thing. She ran into the room and saw it, hoverin' over her dead baby."

"What did it look like?"

"She just keeps on sayin' *giant black wings* over and over. Giant black wings... Somethin' that steals the souls from the living, drains 'em of their vitality. I mean, if I didn't know any better, I'd say it sounds like a dang raven mocker to me."

"Hm," Will scrunched his eyebrows. "Witches, right? Evil spirits?"

"Well, there's a lot of different versions of the stories, but yeah. Basically. Can't rightly say exactly what they are 'cuz I never met anyone who's actually seen one in all my years. And I turn into a dang *bear*. I seen every kinda' monster and spirit that walks this Earth. Never seen me no raven mocker, no sir... But the stories make sense. A black, evil spirit, feeding on the souls of the living."

"But wasn't the whole thing with raven mockers that they would come to take the souls of the sick and dying? Like the Cherokee version of the angel of death." Will shifted in his seat and paused as their waitress walked by, glancing to see if they needed anything. Once the coast was clear he resumed. "So why this now? If this is a raven mocker, why is it coming after newborns?"

Jimmy shrugged. "That's what I'm hopin' you'll help me find out."

"I don't know, Papaw..."

"Ain't this what you do? Child rescue? Helpin' kids?"

"I mean... we moved to Harlan when I was what, two? I don't know that Cherokee culture anymore, don't know anybody there. And I have no authority there. I don't know..."

"Boy," Jimmy leaned forward. "These are your people. And I am an old man. I cain't do this on my own."

Will looked into his coffee cup and sighed.

6

A WELL RESPECTED MAN

SNOHOMISH, *Washington*

THE OLD MAN CRACKED THREE EGGS INTO A BOWL, sprinkled salt and pepper, and beat the mixture together with a whisk. Coffee was already brewed and hash browns sizzled in a small cast-iron frying pan. He dropped the eggs into a larger pan and they instantly began to crackle and cook.

The morning sun came through the window, and he looked out with a smile. A tall, husky white man, with long bone-white hair pulled into a tight ponytail, he had a ruddy complexion and round features, with white beard stubble that was starting to itch. His pajamas consisted of a simple shirt and sweat pants, stained from years of not giving a damn.

The space inside the one-story cabin was claustrophobic. Books and old VHS tapes and vinyl records were stacked and strewn wherever they would fit. The oak floors and walls had seen better days, but the old man did his best to dress them up with American Indian-style decorations. A hand-knitted Hopi throw rug. An Apache dream catcher, flutes, ashtrays, and trinkets.

A large painting of a white lion hung over his bed.

The whole space was one room, save for the bathroom and closets. Aside from the pathetic old TV and record player, there were no electronics. No computer or cell phone. An old Royal Classic typewriter sat on a humble desk amidst piles and stacks of papers, folders, and miscellaneous, useless crap. Besides the few pieces of Native American art on the walls, there were no other photos or decorations. No family portraits hung over the mantle and no pictures of grandchildren or cousins were displayed in frames or stuck with magnets to the fridge.

The old man hummed a happy tune and stirred his eggs and hash browns, looking out at the dewy-green country outside. Cedar waxwings flitted through the leaves and insects scuttled in the dirt. Outside, two of the old man's workers were already going about their duties. The young woman tended the garden and flowers, while her male counterpart raked and trimmed the trees and hedges.

It was a decent-sized plot of land on a mountain road. Ponderosa pines and black cottonwoods towered all around and a scenic vista of lush, green forest expanded in all directions. Neighbors were close enough to see from the front porch, but far enough that the old man wasn't worried about privacy. His home was small but cozy, and well-kept. The lawn and garden were immaculate, the fence around the front yard kept coated with fresh paint.

Under the porch was a pile of fresh-cut kindling. In the driveway was a humble 1997 Jeep Wrangler SE that still ran just fine.

The old man scooped the cooked food onto his plate, poured a cup of black coffee, and sat at the kitchen table, looking out the window. He turned on an old TV/VCR combo and popped in an ancient VHS tape. The screen fizzed with life, and on came his favorite Dixie Chicks live concert performance. He enjoyed the music and scooped breakfast into his mouth and picked up the latest People Magazine, which was already turned to the crossword section. With half of the answers finished, he continued with the rest as he ate his breakfast.

He walked outside, dressed and shaved.

The two young landscapers stopped what they were doing to greet him as he clomped down his front steps and gave his big belly a satisfied slap. He beamed a charismatic smile and waved to them as he made his way to the Jeep.

"Morning, Andy!" he said. "Morning, Sue! Looking good!"

"Morning, sir!" the young girl waved.

"You want the floor mopped today, sir? Any cleaning on the inside?"

"Nah, I'm good. Thanks buddy," the old man said, pulling out his car keys. He wore simple blue jeans and an American Indian-patterned jacket, hiking boots, and a small totem bag hung from his neck like a pendant. "Not today."

"Meeting tonight?" Sue asked.

"Oh, you know it," he said, climbing into the vehicle. "See you then!"

The old man drove off into the sunny mountain day.

He cruised down the winding road, lined with firs and spruces, and log cabins on either side. He passed a small grocery store, a gas station, and a vendor selling kindling. The high-altitude air whistled around him, crisp and invigorating. The green of the trees, the blue of the sky, the old man enjoyed it all. The beauty, the majesty. Nature. Life. He smiled, the lines crinkling around his blue eyes.

He made his way into the rustic hamlet of Snohomish, where the largest building was two stories and the antique shops outnumbered the bars and restaurants. Senior citizens waddled and shuffled around from store to store, buying groceries from the small market, getting a trim from the barber, and of course, shopping for antiques.

The old man parked and climbed out of his 4x4, saw someone he recognized across the street and gave him a smile and a wave.

"Morning, Rodney!"

He continued down the street, breathing clean air and feeling good. A woman walking her dog across the street smiled and waved. Then another. He crossed to the little bakery and picked up his second cup of Joe and a couple of his favorite butter biscuits. The cashier was a diminutive, kindly older woman with a mop of dyed-brown hair. She handed over the change with an expectant gleam in her eyes, her fingers gently caressed his.

Other people were around, so he just smiled and gave her a knowing wink.

"We have a meeting tonight, *sir?*" she asked.

"You know it, Maggie," the old man happily replied.

He sipped his coffee and made his way down the street to the post office. Two more pedestrians waved and said hello. Inside the small government building, he found his P.O. Box and opened it. There were only a few letters inside, mostly junk mail. He pulled them out and continued along on his way.

He stopped at the market to buy a quart of milk, broccoli, toilet paper, butter and cookies. Carrying the brown paper bag of groceries in one arm, another man greeted him on the street, this one younger.

"Morning, sir! So, tonight. Do we, uh...?"

"Yup. Same time, same place," the old man replied. "See you then, Chuck."

He continued down the street to the public library and walked inside. It was a dusky, dim place, with tables and decor that hadn't been updated in forty years. A meager selection of dusty books as well as old movies and music were on display. In a side room to the right were two rows of tables with computers for internet use. The machines were at least twenty years old and it was a miracle that they could get online at all. The old man pulled out a chair, sat down, and entered his code to log in.

He pulled up his email account and scrolled through the messages, deleting obvious spam. One message was from an account he recognized, so he opened it. The message simply read, *Have you seen this?* And was accompanied by a link. He clicked on the link, which took him to a North Carolina local news headline: *Third mysterious infant death on Cherokee Rez.* The old man sighed and continued to read.

The librarian approached, a pudgy old matron who played the part to a T. She timidly tapped the old man on the shoulder to get his attention. He turned to her with a polite smile.

"Morning, Marjorie," he said.

"Good morning, Keonee," she said. "Do we, um... Are we...?"

"Yes, ma'am," he said. "At the theater. I'll see you there."

"Yes, sir," she beamed. "I'll let you get back to what you were doing. Have a lovely rest of your day. See you tonight!"

Keonee smiled and nodded, but his eyes were troubled.

He turned back to the computer after the librarian left, contemplating what he should do. He went back to his email page, clicked *compose new email*, and entered an address he hadn't used in a long time. He sighed and began to type.

THE SOUNDS AND SMELLS OF SEX FILLED THE MOTEL room.

The light from one small table lamp cast the space in a dim, sickly-yellow hue. A man's clothes were strewn across the floor. The counters were littered with empty beer cans and a makeshift bar of mostly empty bottles was set up in the cove beside the bathroom. A small iPod speaker dock was plugged in by the bed, pulsing with alternating colors, and playing the sweet sounds of Étienne Nicolas Méhul to offset the filth and funk.

The man grinded. The woman had her face down in the pillows, her ass up in the air. He slapped and squeezed, growling through a gold-toothed grin. He was a black man with medium-brown skin, nearly every inch of which was covered in tattoos. Beads of sweat glistened on his flexing muscles and bald head. He pounded himself into her, grinding deep, losing himself in her warmth.

"Ohhh yeah, baby... that's it. Such a good little bitch..."

The woman did not respond or make a sound. She felt him pounding harder, faster. His fingers dug deep into the pillows of her ass as he strained all the way in, exploding in triumph. He groaned and howled as he came, laughed in exasperation, and collapsed onto the bed, a cum-filled condom gripping his cock. Satisfied, he slowly caught his breath as she rolled onto her side, looking away from him.

"Damn, that was good, boo," he said, reaching for his cigarettes beside the bed. He lit one up, taking notice of the classical composition flowing through the speaker, and rolled his eyes. "I don't know why you be listening to this old-ass shit when you fuck, but whatever. I don't care."

The woman didn't answer him. Her nude body lay still as a statue. Her skin was darker than his, her physique lean and firm. Her hair was shaved nearly to the scalp, and she wore no jewelry or tattoos. She sighed and swung her feet off the bed, sitting up. Her dark, almond-eyes were beautiful, but blank and empty. Her perfect bone structure and sumptuous lips had fallen flat, with dark circles under her eyes threatening to overshadow her natural beauty.

Janae Jones went to get another drink.

Her lover of the moment watched her walk, admiring the feminine swish of her hips and perfect ass as she made her way to the bottles of booze. She didn't say a word or acknowledge him at all as she took a motel glass and filled it with Ketel One.

"Damn, baby. You are so fine. Mm mm..." he murmured mostly to himself.

She answered by simply taking a sip of her drink, facing away from him. An electronic chime came from her phone, indicating a new text or email. She ignored it and continued to drink.

"Hey, I'm a' turn this shit off now, okay?" he said, reaching for the iPod dock. "Don't know how you can listen to this boring old-white-man music anyway... 'Ey yo, pour me a drink." He switched off the music, dropping the room into an empty, silent void. "Whiskey and soda."

Janae sighed but did not obey. Instead, she scooped up her panties and a t-shirt, slipping them on in the shadows. She took a sip of vodka and turned around, fishing his clothes off the floor and tossing them onto the bed.

"Take a hike," she said, not even looking at him.

"What?" the man's voice shot up an octave and he bolted up. "Bitch, what did you just say to me?"

"We had a nice time. Thank you," she said. "Now I want you to go."

"Oh *hell* no, you ain't playin' me like that," the man was on his feet in a second, stalking over and grabbing her by the arm. "You think you just gonna tell me what to do like that? Fuck you, bitch!"

"Get your hand off me right now, nigga," she warned.

"I said fuck you, bitch! I ain't going nowhere. Now go get me a fuckin' drink."

Janae finally looked him in the eye.

"And I said..." Janae's pupils began to dilate, and the man felt himself being drawn into them like quicksand. Soon, he had helplessly fallen into the trap of her eyes, swirling deep into her abyss. "Get your hand off of me."

The man finally let go, dumbfounded.

"Now I want you to put that cigarette out on your arm."

He didn't know why, but he obeyed, grinding the hot tip of his Marlboro into the meat of his forearm. His flesh hissed and smoked, and he staggered back, grunting in pain. His eyes burned with tears and confusion.

"Agh! What the fuck, bitch! What the... How did...?"

"Now," she said, stepping forward, her hypnotic eyes locked on his, "I want you to take your shit and get out of here. In fact, I want you to go walk out into traffic."

"I... Huh?" The man was stupefied by the order.

"I said," she stepped closer, drilling her pupils into his. "I want you to go walk out into traffic. Understand?"

He nodded.

"Good. Now fuck off."

She gulped down the rest of her vodka, feeling the heat rolling down into her belly as her spellbound lover began getting dressed. She lit a cigarette of her own and turned the Méhul back on. She swayed with the music in a drunken buzz, closing her eyes as the symphonic notes coursed through her being. She went to her bar and poured another drink.

Loverboy finished getting dressed and went to the door, stopping to give her a last look before leaving. "Bye..." His eyes were dazed. She did not turn or acknowledge him, concentrating on her drink. He turned back to the door and walked out into the brisk night, heading for the nearby interstate. Perhaps the spell would break before he could do any harm to himself, she thought. Or perhaps he would simply stay mystified and walk headlong into a speeding cement mixer.

Either way, she was not concerned.

Janae went to the open door and closed it, locking it behind her. She took a puff from her cigarette and another sip of Ketel One. Then she remembered. Her phone. There was a message. She tried to ignore it, but curiosity got the better of her. She walked over to the device and scooped it off the counter. *New mail: 1, from Keonee.*

She sighed and opened it.

Janae, I don't know if you're alive or dead, or if you still even check this email. It breaks my heart that you left us. I've tried calling and texting, and I hope you're okay. It's been almost two years, and I miss you. If you don't want anything to do with me or The Council anymore, I don't understand, but I will respect your choice. But if you do get this email, I could really use your help right now. We have trouble.

Will Shaw is back.

7

SWEET TOOTH

CHATTANOOGA, *Tennessee*

SHENANDOAH OPENED THE DOOR TO FIND TWO generations of Shaws standing on her front porch. She wore gray sweats and a stained baseball shirt, her hair a tussled mess, her eyes opening wide at the sight of the two tall Indians. Will smiled.

"Hey, Copper."

"Will..." It was impossible for her to stay mad at those dimples. "W-What are you doing here?" She looked from Will to the old man, who smiled and nodded politely.

Will took a step closer. "Can we talk?"

"Uh, sure. Come on in." She stepped back and opened the door, letting them into the modest den. Family photos lined the walls, along with her formal police headshot and a picture of her receiving her badge years ago. Coats hung on the rack by the window and both adult and child-size shoes were strewn across the floor. Shenandoah gingerly kicked them aside along with a toy firetruck, clearing the path for her guests.

"Papaw, this is my friend, Shenandoah."

Jimmy chuckled, sizing up the diminutive White girl. "Shenandoah, huh?" He reached out a hand and she shook it. "How do you do? I'm Geronimo."

"Uh, hi. Good to meet you."

"This is my Pa-my grandfather, Jimmy," Will said.

From the other room they heard the sounds of cartoons and a young child playing. The sounds of small feet running on the hardwood floor. The sound of his voice before he even rounded the corner.

"Mom, who is it?" A little boy slid into the room, his socks threatening to droop off his feet. He was small for an eight year-old, with a spiky head of blonde hair, and big blue eyes that lit up at the sight of his favorite person. "Will!"

"Hey, Luke!" Will beamed and dropped to one knee, opening his arms as the child ran to him. If Calvin ever left Hobbes and materialized into a real person, he would become little Lucas Glass. With a toy helicopter in one hand, he launched himself into a flying hug. Will squeezed back, grinning. "Ahhhh, how ya doin', big guy?"

"Good. One of my teeth fell out. See?"

Luke pulled back and smiled, displaying the gap where his upper incisor used to be. Will nodded, impressed.

"Wow, look at that. You know what that means, right? Means you're growing up, getting big. Soon you'll be as big as me."

Shenandoah rolled her eyes. "God, I hope not."

Will tickled and tussled with Luke, who giggled uncontrollably. Will threw him into the air, turned him upside down, shook him around. Luke loved it. Will plopped the boy back down and rustled his hair.

"Come on, Will! I want to show you my new game!" Luke took Will's hand and started pulling him toward the den, but the adults all made eye contact with each other and everyone knew there was business to discuss.

"Say, buddy," Will stopped the little dynamo, kneeling down again and pulling him in. "Listen, I have to talk to your mom for a minute, okay? But guess what. I got you your favorite..." Will pulled from his pocket a cherry Blow Pop and handed it to the eager boy. "If it's okay with your mom."

Shenandoah sighed, "Sure. He's had his dinner."

Luke bounced up and down as he opened the wrapping and put the sucker in his mouth. Will winked at him and pulled a second sucker from his pocket.

"Got one for myself too, for later. Shhhh." Will put his finger to his lips and slipped the candy back into his pocket. He glanced over at Jimmy, beckoning him over. The older man knew what was required of him and hobbled closer.

"Hey Luke, you know who this is?" Will asked. "This is my grandpa, Jimmy. I call him my papaw. Weird, huh?"

"Hi, Luke. Nice to meet ya," Jimmy said.

"Hi."

"You think *I'm* tough?" Will said. "This here is the guy who taught me to be tough. He's a real Cherokee warrior. Isn't that cool?" The boy nodded, looking up at the big Indian. "He really likes games too, don't you, Papaw?"

"Oh, yeah! Absolutely!" Jimmy lied.

"Why don't you show Papaw Jimmy your game while I talk to your mom for a couple minutes, okay?"

Luke shrugged. "Okay. Come on, it's in here." Luke gestured to the other room and led Jimmy around the corner and into the den.

"Okay, great," Jimmy smiled. "Let's see what you got."

They disappeared out of sight and Will turned back to face Shenandoah. She stood with her arms folded for an awkward moment.

"Nice of you to decide to drop by," she finally said.

Will sighed and took a step forward. "Listen…"

"You need my help," she cut him off.

He reached out and gently took her by the shoulders. "Can we go out to the patio and talk?"

She rolled her eyes and let her arms unfold, hands slapping down onto her thighs. "Fine," she said, turning and leading him through the kitchen. "Come on."

JIMMY LOOKED AROUND AT THE DEN AS LUKE MADE grumbling-engine noises and swooshed his toy helicopter around, sucking on his lollipop. On the thirty-inch flat screen, a new video game was paused, the image of two cartoon-fantasy warriors frozen in combat. Jimmy smirked and stepped around the minefield of toys to get a better look at the screen.

"So what game is this, now?" he asked.

"It's called *Smash Arena*," Luke said, tossing aside the helicopter and snatching up the game controller. "You can pick whichever guy you want to be, and you fight, and you can have different powers."

"Different powers?"

"Yeah, so..." Luke exited the game and went to the main menu, selecting the section where you can choose your character. One after another, Luke began to point them out. "That's T-Rex. He's super strong and has sharp teeth. And that's Nitro. He can like, shoot fire out of his hands like this, *fwooosshhhh!*" Luke held out his hands and demonstrated. Jimmy chuckled. "And this one's Chopper, and he has swords that come out of his hands. That's Yukio, she can shoot lightning and stuff. And this guy's called Gator, and he turns into like, a big alligator..."

"I knew a guy like that once," Jimmy mused.

"Yeah, so you pick who you want to be, and you fight. And everyone has different powers and you can like, be a super fighter and do super-hero stuff, like Will."

"Oh, really?" Jimmy raised his eyebrows. "Can Will do super-hero stuff?"

"Of course!" Luke said, choosing a character and starting a new fight. The game came to life and two badass fantasy characters began to battle on screen. "Will saved my life," Luke continued, his thumbs clicking away at the controller, his eyes focused on the game. "He came and saved me after the bad men took me. They had guns and everything, but Will beat them all up anyway! Nobody can stop Will!"

"Aha..." Jimmy chose his words carefully. "Did you see this happen? Did you see Will, uh... beat them up?"

"No. They had me tied up and my eyes were covered. It was really scary. But I heard like, fighting and screaming and gunshots and stuff... And then Will took me out of there. And that's how he met my mom. He's her boyfriend."

"Wow, that's one heck of a story," Jimmy said.

"Yeah. Will's the best."

THEY STOOD IN THE DARKNESS ON THE PATIO.

"Jesus," Shenandoah whispered, "that's terrible. What do you think is happening?"

"I don't know yet," Will said, pacing in small circles. "We have to go check it out. But I need to know if this is a localized thing, or if there's any more reports like this outside The Rez. And that's where you come in."

"Mm hm."

"I need you to cast as wide a net as you can," Will said, stopping to look her in the eye. "I need you to talk to whoever you know on the force, if you have any connections with state police in North Carolina... You said you have a friend in the FBI, right?" Shenandoah nodded. "Good. Ask around. See if there's any strange or unexplained infant deaths or abductions goin' on outside The Rez."

Shenandoah nodded again, her eyes contemplative. "Three babies. All on the Cherokee reservation. All... drained of life." She shivered.

Will nodded. "And all boys. Somethin' very weird is going on here. Could be some kind of... I don't know, demon? Maybe another skinner, or shapeshifter? Either way, this is dangerous. So ask around, but be careful. Let me know who's down there investigating, let me know what their reports say, get me as much intel as you can. But other than that..."

"Stay out of it," she finished for him.

"Right." Will squeezed her shoulders, the look in his eyes somber. He let her go and turned to head back in the house. "Come on."

"Um, excuse me," Shenandoah said, hands on her hips, an expectant look in her eyes. "Are you forgetting something, mister?"

Will turned around and chuckled, ambling back over to her. She tried to maintain an irritated expression, but a smile forced its way out. He wrapped his strong arms around her and she melted into him as they kissed.

THE VISIT REACHED ITS CONCLUSION, AND Shenandoah opened the front door to let her guests out. Luke stood by his mother's side, still sucking on the pop and trying to get to the bubble-gum center. Will turned to give the little man a final hug.

"Gimme five," Will said, holding out his hand.

The boy slapped it and smiled. Will looked at Shenandoah again.

"Bye," he said, giving her a quick kiss. "Let me know if ya hear anything."

She nodded, clearing her throat.

"It sure was nice to meet ya, ma'am," Jimmy said with a smile. "You too, little man. You protect your mamma, now." Jimmy mimicked a couple of mock-Karate moves and the boy giggled.

They said their goodbyes, and the two visitors walked back down the driveway to Will's car. Shenandoah wrapped her arm around the Luke's shoulders, gently pulling him back inside and closing the door.

Jimmy winced as he made his way down the slope of the driveway. Will took notice, scooping the car keys from his pocket.

"You okay, Papaw?"

"Oh yeah, just these ol' hips. Need to get offa' my feet."

"It's more than that," Will said. "You been quiet all day."

They reached the car and Jimmy sighed, leaning against the passenger door. Will stood at the driver's door, waiting to get in. The old man was clearly bothered.

"Come on, what is it?"

"Y'know, boy," Jimmy said, "this here might not be such a good idea after all."

"What are you talkin' about? These are our people. If somethin's happenin' on the Cherokee Rez, somethin'... *evil*, then it's our responsibility."

"Yeahp, that's true," Jimmy nodded. "It's also the responsibility of The Spirit Council. My old friend Keonee, remember? If they find out about this... hell, they may already know. They'll be comin'. And as far as we know, Keonee wants you dead."

"I'm not afraid of him."

"Oh no? You fixin' to go in there with no backup besides this here broke-down ol' man? Boy, they got strength in numbers. Keonee has 'em wrapped around his finger. When he took control of The Council, he twisted it into somethin' ugly. He got people planted everywhere, in all walks a' life. Now they all just follow him blindly, worship him like some damn messiah. Like that little girl you cain't get off your mind."

Will flexed the muscles in his jaw. "So what are you sayin', we just give up?"

"I'm sayin'," Jimmy said as he opened the passenger door, "to be ready for a fight." The old man plopped down into the car and slammed the door closed.

Will mused on that last comment a moment.

He jumped into the driver's seat and started the engine.

They sped off into the night.

8

———————

DYNAMIC DUO

SANTA MONICA, *California*

THE ROBBERY HAD GONE SOUTH FAST.

One of the robbers was killed by police on the scene, while the other three managed to escape. Brian Fitch and Jackie John Smith made it to the getaway car and peeled away. Shane Smith fled from the scene on foot, a backpack full of money slung over his shoulder. With sirens in the distance growing louder, the young man with the sandy buzz-cut, jeans, and Aerosmith t-shirt huffed through an alley and onto a side street. The look of rage and panic was in his eyes. They had run out on him.

Behind him, footsteps.

He could smell the salt water. In another couple of blocks, he'd be at the Pacific. Palm trees and cool breeze. A good place to get lost in a crowd, or steal a car. While he deliberated between going to the pier or Third Street Promenade, the footsteps behind him increased in speed.

Shane pushed himself harder, his heart and smoker's lungs straining at full capacity.

"Shit shit shit!" Shane cussed under his breath as he powered ahead.

The man in pursuit was gaining. He wore tactical boots, gray khaki pants, and soft-body armor labeled FBI. Most men in their early fifties spent their days in an office, polishing a chair with their asses. Special Agent Michael Warren was not like most men his age. With close-cropped silver hair and the wrinkles of time accentuating his chiseled face, he charged forward with the vigor of a man half his age.

"Golf 1 to Golf 2. Suspect heading west on 6th towards the PCH," Warren spoke into his radio headset, his standard-issue Glock 19M trained ahead.

He sprinted across the bustling Ocean Boulevard, timing his crossing between the speeding traffic, tourists, and numerous homeless camped out in plain sight. With powerful legs, the federal agent bolted forward across the lawn of Samo Ocean Park and into an area of overgrowth.

Not far ahead, Shane Smith reached the end of the wooded area, slapping face-first into a chain-link fence. Gasping for air, he looked ahead at the Pacific Coast Highway raging at the bottom of the hill below him, and the majestic Pacific Ocean directly beyond. With no time to hesitate, he climbed the fence and heaved himself over to the other side.

A steep hill of rocks and mud and overgrowth awaited him, and Shane had no choice but to go down. With the agility and grace of a pregnant yak, he slid and tripped and stumbled his way to the bottom. Hissing and cursing, he tried to keep his feet under him as he descended the highway.

And then there it was, the PCH. Shane gulped in the ocean air as he stared out at the imposing interstate. Six lanes of speeding traffic stretched north and south before him, blocking his path to the beach, the pier, and tourists he might rob or take hostage. The smells of gasoline and rubber merged with the scents of the sea, and seagulls overhead provided the soundtrack. It was now or never.

He climbed over the divider and began across the highway.

Agent Warren collided with the fence up above in time to see the determined scoundrel dodging traffic across the PCH. One option would be to jump the fence and charge down the hill right after him, but the fed preferred not to muddy his shoes. Directly to his left, he saw a pedestrian foot bridge spanning over the highway and connecting with the beach. It was an easy decision.

"Golf 1 in pursuit. Suspect heading for the pier," he said, running for the bridge.

"Golf 2 copy," a female voice crackled in his headset.

Drivers leaned on their horns and hit their brakes as Shane cut in front of them, the Cali sun reducing him to a sweaty mess even in October. Gripping his bag tightly, he clenched his teeth, cursing at himself and God all at once, and finally made it to the other side. Shane hopped over the dividing wall and onto the long-stretching board-walk, where he now had to dodge rollerbladers, dog walk-ers, bike riders, and tourists. He charged towards the closest parking area, pushing past unsuspecting civilians as he looked for a car to steal.

"Get out of the fucking way!" he screamed.

Warren sprinted across the bridge, closing the distance.

He reached the other side and bounded down the cement staircase. The agent pushed himself hard, beads of sweat rolling down his forehead. Up ahead he saw a commotion in the crowd and heard screams from the startled pedestrians. His target was not far away.

"Move it! Move!" Shane demanded as he ran into the parking lot.

He reached into his bag and pulled out his father's old six-inch, nickel-plated Colt Python, causing anyone in his way to scatter. Up ahead, he found what he was looking for. A victim with a car.

The woman was nearly fifty, and taking her Corgi to the beach for a walk was a daily ritual. She was climbing out of her lime-green Ford Fiesta and clipping the leash onto her dog's collar when she noticed the young man barreling towards her. Then she saw the gun. And the intense look in his eyes. Before she could react, Shane was right in her face with a .357 magnum aimed at her heart.

"Give me the keys!" Shane demanded.

"Oh, my... I-I..." the petrified woman stuttered.

"Give me the fucking keys, bitch!"

With a trembling hand, she held out the keys as her little dog yapped angrily at the bad man. Shane snatched them from her hand and shoved her away, running for the open car door. Once he got out onto the highway, he could cut off onto a side street, lose the car, and disappear into a crowd. Agent Michael Warren had other ideas.

"Stop right there, Smith!" Warren ordered.

Shane whipped around to see the fed poised behind him, ready to send 9 mm Hornady hollow-points into his chest. Without a second thought, the two-bit crook acted on impulse, lifting his revolver and firing two shots at his pursuer.

"Fuck you!" Shane shouted as the .357 kicked like a horse.

Pedestrians screamed and ran for cover. Warren stayed calm. Aimed.

BOOM! BOOM! BOOM!

Two shots went wild, but the third struck Shane in the shoulder, shattering his rotator cuff and sending hot pins and needles of agony racing down his whole arm. He yelped in pain, having no choice but to drop the Python to the ground. His blood spattered the driver's window of the Ford as he tripped and stumbled away, determined to not get caught.

Warren lowered his weapon and followed calmly.

With the sounds of police sirens and helicopters approaching in the distance, Shane continued his futile attempt at escape. Clutching his bleeding shoulder, he staggered through the parking lot, heading for the beach. The fed was close behind, and Shane was not about to go down without a fight. He reached into his jeans and pulled out his backup pistol, a little Ruger LCP MAX.

Intending to go out in a dramatic blaze of glory, Shane whipped around, determined to take this pig down with him. He leveled the compact .380 with his left hand, aiming squarely at Warren's head. The agent's eyes went wide, realizing too late that he would not be able to aim and fire fast enough. Shane began to squeeze the trigger.

A black Audi A8 with federal plates screeched through the lot.

Shane saw the car just in time for it to smash into him.

The air blasted from the lowlife's lungs as he rolled up onto the hood of the car and cracked the windshield. Brakes squealed and the Audi skidded to a halt, throwing the wounded robber away like an old dish rag. He toppled over the divider and out of the parking lot, rolling down a sand bank at the edge of the beach.

Special Agent Winona Lambert stepped out of the Audi.

"Hey," she said to her partner.

"Hey," Warren said with a casual smile, holstering his sidearm.

A few years younger than her counterpart, Lambert closed the door behind her and sauntered forward with confidence. She was petite and fit, clad in the same khakis and blue soft-body armor and weaponry as Warren. Her hair was jet-black and pulled back tightly into a severe bun. Her face could have been described as pretty were her features not so sharp and intense. Aviator sunglasses concealed her eyes just as her cold demeanor shrouded her emotions.

"Good timing," Warren said as she strolled over to greet him.

She allowed the corners of her lips to twist into a smile.

"What would you ever do without me?" she said and

kissed him on the lips. He kissed her back and smiled, giving her a playful slap on the butt.

"Shall we, agent?" Warren asked, gesturing towards their culprit.

"Oh, after *you*, agent."

The duo stepped over the dividing wall and began walking down the sandy slope, where a broken and bloodied Shane Smith continued trying to crawl away. All around him, spilled into the sand and twirling in the wind, were hundred-dollar bills from the failed robbery. Grunting in pain and frying in the sun, Shane tried to ignore the sound of the footsteps behind him. His Ruger had fallen and was only a few feet away. If he could only reach it —

Agent Warren walked past him and easily kicked the firearm away. Shane exhaled, finally giving up. His shoulder was bleeding, and at least a few bones were broken. He knew this was it.

"Okay, fine. *Nng!*" Shane grunted, badly hurt. "You got me."

Warren checked his own pulse, uninterested in what the crook had to say. Impressed by his own heart rate, the silver-haired fed made a face as if to say, "not bad!" Lambert flanked the broken crook on his left, looking down at him through her tinted lenses.

"Okay, okay! You got me, I said! Now get me a fucking ambulance!"

"I'm feelin' Ruth's Chris tonight," Warren said. "How 'bout you, babe?"

Lambert shrugged, "Yeah, that sounds good. I could go for a steak."

The other feds and police would be there soon, the sounds of their sirens filling the air. Warren looked at his partner, feeling their time running out.

"We don't have long till the others get here," Warren said. "You want to, uh...?"

"Sure," Lambert said, taking off her sunglasses.

"What the fuck is with you two?" Shane seethed. "What are you talking about?"

"Oh, we just need you to tell us where we can find your other two accomplices, that's all," Warren said. "Jackie John and Brian. Where are they, Shane?"

Shane Smith snorted in laughter, then hissed in pain.

"Oh please, fuck you," Shane said. "You think I'm gonna give up my own brother? Just get me an ambulance and a lawyer, *pig*."

"I think you should just tell us," Warren said, pacing. "Do it the easy way, or we'll have to *make* you tell us."

"Oh, yeah? What you gonna do, huh? Beat it out of me? Torture me right here out in the open? *Hnng!*"

Warren laughed, "Oh no, nothing that barbaric," Warren said. "But you see, my lovely partner here has certain... talents. She can make anyone tell the truth. It's really pretty cool. I'm jealous. I myself am a pretty blunt instrument, don't really have any special talents..."

"That's not true, baby," Lambert said.

"Oh, no? What talents do I have?"

"You're handsome."

"Ah! Well yes, that's true," Warren said, chuckling as he paced in front of the downed man. "But seriously though, my advice is to just tell *me* now, because if *she* asks you, it won't be very pleasant."

"Fuck. You. I'm not telling you shit."

Lambert squatted down beside Shane and looked him in the eye.

"Where can we find Jackie John and Brian, Shane?" she asked.

"Fuck you! Can someone just arrest me already, please?"

"Where can we find Jackie John and Brian, Shane?"

"Look lady, go fuck your—" Shane stopped.

Something felt strange, a sensation he was unfamiliar with. It was a slight pressure, right in the core of his cerebral cortex. Like a finger pressing into the center of his brain. The FBI lady had dark eyes, sure, but he could swear that her pupils were actually dilating. Soon, her irises had gone completely black, unblinking as she stared deep into his soul.

Shane began to tremble. "W-What are you...?"

"See what I mean?" Warren said.

"Where are Jackie John and Brian?"

"N-No way... I won't... I won't..."

The pressure became an unyielding knife in Shane's head. He tried, but knew his strength was rapidly fading.

"Where are they, Shane?" she asked one last time, the whites of her eyes now flooding completely with inky blackness.

"We have a place is Simi!" the crook blurted out. "I-It's an old ranch in the hills! 1501 Tierra Rejada Road... That's where they'll be going..."

Ashamed of himself, Shane slumped to the sandy earth, defeated.

Agent Lambert stood back up, her pupils returning to

their normal size. Warren smiled at her, then keyed the mic on his headset. "Golf 1, dispatch. Suspect is down, I repeat, suspect is down. Let's get a bus down here with a stretcher, over."

While Warren called in the cavalry, guiding the patrol cars and choppers to their location, Lambert put her shades back on. She pulled out her cell phone and checked the screen. An alert displayed: *One new text message from Keonee.* Her jaw clenched as she began to read.

Shane Smith quietly wept, crumpled into the fetal position as a small army of police and FBI swarmed onto the scene. One of two helicopters hummed directly overhead, kicking up wind. Bystanders hungrily tried to grab the stolen money dancing around them in the air over the salty shore.

Warren stepped aside and let a team of junior agents read the perpetrator his rights. He looked over at his partner and could see the concern etched on her face. Her phone was in her hand. His cocky bravado dissipated, and Michael Warren stepped up close to his partner and spoke softly.

"You okay?" he asked. "Orders from D.C.?"

"No," she said, turning to face him. "From The Council. It's time."

9

THE REZ

US HIGHWAY 19 WEST, *North Carolina*

FAST. WARM SUN. WIND IN HAIR. FREEDOM.

THE BLACK 1970 CAMARO Z28 TORE THROUGH THE southern landscape. John Fogerty sang on the one oldies station that got reception, his voice pulled through the open windows and sucked out into the October wind. Orange and purple leaves lined the trees. Dead brown leaves collected on the ground. A red-tailed hawk soared high above. There was no traffic, no clouds, no ugliness to be found in the world. Everything was open roads, sunshine, and freedom.

Will savored the moment, gently holding the steering wheel.

Papaw Jimmy fidgeted in his seat, a twinge of pain

crinkling the skin around the corners of his eyes. He adjusted his posture once, then again, but it was no use. He looked over at his grandson, the young warrior lost in thought.

"Hey, boy," Jimmy said. "You got any Aleve in here? Or Tylenol?"

"Yeah," Will said, pointing his thumb toward the back seat. "In my backpack. Top pocket."

Jimmy looked over his shoulder and saw the bag in the back. He turned around and grabbed it, pulling it onto his lap and un-zipping the pocket.

"Your knees again?"

"Yeahp," Jimmy grumbled, digging through the pocket. It was loaded with junk, including keys, old receipts, pens, lozenges, and candy. He fished around until he found a small bottle of Tylenol and grabbed it, a tangle of other items spilling out along with it. He pushed a couple pens back into the pockets along with some hard candy, then a metal glint caught his eye. It was a thin, aluminum chain with two rounded, rectangular ID plates at the end. Will's Army dog-tags. "Here. You forgot to put these on," Jimmy said, passing them over.

"Nah, I don't really wear 'em. You can put 'em back."

"Huh," Jimmy grumbled, pulling the tags back and taking a closer look. "Thought you were purty proud a' your time in the service."

"Oh, I am," Will said. "Wouldn't trade it for anything. But the dog-tags, I mean... it's just a necklace. Not every veteran wears them."

"Yeah, but... I don't know. It's like a talisman, or somethin'. It's special."

Will chortled. "It's a necklace."

Jimmy shrugged, turning the stainless-steel tags over to see better. Stamped into the metal was Will's name, military ID number , and social security number. Jimmy shrugged, returned the tags to the backpack pocket and tossed two Tylenol into his mouth, swallowing them down.

"Drive faster," Jimmy said.

WILL TURNED RIGHT ONTO ROUTE 441 AND CRUISED toward town. At first, there was not much to see; an animal hospital, then a visitor's center, and a river bisecting a strip of land known as the Oconaluftee Island Park. A gas station. Two motels. Signs in both English and the native Cherokee language. The buildings were sparse and not a soul was in sight. But then they rolled into the downtown area and Will's jaw nearly dropped open.

A vista of tourism and commerce opened up in front of them. The main strip boasted a large collection of souvenir shops, restaurants, bars, motels, and more souvenir shops. White tourists hustled around with camera-phones and bags of goodies, taking in the sights, as Will and Jimmy cruised down the street.

There was a museum, the Bureau of Indian Affairs, the police station, a billboard promoting the show "Unto These Hills," and signs pointing the way to the old Oconaluftee Village. More gas stations, more restaurants, more coffee shops. Tourists and locals hurried around with their families, texting, sharing their trips with the world on social media. A giant statue of a stereotypical Indian brave known as The Muffler Man stood outside the Native Brews Tap & Grille, holding up his hand in the cliché Indian-how gesture.

The new crown jewel on The Rez was Harrah's Cherokee Casino Resort, a luxury 21-story hotel and casino sprouting up from the rolling hills and completely native-owned. Tourists and locals alike flocked to pour their money down the drain, drink overpriced cocktails and bask in the greed and glow of the modern world. Jimmy watched in disbelief as cars lined up to get a parking space inside the massive, four-story garage. This was a far cry from the reservation of his youth. The old man wilted in his seat, looking down at the floor.

"My God," Jimmy whispered.

"Not exactly what I was expecting either," Will said.

"Just, um... Just look fer a place called Pete's Pancakes. That's where we're meeting up. Maybe we can ask someone fer directions..."

Will took out his phone, opened up his nav-system, and spoke, "Find Pete's Pancakes." The app whirred into action and started them on a course.

"Or I guess you could just do that too," Jimmy shrugged.

PETER LITTLEJOHN WAS THE PRINCIPAL CHIEF OF Cherokee, NC and the owner of Pete's Pancakes, the best breakfast spot in town. The old timer was a stocky, squat little man, like a tree trunk with arms and legs. Pete was as old as Jimmy, but sported a mop of black hair unusual for his age, wore thick glasses on his round, red face, a blue blazer over a white shirt, and a hand-made Cherokee beaded medallion around his neck. He stood in the sun, smiling warmly and greeting the guests as they came in, chewing the fat with the locals.

He didn't recognize the black muscle car as it pulled into a parking spot, but the face of the man in the passenger seat set off an alert in his head. He was a stranger, yet familiar. An old man Pete hadn't seen since he was a young man. Pete's jaw clenched and he stood at attention without realizing it. Customers smiled and waved at him as they came and went, but Pete's focus carried him across the lot to greet the strange newcomers. He approached the passenger door as Will and Jimmy got out.

"Well, I'll be damned," Pete said, a smile crackling across his old lips, "Jimmy Shaw." He chuckled as Jimmy froze in mid-stretch and turned to see him.

"Son of a bitch." Jimmy smiled.

Will watched as the two old goats came together, sizing each other up after over five decades. Jimmy put his hands on his hips, looking Pete up and down.

"You haven't changed a bit," Jimmy said.

Pete busted out into a booming laugh, slapping his thigh and holding his arms open to greet his old friend. "Get over here, old man!"

They came together and hugged, slapping each other on the back before stepping away. Pete patted Jimmy on the shoulder and gave him a good, loving shake.

"So how the hell are you?" Pete asked.

"I tell ye," Jimmy smirked, "if I were any better, I'd be twins. How are you?"

"Old. Fat. Ahhh, remember when we were young and in shape?"

"Now now, Pete, don't say that. Round is a shape," Jimmy joked, reaching in to slap Pete's bulging belly. The two old friends laughed as Will came around to meet them, wearing his best courteous smile. Jimmy reached out and slapped his grandson's shoulder.

"Pete, I want you to meet Will," Jimmy said.

Pete reached out to shake his hand, a look of awe and reverence in his eyes. Will felt like a rock star meeting his biggest fan.

"Afternoon, sir," Will said.

"Hello, very nice to meet you," Pete said, forgetting to let go of Will's hand. "So you are, uh...? He is a...?" Pete looked over at Jimmy, who nodded. He kept shaking Will's hand, looking him up and down, taking in his impressive, statuesque physique. "Wow. Very cool. Thank you, thank you for coming... Oh, sorry." Pete finally gave Will's hand back.

"Hey, Pete!" A middle-aged man said, waving as he and his wife walked out the front door with full bellies.

"Hey, Ronnie! Hey Jan!" Pete beamed his politician smile and waved back as the married couple walked to their car. "Good to see you!"

"Not a bad gig," Will said. "Principal chief *and* owner of the pancake house."

"Ha! I don't run the restaurant so much anymore," he said. "I let my daughter handle the business. I just come in when I want a free meal! Speaking of which, Will... Do you like blueberry pancakes?"

WILL POURED MORE BLUEBERRY SYRUP ON HIS blueberry pancakes.

Pete watched his two guests eat, opting only for a cup of coffee himself. Will scarfed down the pancakes, stabbing bacon onto the end of his fork, his eyes rolling back in his head with each orgasmic bite. Jimmy ate a simple BLT.

They sat in a corner booth away from the other diners. The decor was clean and rustic, with wood-paneled walls and graphic art of chickens and roosters everywhere. The staff were peppy in purple t-shirts with the company logo on the breasts, and classic Motown pumping through the speakers at a comfortable decibel level. Eggs, bacon, pancakes, waffles, coffee and more circled the room, filling the air with a decadent swirl of aromas.

Pete fidgeted with his coffee cup, trying not to stare at Will's impressive biceps and vascular forearms. He looked closer, as if he might be able to see Will's skinner spirit if he looked hard enough. Will tried not to notice.

"So, are you like, um... a bear?" Pete whispered. "Or a wolf?"

Will froze, suddenly embarrassed. He may as well have been asked how big his dick was. He chuckled and washed down his food with sweet coffee.

"Uh, no." Will shot an uncomfortable glance at Jimmy, then returned to his food.

"I-I mean, I know wolves are the most common type of, y'know..." Pete looked around, making sure no one was listening, and then whispered again, "...skinners. So I just figured..."

"Cat," Will said, chewing his food.

"Ahhh, a cat!" Pete caught himself and checked his volume. "Right on, that's cool. A cat. Blue Clan! Oldest clan of the Cherokee people. Very nice. And the bear, also a subdivision of the Blue Clan!" Pete gestured to Jimmy. "Very cool. Did your papaw tell you he saved my life once when we were young? Some good 'ol boys were drunk, wanted to kill themselves an injun, I guess... Damn near beat me to death. Then your papaw showed up and..." Pete cackled at the fond memory. "Well, you can pretty much imagine what happened next."

"Pete," Will said, wiping crumbs from the corners of his mouth and getting down to business, "tell me about what kind of resources we have here."

"To handle something like this? Not much. We have a couple psychics, including my wife. She practices shamanism, but I mean, she reads tarot cards and astrology and stuff. Makes dreamcatchers and amulets to sell in souvenir shops..." He threw his hands up. "Not exactly powerful sorcery."

"What about your marshal service?"

Pete shrugged. "They're a modern police force. They have fancy weapons and technology, body armor... Heck, they even have a S.W.A.T. team and a bomb squad now! But still, nothing to handle something like *this*." Pete slouched in his chair, his eyes downturned. "That's why I called ya'll. We need all the help we can get."

"So then what's the plan, ye ol' geezer?" Jimmy asked, taking a sip of coffee.

"Every night, we've had patrols set up. Police and volunteers have been setting up in different spots around The Rez. They have walkie-talkies, they have guns... they don't have a clue. Even if they do spot this thing, whatever the hell it is, what are they gonna do?"

"Can we interview any of the victims?" Will asked.

"I know the Tsagasi family. They were the first. They're still... Well, I think I can get them to talk with us."

Will said, "I want to drive around, get familiar with the area, investigate however we can."

"Sure," Pete said, "but keep in mind, the Cherokee Nation Marshal Service is in charge. We can't just go barging into crime scenes or anything. We have to be sly."

"Oh, I can be sly," Will said and chomped into a forkfull of pancake.

"Good," Pete said, finishing his coffee and plunking the empty mug down. "But first thing's first. I want you to meet some of the boys. Lieutenant Ballard and some of the others are down at the football field today letting off some steam before patrol tonight, playing a little stickball."

Will stopped mid-chew.

"Stickball?"

10

STICKBALL

BY THE TIME they arrived at the high-school football field, most of the players had already assembled. Cars and trucks filled the parking lot along with a few police SUV's. Children ran and played along the edge of the field, while their parents lounged in folding chairs, sipping brews from the coolers they brought from home. Vendors sold everything from nachos and cheese with jalapeños, to hot tamales, street corn, and everyone's favorite Indian tacos at the food truck. A small group of teenagers played frisbee off to the side while munching on a basket of fry-bread coated in powdered sugar. Everyone came out when there was a stickball game.

"I don't see the point in this at all," Will grumbled as he climbed out of his driver's seat and closed the door. "We're here on a hunt."

Papaw Jimmy and Pete Littlejohn got out and ambled over to Will, all three of them gazing out at the bustling, sunny field.

"Patrol doesn't start till tonight," Pete said. "It's only

one in the afternoon. Plenty of time. Besides, this is important. This is part of our culture and you're an outsider. The boys will trust you more if you prove you're worthy."

Will shook his head in disbelief as they approached the field, the sweet and savory aromas coming from the street vendors making his mouth water. He looked around, taking in the scene. The children playing. The tourists taking pictures with their cell phones. The sun warm and high in the sky. A hipster college student sat at the foot of a tree, singing and strumming an acoustic guitar, hoping for cash and coins to drop into his instrument's beat-up case. Will listened to the boy's song, a melancholy march in A-minor 7, his voice a bittersweet croon.

"Mama rocks the child awake - He with waves casts fingers in sand - Sleeping body carries him to shore - Against red sky the blackbirds dance...

And mama sings rise, morningbird, rise - Blackbirds dance - Morningbird rise - She sings rise, morningbird, rise - Blackbirds dance - Morningbird rise..."

The shaggy young man continued to play and sing, picking and strumming. Will stopped to listen as Pete waddled ahead towards the group of players, calling back to Will and Jimmy.

"Gonna tell the boys you're here," Pete said.

Will glanced at Jimmy, annoyed.

"This is ridiculous, Papaw. I've never played this game before."

"Ah, it's easy," Jimmy shrugged dismissively. "You run around like an idjit and try to pick up a leather ball with a couple a' sticks, throw it through a... a thing, try not to get tackled. Ain't nothin' to it."

"Oh good, now I feel much better," Will muttered, watching as Pete spoke and shook hands with a group of shirtless stickball players. He touched one on the shoulder, a handsome middle-aged man who carried himself like a leader, then gestured back over to Will and Jimmy. Will grumbled, uneasy.

The street musician continued to play and sing.

"Awake now he stands - Just up to her side - On his shoulder she rests her hand - As the sun does rise...

And we sing rise, morningbird, rise - Blackbirds dance - Morningbird rise - We sing rise up, morningbird, rise - Blackbirds dance - Morningbird rise..."

Pete returned with the other man, a Cherokee native standing just over six feet-tall, with short salt-and-pepper hair and a handsome mustache beneath his robust nose. He was shirtless and well-built for a man in his early fifties. There was a gleam of confidence and charisma in his eyes; Will immediately recognized him as an alpha male.

"Jimmy, Will," Pete said as he gestured to his friend, "I'd like you to meet Lieutenant Ben Ballard with the CMS. He's heading up the task force."

"Pleased to meet you, Jimmy," Ballard said, shaking Jimmy's hand. "Will," they shook hands. Both gripped with strength. "I've heard a lot about you. Bounty hunter, special ops rescues, Army Ranger..."

"Well, I don't like to brag," Will chuckled.

"...Five years for aggravated assault."

"Yeah, well uh..." Will was at a loss. The tension was

palpable. The handshake held firm. Jimmy and Pete watched in suspense as neither Will nor Ballard broke eye contact. Finally, a smile broke across the lieutenant's face and he slapped Will's shoulder.

"Ahhh, I'm just playin' with you, Will," Ballard said with a hearty laugh. "Glad to have you. We can use all the help we can get."

"No problem. Happy to help," Will cleared his throat.

"So, your family left The Rez when you were just a baby, huh?"

"That's right."

"Well around here, stickball is pretty big. We play it to settle disputes, or like today... to prepare for battle. You ever play?"

Will glanced over at Jimmy. "Oh yeah, it's my favorite game."

Ballard hooted at Will's overt sarcasm and slapped his shoulder again.

"Ah, you'll be fine," Ballard said. "I'll show you what to do. We do shirts versus skins. We're skins. Hope you're not shy about taking your shirt off."

Will made a face and accepted the challenge, peeling off his t-shirt and exposing a physique sculpted by years of combat and martial arts training. Ballard swallowed his Adam's apple and tried not to appear visibly intimidated. Pete and Jimmy shared an impressed look. Women sitting around the field quickly took notice. Will tossed his shirt at his grandfather's face and the older Shaw caught it, laughing and shaking his head.

"Let's do the damn thing," Will said.

They walked out onto the grassy field to meet the rest of the boys. All eyes turned to the stranger. Including Ballard, there were eleven men of varying ages and body types, tall and short, fat and thin, each ready for battle. Ballard greeted them all, politely gesturing to Will as they mixed into the group.

"Boys, this is Will. He's playing with us today." Heads nodded and greetings were spoken. "He's a newbie, so help him out, okay? Cody, get him some sticks."

A slender young man nodded and dutifully went on with the task.

"John, this is Will," Ballard said as another man approached with an extended hand. Will shook it. "Will's gonna be joining us on patrol tonight. Will, sergeant John Sneed. Toughest sonofabitch on The Rez. Man's a damn grizzly bear!"

Oh no he's not, Will thought. Sneed was a husky and stout man, but only a man. Will smiled politely as he noticed the sergeant sizing him up.

"Nice to meet you, sir."

"And that there is Officer Paul Kituwah, and Officer Charlie Saunooke," Ballard gestured to two more young men, both strong and stocky, but hardly athletic in appearance. They both waved and nodded at the newcomer.

"Hey," Kituwah said.

"How you doing?" Saunooke added.

Will looked at the other end of the field, watching as the shirts-team gathered and prepared for the game. They looked like a herd of buffalo getting ready to charge. Will took a deap breath and let it out slow, and the younger officer returned with two stickball sticks for Will.

"Here you go," the youth said. He was in his early twenties with a physique that could be blown over by a stiff gust of wind and acne threatening to break out on his cheeks and forehead. "Cody Ray, good to meet ya."

"Officer Owle. My youngest on the force," Ballard said, playfully jabbing his subordinate in the stomach. "Real killer."

Will inspected the sticks, his eyebrows furrowed in puzzlement. Each stick was two-feet long and crafted from hickory, with the ends bent into a teardrop-shaped pocket. Within each pocket was a web of deer hide sinew, resembling a snowshoe or a tennis racket. Will waved the sticks around, completely baffled.

"Umm…"

"Here," Owle laughed and held his own sticks out to demonstrate. "You have to use the sticks to pick up the ball…" he tossed a small, soft ball made of deer hair and hide onto the ground, then proceeded to use the two pockets at the end of his sticks to scoop it up. "Then you run the ball to the other end of the field, and you hit their goal post with it. You can either throw it, or hit the post with the sticks. Each time you hit is a point, twelve points wins the game. Twelve-man teams."

"That it?" Will asked.

"You ever play football?" Owle smirked.

"Yeah."

"Then you should be fine."

The players aligned on the field, poised for battle, their sticks gripped tightly. Muscles flexed, eyes bored into those of the opposing team like lasers. The wind blew. The crowd watched. The street musician continued to play.

A referee issued a call to battle and tossed the deer hide ball into the air. Will watched as it fell, time seeming to slow down as it neared its collision with the ground. With a soft, leathery *thump*, the ball hit the grassy field. Then all hell broke loose.

The players erupted into a flurry of action, each fighting to be the first to scoop the ball up between their sticks. Will was caught in the melee, smashed amongst the crowd of aggressive, sweaty bodies. He tried to reach with his sticks but couldn't even see the ball. Shouts and grunts filled his ears. Grass and earth kicked up into the air. The ball went flying and everyone chased it.

A stick cracked against Will's shin out of nowhere and he was almost knocked over by the stampede of play-ers. He cursed and bolted after them, watching as Ballard and two of his other teammates reached the front and fought for control of the ball. Officer Kituwah scooped it up but was promptly tackled to the ground. Ballard swiped up the ball and tossed it in Will's direction before he too was tackled.

"Will!" Ballard shouted as a burly man ruthlessly took him down.

"Oh, shit..." Will watched as the ball sailed past him, then chased after it. He put the ends of his two sticks together, desperately trying to pick the ball up into the pockets, but the task was much harder than it looked. Sweat glistened on his body as he used one stick to push the ball into the pocket of the other, the swarm of players charging straight at him. Finally, he snatched the ball into his grip, holding it between the two sticks, and stood up proudly. "I got it!"

Smash! A huge man made of fatty flesh and muscle collided into him, knocking the air from his lungs and the ball from his grasp. Will crunched into the ground, the sweaty brute smiling down at him. The ball went sailing and everyone continued to chase after it. Will rolled onto his side and watched as the small war continued.

"Jesus Christ..." he said, pulling himself back to his feet.

Jimmy and Pete watched as the battle raged on. The opposing team scored the first point. Then Will's team. Back and forth it went, a spectacle of tackling, throwing, slapping, shouting. The crowd cheered on their favorite team, and the women secretly kept their eyes trained on the muscular stranger. Will managed to catch the ball between his sticks, seeing Ballard open downfield, and successfully tossed the ball over to him. The lieutenant snatched up the ball, ran to the goal post and scored a point. Pete smiled, impressed.

"Not bad for a newbie," he said.

Jimmy nodded with a polite smile, digging into an Indian taco he'd bought from the food truck, enjoying the mixture of savory flavors.

"Mm, been a million years since I had one of these," he mused. There was a sadness in his eyes that did not go unnoticed.

"What is it?" Pete asked.

"Nothin'," Jimmy mumbled. "Y'know. Bad business goin' on here. Bad feelin'."

"You're right," Pete answered, his own spirits deflating as he remembered their current situation. "But that's why I'm glad ya'll are here. I know you can help."

"Mm," Jimmy mused, his expression solemn and distant. "We'll try."

The crowd cheered as the game charged on.

The young street musician continued to play.

"Long since she has passed away - Into sea froth and spray - Old man now, he sits alone - With wife and little ones in his home...

And we all sing rise, morningbird rise - Blackbirds dance - Morningbird rise - We sing rise, morningbird, rise - Blackbirds dance - Morningbird rise..."

THE SPIRIT COUNCIL

SNOHOMISH, *Washington*

THE LIGHTS WENT OUT IN THE FRONT WINDOWS OF The Canary community theater. Posters advertised the venue's upcoming shows: a performance of "The Taming of the Shrew," a poetry showcase featuring fifteen local wordsmiths, and the annual Christmas extravaganza. It was a small building of brick and stone, perched between an antique shop and a vegan sandwich bar, and across from a run-down watering hole.

Wilbur Husky locked the front entrance of the theater.

He twirled away from the door with a spring in his step, grabbing a broom and continuing his nightly ritual. He whistled and hummed, his barrel-belly swaying and jiggling with each movement. He had neatly-combed brown hair, round features and kind eyes, and most people assumed he was younger than his sixty years.

Erupting into his favorite song from "Seven Brides For Seven Brothers," Wilbur gleefully swept the floor of the lobby, wiped down the counters at the concession stand, and locked the back office.

He parted two red curtains and shuffled into the theater. One hundred old, wooden seats were poised before an old stage, a Kingsbury piano set up on stage-right waiting to show off its voice. Wilbur climbed the stairs to the stage, tucked four folding chairs from back-stage under each arm, and brought them out. One by one, he unfolded the chairs and set them up in a semi-circle. He checked his watch, realized it was later than he thought, and hopped into action, shuffling back down the stairs and off to the side of the stage, where the building's back door was positioned.

Wilbur unlocked and swung the door open, letting the cool night air in. Standing patiently in the lights of the back parking lot was a young man with his hands in his pockets. He stood up at attention at the sight of Wilbur opening the door.

"Evening, sir," the young man said.

"Welcome, little brother," Wilbur smiled. "Come on in."

They exchanged pleasantries as Wilbur let him enter, then went about tucking a doormat under the door to jam it open. He took a peek outside and saw other figures approaching in the distance, coming down from the streets, into the parking lot and to his back door. Another young man came, then another. Then Marjorie the librarian arrived. Wilbur greeted them all with a smile.

The door began to slip and swing closed, but a well-manicured hand caught it. Agent Michael Warren pushed the door open, smiling confidently. Beside him as always, Agent Winona Lambert. He wore a Hawes & Curtis slate-gray suit to complement his silver hair. She wore a cheap JC Penney black suit to complement her tight bun of black hair.

"Hey, party people," Warren said with a warm smile and an extended hand.

"Haha! Come in, Mike! Come in!" Wilbur said, waving them in.

"Good to see you," Lambert said as he embraced them both.

Wilbur shook hands, gave hugs and smiled as the group arrived and took their positions inside. The younger people found chairs in the front rows while the elders went up to the stage, taking seats in the semi-circle of folded chairs. The older woman from the bakery arrived, smiling and presenting a tray of cookies covered in plastic wrap to Wilbur, whose eyes lit up.

"Ooh! Thanks, Maggie!" Wilbur realized his blunder as the pint-sized woman shot him a disapproving look. "Uh, I mean Orenda. Sorry. How are you?" Wilbur corrected himself, using her secret Council name, and giving her a half-hug and a kiss on the cheek. Orenda grinned and handed over the platter of sweets.

"Good, Takoda, good," she said. "These are for the kids. Oatmeal raisin."

"Well, it's a good thing for me I'm just a big kid!" he chortled, spinning to bring the snacks inside. He set up a folding table and put the cookies down, also bringing in a cooler with an assortment of sodas, napkins, and paper cups.

Orenda went about greeting the guests while Wilbur fussed over being the perfect host, and others continued to arrive. A large, brawny black man in a suit. A short, rotund woman with a red bob of hair. A young American Indian man with long black hair and piercing eyes. They greeted each other, made small talk, and ate cookies.

The back door swung open and Keonee walked in.

"Hello, children," he said with a smile.

The room went quiet as everyone stood at attention to greet the man with the silver ponytail. Everyone smiled and nodded, some waved at him and some offered greetings like "evening, Father" and "hi, Father." He grinned, shook hands, and slapped shoulders as he made his way around.

"Welcome, Father," Wilbur said, shaking Keonee's hand.

"Thank you, Takoda," Keonee said.

He stopped in front of Warren and Lambert, shaking their hands.

"Nayati, Kasa," he said to each respectfully. "Thank you for coming."

"Of course, Father," Warren said.

Keonee smiled and crossed to the snack table. "Mmmm, what have you brought for us tonight, Orenda?"

Keonee reached for a cookie and Orenda playfully swatted it away.

"They're for the kids!" Orenda said with a chuckle.

Keonee laughed and everyone else joined in as he

grabbed himself a cookie anyway, taking a big bite. He chewed the oatmeal-raisin goodness and scanned the room of expectant faces.

"Everybody doing good tonight?" Keonee asked.

Each attendee answered in the affirmative.

"Everybody here?"

"Um," Wilbur muttered, looking around. "I think so."

Agent Warren pointed toward the lobby and said, "I hear someone out front." He cleared his throat. "I uh, I smell him too."

Wilbur turned and scrunched his eyebrows, listening closely. There indeed was a faint tapping on the front window. Wilbur huffed his way back up the aisle, through the curtains and into the front lobby. There indeed was the shadow of a figure standing outside the window. The hefty theater owner let out a sigh as he realized who it was, heading over to open the door.

Old Carl Wexford teetered from side to side, a fresh buzz from cheap booze running through his scraggly head. He was a filthy mess, with long, gray hair and beard, and clothes that used to have individual colors but were now all a faded, shabby brown. The old hobo swung around to face Wilbur, blue eyes piercing through the veil of grime that was his face. Lips parted to reveal a nicotine smile as he lurched toward the door.

"Evenin' Wilbur!" Carl said as Wilbur held the door open and stepped aside.

"You're supposed to come to the back door, Nodin."

"Baaaah!" Carl dismissed Wilbur with a wave of his filthy hand and slipped past him into the building.

Wilbur smelled the alcohol on the old bum's breath and shook his head, closed the door again, and locked it tight.

Carl bursted through the back curtains with a smile and a wave to everyone as he strode down the center aisle towards the stage, an incredulous theater owner in tow. The younger attendees in the front rows turned and nodded to the old hobo with respect as he reached the front, giving Keonee a friendly slap on the shoulder.

"Okay, let's do this!" Carl said. "Ooh! Cookies!"

Carl snatched one from the platter and stuffed it into his mouth as he ascended the stairs to the stage. Keonee and Orenda shared a look of annoyance but chose not to say anything. Wilbur just shrugged and headed up to the stage himself. Carl smiled at the others already seated as he made his way to his reserved chair, cookie crumbs falling into his beard.

"You're drunk, Nodin," Keonee said sternly.

"I'm fine, I'm fine. Hey, everybody," Carl said, waving at the others. "Hey, Chelsea. Bob. Mike. How you guys doin'?" Carl plopped down to his seat and continued to munch.

"Council names only, brother," Orenda said, restraining her annoyance.

"Yeah, yeah..."

"Okay, let's call this meeting to order, shall we?" Keonee said.

"All be seated!" Orenda called out, and anyone not already seated dutifully obeyed. She and Keonee walked up the stairs to the stage, and she took one of the two empty seats left. Keonee nodded respectfully to the seven other senior members seated behind him onstage. He turned and nodded to the junior members in the front rows as well.

"My children," Keonee began pensively, "thank you for coming. I know many of you traveled a great distance. We honor you, as we honor the sun, the moon, the great Mother Spirit. I honor the great spirit of the lion." Keonee gestured to the seven senior council members behind him, starting on the far left with Wilbur, who stood up proudly.

"I honor the great spirit of the bison," Wilbur said, then sat down.

Chelsea Jarvis, the mousy redhead to his right then took her turn, standing. "I honor the great spirit of the fox." She returned to her seat.

Next came Michael Warren and Winona Lambert, in their gray and black suits. Each took their turns, declaring, "I honor the great spirit of the wolf."

Bob Calloway, the large black man, wearing a suit ready for Sunday worship at a Baptist church, rose to his feet and said, "I honor the great spirit of the bear."

Orenda stood. "I honor the great spirit of the scarab." She sat.

All eyes turned to the last person seated on stage, but Carl just munched away at the last remnants of his cookie. Keonee sighed. Calloway gently nudged Carl, who suddenly remembered where he was. The old hobo cleared his throat and stood up.

"I honor the great spirit of the coyote," Carl grumbled, and sat back down.

Keonee shook his head at the old bum. "You are a pitiful sight, Nodin. Undeserving of your seat at this council. Just go home."

"Home?" Carl stood up, ire in his eyes. "What home? I'm your man on the street. Remember, *Father?* Dirty and poor, that's how you want me!"

"Sit down, you fool," Orenda said. "You dishonor yourself and this council."

"Oh, shut up, *Maggie!*" Carl turned to face her, spitting his words. "He wants me on the street, so I'm on the street. I'm your little spy that no one notices, no one cares about. So yeah, I stink! And I fucking drink! Okay? I'm sooo sorry!"

"Silence yourself, Nodin," Keonee said, "or we will silence you."

"Oh yeah?" Carl challenged, kicking his folding chair out of the way and taking a sloppy, aggressive step towards Keonee. "What are you gonna do, *Father?* Huh? You want to shut me up? Well, shut me up! Come on!"

Everyone in attendance watched in suspense.

"Don't be ridiculous," Keonee said.

"Come on, big shot! Let's go!"

Carl began to change. He stood defiantly before his leader, the physical reality of his human self warping away. Claws started to appear, and a muzzle with sharp canines began to phase into existence. Unimpressed, Keonee stood and did nothing. Carl made it nearly halfway through the transformation into his coyote self when he heard the voice.

"Weak," was all Orenda had to say.

Suddenly, the energy that fueled Carl's transformation was gone. Orenda's command stopped him in his tracks, her psychic energy cutting deep into his brain. In an instant, the coyote spirit stopped materializing and dissipated like smoke, leaving the old drunk stupefied. "Weak," she said again, and he felt every ounce of strength draining from his body.

Carl sunk to his knees like a deflating balloon, fighting her spell briefly before finally succumbing. He collapsed to the stage floor, defeated.

Keonee looked over at Warren and Lambert, and they understood what he wanted. The two federal agents rose from their seats and pulled Carl off the floor, helping him back into his chair. The hobo looked down at his feet and wisely decided to remain silent.

Keonee cleared his throat and got back to business.

"We have much to talk about tonight. A lot is going on," Keonee said, strolling deliberately around the stage, making eye contact with his senior council members as well as the junior members in the audience. "Balance has been compromised. There is sadness in the heart of The Great Spirit. Up north in the cold country there have been suspicious disappearances, *monster* sightings. Our friends in Brazil are dealing with their own problems, as are the Russians, but we're not going to even touch on that right now. Those guys do their own thing."

Keonee shook his head and got amused chuckles from his audience.

"I'll be sending three of you to Brazil tomorrow as emissaries, but we'll get to that later. For now, the pressing issue is what's happening in North Carolina, on the Cherokee reservation," he continued, pacing like a college professor. "Babies are being killed. Locals are talking about evil spirits. I myself have seen visions in my dreams, seen the bad omens. Something not of this world is crossing over and attacking the innocent. Taking the lives of children, the most *sacred* among us. Brothers and sisters, I'm sure I don't need to tell you, this evil must be *stopped*."

"Is this the prophecy, Father?" one of the junior members asked.

"It just might be," Keonee answered. "The deaths of the innocent. The rise of corruption both in the spiritual realm and in the world of men. The pollution of the Great Mother... I have been expecting this my whole life."

"You think it's Shaw?" an intense young Chicano with a shaved head asked.

"We just don't know yet, Karuk," Keonee said. "His family is tied to the prophecy. A Shaw will come to threaten, possibly overthrow our whole council. Upset the balance. Plunge the world into darkness... But we have to be sure. Who knows what powers he has, what forbidden doors he's opened using the dark arts. We need to be there and stop whatever this evil spirit is. If it's Will Shaw, the evil must be cleansed from his body with fire. Nayati? Kasa?" Keonee looked at the two feds, who sat forward attentively. "I think we could use some FBI presence down at the Cherokee Rez. What do you say?"

"You got it, Father," Lambert said.

"You go with them, Redhawk," Keonee said, looking

now at the steely-eyed young Indian sitting in the first row. The youth with the long, black hair nodded solemnly, all business. "Ask around. Keep your eyes open. Find whatever foul creature is responsible for this. And if it's Will Shaw... bring him to me alive."

12

PREMONITION

CHATTANOOGA, *Tennessee*

Casey Madison was caught in a triangle choke.

Big Derek was good at those. He was a two-stripe blackbelt, over two hundred-fifty pounds of muscle, with a shaved head and tattoos covering nearly every inch of him. With Casey's head and arm caught between his legs, Derek gave a firm but gentle squeeze until the young girl was forced to tap out. The big man released the choke and Casey fell to the mat gasping for air, a sweaty mess. She smiled and shook her head, getting back in position to start again.

"Remember to posture up when you feel that triangle coming," Derek said.

"Yeah yeah," she laughed. "You're too good!"

"You're getting better. Come on."

Derek waved her forward. She scooted up to him on

the mat, they slapped hands, then bumped fists, and resumed their roll. There was just over two minutes left on the timer before she would have to roll with someone else. All around her on the sweat-streaked mats were pairs of sparring partners, all trying to hone their game and either get a submission victory or at least trying to not get submitted.

Casey much preferred the stand-up classes. *Pop pop*, in and out. Jab, punch, kick, head movement, footwork. That's where she excelled and was most comfortable. But as Will told her many times before, the ground game is incredibly important. What if a big, strong brute like Derek started smashing her into the ground in real life? She'd probably just turn into the cheetah and tear him to pieces, she thought. No no, Will would say. She had to control the beast... Will.

He was not there at class, and she hadn't heard from him. This was not in itself unusual, as he was always running some secretive mission that he'd never take her along for. He still didn't think she could handle herself, still treated her like a child. Casey scoffed as her mind wandered, while Derek allowed her to take his back and practice in a more dominant position. She thought of Will, picturing his face, wondering where he was. Another search and rescue mission? Maybe taking down a drug dealer?

As her mind drifted, she felt a fluttering within herself, saw a flickering of colors intruding on the edges of her vision. It was happening again. She could see things, sometimes past, sometimes future. Her own unique skinner gift, Will called it. Still, it was anything but pleasant and more often than not, frightening.

She couldn't stop it, couldn't understand it. They came out of nowhere, vivid dreams jolting into her head while she was still awake. The flickering colors began to take form, and Casey didn't even notice Derek throwing her off his back and reversing the position. She saw Will in her mind's eye.

He was slumped on his hands and knees on the center of an old, ornate stage. Gaudy swirls of bronze molding and red-velvet cushions accented the dark, Victorian theater. A spotlight shone down directly on him. He wore stage makeup to make him look bruised and bloodied.

Several other actors stood on stage, all draped head-to-toe in black, surrounding him. Another actor lay on the stage beside him, playing dead. One of the black-cloaked figures stepped up to Will and pushed a gun against his temple. The set around them was constructed to look like the forest at night, with painted trees and stars in the background, and a pyrotechnic rig simulating small fires in the foreground.

Skinners made up the entire audience. Sitting in the opulent rows of seats and in balconies above. Wolves, bears, cats, raptors, snakes, all dignified in their finest evening wear. Tuxedos and ball gowns, gold chains and diamond earrings. They were here to enjoy the show. The upscale beasts watched with vested interest as the actor in black wrapped his finger around the trigger and began to squeeze...

"*WILL!*" CASEY SNAPPED OUT OF IT.

Derek had his rear-naked choke set, gently squeezing and expecting her to defend. Instead, she spasmed and flailed. He immediately let her go.

"Casey, hey! You okay?" he asked.

She collapsed to her hands and knees, panting as sweat ran down from her braided corn-rows to the tip of her nose. The images and sounds from the vision echoed in her head like church bells. One thought above all else rang crystal clear: Will needed her help. Derek placed a caring hand on her shoulder but Casey bolted up and stalked away to the women's locker room.

She snatched up her gym bag and took her phone out, dialing Will and pacing impatiently in the small, empty locker room. The phone rang but went to voice-mail. She cursed, hung up, redialed. It rang and rang but once again, voicemail. Casey hissed and grumbled, trying to think. Finally, she decided to send a text.

Hey old man, how's it goin? Everything ok?

That would have to do for now. Her mom would be there soon to pick her up. Casey peeled out of her sweat-soaked rash guard and shorts and stepped into the shower. She leaned against the wall and let her body rest as the hot water ran over her skin, but the thoughts in her head raced and pounded like a storm.

Will needed her help.

Bri Madison parked her silver 2014 Civic in the

parking lot as the sun began to set, ready to hop out and catch the tail-end of her daughter's class as she usually did. Casey strode through the front door in her clean sweats, gym bag slung over her shoulder, making a bee-line for her mother's car. Before Bri could switch off the ignition, Casey opened the passenger door and jumped in.

"Hey," Bri said, surprised. "Class end early?"

"Nah," Casey said, closing her door. "Tweaked my neck a little."

"Aw. Well, I'll get you some Ibuprofen, maybe some Icy-Hot. Okay?"

Casey smiled and nodded. She'd gotten good at lying.

As Bri drove the car off into the darkening night, Casey pulled out her cell phone and saw she had one unread message. It was Will's reply to her text:

"*Fine. Working a case.*"

She shook her head and pocketed the phone. Always a man of few words. In any case, he was still alive. Casey still had time, but how much? She had to think of something to both help Will and cover her own tracks. She couldn't just disappear again on some rescue mission; she'd scare her poor mother to death. And she could hardly tell the truth either, unless she wanted her mom to know that her daughter was a shapeshifting were-cheetah. She needed a good excuse.

A smile curled onto Casey's lips. She had an idea. Her thumbs flew into action, quickly texting a new message to her best friend, Ieshia.

Hey girl, I need a big favor. Meet me at my house in 20 minutes! Important!

. . .

Iᴇsʜɪᴀ ᴡᴀs ᴀ ʀᴇɢᴜʟᴀʀ ɢᴜᴇsᴛ ᴀᴛ ᴛʜᴇ Mᴀᴅɪsᴏɴ home, and Bri let her in with a smile. Casey whisked her friend away to her bedroom, trying to act casual and not arouse her mother's suspicion. But there was trepidation in Ieshia's eyes.

"What's going on?" Ieshia asked as Casey closed and locked her bedroom door. "You're acting weird."

Casey's room was a mess, and she flung clothes and pillows aside as she jumped up onto her bed. On the wall where most girls would hang posters of their favorite teen idols and boy-bands, Casey had posters of Jackie Chan and MMA champions Valentina Shevchenko and Israel Adesanya. With a fervor, Casey tore her photos down from the wall and kicked everything to the floor. Ieshia watched as her friend stripped the wall down to its bare-white foundation.

"You know I still have some packing to do, right?" Ieshia continued. "I gotta go to sleep early too. Tomorrow's the big day... Hello?"

Casey barely acknowledged her friend, jumping off her bed and crossing to the closest. She dug through a pile of junk until she located her digital projector.

"Yeah, I know..." Casey finally said. "And that's why I need your help. I'm coming with you. Or at least, that's what I need my mom to think."

"Huh?"

Casey plugged the projector into the wall, then ran a USB cable to connect it with her laptop. On the computer screen were multiple thumbnail images of a beautiful amusement park. Roller coasters, grand fountains, games, a luxury resort and pool. She selected a photo of a sprawling vista of tourists in front of a ferris wheel, sent it to her projector, and shot the image onto her blank wall. With a few adjustments of the lens, she blew up the image to take up the whole surface like a movie screen. She smiled.

"You and me are gonna take some pictures," Casey said. "A few outfit changes, a little white lie... And I'll owe you forever. Now, pay attention."

"I hate you so much."

Bri was only half-paying attention to the latest dating reality show on Netflix and sipping on a nice white zin when Casey and Ieshia ran into the living room. Casey's eyes were wide with excitement, her smile stretching from ear to ear.

"Mom! Mom! Guess what!"

Bri shifted on the couch, looking quizzically at her daughter.

"Mm hm?"

"Well, remember I told you that Ieshia and her family were going to Paradise Park this week? Well, Ieshia's mom and dad invited me to go with them!"

Ieshia smiled and played along. "Yeah, they said it's cool. Besides, I'd rather have a friend there with me than just spend the whole time with my parents and my brother. Ew."

"But..." Bri started to protest. "You wanna go away

for a whole week? I don't know, baby. That place is very expensive..."

"Oh, please mom! Please!" Casey begged.

"Yeah," Ieshia added, "my parents said they'll take care of everything."

"I'll take my taser with me. I'll call every day. And send pictures! I promise! Oh pleeeeaase, mom! Please please please please pleeeeaaase??"

13

MEDICINE BAG

WILL COULD HEAR the croon of Van Morrison coming from inside as they walked up to Pete Littlejohn's front door. There was a brick entryway set into a ranch-style home in the upscale part of town. The lawns on this street were well kept, the cars new and equipped with navi and bluetooth. There were no trailers parked or old sofas rotting at the edge of curbs, no stray dogs running amok in the streets. Pete turned to smile at his two guests as he unlocked the front door.

"Smells like Leah's cookin' some pot roast," he said, letting them in.

"Oh yeah," Will breathed in the savory aroma as they entered the cozy, mid-sized abode. Van Morrison continued to sing as a female voice voice harmonized from up ahead in the kitchen. Will could see glimpses of her moving in and out of the doorway, dancing and singing as she prepared the hot meal.

"Babe, we're here!" Pete called out.

"Ooh! Okay okay!"

Leah Littlejohn skidded into the kitchen's doorway, hastily wiping her hands off on a towel and eyeballing the two strangers. She was short and stout to match her husband, with chubby cheeks and streaked-grey hair. She was half Indian and half White, and with her flowing garments and purple bandana, she was as much a flower child as she was a Cherokee princess.

"Is this them?" Leah cooed, flustered. "I mean, obviously it's them. Obviously it's you! Hi, I'm Leah. Welcome!"

They all exchanged greetings but Leah's eyes were stuck on Will. She held onto his hand after she shook it, reaching up with her left to touch his arm. She may as well have been a little girl in the 50's meeting Elvis.

"Wow, so you're him... I mean, uh... I heard a lot about you. I've been a psychic and astrologer my whole life, believe in all ranges of spirits and beings... and now there's a real skinwalker standing in my living room!"

"Uh," Jimmy cleared his throat. "I'm here too, yknow."

"Oh my God, I'm so sorry! I forgot. I didn't... I'm sorry. Of course, you're both... wow." She eyeballed Will's filthy state from head to toe and made a face at her husband. "You made him play fuckin' stickball, didn't you?"

"Leave me alone, woman," Pete grumbled as he crossed into the kitchen.

"Will, do you want me to wash those muddy clothes for you?" Leah offered. "Have it all ready by the time we finish dinner."

"Oh, no. Um," Will looked down at his sordid state

and thought twice. "Well, I do have a change of clothes in the car..."

"Here. Go get your clean clothes and give me these dirty ones! Shannon!" Leah turned and called behind her.

"What?" came a muffled voice from another room.

"Get your ass in here, that's what! We have guests! *What*, she says."

Shannon Littlejohn strode into the room, and aside from being thirty years younger, and with black hair instead of gray, she was a mirror image of her mother. She stopped in her tracks at the sight of the handsome stranger in her home.

"Uh, hi..." Shannon consciously stopped herself from drooling.

"This is my daughter, Shannon," Leah presented formally.

"Pleased to meet you, ma'am," Will said, shaking her hand.

"Shannon, please take Will's clothes and put them in the wash."

"Okay..." she almost started undressing him right there.

Will laughed and threw up his hands.

"After I come back from the car!" he joked, skipping back to the door and heading back out to the car. Jimmy rocked uneasily on his heels.

"I'm Jimmy," he said.

LEAH SPARKED UP A BIG JOINT.

She held the breath of savory cannabis in her lungs for a moment, regarding the family and guests sitting at the dinner table around her. The scant remnants of roasted wild pig, potatoes, okra, and green beans colored their plates. Will had just finished a slice of Shannon's homemade blackberry cobbler and felt about ready to burst. The young woman smiled and held out the pan, offering him more.

"Want another slice of pie, Will?" she asked, starry-eyed.

Will could tell she was offering more than just blackberry cobbler, and politely cleared his throat and waved it away.

"Oh, no thanks, ma'am. I am stuffed to the gills."

Leah exhaled a cyan puff of smoke and continued the story she was telling.

"But to answer your question, Jimmy, no. I'm not clairvoyant. I mostly do tarot readings, astrology, that kind of thing. I do some shamanic work, like spiritual journeys, mostly for white tourists looking for a taste of Indian spirituality in their boring-ass lives. Oh, want some?" Leah held out the burning joint to Jimmy, who politely waved it away.

"No thank you, ma'am. We're fixin' to get to work in just a bit," Jimmy said.

"Right, right. Sorry," said Leah, taking a big pull and then passing the joint over to her daughter, who gladly took a hit. Jimmy looked across the table at Pete, who just shrugged, and the two old coots nearly cracked up laughing. "But I do have my moments," she continued. "Remember when Great Aunt Marie had a stroke and we didn't know if she would make it?" Pete and Shannon nodded. "Well, I had a dream one night that she was sitting at a big dinner table, kinda like this one, and Grandpa Pat was there, and Uncle Willie, all our family who'd passed on... They were smilin' and laughin' and havin' a great time... Then when I woke up the next morning, I got the news that she'd crossed over."

"Wow," Will said, pretending to be impressed.

Leah nodded proudly as Shannon passed the fattie back over.

"Yeahp," Pete said sarcastically, "you're a real soothsayer."

"Kiss my grits," Leah replied, taking a long pull of indica.

Shannon laughed at her parents' banter and Jimmy joined in. Will saw the cloud of smoke filling the room despite the open windows and fan blowing. A little longer in there and he'd have a contact high. That plus Shannon's hungry eyes looking at him, and Will was ready to bolt. His phone began vibrating in his pocket and he quickly pulled it out. The screen read, *Shenandoah calling*. Will almost said "thank God" out loud as a feeling of relief washed over him.

"Um, I have to take this," Will said, standing up. "Please excuse me." He walked across the room to the sliding glass door, opening it and slipping out onto the patio, now lit only by moon and stars. He hit the answer button and held the phone to his ear with a smile. "Hey, Copper."

"Hi, stud." Her sweet twang was music to his ears.

"Got anything good for me?" Will asked, absently pacing the patio.

"Oh, I always got something good for you."

"Something good about this *case*, Copper."

"I asked around. Talked to my friend in the North Carolina State Troopers, talked to my contact in the FBI, searched every database... Nothing. Whatever's going on up there, the Cherokee Marshal Service is keeping it pretty close to the chest."

"Hm. Okay, thanks."

"So, how's The Rez?"

"It's, uh... different."

"Not like you remember, huh?"

"I don't remember it at all," Will looked up to the speckled sky, kicking absently at the gravel as he paced the patio. "Just not like I expected is all. People here are scared, and I can't blame 'em."

"I bet," Shenandoah said. "Anything else I can do?"

"Just keep your ear to the ground, sweet tea. You've done enough. You just rescued me from a very awkward dinner. So, thank you!" Will chuckled.

"Okay," she giggled in return, "so where are you stayin'?"

"Nowhere. Least not yet. Up all night tonight on patrol, lookin' for whatever this damn thing is. 'Bout time to head out. Don't know how long I'll be here, so... yeah, we'll see."

"Well, be safe. Let me know if there's anything I can do."

"You got it, Copper. Thanks again."

They said their goodbyes and ended the call. Will

stood for a moment in the cool night air, looking at the moon. His belly was full, but deep within the big cat was hungry. It was time to go.

Back inside, Leah was regaling Papaw Jimmy with the stories behind every piece of artwork on the walls, while Pete and Shannon cleaned up the dinner table. Will came back in and Shannon perked up.

"Oh, Will! Just a minute..." she said, skipping off to the laundry room. She returned a moment later with his shirt and pants. Will smiled politely as Shannon bounced up to him, beaming as she proudly presented the clean laundry. "Here you go. All cleaned and folded."

"Thank you, ma'am," Will said, feeling her eyes all over him. "Well, we probably better get goin' now, right?"

"Yeah," Pete said, drying off his hands with a dish towel, "Ballard and the others are meeting at Veteran's Park in a little bit. We should be heading over."

"Okay, wait. Before you go, I got somethin' for ya!" Leah placed her joint into a handmade ceramic ashtray and scooted into her art studio. Will and Jimmy heard the sounds of clinking and shuffling, a drawer being opened and closed, and a moment later, Leah returned with a necklace in each hand. "One for each of ya!"

Each was a leather lanyard with a small pouch at the bottom, one brown and one black, each adorned with beads and a tiny feather. Leah handed Jimmy the brown bag and Will the black.

"Thank you, ma'am," Will said, perplexed as he looked at it.

"They're medicine bags," Leah said. "Made 'em

myself just for you. Said a special blessin' over 'em, help keep you protected."

"What's in it?" Will asked, feeling the stuffed, small leather pouch.

"Mostly tobacco and sage. It will keep you in tune with your spirit and the spirit of the people. Think of it like a good luck charm."

"Medicine bags are powerful talismans, boy," Jimmy said, slipping his over his head and smiling with gratitude. "Especially when blessed by a high-medicine woman. Thank you very much, Leah."

"Yeah, *high* medicine woman is right," Pete joked, and was met by a quick slap to the shoulder from Leah as he slipped into his jacket.

"Shut up, ya idgit!" Leah snapped, then turned back to Jimmy. "You're welcome, Jimmy. I hope they help keep you safe and strong."

Will, not wanting to be impolite, slipped the leather loop over his head and let the medicine bag hang from his neck. "Thank you, Leah. I appreciate it."

"Blessed be, boys," she said. "I hope you can find this evil out there and kick its fuckin' ass. I'll be prayin' for you."

"Me too," Shannon added. "Be careful."

"We will," Pete said, leading Will and Jimmy to the front door. "Come on, boys. Let's go kill us a demon."

The three men strode out into the night, Pete unlocking his silver Ford F-150 and climbing inside. "All right now, just follow me, okay?"

"Copy," Will said, he and Jimmy both sliding into

Will's sleek-black machine. Jimmy clicked on his seat belt as Will fired up the engine.

"You ready for this, son?"

Will just made a face and shot his papaw a look.

Of course he was ready. Will shifted the car into drive, but stopped before pulling forward. There was one more thing left to do. He pulled the medicine bag off over his head, tucking the leather pouch and lanyard into his jacket pocket. Jimmy watched, disappointed, but didn't say a word. Will released stepped on the gas and they followed Pete as he led them off into the night to find a monster.

14

WITCH HUNT

BY THE TIME they arrived at the Cherokee Fairgrounds, the crowd had already amassed. Lieutenant Ballard and his officers had cleaned up nicely and wore their black uniforms and silver badges. Officers and civilian volunteers buzzed around the square, carrying flashlights, walkie-talkies, and to-go cups of coffee. Ballard had a large map spread across a table, and he was busy pointing out what sectors each search group was covering.

Will and Jimmy parked and joined up with Pete, the three men funneling into the crowd. Pete pushed his way through, regarding everyone and shaking hands. The chief led Will and Jimmy to the center of the crowd, where Ballard was giving instructions to the volunteers. When he saw Pete approaching, he stopped and smiled.

"Evening, Ben," Pete said with a warm smile.

"Glad you could make it," Ballard said and turned to Officer Owle. "Get these men some radios, Cody." Owle nodded and complied, giving Will, Jimmy, and Pete each a walkie-talkie. "We're on channel three. You guys will be in group four with Cody."

Will's eyebrows furrowed. "Group?"

"Yeah, group four."

Ballard continued giving instructions, and Will turned to Jimmy and Pete, his eyes concerned. "Guys, I don't want to be in no group," he whispered.

"Well, that's how this is set up," Pete shrugged. "Each group has one police officer leading it, we all split up and patrol different sectors in town—"

"Groups with police officers leading them," Will repeated, shaking his head. "Guys, I work alone. I need to be able to just do my own thing. If I see this raven mocker, I'm not gonna radio it in. I'm gonna let the panther rip it to pieces."

"Look, fellas, we'll figure it out, okay?" Jimmy said, trying to calm Will.

"Everything all right over here?" Ballard cut into their private conversation.

Will, Jimmy, and Pete shared a look. Will sighed.

"Yeah," Will said.

"Good," a female voice interjected. "Because we need all the help we can get." Captain Lynn Oocuna was a tall, handsome Cherokee woman whose presence commanded respect. All eyes turned to her as she strode to the center of the group and locked her steady brown eyes on Will. "This community is living in fear, mister...?"

Will cleared his throat. "Uh, Shaw. Will Shaw, ma'am."

"Will, this is Captain Oocuna," Pete gestured politely. "She's in charge of the task force."

"Thank you, chief," the captain continued. "Now listen up, everybody. I hope you all took a nice nap, 'cause it's going to be a long night. Everybody stick with your groups and stay in your sectors. We're spread thin but we should be able to cover all the residential areas on The Rez. Just keep your eyes and ears open. We are going to catch this son of a bitch, whoever he is, and put him where he belongs. And I don't want to hear no more talk about a demon, or a phantom, or whatever. People 'round here are scared enough as it is, understand?"

The crowd begrudgingly murmured in agreement. Ballard and some of the other officers looked at the ground, or off in the distance, not wanting to make eye contact with their captain. Will, Jimmy, and Pete shared a look, feeling the tension and division amongst the local law enforcement community. Ballard cleared his throat and folded up the map, gathering up his things.

"You all know where you're going," the lieutenant said. "Just keep your eyes and ears open and use your radio if you see anything out of the ordinary." He looked straight at Will and said, "And stay with your groups. Good luck, everyone."

Will grumbled in Ballard's direction as the crowd began to disperse.

"Okay," Officer Owle clapped his hands, "so who's with me? Who's group four?"

In addition to Will, Jimmy, and Pete, six other civilians raised their hands.

"Good," Owle said. "Everybody get to your cars, and

we'll all meet up at the fountain by the Welcome Center. From there we'll disperse and patrol a tight grid, moving street by street. Okay?"

The small group muttered in the affirmative and disbanded.

Will looked at Pete. "The Welcome Center?"

"Just follow us," Pete said, and the two old timers lurched over to Pete's truck.

Will sighed and looked up at the moon. A three-quarter moon. He had his 9mm Canik TP9 holstered on his waist and concealed by his black leather jacket, a Glock 42 strapped to his ankle, and his favorite folding knife in his pocket. That plus clean clothes and a full stomach, and he was ready for anything. He spun on his right heel and went to his Camaro, sliding behind the wheel and starting her up.

GROUP FOUR CONGREGATED AROUND THE OLD fountain by the Welcome Center. Officer Owle regarded his eclectic group as they all filed in. There were a few old men, two young braves, a middle-aged woman, Chief Littlejohn, and the two strangers. The lanky young officer regarded Will with a sheepish nod.

"Okay, does everyone have a partner?" Owle asked.

The volunteers nodded and said yes.

"Everyone on channel three?"

They all checked their radios and confirmed.

As the officer gave his last-minute instructions, Will looked around, scanning the area. The park sat as the centerpiece of the modest neighborhood. Highway 441 stretched out left and right, with smaller residential streets splitting off into the darkness. A light breeze came in from the east. Most of the critters had settled down for the night, save for the odd squirrel rustling through the branches. The main street and its tributaries were darkened, lit only by the moon, a speckling of lights from the nearby houses, and an odd blueish-purple illumination coming from the streetlights. Will furrowed his eyebrows, puzzled.

"What's the deal with the blue streetlights?" Will asked.

"Ask the fine folks over at Duke Energy," Owle snickered. "It's a manufacturing defect in the LED bulbs. They start out just fine, but after a while, *pffft*, they start turning blue." The officer shrugged and glanced over at Pete.

The chief sighed, getting a little tired of fielding complaints about the blue streetlights. "We installed them to replace the sodium vapor lights that've been here since the 70's," he told Will, then directed his next words at Officer Owle, "and yes, we're *working* on it."

Will shrugged. "Looks pretty cool to me."

Officer Owle chuckled, stepping up to Will, admiring the lights.

"Yeah, kinda like blacklight, huh?" Owle joked. "Feels like a night club!"

Will chuckled, "Yeah, kind of."

"How you feeling after that stickball game, huh?" Owle asked. "Sore? Hey, do you mind if I ask what you use for soreness? See, I'm tryin' to gain some mass. Been workin' out, y'know?"

Will tried not to roll his eyes. Another young guy wanting fitness advice.

"I read this one article that said you need a lot of potassium right after a workout, but then this one guy at the gym said to try turmeric. I don't know, I'm trying, but it's just so hard to put on any weight..."

"Just stick with it," Will said. "Exercise, eat healthy foods. That's about it."

"Do as he says, not as he does," Jimmy cackled. "Will's idea of healthy food is Pop-Tarts and ice cream!"

"Well, I got a weird metabolism. What can I say?"

Cody Owle nodded, smiling with the eagerness and innocence of a puppy. "So what do you say, Will?" the officer asked. "You and me, huh?"

Will suddenly realized the cop was asking him to partner-up for the night. He casted an uneasy glance over at Pete and Jimmy. "Oh, uh... I'm ridin' with my papaw tonight, Cody," Will said.

"Yeah, I cain't be on my feet too long anyhow," Jimmy added. "Gotta stay in the car, patrol around like that."

Owle tried to hide his disappointment. "All right, looks like it's you and me, Mr. Littlejohn." He flashed a polite smile at Pete, who returned the gesture.

"Great," Pete said, then turned to Will and Jimmy. "Good luck out there, boys."

"You don't need good luck when you're good lookin'," Jimmy snickered, jabbing Will's shoulder. "Right, boy?"

Will chuckled and waved to the others, turning to join his grandfather as they walked back to the car. When they were out of earshot, Will spoke.

"So, you pickin' up anything on that radar of yours?"

"Yeah," Jimmy said, "whatever this thing is, it's close."

"And we'll be ready. Once we get away from the others, I'll be off on foot. You good to drive a stick?"

Jimmy sneered. "Don't make me have to pop you in your mouth, boy."

Will laughed and slapped Jimmy's back. He handed his papaw the keys and they climbed into the Camaro, starting the engine, and growling off into the blue-washed streets.

15

OUT OF THE BAG

LET ME LOOSE. **LET ME GO.**

WILL FELT THE DESIRE OF HIS OTHER SELF BREWING, the need for the big cat to be released from his small cage. It paced and grumbled and grew impatient. Will's heartbeat quickened and his mouth watered. He drummed his fingers on his knees as Jimmy calmly steered the Camaro down Yellowhill Road. The locals had settled in for the night and all was quiet.

"Sure don't seem like everyone's on the same page around here," Jimmy said. "That captain lady? She thinks we're just lookin' for some crazy *guy*. Sure, like some psycho could just drain the life right out of a child." The old man shook his head.

"She's scared," Will said. "They're all scared. "Most people won't believe until they see with their own eyes. Shit, even then..."

"Well, she'd best start believin'. She don't know what kind of evil she's dealin' with. If it's a raven mocker..."

"Then I'll tear its damn throat out," Will finished.

"Don't get cocky, boy," Jimmy said. "They ain't entirely physical, ain't entirely spirit. I never faced one before, don't know if they can even be killed at all."

"If it can be killed, I'll kill it."

LET ME GO! I WANT OUT!

"Let me out right here," Will said as they approached the next intersection, feeling the beast straining to be set free.

Jimmy obliged, pulling off to the corner and stopping. He turned to Will, putting a loving hand on his grandson's shoulder.

"You gotta fight this thing with your spirit, son. Not your claws."

"Okay, whatever that means," Will chuckled, kicking open the passenger door and hopping out. "Just keep drivin' around, Papaw. Radio me if you see anything."

"And if you're the cat, you gonna hear the radio?"

Will shrugged. "If not, the others will. We'll do our best, okay? We'll get this thing one way or another." Will closed the door and bent down, looking through the window at Jimmy. "Don't worry."

Jimmy sighed. "Be careful, boy."

Will smiled and flashed the hang-loose hand sign as Jimmy drove away.

Finally alone. Will stood and breathed the air, felt the pavement beneath his boots. Indigo streetlights and a silent breeze. Darkness. Freedom. Power. He felt the night, every murmur and hush, every shadow and secret. He was tall and strong and his heart pounded like a bass drum. The night belonged to him.

LET ME OUT! LET ME OUT!

WILL STARTED WALKING. HIS SENSES WERE OPEN and alert. He looked for a place untouched by light, a dark pocket in the quiet neighborhood. Behind the row of houses to his left was a narrow strip of woods dividing the streets. The feeling inside him was growing in urgency; he could ignore it no longer. With practiced stealth, Will made sure nobody was watching, and slipped between houses and into the wooded area.

The shadows and crickets welcomed him. He stood amongst the trees and closed his eyes, took a relaxing breath, and allowed himself to phase away into the ether between worlds. Reality shimmered and warped around him. The man flickered away and the black jaguar came into being.

Will opened his yellow eyes.

He was the cat, black and strong and fierce and fast. A satisfied growl breathed through his fanged muzzle. He flexed his powerful muscles, dug his clawed toes into the dirt. One with the shadows, he began to slink between the trees, looking for anything out of the ordinary.

There were silhouettes moving behind closed curtains, the muffled sounds of televisions, conversations, washing machines. The mouth-watering scents of fried chicken and hot chocolate. Residents of the humble street went about their lives, unaware of the silent, dark protector patrolling the night.

Will caught the familiar, unpleasant scent of dog, and a moment later, a German Shepard lunged at him. The beast hit the end of its run with a sharp *snap* and the leash yanked it back. Will side-stepped through the cover of trees at the edge of the yard as the canine frantically barked in alarm. He focused on the animal's teeth, its ferocious eyes, and his mind suddenly flashed to his brother. Mason.

"Hey, buddy."

Mason's voice echoed in Will's mind as he recalled that last night. The train, the fire, the rage in his brother's eyes. Watching those eyes go dull as he took his last breath. The flashes of imagery quickly faded, like they always did. Mason was gone.

Will continued through the darkness as he heard the dog's owner behind him, coming out to see what the mutt was barking at. The black cat slipped away between the trees, his powerful haunches absorbing the impact of each step, making him as silent as a shadow.

He came to the end of the row of houses, circled around to the right, and found himself in the park. Across the vast lawn, he could see the cars of the group-four search party in the parking lot by the fountain. Will moved on, inspecting the perimeter of the rustic park, enjoying his stroll in the moonlight. There was a jungle gym, a basketball court, and a pond. There were restrooms and water fountains. But there were no demons or soul-sucking wraiths anywhere in sight.

A familiar and unpleasant feeling began to sink into his bones. Boredom. He had claws and fangs and anger, and he was ready for a fight. Crickets chirped. Will growled. He wondered what his papaw was doing, where the others were, if anybody had seen anything, or would see anything. He wondered if he was even in the right place. With the walkie talkie deep in the ether along with his human self, he wouldn't hear if anyone tried to call him. Will paced and growled, debating what to do.

Leaves rustled and twigs snapped.

Will froze, listening more carefully. He smelled the breeze and caught a scent. His mouth watered as he turned his gaze in the direction of the sound. It was a young elk, very common in these parts. The corners of Will's savage muzzle pulled up into a smile and the ebony hunter slinked through the darkness towards the unsuspecting herbivore.

Closer he crept, watching the animal at it strolled casually across the lawn without a care in the world. Closer. Will closed the distance. He knelt down, coiling into a ball. His curved claws flexed. His eyes focused on the target. He pulled the trigger.

The elk screamed and exploded into a mad sprint for its life as the predator sprung from the shadows. Its hooves pounded into the grassy turf, its eyes bulging with panic and fear. The black cat powered forward and sank his claws into the rear haunches of his prey. The elk trumpeted a chilling shriek as its killer tackled it to the ground and wasted no time jumping on top and sinking his fangs into its throat. Will bit down hard, crushing the animal's windpipe and holding the pressure. After a few moments of struggling, the elk's body went limp.

Will proceeded to tear his prey apart and feast on its bloody flesh.

JIMMY STEERED THE CAMARO AROUND THE neighborhood. His eyes were growing weary and his knee was aching again. Once in a while the radio would crackle and one of the group leaders would ask for the volunteers to check in. The classic rock on the radio wasn't doing a very good job of keeping him awake, and any more coffee would be murder on his prostate. The old man toughed it out though, patrolling the streets, looking for a monster. He checked his watch and the time was 1:15 a.m.

Up ahead, he saw a large man walking toward him on the sidewalk. The old man tensed up in apprehension, squinting to see better as the figure drew closer. It was Will. Jimmy relaxed as his grandson came into focus, strolling down the street, back in his human form. Jimmy slowed to a halt as Will walked to the passenger side, opened the door, and slid into the seat.

"Hey hey," Will said. "Any action?"

"Pssh. This town's quieter than a whorehouse on Sunday," Jimmy said. "You?"

"Nope. Just had me a little midnight snack, but that's about it. You gettin' tired, want me to drive?"

"Hell naw," Jimmy lied, taking his foot off the brake.

"I'm doin' just fine, thank you very much. I may be old, but the night is young, and we got us a monster to kill." He pulled away and continued down the street as Will smiled, clicking on his seatbelt.

Down the street, Redhawk silently watched them. The tall, young Indian stood like a sentinel in the shadows, his dark eyes severe and focused, his long black hair catching in the breeze. His face betrayed no emotions, a silent soldier obeying orders and following his target. Light and shadows began to bend around him. Reality warped and wavered, flickering and shimmering as the man shifted out of this reality and something else took his place.

Powerful feathered wings of brown and gold hues flexed and stretched open, and in an instant, he shot up into the night sky like a rocket.

16

RESCUE MISSION

CHATTANOOGA, *Tennessee*

CASEY MADISON DID NOT GO WITH HER FRIEND'S family to the theme park that day. Instead, she snuck over to East Brainerd with a backpack full of supplies and a wad of cash withdrawn from her college savings account. She hopped off the 8:15 crosstown bus, took out her phone, and confirmed the address she was looking for. Pocketing the phone again, she powered through the misty morning streets.

Finding her way to 21 Diamond Lane without difficulty, Casey hesitated for a moment before opening the front gate and walking in. It was a modest and well-kept home, with blueish-gray walls and a manicured lawn and garden. She smelled home cooking and heard cartoons coming from inside. Taking a deep breath, Casey climbed the four steps to the front porch, stepped up to the door, raised her finger, tensed up with fear, and finally rang the bell.

Her heart raced as she heard approaching footsteps. She controlled her breathing. The door unlocked and swung open.

Shenandoah Glass stood in the doorway.

"Hi," she said, "can I help you?"

"You're Shenandoah, right?"

"Yeah." She was glistening in a layer of sweat, wearing spandex shorts and a cut-off sweatshirt top, her favorite workout clothes.

"I'm Casey Madison."

It took a second for the name to register, then, "Oh... *Oh*."

Shenandoah took a step back, trying to keep her cool.

"Will gave me this address," Casey said, "in case of emergencies, y'know? And, well... this is an emergency. Will needs our help."

The lady cop exhaled and stepped aside, opening the door for Casey to enter.

Lucas popped his spiky-blonde head up from the top hatch of his own homemade time machine, constructed out of cardboard boxes and silver spray paint. He oogled the teenage girl as she came in, and noted the uncomfortable tension in the room. "Who are you?" he asked.

"Um, Luke, this is uh..." Shenandoah stammered.

"Hi, I'm Casey," she said with a pleasant smile.

"I'm Lucas. Wanna see my time machine?"

"Luke, baby, um... maybe a little later, okay? Right now me and Casey need to talk. I need you to go play in your room now, please."

"Oh, *Mom!*"

"Go on now, munchkin. Don't make me tell you twice. I'll come get you in a little while, okay?"

"Fiiiiine," Luke sighed, climbing out of his recyclable temporal displacement device and shuffling out of the room. "Bye," he moaned as he turned the corner and climbed the stairs. Shenandoah rubbed her shoulders, nervously shifting her weight from foot to foot.

"Cute kid," Casey said.

"Thanks. So, you're a... you're a... right? You're...?"

"A skinner? Yeah."

Shenandoah tried to remain cool, considering she now had a shapeshifting teenage girl with an emergency standing in her living room. "Wow. Cool," was all she could say.

"Will's in trouble," Casey pressed. "Do you know where he is?"

"Yeah, he's at the Cherokee Reservation in North Carolina, working a case," the cop said. "What's going on?"

Casey paced, unable to be still, struggling to find the words she was trying to say. "Something... something bad's gonna happen to Will. If we don't help him. That's all I know."

"What do you mean? Where are you getting this from?"

"I... I had one of my things," Casey said. "My visions, or whatever. I saw Will, he was all beat up... with a gun to his head. There were so many skinners around him. This is... this is going to happen soon. I know it. If we don't get to Will and stop it... he's going to die."

"If *we* don't stop it?" Shenandoah raised an eyebrow.

"I can't do this on my own," Casey said.

"Uh huh. And does your mother know about this little expedition?"

"No way, she'd flip her shit. Oh, but thanks for reminding me..." Casey took out her phone and quickly texted her mother —

Hey! We're on the road! In a few hours we'll be at Paradise Park!! OMG so excited!! Ekkkkkk!!!

Casey tucked her phone away and looked back at Shenandoah expectantly. The state trooper brushed the blonde bangs away from her eyes and paced the room, trying to think. The urgency in the teenager's glare was clear.

"Look, Casey. I have my son here. I can't just take off for North Carolina for a few days—"

"Can't someone watch him for you? Your ex? Tell him it's an emergency, I'm sure he'll understand."

Shenandoah grumbled. She knew the girl was right. While not a great husband, her ex had always been a good father, always willing to watch Luke when she was in a bind.

"Okay, look," she said, shifting into her stern mother-voice, "Even if I'm able to go up there and help Will, you are not coming with me."

"Yes I am."

"How old are you, fourteen? I am not putting you in danger. It's not even up for discussion. God, your poor mother..."

"Look," Casey stepped up to Shenandoah, already the same height as the adult, and looked her in the eye.

"Will needs me. And I'm not just some kid. I can take care of myself. Now, I'm going one way or another, with or without you. Will needs as much help as he can get."

Shenandoah sighed. "You won't let go of it, will you?"

"I saw what I saw."

"So me and a fourteen year-old girl are gonna bust in there and save the day, huh? That's your plan?"

"Actually," Casey said. "I know someone else we can ask for help. We need to call in the big guns."

VICTIMOLOGY

CHEROKEE RESERVATION, *North Carolina*

THE CURTAINS IN THE CHEAP MOTEL ROOM BLOCKED out most of the morning sunlight, but there were still a few golden beams cutting through. Will had kicked off his boots and slept in his clothes on top of the covers. Jimmy was in the second bed, tucked under layers of nylon bedding and snoring peacefully. After an uneventful first night on patrol, they had come back to their temporary abode to crash only three hours earlier.

It was now 10 a.m. The bedside phone rang.

Jimmy jolted in his sleep, his mess of white hair poking up from beneath the covers. Will stirred in his bed, but the abrasive metallic bell failed to immediately wake him. Jimmy grumbled and coughed, looking over at the old-fashioned rotary as it continued to shriek. He pulled himself to the edge of the bed, cleared his throat, and picked up the receiver.

"Hello?" Jimmy said, his eyes half closed. "Pete?"

Will began to wake up, stretching and yawning. He pushed up onto his elbows and looked over at Jimmy. The old man sat up on the edge of the bed, concern and confusion in every wrinkle on his face.

"What? You're shittin' me! Oh, no..."

Will sat up and rubbed his eyes, listening intently.

"Uh huh, yeah..." Jimmy continued. "Yeah, of course, we'll be right over." He hung up the phone, stupefied, then looked over at his grandson.

"What's goin' on?" Will asked.

"That was Pete," Jimmy said. "It happened again last night. Another baby."

Will's veins flooded with fire.

THE CROWD AROUND THE SMALL SUBURBAN HOME bristled with anger, fear, and curiosity. Police cruisers lined the street, and every officer on the force stood guard to keep the surge of onlookers from breaking through the yellow crime scene tape. Captain Oocuna and Lieutenant Ballard spoke with the forensic team on the front porch, while officers Owle, Kituwah, and Saunooke, among others, handled crowd control. A young couple sat on the front bench, huddled together in shock, as investigators swarmed in and out of their home.

The closest Pete Littlejohn could park was two blocks away. As he, Will, and Jimmy hopped out of Pete's truck, their sense of dread was palpable. Will could practically smell the heartache in the air. The three men hurried forward, dodging and pushing through the crowd to get to the scene. When they reached the yellow tape they were met by the young and tough Officer Sarah Apachito.

"Please stay back," she said, holding up her hands. "I can't let you through."

"Officer, it's me, Chief Littlejohn," Pete said. "We have to get up there."

"I'm sorry, Chief. Strict orders."

Will strained to see what was happening at the house beyond the barrier. The husband and wife trembled as a plain-clothes detective spoke with them. Ballard was whispering orders to some and barking orders at others.

"Officer, please," Pete urged. "This is important. These men are here to assist in the investigation."

"No civilians past this point, I'm sorry," Apachito said. "You're welcome to wait here to speak with the lieutenant. Might be a while though."

Will, Pete, and Jimmy shared an impatient look between them. Pete glanced to his left and saw Cody Owle holding back the throng of angry civilians and pushed his way over to him, with Will and Jimmy in tow. Pete waved his hands and called out to get the young man's attention.

"Cody! Hey, Cody!" he shouted.

The lanky young cop saw the three men approaching, pushing their way through the crowd. Judging by Owle's sunken eyes and unshaved chin, he had clearly not slept at all.

"Pete," Owle said, nodding to Will and Jimmy as well.

"What can you tell us?" Pete asked.

"Second verse, same as the first," Owle said, tired and annoyed.

"Nobody saw anything?" Will asked. "I thought we had this whole town buttoned up tight? Every family with a newborn was under surveillance, right?"

"Right," Owle said, "only this time it wasn't a newborn."

A chill ran through Will's bones, and he shared a concerned look with Jimmy and Pete. The chief leaned in closer. "Well then, who...?"

"Oh, it was still a baby," Owle said, "but not a newborn. This one was a toddler, little boy, almost two years old." The officer shook his head in disgust.

Pete stepped back, shocked. Jimmy touched the medicine bag that Leah gave him, closing his eyes and saying a silent prayer. Will's mind raced.

A shriek turned into a sob and all eyes turned to the front porch. Two forensic examiners wheeled a gurney out through the front door, a black body bag on top. Inside the bag was a child-size lump. The cries belonged to the young mother, needing to be restrained as they wheeled her child's body to the ambulance. Her husband held her back, himself weeping, and they collapsed to the deck as Captain Oocuna and Lieutenant Ballard tried in vain to console them.

Will fumed. He spun around, pushing back through the crowd.

"Come on," he said. "Let's go."

"Where to?" Pete asked.

"To get some answers."

.   .   .

HECTOR TSAGASI CRACKED OPEN HIS FRONT DOOR TO find three men standing on his front steps. He recognized the principal chief right away, but the other two he'd never seen before. Strands of long, black hair hung in front of his perplexed eyes.

"Chief Littlejohn?"

"Mr. Tsagasi," Pete said gingerly, "sorry to bother you at home. These are my friends Jimmy and Will Shaw." They both nodded politely. Will could smell the 9 a.m. Jim Beam on the man's breath. "We were hoping we could talk to you for a few minutes?"

Hector eyed them suspiciously, still hiding halfway behind the open door.

"What about?" he asked.

"Well... about Benny," Pete said as tenderly as possible. "May we come in?"

"Already told the cops everything I know."

"We're not cops," Will said.

"They're private investigators," Pete said. "Specialists. They're here to help."

"Help," Hector scoffed the word. "Sure, why not? Come on in." His tone was sarcastic and defeatist, but he pushed the door open and lumbered back inside, allowing them to follow.

The blinds were drawn, the house was a mess, and the air was stale. Empty bottles of spirits decorated the countertops. Family photos hung crooked on the walls, but all the ones of little Benny were perfectly straight. A shrine had been set up in memoriam of the fallen infant, complete with candles, flowers, and cards of condolences. Hector Tsagasi's face was blank, a countenance drained of emotion, his eyes had no tears left. His well had clearly run dry, and he was doing his best to fill it back up again with cheap bourbon.

"So," Hector said, throwing up his hands and letting them slap back down to his thighs, "how's everything?"

"Mr. Tsagasi," Pete said, "we'd like to hear your version of what happened."

"So you can call me crazy too? So you can laugh? Nobody believes us, so why should you?"

Jimmy lurched forward on his aching, old legs. "That ain't true, young fella. A lot of folk around here believe. We believe."

"The whole town's scared, Mr. Tsagasi," Pete said. "It happened again last night. Another little boy. We need to stop this thing. We were hoping we could ask you and your wife some questions."

"My wife," Hector said, rubbing the back of his neck and glancing down the hall at the closed bedroom door. "She doesn't really... she won't talk to anyone."

"Sir? May I just have a look in the baby's room?" Will asked.

Hector sighed and nodded, gesturing for Will to follow. "Sure."

The wilting man led his three guests down another hallway to a door decorated with stickers, cartoon decals, and a small whiteboard with "Benny" scribbled in purple. He opened the door but dared not go in. It was dark; the one window had been hastily boarded up after being shattered by the intruder. Will stepped into the room, feeling the darkness for a moment before flipping on the light switch. The other three men watched from the doorway as Will went to the center of the room, just standing there and looking around.

"What are you doing?" Hector asked. Will didn't answer.

Pete leaned in and touched the man's shoulder. "Um, let's just let him do his thing. Why don't we go to the living room and talk?"

Hector hesitated a moment, unsure about leaving this strange man alone in his baby's room, but let Pete and Jimmy lead him away. Will stood alone in the nursery. He took a deep breath and focused his energy.

When he first become a skinner and unlocked his powers, Will had no control over the strange, psychic abilities. Every person's aura flared and jumped out, every sound boomed. Every object he touched would send visions flashing through his brain. But since then he'd learned to filter out the noise, to focus and use it only on what he wanted. Now he controlled his breathing, concentrated, and utilized his tactile senses.

He slowly walked around the small room and began to touch. He touched the stuffed animals, the boxes of diapers, the changing table. Each sent sparks of vibrant colors shooting behind his eyes, showing him glimpses of the past. Mr. and Mrs. Tsagasi setting up the room, laughing. Trying to figure out the instructions on how to put together the changing table. Hanging decorations to welcome the new baby. Happy memories.

He touched the handle of the stroller they never got to use, and saw it being gifted to the expectant young mother at her baby shower. She was smiling and wearing a yellow dress. Will reached into a cardboard box of

Benny's folded clothes, and flashes of innocence flickered like an old silent film. Benny squirming, crying, sleeping, looking up into his father's eyes and feeling loved. He saw the child wriggling on the changing table as mommy changed his diaper, heard the newborn cooing as his father rocked him to sleep and sang Bob Marley songs.

Will took it all in, moving slowly around, touching. He felt the walls and didn't get much. He touched the boarded-up window and could sense an air of darkness, but nothing specific yet. The boards had been put up after the fact; whatever kind of evil spirit this was, it hadn't made direct contact with them. The crib called to Will from the corner, and a feeling of dread sank in as he approached it. He lifted both hands, extended his fingers, and wrapped them around the rim of the crib.

Evil. Greed. Death.

Will's body jolted as an electric current of terror shot through his veins like ice water. He could see the beast perched weightlessly on the edge, reaching down with what must have been its mouth. Its acrid, rotten odor stung in his nose. The squish of its slimy tendrils and the sinister, staccato rasp of its breathing rang in his ears. Poor Benny lay helpless as the creature gave him a kiss of death, sucking the life force out of his tiny body. Will trembled, keeping his grip tight on the crib, needing to see more.

He focused on the creature. He didn't sense any intelligence, hatred, or ill will. Like a shark, it simply went about and killed to survive. But there was something more. There was a sense of frustration, of this dark entity not wanting to be there. Will recognized the feeling all too well. It was the feeling of doing a job. Punching a time clock, going to work, wishing you were somewhere else.

"SO BY THE TIME YOU GOT THERE, IT WAS ALREADY gone?" Jimmy asked.

Hector nodded, pouring more JB into his glass. "I heard Maria scream, heard a big crash, I ran in... The window was broken, the crib was knocked over, the baby was..." He stopped himself from saying more, taking a gulp of bourbon.

"So, you didn't see anything?" Pete pressed. "Is there anything else you can tell us?"

Hector sprung to his feet, drunk and agitated. "Look man, what do you want from me? I told you and I told the police, I didn't see nothing! I-I... The devil broke into my house and killed my baby boy! Okay? No, I didn't see anything! Actually, wait. Here..." He stalked over to a bookshelf where there were several sketch pads of various sizes, along with pencils, paints and other art supplies. He scooped up the pad on top of the pile and began to flip through the pages. "Here you go. You want to see what it looks like? Here. Maria drew these."

He handed the pad over to Jimmy and Pete. The image on the page was drawn in charcoal, and simply looked like a big mess. Jimmy turned the page and the next one was the same thing. And on the next page, the same. They all looked like she had simply pressed charcoal into the paper and angrily scribbled everywhere. Mostly a big, black splotch, but with other crazy lines randomly snaking around in no particular shape. It did appear to spread out horizontally, and if you squinted, the shape could appear to be two outstretched, black wings. Jimmy sighed.

"Hector?" a woman's voice called from behind a closed door. "Is somebody in there with you?" Maria sounded annoyed and half asleep.

"Um, ah..." Hector tripped on his words, taking a few steps closer to the bedroom door and trying to think fast. "It's just a couple of friends, um... we're just..."

"Tell them to leave!"

"Babe, they're just..."

"Get out! Get out!"

Jimmy and Pete shared a look, feeling the pain and heartbreak in the poor woman's voice. Jimmy sighed and put the sketch pad down, standing back up on creaky knees. Pete rose to his feet as well, accepting that they had learned all they could here.

Will emerged from the child's bedroom a moment later, his expression solemn. Hector sighed and hung his head in shame.

"You'd better go," he said.

Hector went to the front door and opened it, once again letting sunlight stream into the dark cave. The three visitors quietly made their way out. Pete nodded politely and said, "Thank you, Mr. Tsagasi. I'm so sorry for your loss."

The broken father looked at Will with a tinge of hope in his eyes as he passed. "Well? Was anything in there helpful? Do you find anything...?"

Will considered telling the truth, but finally said,

"No. If we need anything else, we'll let you know." And with that, he walked out the door.

Jimmy sensed no emotion in his grandson's voice, no empathy. Disappointed, the old man stepped back up to the front door, holding his hand out to Hector. The young man shook the old, leathery hand, and Jimmy gently placed his left hand on top of both, looking Hector in the eye.

"Hey," Jimmy said. "You need to know that little Benny is with the Great Spirit now. I can feel his energy. He's okay. And you're gonna be okay too, y'hear?"

Hector nodded, fighting the tears brimming in his eyes.

"Okay," Jimmy said tenderly, slapping the man's shoulder. "We're gonna take this thing down. I promise."

And with that, the three visitors pulled back, and Hector Tsagai retreated back into his home, closing the door.

Will strode down the front walkway to the sidewalk, trying to shake off the residue of the vision he had. Pete and Jimmy were closed behind, meeting up with Will beside Pete's truck.

"Did a coon-dog just crawl up your shitter sideways, boy?" Jimmy asked Will, concern and frustration in his Kentucky drawl.

"I saw it," Will said, trying to describe the experience. "I felt it."

"The raven mocker?" Jimmy asked. Will nodded.

"This isn't random," Will said. "I could feel its intentions. It's not just going after any boys. It's looking for a specific boy."

"Then why does it suddenly go from newborns to a toddler?" Pete asked.

"It's like... I don't know. It doesn't know what it's lookin' for yet. It's searching for the right little boy, and when it does..."

"Well sheeit," Jimmy said, "what now?"

"Now we eat," Will said with a smile. "Pete, you know any good breakfast places around here?"

18

A CALL TO ARMS

CHATTANOOGA, *Tennessee*

JACKSON COOPER TOOK A DEEP BREATH AS HE shifted gears into park and looked out the windshield of his van. The signage of the storefront stood out in bold, blue letters: COOPER AUTO. He controlled his breathing and pushed the anxiety aside. Out on the lot, there were customers and employees walking around, talking, looking at cars. Through the windows of the showroom, there were more people and many familiar faces. Jackson told himself there was nothing to fear, turned off the ignition, and activated the hydraulic ramp to let himself out.

Once on the pavement, he pushed his wheelchair forward from his personal handicap parking space up to the front entrance of the building. His hair was a mess, his eyes were tired, and he was wearing the same track suit he'd had on for days, but he did at least make an effort to shave. Still, he could do nothing to hide the scar etched down the side of his face, his daily reminder of that horrible night. Jackson pushed himself to the automatic sliding glass doors, felt the cool air conditioning inside as they hummed open, and wheeled himself in.

Employees took notice. Their eyes widened and some whispered to each other in surprise, "Look, it's Jackson!" He pushed past several sleek cars posed in the showroom, past the restrooms and lounge area, to the front desk. One portly car salesman waved to him from across the room.

"Hey, Mr. Cooper!" the man said with a big grin. Jackson nodded politely.

"Jackson, hey!" another employee said. "What are you doing here?"

"Hi, Carl. Good to see you," Jackson said, and continued forward.

As he approached the main lobby, the receptionist at the front desk saw him and jumped to her feet. The middle-age woman trotted excitedly around the desk to greet him. She had dyed-black hair, rosy cheeks, and pleasantly plump hips.

"Mr. Cooper! Oh, thank you for coming in!" she said.

"Hi, Chelsea. So what's going on?"

"I don't know. But they wouldn't take no for an answer. Said they needed to talk to you in person."

"Where are they?"

"They've been waiting in your office for the past hour."

"Okay," Jackson sighed. "Thanks, Chelsea."

She smiled again as he pushed himself forward, pity in her eyes. Jackson ignored it, along with all the other stares and looks of concern, as he wheeled past the row of offices. He stopped at the door to his office and looked in through the window. Sitting on the couch across from his desk was a young woman in a blue business suit and a teenage girl. Perplexed and curious, Jackson opened the door and wheeled himself inside.

Casey and Shenandoah stood to greet him.

"Jackson Cooper?" the woman with the short blonde hair asked.

"Yes, hello. How may I help you?"

"My name is Detective Shenandoah Glass, state police," she said, showing her badge, "and this is Casey Madison. Thank you for coming in."

They shook hands cordially, and Jackson wheeled himself around to his desk to face them while the two ladies sat back down. "No problem," he said. "I don't really come in much anymore. I, uh... I mostly work from home these days. But my secretary said there was some kind of emergency...?"

"Yes, Mr. Cooper..." Casey eagerly began before her partner waved an authoritative hand to silence her. Casey sulked, allowing Shenandoah to take the lead.

"We have a... a sensitive situation, Mr. Cooper," the officer said. "We have a friend in common, someone who needs our help. And due to... extenuating circumstances, we are not able to go through official channels. This has to be kept a secret." She struggled to find the words to phrase the awkward request.

"Oh, this is gonna be good," Jackson balked. "Who's this friend?"

Shenandoah cleared her throat. "...Will Shaw."

The color drained from Jackson's face.

"Get out of my office."

"Please, if you'd just—"

"Get *out*."

"Look," Casey bolted to her feet, quickly closing the blinds to block out the curious prying eyes, "this *is* an emergency. Will is in trouble, and a lot of children are in trouble too. Something terrible is about to happen, and—"

"Casey, please," Shenandoah said, gripping the girl's shoulder and pulling her back. "What did I say? I do all the talking, right?"

"But..."

"Look," Jackson said, the expression on his face severe, "I want you both to leave. I don't know what this is about, but Will Shaw is no friend of mine."

"Will is up at the Cherokee reservation right now, working a case," Shenandoah pressed. "Something is up there, something evil... It's killing newborn babies, and no one knows why. Will is up there trying to stop it. Now, Will has told me about your history together, and I know what happened to you and your family..." she watched as Jackson sunk almost imperceptibly in his chair, his jaw clenched. "I know what you've gone through, and I'm so *so* sorry. I really am. But children are being murdered, *babies*. There's some kind of... creature out there, and it needs to be stopped."

"And you want me to what? Go to the Cherokee reservation with you? My fat ass in a wheelchair? To help that son of a bitch?"

Casey's restraint ran out and she pounced forward, putting her hands on Jackson's desk and leaning in to look him in the eye. "Listen. Will is going to die if we don't help him. I saw it."

"Casey," Shenandoah tried to pull her back, but the girl was having none of it.

"What do you mean, you saw it?" Jackson said, confused.

"I saw it... I had a vision."

"Oh, you had a vision. Okay."

"I... have visions sometimes," she continued. "I can see things that haven't happened yet. People like us... sometimes we have, like, powers."

"People like us?"

"Like me and Will," she said.

The implication of her words finally sank in, and Jackson's face drooped in fear.

"Y-you're... you're one of them?" The car salesman pulled back in his chair, his hands shaking. "You're a... you're a..."

"We're called skinners," Casey said. "Skinwalkers. Don't worry, I'm not here to hurt you. We're not all bad."

"Please leave my office right now."

"Mr. Cooper..."

"*Please leave!*"

Shenandoah jumped off the couch and flew around Jackson's desk, kneeling down in front of him and scooping his hands into hers. The crippled man was trembling in fear. She looked him in the eye and spoke in a practiced, empathetic voice.

"I know you're afraid," she said, "and I'm sorry. Trust me, we wouldn't be here if we had anywhere else to go. We need help."

"Even *if* I wanted to help Will, look at me. What am I supposed to do? You really expect me to go fight *monsters* with you?"

"Well, maybe not you," Casey said, "but Will told me you have connections. Friends you knew from the Army. People who have weapons. Some guy named Paul who owns practically every gun ever made. A dude who owns his own helicopter, I think Will called him Batshit Billy, or something like that?"

Jackson bolted to attention. "Batshit Barry?" he asked.

"That's it!" Casey said. "Will told me that guy would do just about anything."

"Will told *you* about Batshit Barry?" Jackson said, stupefied. "Will told a thirteen year-old girl about Batshit Barry Kowalczyk?"

"I'm fourteen," Casey corrected.

Jackson bursted out laughing, then put his face into his hands and groaned. He shook his head in disbelief, certain at any moment he would wake up in bed.

"I wouldn't quite call Barry a friend," Jackson said, looking from the young girl to the lady cop. "More like someone whose good side I want to stay on, if you know what I mean. He didn't get that nickname for nothing, the dude is frickin' *crazy!* I saw him guzzle an entire bottle of Hennessy once, rip all his clothes off, and chopper into battle buck-ass-naked!"

"Sounds perfect!" Casey said.

"This is absolutely absurd," Jackson shook his head. "I am not calling Paul, or Barry, or anyone else, and asking them to go to the Cherokee reservation to fight monsters! I don't believe I'm hearing this, I just... no. No way. Will Shaw ruined my life. How the hell do you know Will, anyway?" he asked Casey.

"He saved my life."

"He saved my son's life too," Shenandoah added, "and *your* son's."

Jackson sat speechless. His guests stood patiently, watching him and waiting for his response. Emotions raced in his eyes. He rubbed the back of his neck, then ran his hand across his jaw, and rubbed his chin and mouth. He processed the new information, remembered the past, and made his decision. His face hardened and his eyes brimmed with anger.

"Get out."

Casey snapped into a rage, jumping forward and slapping her hands on his desk. "Don't be such a *pussy!*"

For just a split second, Jackson saw a flash of the cheetah in the young girl's face. He jolted back and yelped in fear.

Casey instantly knew she'd crossed the line, and sank back apologetically. A moment later, the receptionist burst through the door, concerned for her boss.

"Is everything okay?" she asked.

"Uh, y-yes. Thank you, Chelsea. It's okay. You can close the door."

"We were just leaving," Shenandoah said, giving Casey a stern look. Chelsea withdrew from the room hesitantly, and shut the door behind her. "We're sorry to have bothered you."

"I'm sorry," Casey said. "I got carried away. We can

handle this on our own. We're going up there to help Will, and nothing is gonna stop us."

"*You* are not going anywhere but home, young lady," Shenandoah said.

"What?" Casey's eyes flared with anger. "But you said—"

"I lied. I'm not taking a teenage girl into a fight. Are you crazy? Your poor mother, my *God*. I am taking you home, and then *I* am going to handle this." Shenandoah shook her head and took the girl by the arm, pulling her toward the door. Casey raged and struggled, but the copper's authority and strength was apparent. *She* was in charge.

"That's not fair!" Casey protested as Shenandoah opened the office door and pulled out her keys. She thumbed her key fab and could see her car's lights flash through the office window as the vehicle unlocked. "You can't do this!"

"Look, just go wait in the car," the boss lady said. "I'll be out in a minute."

"But—"

"Do not make me tell you twice, girl."

Casey couldn't argue with that look. Those mature, strong, crystal-blue eyes. The young girl deflated, slouching and shuffling off obediently out of the building. Shenandoah turned to Jackson once again, who had remained frozen behind his desk for the last few minutes.

"Sorry again," she said.

"Oh no, it's been a blast. Let's do it again sometime."

Shenandoah sighed and walked back up to the desk.

She reached into her jacket pocket and pulled out her business card, placing it down before him.

"In case you change your mind."

Jackson swiped the card off the desk, and without hesitation, tossed it in the trash. She sighed and nodded, turning once again to leave.

"Can I ask you just one question?" he said.

"Go ahead."

"Why in the hell are you doing this?"

She thought a moment before answering, "I love him."

Her strong legs carried her out of the building in long strides. She felt the cool autumn breeze as she walked across the lot to her car, a fire engine-red '24 Ford Taurus SHO. Pulling the keychain from her pocket, she suddenly realized something was wrong. Casey was missing.

"Oh, shit... Shit shit shit!"

Shenandoah ran up to her car and peered through the windows at the front and back seats. Empty. She turned around, looking in all directions, down every street, but she didn't see Casey. The determined little diva had boasted that nothing would stand in her way, and she was so far true to her word. Shenandoah kicked the gravel and got in her car, starting it up.

"Wonderful. Great job," she growled to herself, shifting into gear and pulling out of the lot and into traffic. She figured it would take roughly three hours to drive to The Rez, and from there she would track down Will and help however she could. Steering onto the onramp to highway 75, she began her journey.

In the trunk, along with an old suitcase, a spare tire and a jack, was Casey Madison, huddled into the fetal position. Her phone provided the only light in the darkness, as Casey went onto Instagram to post a photo. She chose one of the staged shots of her and Ieshia at the theme park, and wrote:

OMG having such a great timeeeeee!!!!

19

______

TAIL

CHEROKEE RESERVATION, *North Carolina*

AFTER A SLEEPLESS NIGHT AND A HEARTY BREAKFAST of bacon, eggs, and banana pancakes, Papaw Jimmy needed a serious nap. Will dropped the old bear off at the motel and decided to take in the town and learn as much as he could. He cruised and walked the streets, playing the part of a tourist. He checked out the Smoky Mountain community theater and the Qualla art gallery, a rich deposit of native arts and culture. He saw the old Oconaluftee Village, where vendors and artisans sold handmade blankets, baskets, and jewelry, and performed shows and traditional dances for the amusement of White people recording on their cell phones.

Will walked through the Oconaluftee Island Park, admiring a large swath of bamboo forest that was perfect for a scenic stroll. He drove past Native Brews Tap & Grille and shook his head at the fifty-foot red Indian statue outside. He drove past the monolithic Harrah's Casino, tempted to check it out, but knowing full well that he'd emerge drunk and broke.

THE FIRST TWO TIMES HE SAW THE SILVER BUICK Regal, he paid it no mind. The third time, he took notice. It was parked two blocks away, its occupants not clearly visible through the windshield, but he could swear they were watching him as he emerged from Sugarbear's Ice Cream Shop with a cone of mint chocolate chip.

Wonderful, he thought, *I've picked up a tail.*

Will strolled down the sidewalk, checking his peripherals as he licked and slurped his ice cream. He stopped at a touristy gift shop, turning to browse through a display of post cards, using it as an excuse to take a side glance down the street. There was the Buick again. He continued walking. A tall and striking young Indian man with long hair and a brown corduroy jacket stood across the street. Will detected something strange about the man's aura, but didn't have time to focus on it.

Turning the next corner, Will picked up the pace. His eyes scanned the surrounding area, that Ranger training kicking in. He looked for anything that could potentially be used as cover or as a weapon. Anything that could be an obstacle or hazard or give away his position. He was parked over a mile away, so he couldn't jump right in his car.

Taking off his sunglasses, he pretended to wipe the lenses clean, but really he used the reflective surfaces as a mirror to see behind him. The tall, young Indian man had

turned the corner as well, staying on his six. *That aura...
Shit. He's a skinner.*

The Buick stayed behind at a distance, its passengers silently watching.

Will spotted the sign for the Wize Guyz Grille up ahead and ducked inside. Wasting no time, he whisked past the host as she tried to greet him and headed to the back of the restaurant. He passed the kitchen and restrooms, finally pushing through the back door and into the sunlight again.

Will was in the back alley, hidden from public view. There was a dumpster to his left and two employee vehicles to his right. Several other dumpsters and vehicles lined the secluded stretch, along with wooden crates, palettes, and all the filth you'd expect to see in an alley behind a restaurant.

He found a spot to hide behind a worn-out wooden fence. He waited. His first thought was to draw the Canik, but no, far too loud. There was also no way he'd bring the panther out in broad daylight with civilians around. The decision was made to flick open his knife, the good old silent killer. Will remained coiled like a spring, ready to pounce. Watching. Waiting. Finally, the back door swung open and sure enough, his big Indian friend walked through.

Redhawk was taller than Will, standing 6'3", but not as thickly muscled. His features were broad and bold, but still handsome. His eyes were dark and intense beneath thick, furrowed brows. Focusing on the big man's aura, Will could finally see it clearly. There were colors of red, brown, and gold, and the ghostly outline of his spirit animal caught in the sunlight. Will saw a beak and wings, confirming that this skinner was a raptor.

Will prepared to make his move, watching as Redhawk stepped further out into the alley, looking for his mark. With expert stealth, Will rushed his opponent, grabbing the collar of his jacket and slamming him against the side of the dumpster. Will's blade was up against the younger man's throat in an instant.

"All right, bird boy," Will snarled, "who are you and why are you fo—"

Crack!

In a flash, Redhawk knocked the knife out of Will's hand and drove a large fist into his solar plexus. Will staggered back, doubled over as the air was knocked out of him. Without missing a beat, Redhawk shot his knee up and connected with Will's chin, sending fireworks shooting through his head and knocking him to the filthy concrete.

"Hello, Mr. Shaw," Redhawk said calmly, watching the older man squirm on the ground before him. "We should talk."

"Okay," Will gasped, gathering his strength, "let's talk."

Will sprang off the ground, sending a fist flying up at Redhawk's face. His blow was dodged and countered, and the younger man floored him again with a two-punch combination. "Please stop resisting," Redhawk said.

Faced with a younger, stronger, faster version of himself, Will Shaw could see only one option. Keep fighting.

He hooked the big Indian's heel with one foot and

kicked up with the other, sending Redhawk crashing backwards to the unyielding pavement. Will jumped right on top, mounting him and delivering a barrage of punches. Three connected, bloodying Redhawk's nose before the bigger man swept Will to the side and jumped back to his feet. Will leapt back up as well. They squared off.

"I'm with The Spirit Council, Mr. Shaw," Redhawk said.

"Yeah, I pretty much figured."

Will shot forward, throwing a storm of punches. Redhawk blocked a few, but took several strong hits as well. He countered with his own strikes, a one-two combination followed by a front kick to the body. Will staggered back.

"What brings you to North Carolina, Mr. Shaw?"

Will seethed. "Oh, just a little sightseeing."

He blasted a six-punch combination at Redhawk's face, and when the opponent's hands came up to defend, Will ducked down and cinched a body lock. He lifted Redhawk up, twisted him around, and threw him down to the pavement. The air was knocked out of Redhawk's lungs and Will kept throwing punches. The younger warrior reflexively turned to evade the barrage, unaware that giving up his back to Will Shaw was a grave mistake. *Your ground game needs some work, bird boy!* Will thought.

With practiced precision, Will clamped himself onto Redhawk's back, locking his legs around him, and hooking his left arm around his neck. His right arm came in to stabilize, and Redhawk found himself caught in a perfect rear-naked choke. Will held on tight, cutting off the blood flow to his opponent's brain as the bigger man fought his way back to his feet. Will hung on, squeezing as Redhawk staggered around the alley, close to passing out.

Seeing the garbage dumpster in front of him, Redhawk chose his avenue of escape. He spun around, pointing Will towards the dumpster as the ex-Ranger clung to his back, choking him. With a powerful backward thrust, Redhawk launched into the dumpster, smashing Will into the steel surface.

Will's grip broke and he slid to the ground with a moan, pain shooting through his spine. He and Redhawk both gasped for air, each man struggling to regain his senses. Will pulled himself up onto his hands and knees as Redhawk circled him, catching his breath.

"If you're here... because of the murders... you best go home," Redhawk said. "This is Council business... This is not your fight."

"*Nnng*... I'll take it under advisement," Will said, rising to his feet.

"Stop fighting," Redhawk said.

Whack! Crack! Sock! Pow!

The first three punches were partially blocked, but they were really just set-ups for the sidekick. The heel of Will's boot clipped Redhawk's ribs, and he stumbled back, hissing in pain. Will closed the distance and bashed two right hands in a row into his face. Redhawk wavered, his eyes spinning in his head, and Will could have sworn the taller man was just about to fall.

And then came a left hook out of nowhere.

The bony fist collided with Will's jaw and sent shockwaves through his nervous system. He crumpled to the ground, his head spinning, barely clinging to consciousness. Redhawk stood on rubbery legs, himself badly rocked by Will's punches, watching his opponent writhe on the ground. Will tried to stand up, but couldn't, grunting as he collapsed back to the pavement.

Redhawk clutched his aching ribs and lurched forward, catching his breath and composing himself. "Go home," he said, and lurched away.

Will groaned, defeated.

He lay there on the concrete surface, catching his breath, waiting for the world to stop spinning. His eye caught a glint of something metallic under the dumpster, and realized it was his knife. He scooted over and reached under the steel container, his fingertips finding the handle. Will pulled himself to his feet, folding and pocketing the edged weapon. He suddenly realized that he was not alone.

A portly woman with short-pink hair and an apron stood in the doorway of the restaurant he'd passed through. She had a cordless phone in her hand.

"I've called the police," she said.

"Mm," Will grunted and gave her a half-assed salute, stumbling away. He found his way back out onto the street and directed his wobbly legs back to the car.

20

THE PROPHECY

AFTERNOON CREPT TOWARD EVENING, and the sky behind Leah's Psychic Eye bookstore swirled with pink clouds and golden rays. Three cars sat in the small parking lot shared by the bookstore and an out-of-business health food grocery. A painted mural of The Eye of Horus above the front door watched over the premises, and the windows enticed passersby with displays of crystals, handmade jewelry, and of course, books. A black Camaro rumbled into the lot and parked.

Will climbed out of the car and pocketed his keys. Head throbbing and back aching, he grunted and slowly made his way to the door. A tiny bell jingled as he pushed inside and was greeted by the scents of sage and incense and the soothing sounds of native flute music coming from an old stereo behind the front counter. Displays of dreamcatchers hung overhead, Indian-themed paintings and art adorned the walls, and shelves of books filled the spaces in between.

His head swimming from sensory overload, Will

made his way deeper into the mystical lair. Tarot cards and books on astrology. Local-made fine Cherokee crafts. T-shirts for the tourists. Arrowheads for the kids. A young White couple pushed an infant around in a stroller while their five-year-old bounced around and put his grubby hands all over everything. An older woman stood in a far corner, content to skim and browse through old books.

Will looked around for Leah and a moment later she swished into the main showroom, carrying a small pile of folded child-size shirts. The young White family smiled as she approached, holding the first one up with a smile.

"Here we go," she said, kneeling to put the garment up against the little boy's chest to check the size, "let's see if any of these will fit." Leah couldn't help but catch the silhouette of the six-foot beefcake standing in her peripheral vision and turned to see Will, waiting patiently. While the family of customers looked through the shirts she'd brought out, each bearing a colorful design that read *Cherokee, North Carolina*, Leah eyeballed Will's appearance and shook her head. "Excuse me a minute."

She stood up and approached Will, looking him up and down.

"What in the hell happened to you, Will Shaw?"

Will chuckled and said, "Stickball again."

Leah looked for her medicine bag to be hanging from Will's neck, but it wasn't there. Her ego took a hit, but she brushed it aside.

"Mm hm, sure. Well, come on now. I'll get you some aspirin and an ice pack. Your papaw's already here in the back room."

"Oh, okay," Will said, surprised, as he followed her lead.

They went into the employees-only area, passed the bathroom, storage closet, and boxes of merchandise waiting to be priced, and into the break room. It was a small and simple space with a sink and refrigerator, a little TV, a coffee pot, an old couch and a folding table in the center. Jimmy sat at the table, surrounded by books, a cup of coffee beside him and a plate speckled with crumbs from his last snack. He glanced up, took one look at his grandson's condition, and looked back down at the open book in front of him.

"Hey," Jimmy said.

"Hey, Papaw," Will said. "What are you doin' here?"

Jimmy gestured to the spread of books across the table, "Researchin'."

"Me too," Will chuckled. "Great minds, huh?"

Leah patted Will's arm before stepping away. "I'll be right back. Get you that aspirin."

Will groaned, stepping up to the coffee pot and looking for a mug. "Man, coffee sounds good right now." He began to fix himself a cup of mud as Jimmy quietly flipped through his book.

"Been makin' some more new friends, I see," Jimmy said, not looking up.

"Oh, yeah," Will said, shaking his head. "Finally met one of *your* friends from the damn Spirit Council. Real nice guy."

Jimmy stopped reading and looked up. "Who was it?"

"Some big injun," Will said, taking a sip of coffee.

Leah swept back into the room, a colorful native

shawl draped around her shoulders. She handed Will the aspirin and he slapped the pills into his mouth, chugging them down with some sweet coffee. She saw the look of concern on Jimmy's face and sensed the tension in the air. Crossing to the fridge, Leah opened the freezer and took out an ice pack, then handed it to Will.

"Here you go, sugar. Well, ah... if you boys need anything else, you just let me know, okay?"

"Yes, ma'am," Will said politely, pressing the ice pack against his head as she left them alone. Jimmy turned back to his stack of books and papers and Will sauntered over to get a closer look. He rifled through the collection and looked at the covers, chuckling at some, rolling his eyes at others. "*Cherokee Myths and Legends*," he read aloud, "*Shapshifters and Witches, Stories of the Raven Mocker, The First Raven Mocker, Indigenous Folklore of the North East... The Secrets and Mysteries of the Cherokee Little People??*"

"That's right," Jimmy said, not looking up. "Yûñ wi Tsundí. The little people of the forest."

"Okayyy..." Will sighed dismissively, sitting down and taking a sip of coffee while pressing the cold pack against his head. "Well, come up with anything we can use?"

Jimmy grunted and sat back, taking off his glasses and rubbing his eyes.

"Not hardly. All the stories are different. Some say they're evil witches, some say they're shapeshifters. Some say they look like blackbirds, others say they're like Bigfoot. This'n says you could look at one and not even know it, that it can disguise itself to look like an old lady.

And this'n says it's like a genie, you cast a spell and poof, you got a raven mocker to do yer biddin'. And of course most of the stories agree that they come to feed on the life force of the sick and dying, sometimes rip the hearts outta' their chests."

"Lovely," Will said.

"But nothin' about them feedin' on babies. Bottom line is, they're worse than vampires. None of the stories agree. Pretty much what I expected. Ain't nobody never seen a raven mocker and lived to write a daggone book about it. It's all just... stories."

Will slapped the table and smiled, trying to reassure his grandfather. "Ah, don't worry. We'll kick its ass."

"Mm, sure. That's your answer to everythin'."

"What's that supposed to mean?"

"I don't know, boy. Are you here to help these people, or to just get your rocks off pickin' fights?"

Will put the ice pack down, his smile fading. "That's not fair, papaw."

"Oh, no? You ain't actin' like you give a damn about this place, or have any respect for the customs or folklore of your people."

"Oh, come on!" Will stood up, indignant. "I'm here because I care."

"When we were at that house earlier, talkin' to that poor young father done lost his baby? Did you see the pain in his eyes? Could you feel his energy? He was *ruined*. His wife couldn't even come outta the bedroom. And did you show him a shred of compassion, or empathy? Nope. Cold as a Sioux woman's titties. All you want is blood."

"Look, I ain't no social worker, Papaw. I'm a warrior. I'm here because there's something evil to *fight*. And in case you didn't notice, there's more than just a monster to fight here."

"That's right, boy," Jimmy said, standing up to face him. "The Council is here. Which means there's *lots* of monsters to fight. At best, they don't want you here. But really, I 'spect they want you dead. We cain't stand up against them, son. I got half a mind to hotfoot it outta here right now."

"Why the hell are you so scared of them?"

"Because Keonee's got 'em all twisted around his finger, that's why," Jimmy said. "Since he took over, he's made his own rules, changed up the old stories. Since the early days, it's been prophesied that one day a 'chosen one' would come, and that he would bring down the Spirit Council. Well, after me and him had our little falling out, guess what happened? The prophecy conveniently got updated, so now the chosen one is a *Shaw!* All he's gotta do is tell his little cronies 'I've had another vision! The one prophesied to destroy The Council is Will Shaw' and they believe it. He wants to wipe out our whole family. So no, bein' aroun' here with them lookin' for you *ain't* the smartest idea."

"I don't understand," Will said. "How can he make up shit like that and they just go along with it?"

"Ask L. Ron Hubbard!" Jimmy shrugged. "He's a charismatic leader. He knows how to manipulate people. And he is a *little* psychic. Not enough to see things clearly, but just enough to be full a' himself. Like he explained to me once when we were both snot-nosed little shitheads like you, his visions are like watchin' an old TV. You can see the picture sometimes, but it's mostly static. 'Course, his followers all think he's some kinda' great visionary and do whatever he says. Y'see what I'm sayin'?"

Will took a step forward. "Why are you only telling me this now?"

"I was hopin' we could just stay away from them, keep off their radar completely. Hopin' this damn mess would never happen."

"There's something else, isn't there?" Will pushed. "What aren't you telling me? What's on *your* radar, papaw? Huh? What do you see?"

Jimmy released a deep breath, and his gaze fell to the floor.

"Death."

21

STOWAWAY

BY THE TIME Shenandoah arrived at The Rez, the sun had gone down. Her fuel tank was nearly empty, and so was her stomach. Her bladder, however, was quite full. Steering the red Taurus into town, she spotted a gas station up ahead and pulled in, stopping at the closest pump. She jumped out and fumbled through her purse to fish out her debit card, and proceeded to the machine.

While the lady cop was busy making her purchase, Casey waited curled up in the dark trunk for the right moment to make her move. Above her head was an emergency release latch, a security measure available in the trunks of most new cars, and her fingers were wrapped around it, poised. She heard the electronic beeps of the gas pump, the metal clang of the nozzle being inserted into the car, the humming flow of gasoline feeding the hungry machine. Then she heard nothing. Maybe the cop had turned her back, or gone inside, maybe the coast was clear. Either way, she had to take her chances if she was to sneak away and find Will.

Casey pulled the emergency release latch and the trunk gently popped open. She slid her backpack over one shoulder and pushed the trunk open farther, beginning the nimble process of sliding one leg over the rim, then pulling herself out, and throwing the other leg over, oh so quietly. She stepped down onto the pavement, looked around, didn't see anyone, and smiled. The coast was clear. She turned to gently close the trunk behind her and suddenly froze.

Shenandoah stood by the driver's door, texting her ex to check up on little Jake, when she heard a sound and looked up. There was teenage Casey Madison climbing out of her trunk, trying to slink away. The girl looked back at her, a child caught with her hand in the proverbial cookie jar.

"What the..." Shenandoah's blood began to boil.

Casey smiled, guilty and embarrassed, trying to think of what to say.

"Don't be mad?"

"*Fuck!*" Shenandoah stomped the ground, her fists balled up, her face flushed with anger. She paced and spun around and cursed, and paced some more, ire bubbling in her fierce blue eyes as her brain raced to catch up after this unforeseen development. "Son of a... fuck! *Fuck!* I can't believe... how did you... shit! God damn it, you little pain in my... *fuck!*"

"You told me to wait in the car...?" Casey cringed.

"Oh, no! No no no no no!" Shenandoah stalked forward, pointing an accusatory finger at the little rebel. "Don't even try to be cute! Don't even... *ugh! Fuck!*"

"Look," Casey said. "Just pretend you didn't see me,

okay? I'll be just fine on my own. You go your way and I'll—"

"Oh, right! Sure! I'll just let some teenage girl go off on her own to play hero! *Goooood!* That wouldn't weigh on my conscience if anything happened to you!"

"Nothing's gonna happen—"

"Oh, good! That makes me feel so much better! Casey, I'm responsible for you now, get it? You ran away from home, your mother doesn't know where you are... am I right?"

Casey nodded.

"Christ," Shenandoah growled, checking her watch, doing some math in her head. "I've got half a mind to take you back home right now."

"Three hour drive back to Chattanooga, then three hours back up here again?" Casey shrugged and raised her eyebrows. Casey's logic was sound. The detective cursed under her breath and stomped around some more, knowing the kid had called her bluff.

"Fine," she said. "Then I'm gonna buy you a bus ticket and see that your little butt gets on it."

"Oh, please. I'd get off and come right back here."

"Then I'll take you to the local police station and call your *mother*, have her come here and pick you up!"

"Oh yeah? And what are you gonna tell 'em?" Casey raised an eyebrow.

Shenandoah knew the girl was right. There would be a lot of questions, most of which she would be unable to answer without sounding like a complete lunatic. She seethed, her mind racing, and noticed that their argument had drawn the attention of a few motorists gassing up their cars. Grinding her teeth, she marched up to the youth, grabbed her by the arm, and said, "Come with me."

Shenandoah marched off around the building, Casey in tow. She led the girl past the restrooms, looking for a private spot, and found one near the dumpster. It was a dark and grimy corner, and Casey soon found her back pressed up against a cinderblock wall. The blonde lady cop was right up in her face, making sure she could feel the gravity of the situation.

"This is not a game," Shenandoah said. "This is life and death."

"I know that," Casey said, growing annoyed.

"I can't be responsible for protecting you, Casey."

"You're not! I can take care of myself!"

"Casey, for chrissakes, you're fourteen! You're just a kid!"

"I am *not* just a kid!" Casey's eyes flared with gold and she pushed back, knocking the older woman to the ground. Shenandoah landed on her ass and looked up in shock as light bent and warped around the girl. Within seconds, the child had phased away, and a cheetah now stood before her on two feet.

"Oh my God..." Shenandoah marveled, her jaw hanging open.

The young skinner was still not full-grown, but already stronger than any perpetrator the policewoman could ever hope to handle. Her physique was long and lean, toned muscles flexing beneath a spotted, corn-yellow coat. Her hair was short and smooth everywhere but her back and neck, which still had a bit of the longer kitten fluff that would eventually go away with adulthood. Her eyes were like fire. She leaned forward on powerful, haunched legs, peering down at Shenandoah as she towered above. Her fanged muzzle issued a growl of warning.

"Now, you were saying?" Casey's voice rang in the cop's head, though the cat's lips did not move. From the look of shock in her eyes, she was not expecting telepathic communication.

"Wow," was all she could think to say.

Casey stepped back and took a breath. The cat closed her eyes and once again, light and shadows began to warp around her, and the animal shimmered away. Shenandoah looked up in awe at what was once again just a little girl. Casey smiled sheepishly. "Sorry," she said, holding out her hand.

Shenandoah took the outstretched hand and let Casey help her up. She dusted off and composed herself, catching her breath.

"You okay?" Casey asked.

"Yeah... Jesus. Just about ready to pee all over myself, that's all."

"You hungry?"

"Starved."

"Good," Casey said with a smile. "I'll let you buy me dinner."

The teenager skipped away back to the car with a smug look on her face, leaving Shenandoah to stew in her own frustration.

"Little pain in the ass..." the lady cop grumbled.

. . .

THEY SAT AT A CORNER BOOTH AT PAUL'S FAMILY Restaurant, as a disinterested waitress waited for Casey to make her order. The youth's big brown eyes darted back and forth across the open menu as she tried to decide what she wanted. Shenandoah sat with her menu folded, tapping her fingers on the worn vinyl cover, waiting for Casey to get it over with. The waitress also tried to appear patient, though the look in her eyes clearly said, "come on already, kid."

"Hmm," Casey said, leaning forward. "If I get the bison burger, can I replace the fries with a baked potato?"

"Sure thing, sweetie."

"Okay, then let's do that. Oh, and no onions on the burger. Or pickles. Oh, and let's start out with the mozzarella sticks. Gotta do the strawberry milkshake too!"

"And for you, ma'am?"

"Grilled chicken salad," Shenandoah said, "and more coffee." She took a sip from the cup of Joe she was already working on, her deadpan glare leveled at the supernatural juvenile delinquent in front of her.

"Okay then," the waitress said, writing everything in her notebook, "I'll put this right in for ya. Shouldn't take long." She shambled off to the kitchen, leaving silence at the table. Casey pretended to not notice the look of annoyance and disapproval in Shenandoah's eyes. She fiddled with the paper wrapper torn from her straw, balling it up, twisting it around into an abstract sculpture, then looked back up. The policewoman was still staring.

"What?" Casey asked.

"I was just wondering what your plan was, that's all.

You sneak up here in my trunk, you go off on your own, shouting 'Will? Will? Where are you?' Maybe go around to random people on the street, showing a picture, asking if they've seen him?"

"I'd find him," Casey said, confident. She pulled out her phone and her little thumbs went to work. "But first, gotta post some pics to Insta. Show the world what a great time I'm having at Paradise Park." She selected five of the staged photos showing her and Ieshia at the theme park, and posted them to her feed.

Shenandoah shook her head and took a sip of coffee.

"What?" Casey said. "Okay, so what's *your* great plan to find Will?"

"I'm a police detective, Casey. I'm gonna call my friend at dispatch, give him Will's cell phone number, and just have him track the GPS."

"Oh," Casey said. She had no witty retort. "Yeah, that's a good plan."

The cop lady flashed a smug smile and sipped her coffee.

"So, Paradise Park. That's a good one."

"Mm hm," Casey nodded. "Where does your son think *you* are?"

"I just told them I got called in to work. Working a big case. Kinda-sorta technically true," she chuckled. Casey joined in. "I should call him soon, say goodnight before it gets too late."

"Yeah, I gotta call my moms too."

Shenandoah sighed and had another sip of coffee.

"God help us," she said.

22

A CRASH AND A SCREAM

THE NIGHT WAS TOO warm for the leather jacket, so Will opted for a khaki shirt with the sleeves rolled halfway up his forearms. By the time he and Jimmy met up with Pete at the fairgrounds parking lot, a crowd of volunteers had once again amassed. Their faces were illuminated by the dying-indigo streetlights, fear and stress in every pair of eyes. Flashlights and radios were once again passed out, and a few civilians also had hunting rifles at the ready.

Will had the Canik and two backup mags holstered on his waist and his .380 in his boot. Jimmy had Leah's special medicine bag around his neck and prominently displayed. Pete greeted them and shook their hands, apprehensive about the night to come. He'd brought his .30-30 hunting rifle and a thermos full of Black Rifle coffee, and he'd have been in big trouble with the boss lady if he wasn't wearing his protective medicine bag she made for him.

"Here we go again," Pete said, rolling his eyes.

"Yessir," Will said. "Party time."

"I don't know how much more of this I can take," Pete said as Officer Kituwah passed radios to him, Will, and Jimmy. "I'm tired, old, and completely out of shape."

"Now now," Jimmy reassured him, "round is a shape."

Pete cackled and pretended not to notice the bruises on Will's face. He'd heard the story from Leah about his street fight earlier and decided not to mention it. The three men waited as Ballard once again took center stage, dividing the groups and making sure everyone was accounted for. Will scanned the crowd, focusing on the aura of each individual, searching for any hints of malice or evil hidden amongst them.

Each man and woman had their own energy, some glowing brightly, some dim. The usual colors were white, gold, blue, red , and green, some swirling and mixing together like watercolors. Some were dark and muddy, while others were more clean and bright. Nobody in attendance had the pure and innocent white-light energy of a young child, naturally, but he didn't see anything out of the ordinary either.

Officer Owle's energy came closest to the purity of a child, while Kituwah, Apachito, and Saunooke had healthy, mature, earthy tones around them. Sergeant Sneed's aura was dull and muddy, the energy of a middle-aged man who was twice-divorced, overweight, alcoholic, and simply living life on dreary auto pilot. Focusing in on Lieutenant Ballard, Will was reminded of the planet Jupiter. His aura was a swirl of reds, oranges, browns and whites. His was a soul on fire, dancing with anger and discontent, but also not without hope or purpose. Will looked for the captain but didn't see her.

"Where's Oocuna?" he asked.

"Couldn't be bothered to show," Apachito said.

"Sarah, come on," Owle interjected. "She's not feeling well."

"She doesn't know what to do," Pete said, nudging Will's arm. "She's scared. Doesn't believe in all this superstitious nonsense. Doesn't *want* to believe."

"*Shh,*" someone hissed from the crowd. Will and Pete obliged and listened to Lieutenant Ballard's instructions.

"...Now, listen," Ballard continued. "I know a lot of you are packin' tonight. But do not, I repeat *do not* open fire unless your life is in immediate danger. If you see something suspicious, tell your group leader, and radio it in. Just because you have a carry permit doesn't mean you have license to run all over the place shootin' up the dang Rez, got it?" The crowd mumbled in agreement.

"Also, and we don't know if this is connected to this case or not, but an elk was killed over near the Qualla Boundary last night by a large predator. Some kind of big cat, like a mountain lion."

Jimmy made a face at Will, who just shrugged.

"Weren't no mountain lion," a very southern accent called out from the crowd. "Tracks were daggone *huge.*"

"It was some kind of big cat," Ballard continued. "Not native to these parts. Okay? So be careful out there tonight. Ya'll remember what groups you're in? Good. Let's get out there and get this thing, whatever it is. It's never hit two nights in a row before, so we're probably in for an uneventful night. But still... may the Great Spirit protect you all." Ballard clapped his hands and the group began to disperse. He caught sight of Will and Jimmy standing with Pete, noting the battle damage written across Will's face. "What happened to you there, Will Shaw?"

"Cut myself shaving," Will said.

"Uh huh," Ballard grunted, suspicious. "How 'bout you ride with me tonight, Will? I could use some extra muscle."

Will shot a troubled glance at Pete, not sure what to say.

"Unless that's a problem?" Ballard asked.

"Well, no. It's just, ah... If it's all the same to you, I'd rather just do my own thing, y'know? I'm kinda used to flying solo."

"Yeah, I got that impression," Ballard said. "You didn't key in for radio check twice last night. Broke away from your group, huh? What were you doing?"

I was busy turning into a panther and killing that elk, of course.

"Just wanderin' around, keepin' my eyes open," Will said.

"Well, you can keep your eyes open with us tonight," Ballard said. "Regale us with your Army Ranger and bounty hunter stories."

"Look, I uh..." Will started before Jimmy cut him off.

"Son, maybe you should just go with—"

"Papaw," Will stopped his grandfather, annoyed. "I'm sorry, Lieutenant. That's not really how I work. I'll do much better on my own."

Ballard took a few steps closer, his tone firm.

"This is an organized watch, Mr. Shaw. Everyone is accounted for and everyone is in groups. There's no cowboys here. Just Indians."

Pete and Jimmy watched Will, waiting for his response. Ballard stood his ground, not breaking eye contact. Will finally let out a sigh and handed his radio over to the lieutenant.

"Good luck tonight," Will said, then turned and walked away.

Jimmy and Pete hastily followed.

"Come on now, son," Jimmy pleaded, "where you goin'?"

"Goin' to pick a fight, papaw," Will said. "That's all I care about, right?"

"Oh, I'm sorry. Is it that time of the month again?"

"Just leave me the fuck alone, *okay?*"

"That ain't no way to talk to your papaw, Will Shaw," Pete added.

"Look," Will spun around, holding his hands up, "I'm walkin'. You two want to go off in groups and hold hands or whatever, fine. I'm walkin'. If you need me, call my cell. Otherwise, have yourselves a lovely night."

Will turned back around and continued walking, and the two older men let him go. Jimmy watched with disappointment as his grandson stalked off down the blue-lit streets, his boots clip-clopping on the sidewalk.

The main drag was dark and nearly empty, most of the businesses closed for the night. Will turned onto a residential street, letting his instincts guide him. Through the windows, he saw the lights of televisions, heard snippets of conversations, and smelled good home cooking.

He walked to the end of a row of homes, turned around, then turned onto another street. Despite the balmy temperature, he felt a chill, and the little hairs on the back of his neck stood up.

It was the unmistakable feeling of being watched again. *A sedan, about two blocks back, trying to be covert. Those fuckers from The Council again. Damn it.* Will prepared to run, shoot, or fight, whatever was called for, his muscles tensed and ready for action as he sensed the vehicle drawing closer. But then the driver's window rolled down, and he heard that voice.

"Hey, handsome." It was Shenandoah.

Her unmistakable Tinkerbell-twang froze him right in place.

When he turned around, there she was, sitting behind the wheel, a coy smile on those cute lips. Surprise, anger, relief, and confusion hit Will all at once, and he approached the idling car. Shenandoah got out and stepped up onto the curb as Will chuckled and held his hands up.

"What the hell—?" Will began to speak when he noticed another figure in the car, sitting in the shadows of the passenger seat. The door opened and Casey stepped out, looking embarrassed like she'd just been suspended from school. Will stopped in his tracks, his blood beginning to simmer. "What the *hell?* Casey, you... Copper, what did you... What are you *doing* here?"

"Please don't be upset," Shenandoah said.

"*Don't be upset?* I told you what's going on here, right?"

"We came to help," Casey offered.

"Oh good, you came to help! Copper, what the fuck? I can't believe you! You actually brought her here?"

"No! Well, sort of. Look, I can explain..."

"I had to warn you," Casey said, crossing around the front of the car and approaching Will. "I had one of those visions again. You're in danger."

"I know I'm in danger, Casey. This is dangerous. Everything I do is dangerous. It comes with the job. I accept that. What I *don't* accept is *you* putting yourself in harm's way. Do you have any idea what's going on up here? What would I tell your mother if something happened to you? Casey, you're just a—"

"Don't you say it, Will. Not you. I am not just a kid."

"Copper, how could you let this happen?" Will aimed his angry sights at the petite woman standing before him. "She's *fourteen* years-old."

"She's very hard to say no to," Shenandoah winced.

"You're taking her home right now."

"Will, I saw you *die*," Casey said, trying to keep her voice down on the residential street. "You were on your knees, in some kind of theater or something. You were surrounded by skinners. You had a *gun* to your head."

Will clenched his jaw. With no good answer to this dire and unexpected message, he fell back on the reliable, "I can take care of myself," and began to huff away down the block.

"You are lowkey trippin' if you believe that!" Casey shouted.

Will stopped, spun around, and marched back up to her.

"I don't need *your* help. You are just a *little girl*."

"And you're just an old boomer with his head up his ass!"

"Guys, please..." Shenandoah noticed several towns-people peeking out their windows, trying to catch a glimpse of what was going on with the three strangers standing outside. "Let's all just get in the car and go somewhere, okay? We can talk this out, but let's just try and—"

"This conversation is *over*, Shenandoah," Will said, and she piped down. Anytime he spoke her actual name rather than calling her "Copper" or "babe," she knew he was serious. "You've warned me, okay? Thank you. Now, take Casey and get the hell—"

Before Will could finish his sentence, there was a loud crash directly to his left, coming from a home across the street. The shattering of glass and the splintering of wood. Not a second passed before the sharp noise was followed by a high-pitch shriek of absolute terror.

Will, Casey, and Shenandoah looked in time to see shards of glass exploding from a side window in the small home, followed by a dark, amorphous form that spilled out into the night. A tangle of tendrils and two large membranes resembling wings spread open and the black mass filled up with air, floating in the light breeze. It whipped around, and though there were no eyes on its black, oily head, it seemed to stare straight at Will. He stared right back.

The raven mocker bellowed the haunting shrill of an ungodly wraith, and Will understood it as a direct taunt: *Catch me if you can.*

23

WHEN SHADOWS DANCE

KILL. *KILL. KILL.*

THE FOUL ENTITY WAILED AND SLOBBERED AS IT bolted down the side path, knocking over the trash cans and booking it for the forest. Will sprang into action after it, his legs powering him across the street. Shenandoah ran to her car and Casey was right behind, jumping in and buckling up. As Will barreled after the beast on foot, the girls zoomed off by car, trying to catch up.

Will ran past the shattered window, hearing the sounds of a mother and father inside, screaming. It had happened again. The Canik was in his hand and he didn't even remember drawing it. As he charged forward, another cry came from up ahead. Someone else had seen the vile thing. Will cleared the space between houses and sprinted onto the next street. The raven mocker maintained a good lead on him, flying low to the ground, its shape constantly changing like a living Rorschach test.

Shenandoah swerved her red Taurus around the block, her tires screeching as she skidded the tight corner. Casey held on tight, seeing Will up ahead, running up into a cul-de-sac.

"There he is!" she said.

"Hang on!"

Shenandoah stomped the gas pedal and the sedan rocketed up the street as curious neighbors watched the spectacle.

Will saw the creature fly between the houses at the end of the cul-de-sac, vanishing into the dark woods. Civilians began to creep into the street out of curiousity, but Will urgently waved them away as he sprinted as fast as he could.

"Get back! Stay in your homes! Get back!" he barked at them.

Shenandoah and Casey skidded to a halt as they reached the dead end, forced to watch as Will disappeared into the shadows between houses. Casey unbuckled her seatbelt and was about to bolt after him, but Shenandoah's hand slapped down on top of hers.

"Don't even think about it," she said like only a mother can.

Will held his pistol out at half-aim as he dashed through the gloom of the forest, the cat inside of him begging to be set free. He dodged between maples and oaks, tracking a shadow through the shadows. The creature stayed about twenty yards ahead, visible only by the glinting moonlight off its layers of slimy, translucent skins. Will maintained his visual, barely keeping up.

Over a fallen log, down a rocky slope, and crashing

through overgrowth, Will chased the raven mocker. He finally got a clear view, stopping for a moment to level his pistol, and squeezed off four shots. Three of the slugs were right on target, but had seemingly zero effect. It powered forward, its flowing shapes blowing in the breeze like the tattered black cape of an evil witch.

Will snarled, his heart pumping, arms and legs racing.

He took two more shots but the creature didn't even notice. It whisked through the landscape, leading Will into isolation. Up ahead, he saw what looked like a cliff overlooking a deep, wooded valley. The monster shrieked and dove over the edge, sailing down into the murky woods below with ease.

Will had two choices. He could give up and turn back, or...

Fuck it.

He pumped his legs faster, picking up speed. Reaching peak velocity, Will launched himself off the edge of the rock shelf, vaulting into the night sky. He closed his eyes. Held out his arms. Relaxed.

He fell into darkness.

Light warped around him. Reality unfolded.

A man plummeted into the inky void. A black cat emerged from the shadows, absorbing the landing with his powerful haunches. He growled like a steam engine, and dense muscles flexed beneath his shiny-black coat. Curved claws dug into the earth. Electric-yellow eyes scanned the dark countryside, searching for the intruding enemy.

. . .

YES. MY TURN.

A SKINNER IN HIS ELEMENT, THE BLACK JAGUAR crept through the dark hollow. His ears twitched for input, but the crickets and cicadas had quieted down out of fear. Will sniffed the air, detecting the foul and acrid scent of the beast—like wet dog and rotten eggs—but could not pinpoint a location. It was everywhere at once, capable of sliding in and out of any shadow. It was watching him.

Will slinked across the uneven, grassy terrain, poised and ready to strike. It was still here with him somewhere, he knew it. He stalked left, spun right, flexed his claws, and kept looking. His ears picked up a faint rasp, like the reverberating grumble of a reptile or the dying breaths of a lung cancer patient. It was in there with him, breathing.

A black form shot overhead.

Will tensed, ready to fight, but nothing happened. Silence filled the air. Then there it was again, this time to his left, a whoosh of movement through the trees. Then again, this time behind him. Will growled. He opened his fanged jaws and issued a mighty roar, a challenge familiar in any language.

The raven mocker answered, shooting out from the shadows and knocking Will to the ground. The cat sprang back up, snarling, ready to kill. He spun around, then again. He looked up, down, and saw nothing. Silence.

Then again, the darkness came alive and struck him across the face with an audible *crack*. Will grunted and staggered, lashing out with swinging claws, but tearing through nothing but air. Once more it came, this time thrashing its tendrils like whips, one stinging across his back, the others wrapping around his wrists and up his arms.

Will struggled but the demon's grip was unbreakable. The greasy-black mass spun and tossed him through the air, sending him smashing into the side of a towering oak. He absorbed the pain and tried to ignore it, spinning around and lashing out with his claws in a furious blur.

Left-right-left-right, he swung as the foul creature shot in at him, but his claws just went right through the thing. It was like fighting black smoke, intangible and impossible to grab hold of. Yet while Will could not touch the beast, it had no trouble touching him. With the same tendrils and membranes that Will's claws slipped right through, it grabbed hold of him with great physical strength. A cluster of smaller appendages gripped the cat's wrists, while a larger tentacle wrapped around his waist.

Will roared in fury, fighting with all his strength, but to no avail. The beast leaned in with its slick, greasy-black head, and the gruesome hole that was its mouth opened up to scream right back at him. It pulled in closer, as if about to give Will a sloppy kiss. The jaguar fought and thrashed with all he had.

His wrists slipped through the tendrils gripping them, only for them to reform and restrain him again. He pushed the creature back, throwing it from side to side.

With a swipe of his right claw, he sliced right through what must have been the torso of the thing. He tore through the tentacle wrapped around his waist and pushed himself back, gasping for air. The broken bits of the monster reconnected like black ash in the air, and it came for him again.

Whip! Crack! Smack!

The first blow Will felt was a lash across the face, stinging like fire, followed by his legs being swept out from under him. While still in mid-air, the raven mocker spun and struck its longest tentacle across the cat's chest, blasting him back. He tumbled across the ground, rolling to a halt and panting for air.

The monster was on Will in a flash, whipping at him with sharp tendrils and slimy tentacles. He rolled and spun side to side through the dirt to dodge the barrage, but some of the strikes hit their target. Will clawed and bit and fought back, but it was like fighting a cloud of ink in a dark pool of water.

Another *crack* sent him rolling backward down a rocky slope. Will hit the bottom, his head ringing, body aching. He looked up and there was the creature, swirling above him, taking its sweet time. A clicking, chattering came from its twisted mouth, and it took Will a second to realize what the sound was. Laughter. The bastard was laughing at him.

Will sprang up, swiping left, right, again and again, his blood boiling. But his claws and teeth continued to just slide through thing, leaving nothing but a greasy film behind. The strange beast chased and taunted him through the shadowy glen, a black ghost fighting a black cat in the darkness.

Two more hard strikes across the face and body, and Will crumpled to the ground, desperately fighting to remain conscious. He started to sit up but suddenly felt a terrible weight on top of him. His wrists were pinned down in place. It drew in close, spreading its disgusting lips, laughing right in his face. Its breath was like hot vomit, acidic and rancid. Will roared defiantly in its face.

The raven mocker nearly pierced his eardrums with a hitch-pitched shriek, then bolted up into the night sky. Will looked up and saw its ever-changing shape fading away in the darkness as it ascended through the clouds. He imagined that if the thing had hands, it would be giving him the middle finger right now.

24

SCENE OF THE CRIME

RED AND BLUE LIGHTS FLASHED. The crowd surged like an angry tide. A woman was screaming. Every resident of the quaint suburban street had come outside to see the spectacle. Shards of glass lay outside the broken window. Yellow crime scene tape stretched across the lawn. Police cruisers, CSI units, and an ambulance lined the narrow stretch, and a WLOS My40 news crew had also just arrived on the scene.

Lieutenant Ballard did his best to show a brave face as he watched his community falling apart at the seams. Some people wept, others raged. Families huddled together and chanted prayers and blessings. Holding back the raging throng of onlookers, the officers fought to maintain some semblance of order.

Shenandoah and Casey watched from the sidelines, as helpless as everyone else. Other onlookers pushed and shoved, all vying for a closer look as the drama played out before them. Shenandoah scanned every face in the crowd, took in every detail. She held a small pad of paper, and jotted down notes of everything that transpired, from the time of the attack, to when the police arrived, to who was on the scene. She checked her watch: 12:15 a.m., and wrote it down. She doubted it would help much, but still, she couldn't turn her detective brain off. Finally, her eyes settled on a familiar face.

Jimmy and Pete stood not far away, silently observing the tragic scene. They both did their best to be stoic, but their eyes had the glassy sheen of two men holding back tears. Shenandoah tugged on Casey's sleeve and began walking towards them.

"Come on," she said.

Casey followed along with no questions. All her spunk and sass had been replaced by shock and fear. She had seen the creature and it was indeed a foul and evil spirit. The image of its black, translucent form spilling out of that window played over and over in her mind. Hell was real. Evil was real. It was all true and now she knew it. Dazed and stunned, the teenager didn't even feel her feet touch the pavement as she followed Shenandoah through the crowd.

Pete noticed the petite blonde woman and young Black girl approaching them and gently elbowed his companion. "Friends of yours?" Pete asked.

Jimmy turned and recognized the lady detective.

"Mr. Shaw?" she asked.

"Shenandoah," Jimmy said with a polite smile. He shifted focus to the girl and could tell right away that she was different. She was a skinner. "Hey there, young'n. And who might you be?"

"Um, C-Casey..." she stammered as they shook

hands. She could see the faint outline of a grizzly bear around him. "Y-You're a..."

"Mm hm, and so are you." He smiled and winked at her. "This here's my friend, Pete Littlejohn. Principal chief here in Cherokee."

"Ladies," Pete said, shaking both their hands. "Nice to meet you." His voice was a polite, husky whisper. He'd been crying.

"Have ya seen Will?" Jimmy asked.

Shenandoah nodded. "We saw it, he chased it..."

Jimmy and Pete shared a look.

"What was it?" Pete asked.

"It was horrible," Casey muttered mostly to herself.

Ballard and Sneed were in front of the house that had been struck, their voices inaudible from that distance. Officer Owle was guarding the front porch, while Apachito and Kituwah stood guard behind the yellow tape. Officer Saunooke was next door taking statements from the neighbors. More screaming came from inside the house, a man and a woman. Shenandoah pictured the scene inside in her mind, with investigators trying to calm down and interview two young parents who have just had their lives torn apart. Her heart ached for them.

Two blocks over, Will emerged from the woods.

His clothes were a bit ruffled but not otherwise unpresentable. His skin was another story. In addition to the bruises he'd started the evening with, his body was now covered in welts and lacerations from his encounter with the raven mocker. Most of this battle damage was concealed by his clothing, but one whip mark ran across his cheek that he couldn't hide. Fuming with anger and frustration, he stalked along the dark street and followed the sounds of commotion. Reaching the corner of Yellowhill Road, he glanced right, saw the chaos of the scene, and went the other way.

The car's not far away. Head down, maybe nobody will even see me.

"Will?" Shenandoah called out.

Fuck.

Will sped up but Shenandoah and Casey rushed to catch him, with Jimmy and Pete following slowly behind. He kept his head down and tried to shrug it off, but they swarmed around, pawing at him like a wounded puppy.

"Oh my God," Shenandoah gasped, "are you okay?"

"What happened?" Casey asked.

"I'm fine, I'm fine."

Two houses up, Officer Saunooke was taking witness statements from one of the neighbors, an older man in his pajamas and bath robe. While telling his story, the old man noticed the small crowd buzzing around Will, and recognized him immediately. His eyes lit up and he pointed for the officer to see.

"Over there!" the old man said. "That's the guy! When I came outside, he was running into the backyard! It was him!"

Will cursed under his breath as the spotlight was now on. Sergeant Sneed was the first to take notice, coming over with that constantly annoyed face of his to get a closer look.

"Who's that, Shaw?" Sneed asked, squinting to see better. "What the hell are you doing here?"

"Shaw? Will Shaw?" This time it was Ballard's voice,

the lieutenant alerted to his presence. He stormed over in a huff, like a high school principal coming to chastise a misbehaving student. "You just can't keep away, can you?"

Will sighed, "Ah, Lieutenant. Nice to see you."

"What the hell happened to your face?"

Will considered a sarcastic and witty retort, but judging from the angle of Ballard's mustache, he was in no mood. He finally decided on the truth.

"I saw it," he said.

Ballard and Sneed leaned in closer, as did Saunooke and Owle, anxious to hear what was being said. Shenandoah and Casey waited to hear more, as did Jimmy and Pete. Will glanced around at their expectant faces uneasily.

"Saw what?" Sneed pressed.

"The creature, the evil spirit," Will said, then looked at his papaw. "It is a raven mocker. It broke through that window over there and I chased after it."

Jimmy and Pete shared a dour look.

"Uh huh," Ballard said. "So you happened to be walking by just in time to see this monster?"

"That's right."

"Oh yeah?" Sneed said. "What did it look like?"

Will contemplated answering with *your mother* but thought better of it. Instead he just shrugged and shook his head. "Hard to describe," he said.

"And you say you chased it, huh?" Ballard asked. "And?"

"Chased it into the woods," Will continued, "shot at

it several times, but that had no effect. It attacked me, beat me up pretty good."

"And then it just let you go?" Ballard asked.

"Yes," Will said, starting to realize how all this sounded.

"So you just happened to see this thing, went after it, shot at it... and it just let you go. Pretty convenient, don't you think?"

Will's jaw clenched. "Why Lieutenant, if I didn't know any better, I might think you were accusin' me of lying."

Ballard shot his focus back to the witness standing with Officer Saunooke.

"You saw him run past, right?" Ballard asked, pointing to Will.

"Yes sir," the old man said.

"You see a monster?"

"No sir."

Ballard grunted, turning to face two other witnesses across the street, a husband and wife huddled together. "You see this guy running?" Ballard asked.

They nodded.

"See any monsters?"

They shook their heads.

"Look, Lieutenant," Will cut in, "I'm tellin' you the truth. Whether or not you choose to believe me, I really don't care."

"I saw it," Shenandoah said.

"Me too," Casey added.

Again, Ballard grunted. He squinted as headlights swept across his face and a silver Audi A8 sedan rolled up to them. The doors opened, and special agents Warren and Lambert stepped out into the night air. Ballard and Sneed shared a look.

"Uh, hi. I'm Lieutenant Ben Ballard, Cherokee Marshal Service. Can I help you?"

"Special Agents Warren and Lambert. Federal Bureau of Investigation." Warren flashed his badge, as did she. He wore a gray suit, she wore black.

The two agents made eye contact with Will.

He could see they were both skinners, wolves. They smiled at him, then at Jimmy and Casey. The old man's fists clenched and Casey's pulse began to race. If she could see what these agents really were, that meant they could also see her for what she truly was.

"Shiiiit..." Casey hissed.

"Just relax, little missy," Jimmy whispered.

Agent Lambert turned her polite smile back to Lieutenant Ballard.

"We'd like a word, lieutenant," she said. "And of course, we'll need to see the crime scene."

"I'm sorry," Ballard said, flustered, "but who called in the FBI? Captain Oocuna? Nobody told me..."

Agent Warren stepped close enough to Ballard for him to whisper, that sly little smile never leaving his face. "Actually, Lieutenant," he murmured, "we haven't been formally invited to join this investigation. You see, my partner and I head up a special unit in the Bureau that specifically handles this kind of thing."

"This kind of... thing?" Sneed asked.

"Unexplained phenomena," Warren said.

Ballard and Sneed shared an apprehensive look.

"All right," Ballard said, turning and starting to lead them to the scene, "right this way." Agents Warren and Lambert shot wry glances at Will before following the Lieutenant. Ballard pointed piercing eyes at Will as he marched by, saying, "You stay put. I'm gonna need a statement in writing and I may have more questions."

"Yes, we may have some questions as well," Lambert said.

Once they were gone, Will turned and stalked away.

"Fuck this," he said.

"Um, Will?" Owle stammered, making a feeble gesture to stop him. "B-But, the lieutenant said..."

Will shot the young officer a look that shut him right up.

He walked off down the sidewalk, while Shenandoah and Casey trotted behind.

"Will, wait," Shenandoah said. "Will, come on, please."

Jimmy put his hand on Pete's shoulder as he hobbled along after them. "You go on home to Leah now, ol' buddy," he said. "I'll keep ya posted."

"Okay," was all Pete could say. He was staring at the ground and wringing his hands, with thoughts of a twisted, evil spirit terrorizing his community racing in his head as he walked back to his truck.

"Slow down there, boy," Jimmy called out. "I cain't walk that fast."

"Look," Will said, turning around and walking backwards to address them all, "stop following me, okay? Everybody just leave me alone." He turned back around and continued forward at a brisk pace, taking out his keys.

"Baby, please. We're all on your side here," Shenandoah said.

"We need to work together on this, boy."

"I said leave me the *fuck* alone! All of you!" The venom in his tone stopped all three of them in their tracks. Jimmy, Casey, and Shenandoah stood together and watched as Will stalked up to his car and unlocked the door.

"C'mon, boy," Jimmy said, "where you goin'?"

"To get drunk!"

Will jumped in and slammed the door shut.

He fired up the engine and zoomed away.

25

KNOW WHEN TO RUN

WILL TURNED on the radio as he sped down 441, cranking up the volume as the refreshing sounds of Judas Priest blasted through the speakers. Rob Halford screamed about breaking the law as wind howled through the open windows. Cool air and glorious power chords. It helped, but it wasn't enough to drown out the thoughts. The creature. Copper and Casey and Papaw Jimmy. Ballard and his accusatory tone. Will gripped the leather-laced steering wheel tightly, grinding his teeth.

Had he not been so lost in thought, he may have noticed that several cars back, Shenandoah was following him. Jimmy sat in the passenger seat and Casey in the back, each keeping their eyes on the black Camaro up ahead as their driver did her best to keep a good distance. Casey checked her watch—nearly one in the morning. Shenandoah trailed behind Will for several minutes, watching him cruise through the streets of the reservation until he arrived at the one place he had seemingly not yet explored.

Harrah's Casino and Resort was a monolith of greed and commerce, a modern-day luxury retreat for the White Man, sprouting from the heart of the Red Man's clay. The largest hotel in North Carolina, its complex was vast and modern, with a posh hotel, gaming halls, restaurants, arcades, movies, concert hall, fitness center, spa, and anything else tourists could want. An impressive sight to match any Las Vegas casino, neon lights flashed and modern art installations hung above massive indoor fountains. The hotel towered twenty-one stories, and beside it, a huge LED billboard advertised upcoming performances by Adele and Lionel Ritchie. Gordon Ramsay had his own restaurant here. But Will didn't care about any of that, as long as they had booze.

He pulled into the grand main entrance and followed the signs for one of two large parking garages. A pair of security guards with metal-detecting wands stood at each entrance, ensuring no weapons were brought onto the premises.

Shit. I hate going anywhere without a piece. Will contemplated turning around and going to some dive bar, but he was there already, and he figured he may as well see the spectacle. So he pulled up to the kiosk at the north garage and took the ticket the machine spat out.

It wasn't hard to find a space at that hour, so Will parked on the second level and begrudgingly left his weapons in the car. He cleared his throat, straightened his clothes, and marched through the automatic doors. A security guard wanded Will as he entered a long hallway that reminded him of an airport terminal. Guests and gamblers came and went, everything from high rollers, to families on vacation, to bikers and old drunks. Will started down the walkway, following the signs on the walls pointing the way to the main casino. To his right was a wall of windows spanning the hallway and looking out onto the main street. On the wall to his left, a series of jumbo-size abstract paintings. Will soaked it all in and took long strides, already finding the modern, glitzy environment refreshing.

Not far behind, Shenandoah kept her eyes on him, Casey staying by her side. Although they were moving slowly, Jimmy still had a hard time keeping up. His knees throbbed and his hip ached, but in the name of stoicism, he directed his complaints inward as he wobbled along. Casey did not have as much restraint.

"I don't know about this, She-She," she said, her eyebrows furrowed. "Spying on Will like this, feels wrong."

"We're all here because *you* said Will is in danger," Shenandoah said. "And what the hell did you just call me?"

"Sorry, your name has too many syllables."

"The boy ain't thinkin' right," Jimmy huffed from behind them. "Scares me when he gets like this. We gotta keep an eye on him for his own good."

Will walked onto the casino floor.

The massive room was one of many that bustled with hopeful gamblers at all times of the day or night. With lights and colors and sounds and smells coming from every direction, the atmosphere was an assault on the senses. There were reds and yellows and blues, shouting and laughing and radio-friendly pop music, perfumes and colognes and stinking armpits. There were businessmen and whores, tourists and locals, sinners and scoundrels. Will felt right at home.

The gaming floor was built into a recess two steps lower than the outside edges of the room, and divided by brass railings. The carpet was a garish, red monstrosity, clearly designed by someone trying to create a plaid pattern while tripping on peyote. A side area sported a wall of huge LCD screens, showing football, baseball, basketball, horse racing, and practically every other sport that a desperate soul could want to flush their money away on. The walls were lined with slot machines, and tables for every card game imaginable spanned the entire room. Will spotted a large circular bar in an area washed in lavender, wrap-around LED lights, and made straight for it. He trotted up the steps out of the gaming area and got his wallet ready.

Shenandoah found a pillar to hide behind and watched Will from a distance. Casey stuck close to her side, while Jimmy pulled up a chair and caught his breath. They saw him paying for a glass of whiskey with cash, nodding to the bartender, and taking his first sip. He sat on a stool and spun around, leaning against the bar and watching the show of humanity down in the gaming area.

Will felt that cool, pleasant burn running down his throat, the firewater almost instantly warming him up. He pushed off the bar and strolled down into the gaming room, drink in hand, enjoying the spectacle. A small grin began to form as a truly idiotic idea bubbled up into his brain.

Fuck it, why not?

Will crossed over to the cash-out window, smiled at the teller, and pulled several bills from his wallet. He walked back over to the gambling area with two hundred dollars of chips in his hand, feeling frisky. He contemplated poker, blackjack, gin, and the craps table looked appealing, but it was the large spinning roulette wheel that really caught his eye. Only one gambler sat at that table, an old retiree, so Will plopped down into a chair across from him.

"Evening, sir," the dealer said with a professional smile, her blonde hair still teased into a puff the same size and volume as it was back in 1983. "Place your bets."

"Evening," Will said to her, and exchanged polite nods with the other gentleman at the table. "Okay, let's see..." He took another sip of whiskey and jingled the chips in his hand as he contemplated the options on the wheel. The old gambler put his chips down on the table, placing his bet. Feeling the eyes on him, Will took a twenty dollar chip and placed it down in the red square.

"That's a bad move," came a woman's voice from behind him.

Will looked to his left and saw a slim ebony hand reach past him and place a stack of chips onto the black square. Then she pulled up a chair and sat beside him.

"Always bet on black," Janae Jones said.

HER. WOMAN. BITCH. TRAITOR.

. . .

Every muscle in Will's body tensed. There she was, in black leggings and boots, a sleek black-leather riding jacket, her hair shaved nearly down to the skin. She looked at him with those big eyes and his blood began to boil, fists clenched and teeth grinded. The expression on her face was unreadable, the polite smile of a customer service professional who doesn't really care.

"Hi, Will," she said. "Been a minute."

Will couldn't speak. His mouth had dried up and his eyes blazed with fury, staring at her as the dealer spun the wheel and tossed the plastic ball into play. It clacked and bounced and the players waited to see where it landed.

Across the room, Shenandoah watched the interaction, and her pulse sped up. She looked over at Casey and Jimmy, seeing the alarm and recognition in their eyes.

"Is that... her?" she asked.

"Oh yeah," Casey said. "That's Janae."

The lady cop clenched her jaw, seeing her biggest competition in the flesh for the first time. The other woman.

The roulette ball landed on black. Janae won.

She scooped up her winnings as Will continued to stare daggers at her.

"You have got some fucking nerve," he said.

"You don't seem happy to see me."

"Well, maybe that's because the last time I saw you two years ago, you locked me in a burning train car and left me for dead." He debated bashing his fist into her face, or throwing her to the floor and choking the life out of her. But there was security everywhere, cameras, civilians... He knew it would be stupid to try anything here.

The dealer shot a wary glance at the pair seated at her table, feeling the tension in the air, her eyes uneasy. Janae chuckled and leveled her hypnotic gaze at the unsuspecting woman.

"Don't worry, sweetie," Janae said, "you won't remember any of this." She then looked over at the old gambler across the table—also with a baffled expression on his face—and smiled politely, her dark eyes drawing him in. "And neither will you," she told the old timer. "Understand?"

"Yes ma'am," the old man said, and went back to paying them no mind.

"Why are you here, Janae?" Will growled.

"I'm here because of you," she said, eyeballing his beat-up face. "The real question is, what are *you* doing here, other than getting into fights?"

Will laughed and shook his head, taking a drink.

"I'm working a case. And I don't care if you or any of your little buddies from The Council approve. I'm going to find the thing killing these children, and I'm going to stop it."

Janae laughed, shaking her head.

"Man, those dimples, those big brown eyes..." Janae mused. "You fooled me with that pretty-boy charm once, but not this time."

"What's that supposed to mean?"

Janae sighed. "Why don't you make this easy on yourself, Will? Let us take you in peacefully. Don't make a scene."

"Us?" Will said, and suddenly realized she had not come in alone. Standing not ten feet away was Redhawk, watching them patiently. Across the room, agents Warren and Lambert were closing in. Looking around, he could now tell that there were many more skinners hiding in plain sight. They sat at the tables, at the slots, at the bar. He was surrounded. "What exactly is going on here, Janae?"

Janae shook her head and muttered to herself, "Beware the beast with the bright smile, for he is the deceiver, and he is the destroyer of the Spirit Council…"

Will bursted out laughing, shaking his head. "Man, you really have been drinking the Kool-Aid, huh?"

"Maybe you should try some, Mr. Shaw," came a deep voice.

Will turned to see an old, burly White man step up to the table. He wore a white suit, his long, silver hair pulled into a tight ponytail. With piercing blue eyes, he looked at Will and smiled. "I thought I should introduce myself. I am Keonee."

Watching from afar, Jimmy's throat clenched at the sight of his former friend, over fifty years since they last met. Casey could sense that the man in white was not only a skinner, but that he was the leader. She saw the others closing in around Will and squeezed Shenandoah's arm, gesturing for her to see.

"Look, there. And there," she said. "They're skinners."

Shenandoah swallowed hard, feeling the mounting tension.

"How about we take a little walk?" Keonee said. "Let these people finish their game." Orenda came up from behind Keonee and stood by his side.

"You gonna preach to me about your prophecy?"

"We just want to ask you about what's happening to the babies around here," Orenda said. "That's why we're here, to find this thing and stop it."

"Well, I don't know anything," Will said. "Not sure why you think I would."

"Please," Keonee said, gesturing for them to walk.

Will grumbled, downed the rest of his drink, and plunked the glass onto the counter. He stood up, his eyes darting around to Redhawk and the others standing by. Janae smiled politely at the dealer as she collected her chips.

"Thanks very much," she said. "Oh, and give me that stack of hundred-dollar chips, please."

"Yes, ma'am," the dealer said, scooping up over one thousand dollars in chips without thinking twice, and handed them to Janae. "Ya'll have a good night, now."

Will chuckled and shook his head as Janae dumped the chips into her purse. He followed Keonee and Orenda deeper into the grand hall, with Janae to his right, and Redhawk on his left. He looked over at the large Indian and smiled as they walked.

"How you doin' there, player?" Will said.

"The name is Redhawk."

"Oh, sweet. Cool name. I'm Bono."

Shenandoah lost sight of Will and the group of skinners, and strained to see better. No use. They had vanished into the distance.

"Jimmy, come on," she said, tapping his shoulder. "We have to keep an eye on them. Casey, wait here. *Got it?*"

"Fine," Casey rolled her eyes as Shenandoah and Jimmy followed the action. She waited a moment, then figured to hell with it. She crossed over to the left and stayed off the gaming floor, moving at a brisk pace to catch up with them.

Keonee and Orenda led Will to a grand staircase overlooking a lavish entrance below, and an abstract sculpture suspended from cables above. The older man stopped to admire the strange installation hanging in front of them.

"You want to talk about modern art?" Will asked.

"You're a funny guy, huh?" Keonee said, admiring the sculpture. "Look at it, Mr. Shaw. A thing of beauty hanging in the air. Such a delicate balance. What would happen if it were to come crashing down? Would it shatter into a thousand pieces? How many innocent people down there would be killed?"

"Okay, your point?"

"We provide balance, Mr. Shaw," Keonee said. "That's what the Spirit Council does. We've been here since the beginning of time. When a skinner acts out, say, tampers with the dark arts, threatens the balance..." he looked Will in the eye with an accusatory glare, "...we must put a stop to it."

"Wait, you think *I'm* responsible for this?" Will balked. He looked from Keonee, to Orenda, to Janae. "You can't be serious."

"Black magic is very serious, Will," Janae said.

"We have a car waiting outside, Mr. Shaw," Orenda said. "Let's go somewhere more private and talk about this."

"Oh, you want to *talk* about this. Okay."

RUN!

SHENANDOAH AND JIMMY CREPT CLOSER TO WATCH the tense scene. Sneaking in from the other side, Casey got as far as she could without entering the gaming area, so she stepped past the brass railings and moved in, staying close to a row of slot machines. Peaking around the corner of a neon-flashing game, she got a good view of Will, Keonee and the others.

"Let's not make a scene, Mr. Shaw," Agent Warren said.

"Nobody wants to hurt you," Lambert added.

BULLSHIT. RUN!

"LOOK," WILL SAID, ANGLING AWAY AND STARTING TO back up, "thanks for the concern. Really. But it's late, and I'm tired. Been a long day. Maybe we can meet up for lunch sometime? I know a great spot..." He backed up past Janae and Redhawk, past Warren and Lambert, past their crew of backup skinners. "Ya'll have a good night, now, y'hear?"

Will turned and calmly strutted back the way he came. Keonee and Orenda remained at the staircase with Warren and Lambert, watching him walk away. Janae and Redhawk looked to Keonee for instructions, and he simply nodded. With that, they knew what to do, following behind Will and bringing the other skinners with them.

Shenandoah and Jimmy followed the action.

Keonee said to the two federal agents, "I'm in suite 2101, in the Creek tower. Meet me there in twenty minutes." And with that, Keonee and Orenda made their exit, striding across the gaming room with an air of royalty. Casey watched them leave, intent on following behind, when she felt a meaty hand slap down on her shoulder.

"How old are you, young lady?" It was a portly security guard, annoyed at having to deal with another one of these damn kids.

Casey stammered, "Um, uh... I, uh..."

"Come on, let's go. No minors on the gaming floor."

He turned the child around, escorting her out of the gambling area. The first thing to catch Casey's eye was his ID badge and security access card, a laminate clipped onto his breast pocket. She suddenly had an idea and sprang into action.

"Hey! Ow! Let me go!" Casey struggled and protested.

The guard wrestled to keep his grip on the teenager, pushing her forward out of the room. Casey thrashed and caused a scene, trying to force him away, swatting at him, being as difficult as she could manage. Gamblers and tourists turned their heads as the rent-a-cop finally got her to the exit and ousted her from the room.

"Go on now, little girl," he said. "It's past your bedtime."

The guard nodded to two other guards standing watch at the doors, and they returned the gesture. The point had been made clear, and Casey let her head drop, dejected as she slumped away back into the hotel. She made it into the main lobby, saw the coast was clear, and reached into the big pocket in her hoodie.

She pulled out the security guard's ID badge and smiled.

RUN!

WILL PICKED UP THE PACE AS HE MOVED THROUGH the casino. He could feel them following him. Janae, Redhawk, and the others. To his estimation, there were at least six of them, maybe more. Three appeared to be wolf spirits, one was a bobcat, another an alligator. He glanced over his left shoulder, and the skinners were closing the distance. *Shit.* He looked over his right shoulder and saw three more, a coyote, a bat, and what looked like some kind of tropical frog. *Shit!*

RUN!

WILL'S PULSE SPED UP. HE WAS IN A PUBLIC PLACE, surrounded by human civilians. He didn't have a gun.

His car was parked in the garage all the way across the casino complex. Janae and Redhawk were getting closer. They did not want to talk. Will saw the door to the indoor bridge up ahead and knew what he had to do. *Okay, this could get ugly...* He took a deep breath, waited a moment, then exploded.

26

MEAN BONE

WILL SHOT like a bolt across the casino floor.

His pursuers instantly snapped into high-gear, racing after him. Every head in the room turned as the chase erupted like a shot of nitro. Shenandoah sprung to attention and began to follow the chase, but heard a pained gasp behind her, and skidded to a halt. Turning around, she saw Jimmy struggling to follow, clutching at his aching hip. She ran back to help him, knowing there was nothing she could do for Will now, anyway. They were all after him.

Janae and Redhawk sprinted after him, dodging and weaving through the swarm of civilians. Behind them were the three wolf-skinners, going by their Council codenames, Pala, Amaruq, and Opiyel. Behind and to the right was the coyote, Loco, the bobcat, Kentucky, and the alligator, Teoc. To the back and left was Apu the bat, Toho the mountain lion, and Karuk the poison-dart frog.

Will leapt over the brass railing and charged up the stairs, dodging whatever innocent people he could and pushing the others aside. Security guards rushed in from all angles and he saw two of them up ahead at the doors.

"Hey, hold it!"

"Stop right there!"

Will ran faster. A burly security officer who thought he was tough jumped on Will, trying to knock him over like he was back playing college football. But the big Indian simply shifted his weight and spun, throwing the rent-a-cop off his shoulders like an old jacket, sending him smashing into a slot machine. Shards of glass and jackpot coins poured over the man as he crashed down onto the ugly carpet.

Spotting a chip runner pushing a rolling cart, Will grabbed the handle and flung it behind him, sending chips showering onto his pursuers. Janae and Redhawk ducked through it, but the cart smashed into Teoc's face and knocked him down. Will ran faster.

"*Freeze!*" the first guard at the door screamed and drew his pistol.

Will reached terminal velocity and launched forward through the air, delivering a flying-front kick into the man's chest, blasting him back through the doorway. His partner screamed and charged at Will, drawing and aiming his gun point-blank. He suddenly felt his wrist snap as Will twisted the pistol out of his hand and shot a knee into his solar plexus. With a solid punch to the temple, the lights went out and he collapsed to the floor, as tourists gasped and screamed, some recording with their cell phones.

Sorry, guys, Will thought. *Nothing personal.*

He dashed forward without wasting a second, bolting

down the long hallway leading to the parking garage. Hotel guests dove out of his way. Janae had her Sig P320 in hand, but there were too many innocent bystanders to take a shot. She snarled and pushed harder, going after him with fury in her eyes.

Up ahead, two more guards were waiting for him at the end of the hall.

"F-Freeze!" one said, aiming his weapon with shaking hands.

Will was not impressed. He jumped forward into a flying-sidekick, knocking the air out of the guard and smashing him back through the locked door. The other guard spun with his weapon and fired, but Will blocked his wrist and the bullet shattered the window looking out onto the street. Will knocked him out with one punch, then grabbed him by both lapels and flung the unconscious guard behind him. Janae was knocked off her feet and pinned beneath his weight.

"God damn it!" she snapped.

Redhawk helped push the guard off of Janae as Will escaped into the parking garage. The other skinners were right behind them, as well as casino security, and Will assumed the police would be there any minute as well. He jumped down two levels of stairs and ran onto level two, pulling out his car keys.

Boom! Boom! Boom!

Janae fired three shots from her Sig as she raced into the garage, finally getting a clean shot at him. Will leapt over the hood of a Toyota SUV to dodge the attack, the rounds shattering the windows and punching holes into the concrete walls. Janae continued after him, gun pointed ahead, with Redhawk and the others following behind and spreading out.

Will jumped out from behind a row of cars he was hiding behind, making a dash for his car. He hit the unlock button on his key-fab and slid into the driver's door, whipping it open and diving in as Janae opened fire again. Three bullets lodged in his door and one shattered the driver's window. Will grinded his teeth and started the engine. Immediately, *Mean Bone* by Slash's Snakepit blasted through the speakers, and Will smiled. He shifted into gear and hit the gas to the sounds of the hard-rock banger.

The black Camaro jolted out of the parking space, spinning and screeching as it nearly fishtailed into a concrete column. Will zoomed out of the danger zone as Janae continued to shoot, her bullets peppering his car and the vehicles nearby. Her slide locked back as the magazine ran empty, so she popped it out and slapped in a new one as she continued to move.

"Get after him!" she ordered the others, as she sprinted towards her own vehicle. Loco, Kentucky, and Apu tried to continue on foot, but Will had already sped around the corner to the next level down. Redhawk didn't waste his time running. Instead, he crossed over to the elevators and called one. When he stepped inside, he pressed the button for the roof level, and the doors whirred closed.

Will swung the Camaro down the ramp to level one and nearly ran head-first into an oncoming Ford Bronco. The driver of the SUV pounded his horn and Will swerved out of the way, smashing sidelong into three parked cars instead, scraping the bumpers and rear tail-lights off all of them. He cringed and grinded his teeth, gripping the wheel and pushing forward toward the exit.

He saw the mechanical entrance and exit gates up ahead, but another driver was at the exit gate, taking their sweet time finding their ticket to insert into the machine. Not a second to waste, Will swerved into the oncoming traffic lane and aimed for the entrance gate. *Always wanted to do this,* Will thought with a smile as he smashed through the mechanized arm and out onto the street.

A security car with flashing blue lights was already there, driving straight for him. He cut the wheel and swerved around it, smashing over the two-foot concrete divider and crashing down into the inclined driveway exiting the parking structure. The muscle car lurched and shook. Checking his rear-view and side mirrors, he could see more of them coming. Security vehicles, and in the distance, tribal police.

This is stupid this is stupid this is stupid!

Will shook his head and punched the wheel. The song coming through the speakers rocked hard, the beat aggressive, the guitar work vicious. Will snorted out a small laugh, as one glass of whiskey mixed with adren-aline and rock n' roll to create the perfect attitude for a car chase. His smile spreading into an ear-to-ear grin, he cranked the volume all the way up and stomped on the gas.

Redhawk arrived at the roof of the parking garage.

He stepped out of the elevator with a sense of urgency and looked around. There were a few parked cars here and there, but no people. No witnesses. He ran over to the edge and jumped up onto the wall, looking down at the mountains and valley before him. There was Will's car down below, swerving right onto 441 and blasting that awful heavy metal music. Even from this distance several stories up, it was loud enough to make him cringe. He stepped to the edge and held out his arms, closing his eyes. He jumped.

As he fell, light shimmered and refracted around him. Reality bent and warped. Instead of plunging to his death, the man melted away, and something else came into this dimension. Massive wings of brown and golden feathers spread out and caught the wind, sending the red-tail hawk skinner soaring back up into the sky.

Janae rocketed out of the parking garage on her black Ducati Monster 1200 motorcycle, her right knee nearly scraping the ground as she banked onto the street and sped after Will. Loco and Kentucky raced out of the other exit in a black F-150, with Pala, Opiyel, and Amaruq following a moment later in a silver Mustang. They all sped up on the black Camaro, sandwiching it in from all sides.

Will whipped the wheel right and left, swerving through traffic as his pursuers closed the distance. He recognized the rider in black and his pulse pounded even faster as she drew her gun and began to fire. The rear windshield shattered and Will ducked down low, skidding and smashing against a row of parked cars as he pushed his machine forward.

"Okay, bitch! You want to play?"

Will grabbed his Canik from the center console,

along with two extended mags. He whipped right around a corner, momentarily giving him a straight angle at his attackers through the passenger window. He leveled his iron sights and fired. *Boom! Boom! Boom! Boom! Boom!* One 9mm hollow-point round grazed Janae's thigh, making her wobble and nearly crash, and several more punched into the engine block of Loco's truck.

They opened fire in return, spitting hot lead into the black Camaro. Pala slammed her gas pedal and raced up alongside Will on his left, wasting no time in smashing into him. Amaruq and Opiyel blasted at him with 9's and .45's, blowing holes into Will's car as he desperately tried to stay on the road. Loco swerved in from the right, smashing into Will from the other side. As they progressively mashed the Camaro into scrap metal, Janae glanced in her mirrors to see police racing up behind in the distance.

Redhawk sailed overhead, cool wind catching in his feathers as he watched the action from two hundred feet above. The Camaro swerved and smashed and raced along the serpentine road below, trying to make it to the interstate as the team of skinners attacked from all directions.

The road opened up in front of them, giving Will more room to maneuver. Seeing the Cherokee welcome center coming up on the left, he pumped the brakes, letting Pala sail ahead of him, then pounded the gas again. The Camaro shot forward, hitting the Mustang's back bumper in just the right place, causing it to spin wildly out of control.

Pala and her two cohorts screamed as the car

hydroplaned across the empty parking lot, smashing through the front windows of the Native Earth gift shop. They blasted through aisles of merchandise and the front register, coming to a halt as t-shirts and postcards reading "Cherokee, NC" fell onto the windshield.

Will powered forward, Janae right on his tail. He ducked as she fired off several more shots, one of them ripping through his left-rear tire. The car lurched as the whole tire blew out, and sparks sprayed as the wheel block scraped against asphalt like a match. Will struggled to steer, turning left at the intersection of 441 and Acquoni Road, hoping to make it to the interstate. Suddenly, multiple headlights glared in his eyes and he nearly ran headlong into a squad of police cars, their lights flashing and sirens blaring. Will cursed at himself and spun the wheel right, leaving a trail of blazing sparks behind him.

Janae and Loco each hit their brakes as the Cherokee Marshal Service troopers cut them off, six cherry-tops in total. With no choice now but to follow behind them, Janae growled in frustration, and Redhawk continued to monitor the action from above, camouflaged by the dark clouds.

Racing along the dark, two-lane road, the Oconaluftee river flowing to his left and a mountain to his right, Will could only go forward. His hands strained to keep the wheel straight. Sparks flew. Slash shredded.

Will went off-road, bouncing over a sidewalk, skidding across another strip mall parking lot and rumbling onto a large, open field. His mortally wounded vehicle would not allow the maneuver, sending him into a spin across grass and dirt.

He jolted forward as his beautiful black baby crumpled head-first into a large, steel post. Slash abruptly stopped shredding. The Camaro groaned its death rattle, plumes of thick, white smoke pouring out from the engine block. His head ringing, Will looked for his Canik, but it was gone, lost somewhere in the night. The party was over.

Will couldn't open his door, so he instead slipped through the shattered window, collapsing onto the grassy surface. He looked up to see the cops blocking off the surrounding roads. At first, he thought he'd run into a tree, but as his gaze moved up the object, he could see now that it was a goal post. He had returned back to the football field where he'd played stickball just the day before. Will scoffed.

"We have you surrounded! Come out with your hands up!"

Will pushed forward into the gloomy, dark football field. Behind him, several police and S.W.A.T. officers closed in, shining lights. At the other end of the field he saw the lights of more law enforcement officers coming his way. He looked up to the sky, hearing a familiar echoing reverb filling the air. It was a police helicopter, its HID light beam shining down on him. A sense of peace came over him. This was it. Nowhere to run. They had him.

"Show me your hands! Do it!"

"On your knees! On your knees!"

Will obeyed the commands as they closed in. Within

seconds, they were on him. He closed his eyes and hummed a tune while the boys he'd been playing stick-ball with on this very field pushed his face into the mud and cuffed him.

Janae watched from behind the rows of police cruisers as they took him away. She revved her engine and angrily spun around, speeding into the indigo night. A dejected Loco and Kentucky followed her in their pickup, unable to finish the job without blowing their cover.

Up above the action, high in the trees, sat a silent sentinel.

Redhawk observed from the shadows. He gripped the tree with his clawed feet and hands. His curved beak was a formidable weapon, his intense eyes like night-vision binoculars. He perched with his wings folded, peering through the leaves at the activity on the ground. The raptor stood up and unfolded his wings.

He bolted up into the clouds.

27

HIGH ROLLER

CASEY STROLLED AS CASUALLY as she could manage around the outside perimeter of the Creek tower at Harrah's. Traipsing around a casino at one-thirty in the morning was never a position she expected to be in. Her hands trembled as she held the security guard's stolen access badge, a jittery skip to her walk as she scanned the building for a way in. This was way past her bedtime.

As she rounded the next corner she saw a loading dock, presently unoccupied by workers. She jogged up the concrete ramp to the platform and went to the automatic door. There was a keypad and magnetic swipe-sensor on the wall. Casey's heart fluttered and she took a deep breath. This was her last chance to turn back.

Fuck it. She swiped the badge. The sensor buzzed and a green light popped up on the keypad. Casey smiled and watched as the doors swung open for her. She pranced inside, hoping to God that nobody in the security office was paying close attention to their video monitors.

Casey stepped cautiously into the industrial belly of the hotel. A loading area full of cardboard boxes, shipping palettes, and clean stacks of laundry led to two nondescript, blank hallways. A mechanical whirring was coming from somewhere. The sounds of employees talking and working came muffled through the walls. She sniffed the air and smelled cleaning products.

Psyching herself up for the mission ahead, Casey chose the hallway to the right and moved with a sense of urgency. She remembered the old man in white saying "suite 2101, the Creek tower, twenty minutes." Time was ticking away and she figured as long as she could find an elevator, the high-roller suites must be on the top floor. If the old man was the leader of this council thing, and they were the official body designated to investigate this sort of case, then maybe she could sneak in and learn something that could help Will. That was the theory.

She suddenly stiffened as a maid came around a corner, pushing an empty cart to replenish her supplies. An older Indian woman, a puzzled look came over her as she saw the young girl. Casey thought quick.

"Oh, good!" she said. "I'm totally lost. I'm trying to get back to my room, but I think I went the wrong way."

"That's okay, hon," the lady said with a smile. "What room are you in?"

"Uh, 2101."

"Ohhh, the presidential suite. Very nice. Yeah, you just keep going down this hallway, make another right. You'll come to two elevators, one is a freight, so take the other one all the way up." The maid gestured behind her and Casey beamed.

"Great, thank you so much," Casey said. "You have a great night!"

"You too, hon."

Quite proud of her deception, Casey continued along the hallway and followed the cleaning lady's directions. Two minutes later, she was standing in a posh elevator, going up. Twice, hotel guests got on and got off, and Casey nodded pleasantly at them. She could feel her heart pattering in her chest, and by the time she reached the top floor, it was banging like a kick drum. The doors slid open with a *ding* and Casey stepped out into a lavish hallway. The carpet was imported from Turkey, the trim and fixtures a fine gold leaf. The paintings on the walls were high-end gallery pieces, not the usual hotel fare of scenic mountains and watercolor sunsets.

Her throat was dry. Her heart raced. Casey forced herself forward, looking at the room numbers as she passed. It took a minute, but then at the end of a long hallway, there it was. Room 2101. She approached the door, trembling, and pulled the stolen access badge from her pocket. She was about to swipe the card when she thought twice. It would be foolish to not check first.

Casey knocked on the door. She waited a minute with no response, then tried again. Nothing. After determining that the old man in white had not yet returned, she knew this was the moment. She took a deep breath, closed her eyes, and swiped the badge. The digital lock beeped, the green light flashed, and the door opened. Casey smiled and walked in.

A luxurious hotel room was what Casey was expecting. She was not prepared to walk into a miniature palace. Her mouth dropped open as she stepped into the foyer of the massive, dark space. Even with all the lights off, it was an opulent sight to behold. White marble floors stretched out to a huge wall of windows reaching up two stories into a vaulted ceiling. The lights from the town outside twinkled through the windows, illuminating the spread. There was an inlaid couch placed before a wall-mounted, eighty-inch flatscreen, and a fireplace big enough to fit a king-size bed. There was a bar—not a mini bar—that was an offshoot of the massive kitchen.

Casey explored the space, careful not to disturb anything. There were a few suitcases and articles of clothing in the first of two large bedrooms with king beds. The second bedroom was empty and untouched. She passed by a small bathroom, then a second one which was much larger and came equipped with a multiple-water jet shower. And then a second kitchen. Casey shook her head.

"Holy shit," was all she could say.

She went to the glass doors that led to the balcony and pushed them open. Stepping out into the chilly night air, her jaw dropped open even more. This was no mere balcony. It was a platform that wrapped around the entire corner of the building, complete with chairs, tables, umbrellas, and of course, a high-end jacuzzi. Casey made a mental checklist of all the items she would have when she grew up.

Then she heard a *click*. Someone was coming.

Casey bolted back inside, running on her tiptoes and closing the patio door as quickly and quietly as possible. She heard voices and knew she had only a split second to hide. The bar presented itself as her best option, and with three running steps, Casey jumped into a forward-roll—a different experience on a marble floor than on the mats at BJJ class—and landed behind its polished stone counter. She scooched down low and tight against the cabinets, her heart thumping.

The front door opened and light from the hallway flooded in as two figures entered the room. Keonee hummed a tune as he guided her inside, his hand in the small of her back. He took off his white jacket and draped it on one of the chairs. Orenda switched on the lights and the room came alive with sparkle. Although still hidden, Casey suddenly felt exposed and knew she had to find a better spot. She looked around at the drawers and cabinets under the bar and began to silently check for a space she could fit in.

"What a day," she heard Keonee say.

"How are you feeling?" Orenda asked, sitting down to take off her shoes.

"Eh, you know. Starting to hurt a little," he said, unbuttoning the top two buttons of his white shirt and rolling the sleeves halfway up his forearms. "It'll be here soon. I'll be fine."

Casey gingerly opened the first cabinet and found a wine rack inside. She checked the next one and there were three shelves inside filled with glasses and bar equipment. *Come on, damn it!* she thought. The third cabinet was simply a large open space, with nothing inside but a blender and small coffee pot. Casey eagerly pushed the items aside and slid into the dark hiding spot, easing the door closed behind her.

A sliver of light reached into the darkness with her, a small gap between the cabinet and the marble counter-top. Casey leaned in and peered through, finding she had a clear view of the suite and the two mysterious figures. She smiled and hunkered down, enjoying the show. *Now all I need is some popcorn.*

"Would you like a drink?" Orenda asked Keonee, stroking his shoulders.

"No thank you, my love," he said with a slight wince of pain, giving her a small kiss as he went to the sliding balcony doors. Casey noticed that one of the doors was still open a crack from when she'd gone out there and hadn't closed it all the way. She cringed for a moment that seemed to linger in time, but then breathed a sigh of relief when he went through, not noticing. He gazed up into the sky as if looking for something and breathed in the cool night air. "Any time now... man, I used to play stickball with Jimmy Shaw when we were kids. We got drunk together more times than I can count, hooked up with a few girls, got into a few fights... Never would have thought it would come to this."

"It has to be done," Orenda said, walking to the bar to get herself a drink. Casey stiffened up as she heard the woman come within a foot of her, the sound of fine crystal clinking on the counter just above her head, ice cubes dropping into the glass, alcohol pouring. "Will Shaw is a threat to the balance. He's dangerous."

"Oh, absolutely..." Keonee trailed off in thought.

There was a knock at the door.

Keonee nodded to Orenda, who crossed around the bar and went to answer it. Agents Warren and Lambert followed her inside, his arm around her waist, each taking in the accommodations with wry smiles.

"Not too shabby," Warren said.

"High roller suite, baby!" Keonee said with a big grin, holding his hands out in the air and waved them in. "Get over here!"

Keonee embraced his old friends, each still regarding him in the formal manner dictated by the council. They nodded their heads and each said, "Father."

"My children," Keonee said with sincere warmth.

"I could get used to this," Lambert said, appraising the digs.

"Drink?" Orenda offered.

Lambert declined, but Warren replied, "Sure, why not? Never turn down free booze, babe. Scotch, please."

Casey watched from her hiding spot as Orenda came behind the bar again to prepare the beverage. Keonee grasped each of the agents by a shoulder, enthusiasm in his eyes. "It's almost time. We're so close. Well, what happened out there?"

"Shaw has been arrested by local PD," Warren said. "Crashed into the football field, the idiot. They got him locked up now at the station."

Casey's stomach felt like it dropped.

"Good," Keonee said. "Tomorrow you two can show up to transport him into federal custody, and then he'll be ours."

"What about the baby?" Lambert asked. "Was tonight the right one?"

"We're about to find out," Keonee said. "And if not, we'll find him. I'll find him." A rude wind blew through the open balcony doors, sending shivers through Casey's spine and making her teeth chatter. She watched as the leaders of the Spirit Council turned towards the doors, waiting as the drapes danced with the cold breeze. Keonee smiled and approached the open doorway. "It's here."

Something appeared in the black sky past the balcony.

At first, it looked to Casey like an errant black plastic bag, torn and twisting and dancing on the wind. It pulsed and undulated, floating weightlessly yet still moving with a purpose over the balcony, and finally, through the glass doors and into the palatial suite. Casey's throat seized up and her pounding heart suddenly seemed to stop.

"Welcome, my friend," Keonee said.

The raven mocker drifted into the suite.

All the lights dimmed and flickered in its presence. Keonee stepped forward as Orenda, Warren, and Lambert watched quietly. Black, oily tentacles and membranes swirled into abstract shapes, changing with each passing second. A circular mouth with putrid, gray gums and no teeth swirled through the translucent forms as it faced the old man. Keonee held his hands out and smiled.

"Come," he said. "Let's see what you brought for me."

The dark entity obeyed its master, slithering through the air, its awful maw unfolding as if to give him a kiss. Keonee closed his eyes and opened his mouth as it came right up to him, exhaling what appeared to be a flowing, white smoke. As the creature breathed out, Keonee breathed it in, the strange mist pulsating with an etherial light as it flowed from one host to another.

Casey snapped out of her shock and reached a trembling hand into her pocket to pull out her phone. She turned it on, switched it to camera mode, and began recording video as she placed the lens up against the gap in the cabinet. She watched in horror as what she knew must be the life force of an innocent baby flowed into the old man's mouth. Finally, the last of it vanished down Keonee's throat, and the raven mocker floated back to await his reaction.

Keonee took a deep breath, as if smelling the freshest air at the top of the Alps, a slight smile of relief tweaking his lips. He opened his eyes, exhaling with satisfaction. Orenda took a step forward, hopeful.

"How do you feel, darling?" she asked.

"Good," he said.

"Just good?"

Keonee turned to face his team, a slight twinge of disappointment in his eyes. "Just good," he said with a sigh. "The child continues to elude us. I am replenished, but not for long. Of all the vile and evil monsters I have faced, Cancer is surely the worst. I can feel it... eating me alive."

"Father, please," Agent Lambert said, stepping forward. "I can make Will Shaw talk. I'll *make* him tell us where this damn kid is."

"She's right," Warren added. "We've already done enough to convince the police here that Shaw is their boogeyman. And after tomorrow, there will be no doubt."

Keonee nodded and strolled through the living room,

running his fingers across Orenda's back and then along the back of the couch as he contemplated. "All right," he said. "Use your gift of persuasion, my child. Once I have breathed the essence of the chosen child, I will know no more pain or disease... I'll be immortal. And *we* will be unstoppable."

"And if Shaw doesn't know where the child is?" Orenda asked.

"Oh please," Keonee said. "How could he not know? Either way, after tomorrow night, we'll be rid of him for good." Keonee turned back to face the unearthly wraith floating in his patio doorway, patiently waiting for his word. "Go now, friend. I will call on you soon."

The creature obeyed, making a strange rattling-clicking sound as its black masses swirled and floated backward. It drifted out of the room, across the patio, and up into the sky, where it dissolved into the night and disappeared into some dark, unknown dimension of evil.

Casey trembled as she continued to record, trying to hold her phone steady. She watched as Keonee rejoined his small group of conspirators, slapping their shoulders and laughing in his jovial baritone voice. They joked and made small talk , and Casey decided to stop recording to check her video. She ran it back from the beginning, watching the small glowing screen in the darkness of her hiding place. It was jittery and low-quality video, a hand-held mess shot through a tiny gap in the cabinet, but some of it was still visible. And every word they said had been recorded.

They heard a knock at the door and Orenda went to answer it.

A dejected Janae and Redhawk stood in the doorway. They nodded respectfully to the senior councilwoman, who returned the gesture and stepped aside to let them in. Keonee, Warren, and Lambert greeted them with warm smiles, but their body language had changed. Warren removed his hand from Lambert's waist and any hints of romantic coupling were stowed away. Janae was too angry and frustrated to smile, her hand rubbing the bloody spot on her left thigh.

"Father," she and Redhawk both said.

"My children," Keonee said, then noticed the wound. "You're hurt."

"It only grazed me," she said.

"The police have taken the deceiver," Redhawk reported.

"We know," Keonee said, nodding to Warren and Lambert. "Tomorrow, Nayati and Kasa will take him into custody and his reign of evil will come to an end."

"And the raven mocker?" Redhawk asked.

"Kill the master and you destroy the slave," Agent Warren said. "Whatever black magic he used to conjure that vile beast, when he dies, his spell will be broken."

"Go now, my children. You have had a long day. Tomorrow this nightmare finally comes to an end. You have both earned a chair at the circle."

Redhawk nodded proudly. Casey found it difficult to read how Janae was feeling. The woman's face was flat and expressionless, but she respectfully bowed and did as her master instructed. Together, the two young warriors walked back to the door, where Orenda saw them out.

She smiled and went back to the group, finishing off her drink.

"Well, I don't mind celebrating a little early," she said. "Another drink, anyone?"

"Actually," Agent Warren said with a cocky smirk, swaggering over to the bar, "I'd love another drink. How about..." he went behind the counter, bent down and whipped open the cabinet door. Casey jolted in shock as his hand shot in and grabbed her by the collar, yanking her out into the light. "...a Shirley Temple?"

Casey screamed and thrashed but couldn't break his grip.

"Let me go! Let me go!"

"Hello," Keonee said with a smile, coming closer, "what do we have here?"

"Can't believe you guys didn't smell her," Warren said.

"*I said let go!*" Casey snarled and used a technique Will taught her to twist out of Warren's grip, then shot a front kick into his chest. The federal agent was stunned as she knocked him back and assumed a fighting stance. "Get away from me!" I mean it!" Casey warned, her fists balled tightly as she tried to circle around them.

Orenda was mildly amused.

"Weak," the older woman said.

Casey at once felt light-headed, and heavy fatigue draped over her like a wet blanket. She tried to fight it, to stay on her feet, proud and defiant to the end. But the strength drained from her body, and she fell to one knee, then the other.

Fear pulsed through Casey's body as the four skinners crowded around her. The old man with the white ponytail leaned in close enough for her to smell his hot breath.

"Looks like we have a new guest," Keonee said. "Let's make her feel at home. Tell me," he leaned in even closer and she squirmed, tears welling in her eyes. "Where did you come from, little kitten?"

28

HOT BLOODED

WILL SAT ALONE on his cot in a dark, metal cage.

He had been thrown once again into purgatory. Not living, not dead, simply existing. He was drenched in sweat and dirt, his body ached, and try as he might, he could not turn off his brain. The raven mocker. The casino. Papaw Jimmy, Shenandoah, and Casey. The chase. His poor car. Keonee... Her.

BITCH! WHORE! KILL HER! TEAR HER APART!

Janae's face flashed through his mind, refusing to let him rest. Her eyes, her lips, the way she swung her hips when she walked. The way she tried to pump him full of lead, the way she left him to die in a raging inferno... her skin, her scent, her sultry voice... *stop it, God damn it!*

Will kicked the floor in frustration and stood up, fuming. He paced in the tight jail cell, tempted to skin into the cat and test the strength of the steel bars. The thoughts raced through his neural channels, shooting and twisting and flipping, making it impossible for him to hold a thought longer than a few seconds. Mason, Jackson, the Army, his parents. *Her.*

Will screamed and threw his flimsy cot against the cinderblock wall, then followed it with two hard kicks for good measure. He paced some more, working himself up, breathing heavily. His eyes burned with fury and he wrung his hands together, dreaming of violence and blood.

Then the cellblock door opened.

The sound of footsteps came from down the hall. Will turned to face the door, detecting three sets of shoes clip-clopping his way. He steeled himself for whatever may come as three shadows swept across the floor and two officers stepped up to the cell door. Behind them was a third figure, completely draped in shadow.

"You have a visitor, Shaw," one of the officers said.

The two guards stepped aside and the third figure moved out of the shadows and into the light. It was Janae, standing tall and confident in an Alexander McQueen black business suit and red Louboutin heels. Will's rage began to boil.

"Hello, Will," she said.

BITCH! KILL HER! RIP HER THROAT

OUT! TEAR HER TO PIECES! BACKSTABBING WHORE!

WILL SPRANG FORWARD AND SHOT OUT THE strongest front-kick of his life, blasting the steel cell door off its hinges. The heavy frame knocked Janae back against the wall, pinning her down as Will leapt out into the corridor, bloodlust in his eyes. The two officers who came in with her were mysteriously gone now, but he paid no attention. He grabbed the broken door by its bars and tossed it aside like it was made of balsa wood. Janae squirmed on the floor, dazed and stunned, a huge gash on her forehead bleeding down into her face.

"Fucking bitch!"

He stomped his boot down, smashing her head again and again until it was nothing but a bloody pulp. Ravenous, he straddled her, wrapping all ten of his thick fingers around her throat and squeezing with all his might. Her body twitched and spasmed, and a bloody foam gurgled up from what used to be her mouth. Within moments, Janae went slack, her body a lifeless heap of meat.

And then she was gone. Vanished into thin air.

Will stared down at the empty floor beneath him, shocked and baffled, when suddenly three bullets ripped through his back and exploded out of his chest. He gasped in pain and looked down to see geysers of deep cranberry-red gushing from the wounds. He turned and collapsed against the wall, looking up in shock to see who shot him.

Janae stood above, a smoking Colt 1911 in her hand. She wore a sleek, red miniskirt, the elastic fabric hugging every one of her womanly curves. She was smiling.

WOMAN. LEGS. HIPS. LIPS. GRAB HER, HOLD HER, FUCK HER HARD!

Janae jumped onto Will's lap and began kissing him passionately. He kissed her back, tasting those sweet lips again, feeling her tongue against his. He ran his hands from her breasts down to her ass, and she wasted no time unzipping his pants and whipping out his cock. She hiked up her skirt and sat back down on him, sliding him inside of her with a moan of exquisite pleasure.

Will groaned and groped her delicious flesh as she rode him and grinded hard. Blood continued to pump from his gaping chest wounds, but neither of them minded. Janae smeared it all over her face and breasts as she fucked him harder and harder. He pounded her back. She slapped his face and he returned the blow. Next came her fist, bashing into his jaw and nose again and again as she kept riding him.

Will snarled and flipped her over onto her back and fucked her hard. His gunshot wounds pumped blood all over her. He delivered bone-shattering blows to her face, and she screamed in ecstasy, cumming so hard her eyes rolled back in her head. There was suddenly a knife in her hand, and with one quick stroke, she sliced Will's throat from ear to ear.

His eyes flapped open and he grasped at the wound, fountains of hot blood spraying from between his fingers.

Janae jumped up and whipped her shin into Will's face, knocking him back to the floor. She kicked him repeatedly, viciously doing as much damage as she could. Will found the 1911 she'd used on him laying close by, grabbed it and turned it on her. Four deafening shots rang out, three hitting her center-mass, the fourth blowing her brains all over the wall.

Her body went limp and began to fall, but Will jumped up to catch her. He snarled in anger and ran down the hallway, carrying her lifeless body and heaving it through the exit door.

BITCH! DIE! KILL HER! GUT HER ALIVE! FUCK HER HARD!

WILL CHARGED THROUGH THE DOORWAY AND FOUND himself in a burning train yard. It was that night again. Walls of flames towered around him. Janae stood up, wearing her riding outfit, the same clothes she wore the last time he saw her. Will screamed and charged at her, launching a flurry of fists.

Janae blocked and dodged a few blows, but a couple hard shots landed. She returned fire with her own strikes, including a snapping roundhouse kick to the liver that brought Will to his knees. He groaned in agony, but as the next kick came at his head, he caught her leg, stood up, and whipped her around like a rag doll. He spun and released her, sending her smashing into the side of a burning box car.

Will was on her in a second, and they began exchanging blows again. Janae landed a big shot, breaking his nose, then pulled him in for a deep French kiss. He squeezed her flesh, then pushed her back and kept fighting. He landed heavy shots, bloodying her face as the intense flames raged around them. Janae staggered, but Will pulled her back up, spinning her around and pushing her face-first into the red-hot side of the train.

She screamed as her clothes and flesh caught fire.

Will yanked her pants down and whipped out his cock. With one rough, violent thrust, he was inside her again, pounding her hard. She came in agonizing ecstasy, her cheek melting off as he kept fucking her. Will came hard, screaming in triumph and pushing her face deeper into the flames.

"Die, bitch!"

Janae suddenly whipped back around and lashed out with a vicious punch to his face. But instead of a hard *crack,* Will felt the slice of four razors slashing his cheek open. He staggered back in shock, deliriously looking up as Janae came back at him. But she was no longer Janae. She was the leopard. And he was the jaguar.

Will roared and rushed back at her, his long fangs and curved claws blazing. They fought as the world burned down around them, exchanging blows and tearing each other apart. Her golden, spotted coat became streaked with blood. His amber-yellow eyes blazed with pure hatred.

Then they fucked some more.

. . .

Will woke up in his jail cell, drenched in sweat.

Through sheer exhaustion, he had actually fallen asleep despite being thrown into a cold steel cage. Cinderblock walls. Cold floors. Bars. He looked out the small window at the end of the hallway and saw the first light of morning. He had been arrested, booked, mirandized, photographed, fingerprinted, and questioned. Fortunately for him, his answer to every question was "lawyer." It was a brief interrogation. Then they took him to his new home and he was out like a light.

Jax used to say I could fall asleep anywhere. Will smirked and rubbed his neck as he swung his feet off the side of the bed and sat in the darkness. Somewhere, a faucet was dripping. He couldn't tell what hurt worse, his collection of cuts and bruises or the way the officers had looked at him tonight. Cody Owle especially, a young man who once viewed him with envy and admiration, now had fear in his eyes.

They had put him in a cell in an otherwise empty hallway of cells, five in total. He figured they had cleared out an area just for him. After all, these cops now believed he was responsible for this, that *he* was the raven mocker or its master. Will balled his fists. *Sorry, Papaw. Guess I blew it.*

He sat in silence thinking, calculating the risks of different options he might take, knowing that they had every intention of killing him. Somehow, he had to get out of there. Somehow, he had to get his hands on... her.

29

CHANGE OF PLANS

LEAH SET down two steaming mugs of coffee for Jimmy and Shenandoah. It had been a very long night, and neither of them had slept. They sat at Pete and Leah's dining room table, dejected, the early morning sun shining through the windows like a spotlight on their failures. They had seen Will chased through the casino and been powerless to help. They'd returned to where Casey was supposed to be waiting, but the child was gone. Shenandoah had the look of a worried mother in her eyes.

"I'm sure she'll turn up," Pete said, trying to be reassuring as he absently stirred his coffee.

"They've got her," Shenandoah uttered, staring down into her hot drink.

"We don't know that for sure," Pete said.

"They've *got* her," she repeated. "And they've got Will. They're going to kill him."

"Now now," Pete said, "let's not jump to conclusions. He's in a heavily-guarded police station. They can't just walk in there and—"

"They'll find a way," Jimmy said, his voice tired. "Two of their skinners are FBI. Real FBI. They'll get him outta there nice and legal, and no one'll say a thing."

"There has to be something we can do," Leah said, pacing nervously, unable to sit down. "Babe, can't you just call Captain Oocuna, get her to release him? Or at least to not let them take him, or...?"

"I can try," Pete shrugged.

"It's no use," Shenandoah said. "They have Federal jurisdiction."

"Plus, these are skinners. They can read minds, make people do things against their will..." Jimmy sighed. "They can do whatever they want. They got your little police department eatin' outta their hand. Now everyone thinks Will is responsible for what's been happenin' around here. They think he's a monster."

"But why?" Leah said. "I thought this Spirit Council was supposed to be like, peacekeepers? Good guys?"

"They're supposed to be," Jimmy said. "But Keonee is behind this, somehow. I just know it. They needed a fall guy, and Will is it."

"But why would he do this?" Pete asked. "Why would Keonee send this evil spirit to terrorize our people?"

"I don't rightly know..." Jimmy said, staring into his coffee mug.

A moment of silence passed as everyone let that soak in.

The front door suddenly flew open and Shannon came rushing inside, a brown bag of bagels in one hand, a tray of to-go coffee cups in the other. She was still wearing her shirt and name-tag from the restaurant, and out of breath from all the running around. Shannon plopped the coffee and bagels onto the table and hurried over to her father with worry in her eyes.

"Dad, are you okay? Oh my God, I heard what happened!"

"I'm okay, sweetie," Pete said.

"Is it true that they arrested Will? Is he okay?"

As Shannon continued to pester her parents for information, Shenandoah grew restless just sitting there, and sprung up to her feet. She crossed over to the window, squinting as she looked out into the sun. Her mind spun with thoughts of Will, of Casey, of her own son, Lucas. She pulled a small photo of little Luke from her pocket and looked down at it. There he was, smiling back at her with that spiky blonde hair and cute little smile. Somewhere in Chattanooga, there was a similar photo of Casey. A photo that her mother would look at with tears of sorrow and wonder what happened to her baby girl.

"I can't let them get away with it," Shenandoah said mostly to herself.

"What?" Leah asked.

"They're going to murder Will," she continued, still looking at the picture of her son. "Probably kill Casey too. Blame the whole thing on Will... Can't let them get away with it."

"Who's Casey?" Shannon asked, looking around the table. "Who are *you?*"

"Shenandoah is here to help," Leah told her daughter.

The lady cop turned away from the window to face

them again, determination in her eyes. Jimmy studied her face and knew she meant business.

"Just what're ye thinkin' there, lady tiger?" he said.

"I'm going to break him out of there. And find Casey."

Pete bolted up, waving his hands in the air.

"Hold on, hold on. I can't believe what I'm hearing here," Pete said. "You can't just break into the justice center and bust someone out. There are dozens of cops in there at any given time. They have weapons, helicopters, cameras everywhere, high-tech security... You're crazy if you think you can pull it off."

"I have to try."

"So what are you, like, Will's girlfriend?" Shannon asked.

"Yeah, that's right," Shenandoah said.

"Mm." Shannon's jealous eyes narrowed.

"What do you have, one gun?" Leah balked. "What are you gonna do, run in there like John Wick and kick everybody's ass?"

"I'm a detective with a badge," Shenandoah said. "Maybe I can talk my way in somehow, trick them into releasing him into my custody... I don't know."

"You are really reachin' there, little sister," Leah countered.

Shenandoah snapped, "I have to try, all right? They're gonna kill him if we don't do something!" She pounded the dining room table with her fist, startling everyone present. She sighed and paced around, desperately thinking.

Pete contemplated for a moment. "It would help if I came with you," he said.

"Babe! What the fuck?" Leah shouted.

"I'm the principal chief. I have some pull around here. If I go in with her..."

Leah threw her hands up, flustered, stalking off into another room. "I can't take this madness," she said. "I need a gummy!"

"Dad, you can't be serious," Shannon said, resting her hand on his shoulder.

"These bastards brought a monster here," Pete said. "They brought an ugly, evil monster to *my* town, to murder *our* children. What kind of man would I be... What kind of *chief* would I be, if I just stood by and did nothing?"

"You won't be chief much longer," Jimmy said. "Prob'ly go to jail if ye don't get yourself killed. And *you*," he said, looking at Shenandoah, "a cop breakin' a violent criminal outta jail? You can kiss that badge goodbye."

"I know," she said with a sigh. "And say hello to federal prison..."

"So, you think we can con our way in and out of there, huh?" Pete asked.

"Hopefully," she said. "If not, con our way in... shoot our way out."

Shannon shook her head, exasperated, and dug into the brown paper bag she'd brought with her. "I'm having a bagel," she announced, trying to pretend this conversation wasn't really happening.

Pete looked at his old friend and sighed. "Suicide mission, huh?"

"It's as good a day to die as any," Jimmy said.

"Maybe not," Shenandoah said. "Pete, with your knowledge of the layout of the building, of the people there and the routines... maybe we can get in and out before they notice. If not, once I get to Will and get a gun in his hands, then together... we'll get out of there."

"I guess I'm the getaway driver," Jimmy shrugged.

"And after that, we'll find Casey too."

"Who the hell is *Casey?*" Shannon scoffed.

"Who the hell are *you?*" Shenandoah snapped back. "Eat your fucking bagel!"

"This is my house, bitch!" the rotund young woman jumped up and got in the detective's face. "Who the fuck do you think you are?"

The two women faced off and Pete jumped in between to keep them apart as they bickered and squabbled. Jimmy just shook his head and sipped his coffee. Leah came back into the room, waving her hands, the stress level proving far too much for her.

"Please, please," she begged, "you guys are giving me odgeda! Calm down!"

The room erupted into a melee, everyone shouting over each other at once. Shenandoah threw her hands up and walked away into the foyer, trying to cool down as the others continued to argue. The photo of Lucas was still in her hand. Looking at it, tears began to form in her eyes. She knew she might never see him again.

She felt her phone vibrating, and pulled it from her pocket to look. The number on the caller ID was not familiar. Perplexed as to who it might be, she answered the call, covering her other ear to block the noise.

"Hello?" she answered.

While the lady cop was busy on her call, Leah did her best to put out the fire in the dining room. Pete and Jimmy seemed to have their minds set on this suicide mission, and Shannon was a rambling mess. She was just a restaurant owner and manager, and this kind of craziness was way out of her wheelhouse. Leah pulled Pete aside into the kitchen, ran her fingers through his grey hair and let her hands slide down to his shoulders. Her eyes looked pleadingly into his.

"Baby, *please*," she whispered. "This is crazy. This isn't your fight."

"These are our people."

"That doesn't mean you have to go out there and die. You're not a warrior. You're sixty-eight years-old. I'm an old woman, Pete. I can't lose you."

She began to cry. Pete sighed and tenderly touched her cheek, pulling her into an embrace. He kissed her forehead and stroked her back as he had done for the past forty-five years.

"Oh, my little hummingbird," he said, "you could never lose me."

"We better act fast," Jimmy said, hating to intrude on their moment.

"Don't go, please."

"I have to, baby."

Pete led Leah back into the dining room and gently pulled out a chair for her at the table. Shannon ate her bagel and pretended none of this was happening. They all looked up as Shenandoah reentered the room, a peculiar look on her face. She had finished speaking with the unknown caller and slipped the phone back into her pocket.

"What is it?" Jimmy asked.

Shenandoah smirked and said, "Change of plans."

30

TACTILE

PETE WAS gassing up his truck while Jimmy sat in the passenger seat, touching the medicine bag hanging around his neck, praying softly. Off towards the end of the gas station, Shenandoah stood in a gravely area, making a call on her cell. She was far enough away from the pumps, the snack shop, or any prying eyes, to feel a sense of privacy. Her hair caught the sun brilliantly. She wore the blue backup suit she'd brought and a fresh blouse, and with her badge and gun on her hip, she was all business.

But her eyes were troubled, and her posture was not that of a confident official, but of a scared little girl. She paced and kicked at pebbles as the phone rang. Finally, the line was picked up, and she covered her other ear to hear better.

"Hi, Zeke... I'm fine, thanks... Yeah yeah, everything's okay..." Shenandoah cleared her throat, trying to steel herself for what was to come. "Um, listen, can I talk to

Luke real quick? ...Well then, can you wake him up? Please? It's important ...Thanks."

She waited, taking a deep breath.

Long-haul trucks roared by. The smell of gasoline lingered.

"Hello?" Shenandoah perked up. "Hi, baby! How are you? ...Oh, yeah? Well, I miss you too... Yeah, I'm still here... Yeah, I know. Work sucks sometimes. You and Daddy been playing some video games? Having some pizza?... Good... Oh, I'm sorry to wake you up, baby. I just wanted to hear your voice." She stopped herself suddenly as her throat seized up and tears rushed to her eyes. Trying to not cause alarm, she fought it back, doing her very best to sound like everything was okay. "Oh, yeah? Oh, that sounds good... Listen, baby, I just... I-I just wanted to say I love you, that's all. Just... Mommy loves you. No matter what happens, no matter what anybody says, Mommy loves you. I want you to always remember that, okay? ...Okay. Well, I love you. Goober. Have fun with Daddy... I love you... Bye bye."

Shenandoah hung up and wiped the tears from her face.

She pulled out the small, wallet-size photo of little Lucas, and held it out in front of her with both hands. She closed her eyes, took a breath, and began to speak.

"Will, I want you to listen to me very carefully..."

THE CHEROKEE TRIBAL JUSTICE CENTER BUSTLED with activity. Every officer not otherwise on duty had been called in as extra backup, after all, they had a monster in custody. Or a demon. Or some kind of evil, black-magic witch doctor who summons monsters and demons. None of them had a clue what Will Shaw was. All they knew was what FBI agents Warren and Lambert had told them, and together with the circumstantial evidence they'd seen, they were all convinced. Even Captain Oocuna had put aside her skepticism, accepting that their prisoner was somehow in league with dark forces.

There were four officers posted outside the front door on guard duty, another four by the back door, two more in the lobby, four guarding the hallway to Will's cell, and at least twenty more working or on standby dispersed through the complex. Everyone was on edge. Two officers were required just to bring Will his tray of breakfast and were given strict orders not to talk to him or look him in the eye.

Officer Owle slid the tray of food through the slot in the cell door, his hands trembling. The second officer kept his hand on his sidearm just in case. Will shook his head in disbelief.

"Hi, Cody," Will said.

The young cop didn't answer. The shiver that ran through his body said it all.

"Cody, come on, man..."

Will sighed as Owle left the food and hurried out of there, careful not to make eye contact. The two officers locked the door behind them, thankful to put distance between themselves and the monster. Will just sat on the edge of his cot. He didn't touch the food.

. . .

Captain Oocuna sat at her desk and appeared to be staring into space, but that wasn't really true. She was staring at a small, toy frog perched on her filing cabinet. It had been there for years and she couldn't remember how she got it, but she liked the little ceramic guy. Right now, he was a far more pleasant thing to focus on than the reality unfolding around her. Officers, detectives, and forensics workers came and went through the main hall outside her office, but she paid them no mind. The little frog was slowly drifting out of focus.

Oocuna suddenly snapped to attention when Lieutenant Ballard came into her doorway and cleared his throat. For a second, she tried to do something with her hands to look busy, but quickly gave up on pretenses.

"Hey, Ben," she said.

"Lynn," Ballard said, stepping in. "You okay?"

"Uh, yeah. Sure. What's up?"

"Well, Chief Littlejohn is here to see you, and he's got a detective from the Tennessee State PD with him."

The Captain closed her eyes and groaned.

Detective Shenandoah Glass was not what Oocuna was expecting. She somehow pictured a big, burly man, not this little, blonde pixie. Pete Littlejohn smiled and extended a hand, and she dutifully shook it.

"Pete," she said.

"Morning, Lynn," Pete said. "Like you to meet a friend of mine."

"Detective Shenandoah Glass, Tennessee State Troopers. How do you do?" she said and shook Oocuna's hand.

"Fine, thanks. Little crazy around here right now. How can I help you?"

"I understand you have Will Shaw in custody."

The captain's posture stiffened. "That's right."

"He's the prime suspect in a series of child murders all over Tennessee and Georgia," Shenandoah said. "Nashville, Chattanooga, Memphis... Sometimes little babies, sometimes older kids..." She hammed it up, delivering her best dramatic acting performance. "I've been tracking the bastard for the past five years, but could never catch up to him. Now I hear you finally got him. Congratulations, captain. Great work."

"Thank you," Oocuna said, sharing a look with Ballard. "So what is it you need?"

"There's been another abduction," the detective said. "Six years old. We still haven't found him, and we're hoping he's still alive... I'd like to show the prisoner a photograph, ask him a few questions. If that's all right with you?"

Oocuna stammered, so Ballard took over. "I'm afraid that's out of the question, ma'am," he said. "The Feds are coming to take him later today, and they gave us strict instructions that he's to have no visitors. I'm sorry."

"Please," Shenandoah pushed. "This little boy might still be alive. There might still be time."

Oocuna looked to Ballard, who turned to Sneed. The captain took a deep breath and paced around, trying to think. "How do you two know each other?" she asked Pete.

"Oh, uh..." Pete thought quick, "old family friend."

"Do you guys even know what you're dealing with?"

Ballard asked her. "Do you know what's been going on here? This Will Shaw, he's into some kind of, I don't know, witchcraft or someth—"

"Ben!" Oocuna hissed for him to be silent.

"I know something is going on with him," the detective answered. "I know he's dangerous. I just want to show him a photograph, that's all." She gave her best sad puppy-dog look, and to top it all off, she added, "Do you have any kids, Captain?"

Oocuna closed her eyes and sighed.

BALLARD AND SNEED LED PETE AND SHENANDOAH through the cold, gray hallways of the justice complex. They arrived at the holding area, and the guards at the door buzzed them in. They walked past several hallways of cells, mostly empty, save for the odd prisoner here and there. When they reached D block, they saw Officers Owle and Apachito standing post.

"Buzz us in," Ballard said.

"But..." Owle tried to remind his lieutenant of their order.

"Just do it, Cody."

Owle grumbled under his breath and obeyed. The lieutenant and the sergeant led them down the industrial hall, a row of five cells, the first four being empty. In the last cell was the slouching figure of Will Shaw, and Shenandoah resisted the urge to just run inside and wrap her arms around him.

Ballard and Sneed approached the cell with trepidation. Will looked up from the floor as his visitors drew near, and his body tensed. Pete and Shenandoah. *What the hell are they doing here?* Will thought.

"Two minutes," Sneed said. "That's all."

Sneed and Ballard stepped back, allowing Shenandoah to approach the bars and face the criminal. His eyes narrowed looking up at her.

"Well well, Mr. Shaw," she said. "Funny seeing you here. I'm Detective Shenandoah Glass. Tennessee State Troopers. We finally meet."

Okay, what is she doing?

"I've been tracking you all over Tennessee," she continued, "but where do I find you? North Carolina!" She threw up her hands and slapped them down on her thighs, faking an antagonizing attitude. "It's always the last place you ever think to look. But here you are. Will Shaw. And you're doing the same thing here." She shook her head and looked at him in disgust. "No child is safe when you're around, are they?"

Pete watched silently, impressed with her performance.

"Lieutenant," she said and turned to Ballard. "This man has over a dozen warrants for homicide in Tennessee. If I could just take him there to question him about some of these cases..."

Ballard said, "Out of the question."

"Help us locate some of these bodies..."

"Out of the *question*. Look, the FBI is transporting him tonight. This is a federal case. Now, do what you came to do, but then you have to be moving on. I'm sorry."

Shenandoah sighed and nodded. No way was she

expecting that to work, but she had to try. She stepped closer to the bars, reaching into her jacket, and took out the photo of Lucas.

"Tell me, Mr. Shaw. Do you recognize..." she quickly thought of the name of her first boyfriend when she was thirteen, "...little Eric Dietz? Have you seen this boy?"

She held out the photo of Lucas even closer.

Will's eyes narrowed even more.

Where is she going with this? Let's see.

He stood up and slowly approached the bars.

"Here, look closer," she held it out to pass it to him, but Sneed pulled her back.

"Can't hand him anything," he said.

"Guys, it's such a tiny photo. Look," she said, showing them the wallet-size school portrait. "He can't see it from here. Come on."

"No," Sneed growled. "I think it's about time for you to—"

"Guys, look," Pete cut in. "Come on. Just let her show him the picture. We'll be out of your hair in two minutes."

Sneed shared a look of annoyance with Ballard, who finally rolled his eyes and shrugged as if to say, "whatever." Sneed took a step back and said, "just hurry up."

Shenandoah turned back to the bars and held out the photo.

"Mr. Shaw, please take a closer look at this photo," she said. "Do you recognize Eric Dietz?" He looked at the photo of Lucas. "Take it."

Will played along and reached out slowly, taking the photo into his hand to look closer. The moment he gripped the small rectangle of paper, a hot jolt of psychic energy shot through his nervous system. His tactile sense kicked in and then suddenly, as if watching a recorded video, a message began to play in his head.

He saw the image of Shenandoah standing outside the gas station, holding the photo in both hands, squeezing her eyes closed and concentrating, as if that would somehow make the psychic message work better. Will smirked and played along, pretending to study the face in the photograph as he listened to her secret message.

"Will, I want you to listen to me very carefully..." she said. *"We have to get you out of here. They've taken Casey. And they're going to kill you if we don't do something. Now look, we have a plan, and it's kinda crazy, but you need to be ready to move..."*

"All right," Ballard said, losing his patience, "that's enough. Come on now."

"Wait," Shenandoah stopped him as he reached to snatch the photo from Will's hand. "Just a minute... Mr. Shaw, please. Do you recognize this boy? Can you tell me where he is?"

Will finally looked up from the photo and met her gaze. From the look in his eyes, she knew he understood. He smirked and reached out, returning the photo to her, and backed away from the bars.

"Sorry, Copper," he said, sitting back down. "I've never seen that boy before in my life."

Sneed touched Shenandoah's shoulder and gently began leading her away. "Okay, let's go now. That's enough."

"Wait, please..."

"*Now*, I said. Let's go."

Shenandoah amped up the histrionics, making sure to struggle a little as Sneed pushed her back. Pete protested as well, but Ballard gave him a stern look, and soon, both were being pushed down the hallway.

"This isn't over, Shaw!" Shenandoah shouted. "I'll be back!"

She turned to look back at Will one last time as the two officers escorted her and Pete out of there. He winked at her, and she fought away the urge to smile.

31

THE EXECUTIONER

JANAE JONES PARKED her Ducati Monster 1200 across the street from The Qualla Arts & Crafts Mutual Co-Op. The foot traffic that afternoon was sparse. It had just begun to rain. She hopped off the bike and walked across the street to the gallery as thunder grumbled in the sky. It was a small, one-story building that looked more like a large souvenir store from the outside than a museum. With an adobe-style design painted in warm earth tones, and impressive window displays of authentic weapons and artifacts, it was an inviting local attraction.

Walking through the door and shaking off the rain, Janae found herself in a place much more special than a cheap souvenir shop. Some of the items on display were hundreds of years old, while others were fine crafts hand-made recently by local artisans. The lighting was tasteful and atmospheric, and soothing, native flute music played through the speakers. Fine art hung on the walls, as well as sculptures, weapons, and charms. The price tags on some of these items went from the hundreds well into the thousands. There were no rubber tomahawks on sale here.

A pleasant, young Cherokee woman sat across the room at the front counter. She looked up and smiled at Janae, greeting her as she walked by. There were three large rooms, and less than a handful of customers. Janae didn't see who she was looking for in the main room, so she proceeded onward around a corner. More impressive artifacts lined the walls, including window displays with printed placards describing historical events, and the origin of the items. At the end of the room, admiring a collection of rare pendants and medallions, was a large, husky man with a white ponytail.

Keonee wore a simple pair of blue jeans and a wool sweater patterned with Indian designs stretched over his bulbous belly. He had brown cowboy boots and a necklace of beads, woven and stitched into a kind of amulet. His eyes were a piercing blue. He was silent. Janae walked up behind him and stopped.

"Father," she said.

Keonee did not turn around.

"This one here," he began, pointing to one of the pendants in the glass display, "that's a representation of Selu, the goddess of the harvest according to the Cherokee. Means 'corn.' She planted her own heart in the soil, that the crops would grow, and the people would never go hungry. Handmade. Twenty-five hundred dollars. Pshh."

"You wanted to see me?" Janae asked.

Keonee began to walk, strolling casually as he browsed the collection of rare treasures. She followed him, wary and suspicious of his silence. They passed another customer, making sure to keep quiet until they were once again out of earshot.

"Nayati and Kasa will take the deceiver into custody tonight, after the cover of darkness," he said. "Then we will put an end to his evil once and for all. Are you ready, my child?"

"Yes," she said without hesitation.

"You let him manipulate you, Janae. Developed feelings for him..."

"I was just doing what I needed to get close to him."

"You were weak willed," Keonee said sternly. "You disappeared for *two years*, Janae. Wouldn't answer my calls or texts... And now that you're back, I sense your energy is off. You're resonating at a low frequency, my child. And I have to question whether or not you'll be up to the task."

"Look," she said, stopping him and making him face her. "I was going through some hard times and really just needed to figure some things out on my own. Yes, I'll admit that Will Shaw did have me a little fucked in the head, but I know now that it was all a lie. Trust me, nobody wants him dead more than me."

Keonee nodded and kept browsing.

"Once we have him, we'll let Kasa use her little trick," he said. "Make him tell us who the child is he's been looking for."

Janae's features tightened. "Sir?"

"He's looking for a specific child. The child of the prophecy. While he is the deceiver, the one that would destroy The Council... the child is the one hope we have to save it. A baby boy. Once the deceiver slays the child and breathes his spirit, he will become all-powerful. Immortal."

Janae followed him as he spoke, her face betraying no emotion.

"You were close to him for a time," Keonee said. "Would you have any idea who this child is?" He looked over to see her response.

"No," she said. "He never mentioned anything like that."

"Mm. Well, it doesn't matter. We'll find the boy and protect him. And tonight, the entire Council will watch Will Shaw die... at your hand."

She hesitated and he caught it right away.

"It is the only way for you to earn your seat at the great table of the Spirit Council," he said. "You have to show me where your loyalty lies. You have to prove yourself to me again, my child. I'm sorry, but you need to balance your energies if you ever want to achieve enlightenment. This will help you cleanse any negative frequencies and conflicting emotions, wipe the slate clean."

"There are no conflicting emotions," Janae said, grinding her teeth. "The only emotion I have towards Will Shaw is hate."

"Good. Then tonight he's all yours. Let me hear you say it."

She looked him in the eye.

"Tonight, he's all mine."

32

BLOOD STORM

THUNDER CRASHED and lightning arced across the black sky as a heavy downpour pelted the Cherokee Justice Center. The tempest raged and the wind howled. Storm drains turned to rivers, and the Oconaluftee was nearly overflowing. The hiss and patter of fat raindrops filled the night. All officers not otherwise on duty had been called in, and their cruisers lined the parking lot.

Two black Ford Expeditions pulled up to the main entrance.

Agents Michael Warren and Winona Lambert got out.

Proceeding up the front walkway while the vehicles remained parked and idling, they wore black trench-coats but held no umbrellas, and made none of the usual efforts to hurry and get inside out of the pouring rain. The cold water streaked through Warren's short, silver hair, and glistened on his angular features and frosty eyes. Her black hair was pulled into a tight bun, her pale face devoid of any emotion.

A young officer in the lobby opened the door for them, smiling pleasantly.

"Hoo! Sure is pissin' down out there, huh?" the officer said.

They did not answer.

Instead, they breezed through the lobby, went behind the front desk and all the police personnel, and headed into the back offices. Several officers were sitting at a table in the break room, including Ballard, Sneed, Apachito, and Kituwah. They all stiffened up as the two agents blew in like a cold breeze.

Warren said, "We're here to transport the prisoner."

WILL STOOD IN THE CENTER OF HIS CELL, DOING light shoulder warm-up exercises. He swung his arms in circles. Twisted and stretched his back. He did a few squats and practiced some shadowboxing. After Shenandoah's message, he knew what to expect. A fight was coming. And her plan was so crazy, it just might actually work.

Not exactly like I got much choice, Will thought. *They're coming.*

He could hear the footsteps before he saw them at the end of the hall. Will hopped up and down, getting ready. They were going to demand he stick his hands through the hole in the door so they can cuff him. No matter what, he could not let that happen.

The sound of the footsteps grew closer.

He could smell them now. Aftershave. Rainwater. Fear. There were quite a few of them, clearly not taking any chances. Now through the barred door at the end of the hall, he could finally see them. Ballard, Sneed, Captain Oocuna and four officers in riot gear with shields. Leading the charge were Warren and Lambert, looking the part of death dealers with their long, black slickers.

Will's muscles tightened and his pulse raced. This was it.

"Prisoner," Ballard ordered in his most authoritative tone, "You will please turn around and put your hands behind your back. Then you will step back and place your hands through the slot. Do you understand?"

Will shook out his arms and bounced up and down, a wicked grin on his face and a glint in his eye. "Oh, I understand," he said.

"Don't make this harder than it has to be, Shaw," Ballard urged.

"Turn around *now!* Hands behind your back!" Sneed barked.

Will made eye contact with Warren and Lambert through the bars.

They were smiling at him.

"So nice to see you again, Will," Warren said smugly.

"Come and get it, motherfuckers," Will said.

The armored guards moved toward the door, hands trembling. Ballard and Sneed backed them up, and Oocuna stayed as far back as she could manage. The men braced themselves for a very hard fight, reaching to unlock the door, when suddenly, the lights went out.

"What the hell is this?" Sneed complained.

Faint emergency lights came on outside, but other

than that, the only souce of illumination was the stormy skies. Everyone in the hallway froze in place, tense and petrified. All except for two.

Agent Warren checked his watch and grunted.

"It's the storm," Oocuna said. "The lines are down."

"No, it isn't the storm," Agent Warren said. "It's us."

"What do you mean?" Lieutenant Ballard asked.

Warren sighed and said, "Oh, Will Shaw breaks out of his cell, uses his black magic to conjure demons, kills everyone in the building, and escapes... Sound about right, babe?"

Lambert already had her Smith & Wesson pressed into the gap between Ballard's armor plates. "Nothing personal," she said, and pulled the trigger twice. The lieutenant gasped in shock and fell to his knees as two hot 9mm hollow-points ripped into his guts. Before anyone could react, Lambert continued to fire.

"Jesus Christ!" Will shouted as the massacre ensued.

While Lambert finished off the officers armored in riot gear, a dark shimmer ran over Warren's body. Before Sergeant Sneed could draw his weapon and fire, the agent became a huge silver-white wolf, towering over him. A bone-crunching grip snapped the sergeant's wrist, and he screamed in agony as the weapon dropped to the floor. Warren snarled through his cruel muzzle and tore the man's throat out with one clawed swipe, sending him crashing to the cold floor, desperately clutching at the arterial spray of blood.

"*No! NO!!*" Will grabbed the bars and yanked on them with all his might.

Warren turned to look at him through the bars, a

savage look in his evil, yellow eyes. The silver wolf just smiled at him.

Captain Oocuna had become a blubbering mess as the nightmare rapidly unfolded around her. She wanted to scream, to run as fast as her legs could pump, but her body would only allow her to tremble and stagger back through the dark hall.

"O-Oh...my...God..." she gasped, looking back over her shoulder at Officers Owle and Apachito who stood guard outside the door. "H-Help... help..."

Warren stalked slowly towards her, his massive wolf haunches absorbing his muscular weight, his gray coat nearly the only thing visible in the near-pitch darkness. He snarled, baring his horrible fangs, taunting her. Behind him came another menacing growl, and one more pair of yellow eyes appeared in the gloom. Lightning crackled outside, briefly illuminating the jet-black and hirsute wolf form of Lambert, melting out of the shadows. The two beasts fell in line, slowly stalking side by side and closing in on the captain.

Oocuna finally found her voice, and her legs, shrieking in unbridled terror as she scrambled frantically for the door.

"Help me!! Oh please, God!! Help me!!" she cried.

She tripped and slid across the linoleum, crashing into the steel door before leaping back to her feet. Owle and Apachito looked through the barred window, petrified, as their captain pleaded for her life on the other side. Owle fumbled with the keys, his hands shaking as he raced to find the right one in the darkness.

"Hurry, please!!"

"Hold on, captain! Hold on!" Owle said, finally finding the right key. He unlocked the door and pushed it open, urging Oocuna to hurry through.

But suddenly, a huge jolt rocked the young officer's body. Owle spasmed and tried to scream, but the only thing to escape his lips was thick, oozing blood. Pain and fear filled his bulging eyes. His chest erupted in a fountain of blood as a barbed, black tendril bursted through his rib cage, offering his still-beating heart for Oocuna to see. Apachito screamed and tried to run, but another slimy appendage came from the darkness and wrapped around her throat, snapping her neck like a toothpick.

The raven mocker glided into the doorway, spreading its horrible, swirling-black masses for the captain, arrogant and vain like a nightmarish, macabre peacock. Oocuna tried to scream, to even breathe, but couldn't. She staggered away from the door, her body shaking. She turned back around to face the hall, but Warren and Lambert were right there. The two terrible wolves closed in, flexing their claws, jowls watering. Finally, they pounced on their prey.

Will yanked and kicked at his cell door, furious, as the sounds of the police captain being torn apart echoed down the corridor. He watched helplessly as the wolves shredded and devoured her flesh. They turned and smiled at him, their muzzles dripping with gore, and left to go handle the rest of the unsuspecting police force.

The two beasts stalked past the raven mocker, continuing into the darkened building. Will watched as the black wraith laughed at him, then joined the two wolves to finish the job. Will raged and pounded on the bars with all his might.

"Son of a bitch!" he screamed. Looking down at the floor, he could see Ballard still had the keys to the cell laying on the floor beside him. Will dropped down to the floor, desperately reaching between the bars to grab the keys as the sounds of murder filled the building.

Agents Warren and Lambert stalked through the darkness, their padded paws making no sound as they tore through every police officer that came their way. Guns and flashlights and body armor, none of it helped them. By the time their eyes registered the nightmarish monsters jumping out of the shadows, it was too late. Their flesh was torn into ribbons, their blood and vital organs splashed against the walls and floors. Shots rang out and went wild.

Lambert wrapped her jaws around one cop's throat and ripped all the tissue out, nearly decapitating him. Warren picked up one burly officer by the neck and threw him into the stone wall like a play toy, shattering his skull and spine.

Three officers ran through the holding area, desperately fleeing for the main lobby. From the shadows, oily tendrils and oozing membranes shot out, ensnaring them with ease. They were slashed, smashed, whipped, beaten. Within seconds, the shadow beast had torn them apart, not wasting a second to pounce on its next victims.

Will strained for Ballard's keys.

They were just out of his grasp. Deeper inside the building, he could hear the terrified shouts and screams, the gunshots, the smashing of bones. The utter annihilation of the entire police station. He grinded his teeth, stretching his arm to its limit, desperate to get out of the cell.

Suddenly, a bloody hand slapped onto Will's. It was Ballard. Will looked in shock to see the downed lieutenant looking back at him, barely clinging to life as he bled out from the two gunshot wounds. He gurgled, trying to breathe, though his left lung had now filled up with blood. Ballard's eyes pleaded with Will.

With his last bit of strength, Ballard took the keys and slid them across the floor into Will's hand. Gripping the blood-streaked keys tightly, he watched the lieutenant release his last breath. Will stood up, not wasting any time, and found the master key.

He popped the lock open and flew into the dark hall.

For a brief moment, he knelt down to collect firearms from the slain officers, but then stopped. *No. I don't want a gun for this.*

Will stood back up, clenching his fists. He closed his eyes, took a deep breath, and let himself fall back. Light warped and shadows bent around him. The man fell away and the cat jumped into his place. He opened his blazing-yellow eyes, snarled, flexed his claws. With a raging roar, Will shot down the hall, racing deeper into the darkened building, toward the sounds of carnage.

The black jaguar was at one with the shadows, slinking smoothly around every corner. He stepped over the disemboweled bodies strewn throughout the fortified complex, smelling the copper in their blood and the gunpowder residue in the air. More muffled screams of new victims erupted from further inside the building.

Bursts of gunfire erupted, then went silent. The police were putting up the best fight they could, but it was no use.

Two officers tried to barricade themselves in one of the interrogation rooms, but the slimy mist of the raven mocker oozed through the gap at the bottom of the door. They panicked, blasting away with 9 mm pistols and 12 gauge buckshot, but all they did was blow more holes in the door for the demon to seep through. Retreating to the corner of the room, they trembled and watched hopelessly as the black wraith slithered into the enclosed space with them. Their screams were heard throughout the building as it tore them apart.

Emergency alarms blared all over the Justice Center. Radios squawked with cries for help, then abruptly went silent. The storm outside continued to sing and dance.

Will ran to a railing and looked down to see the main entrance lobby below. He pounced over the rail and landed silently, his powerful, haunched legs easily absorbing the impact of the fall. The floor was littered with the blood and bodies of over a dozen men and women, freshly mutilated. Will's tail thrashed as he looked left and right, his ears twitching and adjusting to hear every sob and scream.

He bolted down a hallway to the left, hearing automatic gunfire and cries of terror. When he burst through a pair of double doors, he found himself outside near the generator and fuel tanks, hard rain stinging his eyes. The chaos continued outside as well, with police personnel desperately trying to escape in one of two helicopters and an armored car.

One of the choppers managed to get off the ground, the horrified faces of the pilot and passengers clearly visible through the cockpit window. The pilot pulled back hard on the stick, ignoring the dangers of flying a helicopter into a lightning storm as he frantically tried to get them off the ground.

Will watched as a familiar black mass of slithering smoke shot through the raindrops, its tentacles lashing around the chopper's landing struts. Within a second, the dark entity stretched out its tendrils and membranes, wrapping itself around the windows and propellors of the bird. Sparks flew and smoke poured out of the dying engine as the raven mocker let itself get tangled in the whirring blades, causing the machine to buck and swing wildly in the air.

The helicopter careened into the side of the main fuel tank.

Steel ruptured and fire howled. The shock wave of the massive explosion knocked Will off his feet. Giant balls of flames bloomed with a primal power. The generator and the backup fuel tank went next. Fire and steel and smoke and helicopter shrapnel and human body parts sprayed across the lot.

The second helicopter caught fire and exploded.

The building was engulfed in flames. Two of the officers trying to escape were still alive, one burned and limping away, the other paralyzed from the waist down and dragging himself across the wreckage in the pouring rain. His face and body were badly lacerated, and his back had been broken, but he kept on pushing.

Will's head was spinning from the concussive force

of the blast. He lay on his back, his black coat sliced and singed. He was covered in shards of glass, and small fires were sprinkled around him as the rain slammed down. His tail twitched, he wiggled his feet and toes, and he rolled his shoulders. One piece at a time, he took inventory of his injuries.

Okay, nothing structural. Only superficial wounds. I got this.

He sat up and shook his head, trying to clean the cobwebs out.

The limping officer suddenly stopped, turned, and what he saw made his soul sink to the ground. He started to run, but the raven mocker dove out of the shadows and pounced on him. He shrieked in agony as it ripped through his flesh.

"*No!*" Will screamed and leapt to his feet.

The raven mocker dropped its victim and turned to the last man, the one dragging himself away. With an ear-piercing shriek from hell, it bolted for the wounded man. Will sprinted as fast as his legs would go, baring claws and fangs as he dove through the air. Before the raven mocker could claim its next victim, the black cat charged into it, swiping his claws through its form, but doing no damage.

"*Go! Get out of here!*" the black cat ordered the injured man.

Will distracted the creature, allowing the broken officer to keep crawling toward safety. He swung and slashed and bit, but the black spirit simply found it amusing. Will slashed through the pulsing rain, while streaks of lightning split the sky open.

The beast danced with him, allowing Will to tire himself out. It clicked its horrible, rattling laugh, while lashing him with its barbed tentacles. The cat felt the stinging pain, but kept fighting, swinging wildly as the Cherokee Justice Center burned down behind him.

With one stout blow, the raven mocker knocked Will flying back through the air. He splashed down onto the concrete pavement, gasping for air as glowing-orange embers danced around him. He grasped at his chest and forced himself to look up.

Across the lot, the raven mocker floated above the ground, unaffected by the rain. It was looking right at him. The monster unfolded its grotesque maw and issued a nauseating scream from the depths of hell. It was a challenge.

Then it shot off into the woods like a bolt.

Will snarled, jumping to his feet.

Challenge accepted, you son of a bitch. Tonight you die.

Fueled with rage, the black cat sprinted into the night.

33

SHOWDOWN

RAGE, *FURY, BLOODLUST. SPEEDING THROUGH THE FOREST.*
  RAIN IN MY EYES. THUNDER ROARS. SO DO I.

Will charged ahead into the dark, wet woods.

He sprinted, swung, and hurdled over every slippery obstacle. Pine, oak, and chestnut trees blurred past. His massive paws splashed through muddy puddles, and his explosive muscles powered him through the uneven terrain. The raven mocker was nowhere in sight, but Will pushed forward, following its caustic stench over a densely-wooded hill, and down into the next valley.

He crossed a paved street, with thankfully no traffic. He did not want any witnesses of a black werecat running loose in town. Up ahead were the bright lights of a large, modern building complex. It was the local hospital. Making sure to stay out of view, he skirted around the edge of the tree-line, tracing the perimeter as ambulances at the ER bay began frantically speeding away.

Guess they just got word of what happened at the police station, Will thought. *Poor bastards, you're in for a long night.*

He kept going, darting around the hospital, up into more densely-wooded hills. The smell of the beast still stung his nostrils, but it remained out of sight. He pushed harder, faster, determined to catch it.

And what'll I do when I do catch it? Nothing I try seems to hurt this thing! I have to figure something out, and fast!

He bounded across two small, rural roads, past an old wooden fence, and into more dense brush. There was a small parking garage and a locked gate. Will made short work of the gate, leaping over and continuing forward more cautiously now. He approached some kind of large building just past the next line of pines, with several lamp posts around the premises. Whatever it was, all the lights were off and it was hidden right in the middle of the woods.

Will crept into a dark clearing. To his right was a large boulder, but on closer inspection, it was artificial. There was a staircase leading into a small space with seating, much like a dugout. Squinting through the rain and darkness, Will moved ahead, trying to figure out where he was. Up ahead, he saw a circular wall with a row of chairs behind it. As he inched closer, he realized there was another row of chairs behind that and another row behind that and so on.

The rows of stadium bleachers stretched far up into

the dark sky, disappearing behind the whipping sheets of rain. It was the Mountainside Theater, the famous venue that hosted the "Unto These Hills" outdoor drama every summer. Will remembered it from his tour around town, only then he was standing up top and during the day. Now, down at the stage level, looking up at the giant semi-circle of 2,900 seats, it hardly seemed like the same place.

Now, he was the actor on stage, gazing up at the amphitheater surrounding him as he took a minute to catch his breath. He could no longer detect the scent of the raven mocker. Still, something was not right. He felt it, tasted it. His body stiffened, his cat's eyes scanning the outdoor theater.

Blinding light suddenly flared all around him.

Will squinted and covered his eyes as all the stadium lights switched on at once. There were four tall light posts with giant, rectangular LED lights and a row of lights just under the control booth in the center. Will struggled to see who was up there in the booth, when he heard a strange sound in the sky behind him. It wasn't the booming thunder, but the high-pitch battle cry of a large bird of prey.

Redhawk dove through the angry storm clouds.

Will barely had a fraction of a second to react as the raptor dive-bombed into him. The cat tried to lash out with his claws, but Redhawk drove him into the ground with a muddy splash. The birdman pinned the jaguar with the powerful talons on his hands and feet, using all of his strength to hold down the furious cat.

Will bucked and roared, kicking the attacker away

and jumping to his feet. He lunged at Redhawk and took a hard swipe, but the raptor bolted up into the air with his powerful wings and swung back around at Will.

Not this time, bird boy.

As the birdman tried to ram the big cat, Will side-stepped and caught Redhawk's left wing. He spun the bird of prey around and whipped him away, sending him crashing into the faux rock wall. Will leapt at him, throwing slashing blows as Redhawk desperately used his wings to cover up. With a frothing snarl, Will pried open the giant, folded wings, and lifted his opposite claw, ready to deal a lethal blow, when he suddenly felt the wind knocked out of him.

Agent Warren's silver wolf smashed into Will like a linebacker, knocking him through the rain and onto the muddy stage. Will rolled, dodged and ducked as the canine skinner came after him.

"How you doing there, Shaw?" Warren said telepathically, an evil grin on his fanged muzzle. "Getting tired?"

"Please. Bring it, White boy."

Wolf and cat swung and dodged and clawed at each other. A black figure streaked through the rain, and Agent Lambert's black wolf landed on Will's back, snapping for a bite at his neck. He thrashed and roared, reaching back with his curved claws, and grabbed her by the scruff of the neck.

With a practiced Judo throw, Will launched the she-wolf over his shoulder, sending her crashing into Warren. The two wolf skinners were on their feet in an instant, and Redhawk jumped onto a perch along the inner wall, ready to pounce. He watched as the wolves attacked Will from front and back, forcing him to spin and swipe, fighting them both at once.

Lambert sunk her fangs into Will's right forearm, and Warren slashed him across the chest, but the ex-Ranger would not back down. He shot a front kick into Warren's stomach, sending him hurtling black, then raked his claws across Lambert's snout, forcing her to let go. She staggered back with four ugly parallel wounds now streaked across her face. Warren jumped at Will again, then Lambert, then Redhawk.

Thunder boomed. Lightning flashed.

Monsters went to war.

Will went from one opponent to the next, biting, slashing, kicking. They had him outnumbered, but he was a member of an elite special forces unit and a trained, lifelong martial artist. Using skill, technique, and rage, he fought back the three attackers, ignoring the pain and exhaustion that was rapidly setting in.

They had him surrounded. Will held them at bay, but they closed in, backing him up against the sculpted-rock wall. They were about to pounce again, to pile on top of the big cat and overpower him, when a voice called out from behind them.

"That's enough," Janae said, emerging from the shadows. "He's mine."

BITCH. WOMAN. TRAITOR.

. . .

Warren, Lambert, and Redhawk backed off, allowing the sultry young Black woman to approach through the rain. Will growled as she came closer. Reality warped around her, light bent, and the image of a pretty young woman rippled away like a desert mirage. Janae became the leopard, her spotted, golden coat wet and shimmering in the bright, stadium lighting. Her predatory eyes were full of hate. Her lips parted to reveal snarling, dripping fangs.

Will stepped forward. So did Janae.

They sprang into action.

The leopard and the black jaguar collided on the muddy stage, whipping through the rain drops in a frenzy as each attacked with claws and fangs. The other three skinners stood around them, watching the black and gold, spotted coats blurring together as they spun in a flurry of action through the pouring rain and whipping winds.

Janae jumped onto his shoulders, trying to knock him down and straining to bite his face off. Will sank his claws in and whipped her against the wall, knocking the wind out of her. Not wasting a second, he spun in a circle and launched her through the air, sending the she-cat crashing down into the first three rows of bleachers.

The leopard was up in a flash, her head still ringing and body aching. She saw Will hop up onto the inner wall, about to pounce at her, and beat him to it. Springing off the metal and rubber seats, Janae jumped down and shot a kick right into his face. He staggered back, stunned, as she continued her assault, slashing her claws at him again and again. Will held up his arms, blocking the blows with his forearms, then shot down low and tackled her to the ground.

They splashed down into a muddy puddle as the rain pounded relentlessly, Will mounting her right away. Janae tried to buck him off, but he was too strong, too heavy. Covering her snout with both paws, Will pushed her head down under the water, trying to drown her. That was when he felt the taloned grip of Redhawk piercing into his shoulders. The fierce raptor flung him through the raindrops, sending him smashing down and rolling through the mud.

Will looked up. All four were closing in on him. Janae stumbled to her feet, while Warren and Lambert circled his left, and Redhawk touched down on his right. Janae growled, blood running through her fur, anger boiling in her eyes.

"Time to die, deceiver," she said.

"You first, bitch!"

The four skinners jumped him at once, claws and fangs and wings thrashing in a blur of violence. Will fought back with everything he had, kicking Lambert away and backfisting Redhawk, sending them both reeling backward. Janae latched onto his back, claws refusing to let go, fangs straining to tear his throat out. Warren attacked from the front, snapping in the cat's face with his vicious, canine jaws.

Will screamed and pushed the wolf's head back, holding him at bay. He positioned his fingers over Warren's eyes, and with a quick flex, popped his crescent moon-claws out of their sheaths. The wolf skinner howled in agony as Will dug his blades in deep, bursting Warren's eyeballs like balloons filled with slime.

With another well-aimed slash, Will sliced open the silver wolf's throat. The once-menacing beast staggered back, blinded, thick blood pumping from the lethal wound.

"*Mike!!*" Lambert screamed as her lover fell.

As Lambert ran to feebly help her partner, Will shot backward, smashing Janae into the fake rock wall. She let go of her grip, and Will once again whipped her over his shoulder and slammed her to the ground.

He jumped back on top of her, set to deliver the death blow, when suddenly, a woman's voice cut through the rain and storm.

"Weak," was Orenda had to say.

All at once, Will felt his energy rapidly draining. He fell back, splashing down into the shallow water, strength suddenly gone. In front of his eyes, his rosette-patterned black coat and claws began to shimmer away. He fought it, trying to keep the panther in the game, but he was helpless against Orenda's power. Within seconds, the skinner was gone, leaving Will Shaw in human form, bloodied and gasping for air, on his hands and knees.

Jesus Christ, what is this? Will thought. *Get back up and fight, damn it!*

He looked up and saw the witch approaching, cloaked in a black, hooded rain slicker. Will snarled and pushed himself back to his feet, desperately trying to charge at the diminutive older woman.

"Weak," she said once again.

Will fell back to the ground, defeated. He could

barely lift his head, unable to do anything but watch his blood mixing with the growing puddles of rain. Footsteps splashed through the water from all directions; they were closing in on him again.

Janae, Redhawk, and Lambert had all skinned back to their human forms, their injuries carried over from their beastly battle. Lambert wept, looking helplessly down at Michael Warren's lifeless body floating in a bog of blood and rain water. Four parallel, slicing wounds raked diagonally across Lambert's face. She leered over at the condemned prisoner, her eyes filled with rage and murder.

"And the prophecy said, a deceiver will come one day and threaten the Spirit Council," Keonee's unmistakable baritone boomed from high up in the bleachers, cutting through the rain. "He will disguise himself as a hero, but he will be a murderer of the innocent, and in league with devils..." Keonee wore a black raincoat, slowly descending through the bleachers as he delivered his sermon. The wind chopped the rain in from all angles, messing up his usually perfect, tight ponytail. "...And here he is!"

Will lifted his head to look Keonee in the eye, helpless to do anything while under Orenda's psychic grip. His teeth grinded and his lips quivered with rage. The old man had a cocky, self-assured look that made Will just want to rip his face off. While Keonee swaggered down to the front row, Will noticed other figures appearing from the stands, popping out of hiding places.

Pala slid out of the shadows, her Nordic features as sharp as the knives in her hands. Karuk hopped up from behind the counter at the concession stand where he was hiding, his haunting eyes almost bugging out of his head. Kentucky and Amaruq emerged from the control booth overlooking the bleachers, each of them dying to get his hands on the evil deceiver. Apu came down the aisle across from Keonee, her skin and long dreadlocks both black as night.

Will recognized the menacing Black warrior Teoc from the broken nose he gave him, as well as Toho and Opiyel, both of whom chased him through the casino. More and more emerged from the shadows, dozens of people he'd never seen before descending into the lower rows of bleachers. They were all in human form, all eager to release their beasts. Keonee turned and held his hand out, welcoming his followers.

"There is no more room for doubt, my children," the old man said, gesticulating and grandstanding for all to see. "He has come for the child of the prophecy! He has come to tear down our sacred Council! He has come to upset the balance and plunge our Mother Earth into darkness!" Keonee turned, pointing a finger up at the control booth and said, "And he has brought a disciple with him! Bring out the spy!"

Loco emerged from the ticket office at the top of the bleachers, carrying a squirming, smaller figure in his clutches. Will could barely make them out through the rain and blinding lights in his eyes, but as Keonee's scruffy henchman descended the stairs and came closer, Will's heart dropped.

It was Casey.

The teenager kicked and bucked, her hands tied

behind her back as Loco kept a vice-grip on the back of her neck, forcing her down the stairs. She winced and cried in pain, but was no match for the bigger, stronger man. Janae recognized her right away. Redhawk had confusion in his eyes, not expecting to see a child brought into this.

"Ow! Let go of me, you son of a bitch!" Casey screamed.

"Look!" Keonee shouted as Loco brought the girl down to him. "The beast has sent one of his followers to infiltrate! Corrupting the very minds of *children* to help him enact his devious plan!"

"You lying sack of shit!" Casey screamed, trying to kick her way free. "Will, he's lying! He's behind this whole thing! He's—"

Without hesitation, Keonee drove his fist into the child's stomach, knocking all the air from her lungs and sending her splashing down to her knees. Redhawk flinched as he witnessed the child being struck. Loco yanked her back up, and Keonee quickly wrapped his meaty grip around her throat. "Keep that venomous tongue in your mouth, serpent. You will be punished along with your master."

Redhawk clenched his jaw. He started to move forward, raising a hand as if to stop them, but thought better of it. The look in the eyes of his fellow skinners was calling for blood. His great leader, Keonee, glistening wet with his hair hanging in his scowling face, lightning painting the sky behind him, suddenly looked different. Benevolence had turned to cruelty, justice to vengeance.

"Father, please," Redhawk finally said. "Surely, we can't hurt the girl…"

"She is in league with the deceiver!" Orenda snapped.

"But she's just a child. We can't—"

Keonee snarled and took a step closer, looking Redhawk right in the eye. "Do not speak out of turn or question my authority again," he said. "Is that understood?"

Redhawk looked down at his feet. "Yes, Father."

Lambert stepped up to Will, rain and blood dripping down her face. Her pupils dilated as she turned on her power to compel the truth.

"Where is the child, Shaw?" she demanded.

"What fucking child?"

"*Where is he?*" The federal agent was getting frustrated. Her intense stare bore down into his, pushing her psychic ability to its full capacity, pupils expanding until her eyeballs were completely black.

"*I don't know what you're talking about, God damn it!*"

A frustrated Lambert turned to face her leader.

Keonee smiled. "The deceiver is strong," he said. "Janae?"

Taking a deep breath, Janae stepped forward, crossing in front of Will. The condemned man looked up at her. She reached into her jacket and unholstered her Sig, holding it at her side. Casey began to struggle and fight once again.

"Janae, no!" Casey cried.

Keonee stepped up beside Janae and said, "It is time, my child."

Janae took a step forward. Will refused to break eye contact with her.

Rain stung and lightning crashed. The entire Spirit Council watched from the bleachers, enjoying the performance. Janae raised the pistol and pressed it up against Will's head. The hatred in her eyes did not waver.

"Last chance, Will," Keonee said. "Where is the child?"

"Go... fuck... yourself."

Keonee sighed, then looked to Janae, and gave her a nod.

"Janae, *please!*" Casey screamed. Her premonition was coming to life and she was helpless to stop it. Redhawk watched. Keonee watched. Everyone watched.

"Goodbye, Will Shaw," Janae said, and began to squeeze the trigger.

34

LEAD THE WAY

THE LAST THING Janae expected to hear in the dark during a thunderstorm was Classic Rock. The noise began distant and muffled, then grew louder and louder. It was "Fortunate Son" by Credence Clearwater Revival, and it was coming from the woods behind the outdoor stage. Then came the headlights.

Janae snarled. Will smiled.

The volume continued to soar until Fogerty's vocals overpowered the rain and thunder. From the small country road leading to the back of the venue, a champagne-colored Chrysler Pacifica van burst through the branches and bushes, followed by a roaring, silver F-150. The vehicles skidded to a splashing halt on the stage behind Will.

Jackson Cooper screamed, "Will, get down!"

Will jumped out of the way as Jackson aimed a full-auto AA12 shotgun from the driver's window of the van. Casey cheered out loud. Shenandoah jumped out of the passenger seat, clad in a bulletproof vest, and armed to the teeth with an FN SCAR LMk2. She took aim with the monstrous rifle.

"Let the girl go, *now!*" she commanded.

Keonee, Janae, and the rest of the cult backed up in alarm, but stood their ground. The back doors of the van popped open and out jumped Sergeant Mike Krysinski and Corporal Claude Powell of the United States Army Rangers, both men geared-up in combat armor, full-auto AP5's, and an assortment of small arms and explosives.

Jimmy and Pete charged out of Pete's truck, guns blazing.

Pete was happy with his old Remington 870 pump 12 gauge, while Jimmy opted for a new Daniel Defense AR-15 with two extra mags. They took cover by the car and aimed their weapons.

"I said let her go!" Shenandoah warned. *"Do it now!"*

They didn't listen.

Keonee and the others slowly began to come forward. Janae's eyes blazed with anger. Keonee and Orenda led the way, challenging the party-crashers.

Will stumbled back to stand with his comrades.

This is not going to end well, he thought.

Light and shadows began to bend around Keonee and his followers. Reality warped and rippled over each and every one of them like a desert mirage. With so many skinners transforming together at once, and the rain and lightning reflecting from their shimmering auras, it was truly a sight to behold. A kaleidoscope of sparkling lights and visual distortions. When the fabric of reality settled back into place, human beings were no longer present.

"Je-sus Christ..." Sergeant Krysinski gasped, "Cooper wasn't kidding..."

Pala, Amaruq, and Opiyel were now savage, menacing wolves. Kentucky was a fierce Bobcat, Loco a snarling coyote, still clutching Casey by the back of the neck, and Karuk a tropical poison-dart frog. Toho had skinned into her mountain lion form. Teoc, an armored and ferocious gator. Apu was now a giant, black bat, her eyes bulging red. There were many more beasts stalking down the bleachers, stepping over the seats.

Most were wolf-skinners, as is always the most common form, but other hulking silhouettes popped out in front of the lightning-filled sky. Orenda was a living nightmare, with six arms and metallic-black, armored plating, she took on the spirit of the scarab. Giant black eyes. Menacing pincers and mandibles. Translucent, insect wings unfolded from her shell.

Keonee's eyes were blazing blue.

His fur was white. His mane blew in the wind.

He was a massive, towering white lion. His eyes bore into Will's with contempt, then shifted over to Jimmy. A face he hadn't seen in over fifty years. They stared at each other, and no words needed to be spoken. The rain poured down as the white lion led his monstrous troop forward.

"Been a long time, *Jack*," Jimmy said to the lion.

"Stay back!" Shenandoah shouted.

They didn't.

Jimmy slung his rifle down around his back. He skinned into the great grizzly bear and unleashed a blaring battle cry into the storm, echoing off every surface in the massive semi-circle they stood in. Jimmy stomped forward, his claws flexing, his teeth ready to tear flesh.

"Oh yeah, motherfucker," Will said. "It's on."

Will Shaw closed his eyes and fell back. He went to a place warm and cozy, a fuzzy and pleasant cloud where he could float peacefully and relax. He felt comfortable and safe in the ether, happy to let his other self take over from there.

The panther took a step forward.

Will snarled, baring his massive teeth and bunching up his oily-black muscles, ready to spring into action. Janae faced him, her full-body leopard print glistening in the rain. Her feline eyes locked onto his.

Jackson's mouth hung open in awe at what his friend had become. He held his shotgun with trembling hands, facing an army of monsters. Memories flooded his mind. The pain of his spine breaking, of Mason Shaw nearly tearing half his face off. A spark of anger and determination began to burn in his eyes. Jackson clenched his jaw and steadied his hands, ready for battle.

The white lion roared and the arena erupted into a melee of violence.

"*OPEN FIRE!!!*" Jackson screamed.

The beasts of the Council split into all directions, some coming straight forward, others swinging around to attack from the sides. Jackson and Shenandoah opened fire, along with Mike and Claude, and Pete.

Will and Janae collided on the battlefield, fighting for the other's blood.

Keonee and Jimmy clashed, the grizzly bear against the white lion.

Casey jumped out of the way and found cover, her hands still bound.

Skinners swarmed at them from all angles. Bullets cut the beasts down, but there were just too many of them. Within seconds, they would surely overpower the small band of weak humans. But suddenly, gunfire came not only from the front, but from the surrounding woods on either side.

Major Paul "Skipper" Curtis and Lieutenant Kazuhiro Hori flanked the ampitheater, sending hot-lead death into the attacking horde of beasts. Skipper held his position on the left, taking cover in the rain behind a row of maples and firing his IWI X95 Bullpup. While he sent short bursts of 5.56mm into the fray, Kazu was twenty feet up in a tree on the right, carefully picking them off with his precision MK22 sniper rifle in.

Both were retired Rangers. Neither had anything better to do that night.

Squeezing off one well-aimed shot at a time, Kazu tore through two wolf skinners, followed by a cougar. Skipper's shots were less precise, but the spray of incendiary rounds ripped through through the wind and rain, tearing through anything in their path. Skinners ducked and jumped out of the way, but his assault reduced many of them to bloody heaps in the mud.

Two wolves and a cougar skinner leapt up into the trees, jumping from branch to branch and attacking the major from above. He turned his fire upward as the wolves pounced at him, sending sheets of blood pouring down on him along with the rain. The cougar skinner tried to be slick and circled around, shooting in on him from the side, but Skipper was too fast. He cut the beast down with a five-shot burst to the chest, then slapped in a fresh magazine.

CASEY MADISON HID BEHIND THE WALL TO THE women's restroom as blood, rain, and fragments of wood, concrete, and plaster exploded all around. She feverishly struggled with the duct tape binding her hands behind her back, watching in terror as bullets punched holes in the venue and the charging monsters.

"*Nng!* Come on, damn it!" she screamed, unable to break free.

Casey felt a stiff burst of wind as a massive bird dove from the sky.

Redhawk landed beside her, flexing his wings.

The teenager kicked herself back, desperately trying to crawl away from the inevitable attack. But instead, the bird man rushed to her side, putting one taloned hand on her shoulder and looking at her with his round, amber eyes.

"Be still," Redhawk said.

The bird of prey reached behind her, slipped a talon between her wrists, and sliced through the tape with one swipe. Casey was free. She looked up at Redhawk and smiled. He winked at her as he stood back up.

"Traitor!" Loco snapped and lunged at Redhawk. Toho joined in as well, the coyote and mountain lion skinners teaming up against the raptor. Redhawk used his claws and wings to beat them back, giving Casey the chance to get away.

She ran to a safe corner, watching the chaos and bloodshed ensue around her. It would be easy to hunker down into the protection of the stone nook, or to run for the woods and keep going. However, Casey stepped forward. She let herself relax, surrendering to the beast inside. Within seconds, she had become the cheetah.

The young cat roared and jumped into battle to help her friends.

WILL AND JANAE CLASHED.

Rain poured down. Lightning and bullets blasted all around. Janae swiped hooked claws at Will, who dodged and circled her, trying to nullify her attack.

"This time, I'm not stopping till the job is done," Janae snarled.

She pounced at him and he caught her wrists, holding her back.

"You're fighting the wrong person, baby," Will said. "I'm not the one playing you. How can you not see that?"

Janae roared and twisted out of his grip, throwing a perfectly-timed sweep kick, sending Will splashing down. She was on him in a second, snapping at his throat with her lethal fangs. Will caught her and spun, throwing her away. She jumped back agai and again. The two big cats rolled and tussled, a blur of fangs and claws in the storm.

. . .

Keonee and Jimmy circled each other, each throwing swiping shots, waiting for a perfect opening. They were two old beasts, a bear and a lion, each slow, scarred and battle-worn, but still every bit as vicious and lethal. Jimmy threw a looping hook and knocked Keonee to the ground, then used his hulking weight to smash down onto the cat. With a quick reversal, Keonee spun and kicked up with his massive haunches, sending the big bear stumbling back.

The white lion was up in an instant with a challenging snarl. He shot forward, smashing Jimmy against a wall and holding him there. They struggled and strained, brawn against brawn, snapping for each other's throats.

"That the best ya got, white boy?" Jimmy scoffed.

"Tonight... your family name... dies forever!"

Keonee broke Jimmy's grip and smashed him back against the wall. With a lunging chomp, the lion sank his long fangs into the bear's neck. Jimmy winced at the piercing pain, but the injury was superficial. The cat's teeth had only pierced the loose scruff around his neck, but he held on to the thrashing bear.

Jimmy slashed across Keonee's chest with a hooked claw, drawing blood. Keonee released his bite and stumbled back, looking down at the wound. The lion roared and plowed ahead, and the two old friends continued their combat.

BLOMBLOMBLOMBLOM!!

Jackson fired a short burst of full-auto 12 gauge buckshot into a wild boar skinner as it charged at him with its upturned tusks. Blood exploded from the beast's chest. The loathsome beast staggered and groaned, uttering a haunting death rattle as it collapsed into a bog of its own guts.

Shenandoah emptied a magazine into a wolf skinner. It staggered and dropped, convulsing in its death throes as three more jumped over its body at the petite, blonde detective. She slapped in a new magazine and blasted them with 5.56, blowing intestines and brains into the deepening swamp of blood and rain water.

"Shit shit shiiiiiiiiiit..." Jackson was singing.

"They just keep coming!" Shenandoah shouted.

Krysinski and Powell held their ground, sending hot lead into the oncoming attackers. Krysinski was casually chewing gum as he fired his custom, full-auto AP5.

Amaruq leapt down from a tree branch, landing just outside Jackson's window. The used-car dealer yelped as the black and gray wolf ripped the driver's door off its hinges, tossing it back into the woods. Jax frantically aimed his AA12, but the beast tore it from his hands, then yanked him out of the cab.

Jackson splashed down into the mud, his legs useless. He flipped over onto his back and drew his Colt 1911, only for Amaruq to stomp down on his wrist. Jackson was pinned, the snarling muzzle of the wolf opening as it drew closer, ready to tear him into bloody pieces.

Casey Madison came out of nowhere, vaulting over the hood of the vehicle, sending a bone-crunching kick into the wolf's face. Amaruq lurched backwards as the young cheetah landed in a battle-ready pose. The massive wolf snorted a laugh, then stomped forward, ready to tear the little kitten in half.

Thoom! Thoom! Thoom!!

Jackson sent three .45 hollow-points into the beast's chest, staggering him back. Amaruq looked down at the bleeding holes in his coat, but stubbornly lurched forward after Casey. Jackson squeezed the trigger again, firing one last slug through the wolf's right eye, finally knocking him dead.

"You okay?" Casey said, running to help Jax sit up.

Shenandoah ran to her side, and together, they helped Jackson climb back into the driver's seat of his van. The lady cop looked out at the carnage in front of her, with Will and Janae center stage, locked in deadly combat.

"We have to get Will out of there before it's too late!" she yelled.

"Too late for what?" Casey said.

"We've got some more help coming in," Jackson said.

Major Curtis and Lieutenant Hori continued to blast away the beasts swarming at them from every direction. Curtis pulled two grenades and hurled them into the crowd of monsters. A second later, a pair of crashing shockwaves erupted, blowing skinners to pieces. The major ejected his mag and went to snap another in, when a raging lynx skinner grabbed him and threw him against a tree.

He kicked it back, exchanging several blows with the feline monster, but it was too strong. It hefted the hardened warrior over its head and slammed him down. Curtis pulled his sidearm, but the creature swiped it from him and laughed in his face. It held him down, ready to bite his face from his skull, when he unsheathed his trusty ol' ka-bar knife and lashed out, slitting the cat's throat.

The lynx skinner sank to its knees, a fountain of blood gushing from the fatal wound. It choked and spasmed, and finally died. Curtis reloaded and kept fighting.

"That was pretty fun," Curtis said.

Kazu picked them off with one precision shot after another from his perch high in the trees. The sniper did not notice that Karuk, the frog skinner, had climbed above him in another tree. With a springing leap, the leathery amphibian took Kazu by surprise, crashing down onto him. He shrieked in agony as the creature wrapped its long, bony fingers around his head and began to squeeze. Its inhuman strength was overwhelming, and Kazu felt his skull begin to crack. He knew death was inevitable.

Drawing his holstered MK-23, he shoved the barrel into the olive-green, fleshy stomach, and began squeezing the trigger. Karuk's bugging-red eyes flapped open in shock as the large-caliber rounds punched through his vital organs and ripped through his back.

Karuk's final act was to finish crushing Kazu's head, sending blood and brains spurting through his eyes, nose, ears, and mouth. The once-menacing frogman skinner collapsed into his adversary, their combined weight breaking the branch beneath them, sending them crashing down. The two warriors died together in a bloody embrace.

Principal Chief Pete Littlejohn stumbled through the battleground.

He had a bad cut on his forehead and was covered in dirt and mud and skinner gore. His hands trembled, but he kept firing that old pump shotgun.

Chk-Chk-Kow! Chk-Chk-Kow!!

Pete's buckshot tore through one wolf's heart, and blew a jackal skinner's head clean off. He reloaded, wandering around in a daze. Blood sprayed in every direction. Fire. Rain. Lightning. Monsters. Screaming.

This was the Mountainside Theater, hosting the drama "Unto These Hills" since 1950. It was a mainstay of the Cherokee culture, a part of their heritage. Pete had taken his own family to the show several times. This was a place for families. For community. And it was being destroyed by evil right in front of his eyes.

Burning tears rolled down Pete's face. *Chk-Chk!*

"This is *my* town, God damn it!" Pete screamed — *Kow!* — He blasted a softball-sized hole through a skinner's head, chambered another round, and cut down another. "These are *my people!*" Another. And another. *"Go back to hell where you belong!!"*

Something large and black buzzed over Pete's head, and in an instant, Orenda landed right in front of him. Her translucent wings fluttered and folded back. Pete screamed and pumped two rounds of buckshot into her abdomen, but the insect's armored shell was far too tough to penetrate.

She lunged forward, her horrible mandibles clicking, and launched two of her barbed pincers at the old man like spears. One punched through Pete's left lung and out his back, the other through his stomach. Pain lit up his whole body as the awful creature leaned in closer, getting right in his face, so that the last thing he saw would be his own dying reflection in her convex, black eyes.

With a hard yank, Orenda ripped her pincers out of Pete's body, allowing him to crash to the wet earth. The principal chief of Cherokee, NC convulsed and bleed out into the muddy soil, fading fast.

With his final wheezing breaths, Pete grabbed the medicine bag hanging from his neck and squeezed, uttering a silent prayer. Then his body went limp.

He was gone.

"PETE!!" JIMMY SCREAMED, SEEING HIS FRIEND FALL across the battlefield.

In a split second, the world seemed to slow down as the massive old bear looked around at the carnage surrounding him.

Will and Janae continued to fight.

Jackson and Shenandoah blasted away.

Skinners were being chopped down by gunfire.

Blood and smoke and fire and rain.

Lambert, Pala, and Opiyel ganged up on Sergeant Krysinki.

He managed to blow away Opiyel in his final act

before the other two took him down, tearing him limb from limb. Lightning roasted the sky and thunder belted out its operatic aria. Jimmy stood in a daze of disbelief, panting for air.

He lost track of his opponent.

The white lion pounced forward and tackled Jimmy to the ground, pinning him down and digging his claws into bear hide. Stinging pain finally snapped Jimmy out of his delirium, and his whole being filled with rage. One of his oldest friends had just been murdered, and another was now trying to kill him.

A growl began in his throat and grew into a furious roar of defiance. Jimmy pushed himself up with all his strength, sinking his claws into the raging white lion. The bear stood up and flung Keonee off of his back, then lunged forward before the cat could find his balance.

Jimmy threw one swiping blow after another, smashing Keonee's face like a heavyweight boxer. The thickly-padded paws collided with his target, sending shockwaves through Keonee's nervous system and knocking him senseless. The white lion fell to his back, his head spinning. He looked up to see the mighty bear towering over him, and knew he'd been defeated.

Keonee scampered away and ran for cover.

WILL DODGED A FLURRY OF SWIPING CLAWS FROM Janae.

The two big cats battled as the violence continued to rage around them. They were both bloody and exhausted, but neither knew the meaning of quit. Bigger and stronger, Will was able to hold the female at bay. He saw openings where he could easily have thrown a killing blow... but didn't.

What the hell is wrong with you, Shaw? Kill the bitch!

Leaping from the fray came Pala, jumping on Will's shoulders to assist her leopard sister. Will roared as the she-cat and she-wolf attacked him from both sides, taking him to the ground and lashing out with claws and fangs. Flailing wildly, the black jaguar tried force them off, but their combined strength was too much.

"Get off of him!" Casey screamed.

The young cheetah sprinted at full speed, blurring past enemies and obstacles, and vaulted through the air. Pala looked up just in time for Casey to kick her front teeth out, knocking her senseless and sending her splashing to the ground.

"Janae, *stop it!*" Casey pleaded, trying to pull the raging leopard away.

Annoyed, Janae stood up and backfisted the child with ruthless force. Casey fell back into a puddle of gore and empty shell casings. Her head spun as blood trickled from her nose and into her muzzle. She looked up at the older cat, someone she once admired, with tears in her eyes.

"Janae, please..." Casey pleaded.

The leopard leered down at the teenage cheetah with a snarl.

"Go home, little pussy cat," Janae said, and turned to face Will.

The jaguar was back on his feet.

He growled and flexed his claws, ready to fight until

the bloody end. Janae assumed a fighting stance. They squared off, ready to pounce again, when suddenly, a new sound came from the sky. It wasn't rain, or thunder, or gunfire. It was a low, grumbling, rhythmic vibration, growing in intensity.

Will and Janae stopped, looking for the source.

The volume grew louder. It was a mechanical chopping, a reverberating growl, a rolling snare drum in the thunderclouds. Casey jumped up and bolted to Will's side, urgently pulling on his arm.

"Will, come on! We have to go!" she shouted.

One by one, the skinner army began to hear the noise, and stopped in their tracks. They all looked up at the storming sky.

"What the hell *is* that?" Janae said.

Will smiled as a light crested over the tree line and the giant sound he knew all too well filled the small clearing.

"Backup," Will said.

35

BATSHIT

CAPTAIN "BATSHIT" Barry Kowalczyk of the United States Army Rangers wore an authentic replica of a Roman Centurion helmet and chest-plate armor over his loud Hawaiian shirt and khaki shorts. On his feet were his most comfortable flip-flops. On his robust, Polish chin, a massive grey beard. Around his meaty neck, US Army dog-tags. In his right hand, a half-eaten Hot Pocket. In his left hand, the control stick for a UH1D Huey gunship attack helicopter, armed with twin-M60 mini-guns and four M134 hydro rocket pods.

A tiny disco ball swung over his head.

As a warrant officer in the 1980's, he'd conveniently "misplaced" the aircraft while working with a National Guard unit. But that was quite common in those days, and the Army didn't seem to care. Since then, he'd tricked out the bird, upgraded her weapons systems, installed Spotify, and named her Katie.

The chopper cleared the tree-line, and Batshit got his first look at the Mountainside Theater below. The mayhem and carnage was everything he was promised and all that he'd hoped for. Hideous monsters raging in battle, fire, explosions, lightning, rain... Bliss.

"Delenda est Carthago," he said, quoting Cato the Elder.

Batshit took a bite of his Hot Pocket and squeezed the trigger.

BUDDABUDDABUDDABUDDABUDDA!!!

The twin mini-guns came to life and sang their duet, spraying 7.62 x 51 NATO into the heart of the ampitheater. Humans and skinners alike ran for cover.

"Get out of here! Go go go!" Will screamed, rushing Casey back to Jackson's van as the heavy artillery ate up the theater around them. Sparks and blood showered and sprayed. The bleachers were blasted apart, pieces of them spinning through the rain and dust and debris. Skinners were torn into bloody chunks as the automatic fire lit up the outdoor theater in the hills.

"Run! Go!" Keonee screamed, leading his people up the bleachers, desperately fleeing for the parking lot. Janae, Orenda, Lambert, and Teoc were right behind him, skinning back to their human forms.

KENTUCKY AND TOHO DID A MACABRE DANCE AS THE chopper blasted them into a grim piece of performance art. Other skinners were also sent flying back as the mini-gun shredded them to pieces. Blood vaporized and turned the rain crimson.

Batshit held the remainder of his Hot Pocket in his

teeth so he could reach the controls for his M134's. He squeezed the trigger.

Hydro rockets streaked through the wind and rain.

FWOOM!! FWOOM!!

A dozen skinners trying to scramble away were consumed by the first roaring ball of flames. Bleachers and chunks of concrete and steel and glass exploded all around. The second rocket hit the stage-right side wall, reducing the support structure of the massive architecture to a cloud of flaming rubble.

The canopy, ticket office, and gift shop collapsed at the top of the stairs, sending burning debris crashing down onto the already-destroyed stage and bleachers. Most were either already dead or running, but two stubborn silhouettes still clashed in the mist.

Redhawk and Loco remained locked in battle.

The raptor used all his strength, but the coyote was just too stout. With a bestial growl, Loco threw Redhawk to the ground as the stadium burned down around them. The hairy beast wrapped his claws around the bird's throat, and Redhawk could barely hold him back.

He looked up to see a sheet of burning debris plummeting towards them. The bird of prey braced for impact. Sections of broken drywall and burning support beams crashed down on the two combatants, covering them both in a pile of smoldering rubble. Redhawk was gone.

WILL AND CASEY DOVE BEHIND JACKSON'S VAN FOR cover.

"Hey, babe," Shenandoah said casually.

Will chuckled and said, "Hey." He glimpsed over to see Jackson sitting behind the wheel, the driver's door torn off. His old friend was looking right at him, finally seeing his true jaguar form. Will took a deep breath and let the skinner slip away. Jackson watched the magical transformation. The beast phased away, and his old buddy, Will Shaw, stood before him again.

"Hey, Jax," Will said, his eyes welling up.

Jackson smiled and held up the "hang loose" hand symbol.

Will returned the gesture. He looked over and saw his old friends, Corporal Powell, and Major Curtis, running back through the bloody mist.

"Fall back!" Curtis screamed. "Fall back!"

"Gang's all here," Will chuckled.

Casey transformed back into a teenage girl as well. She peeked over the hood, watching Katie the Huey lay waste to the ampitheater.

"I'm gonna take a wild guess and say that's Batshit Barry?" Casey asked.

"None other," Jackson said. "Come on, we gotta get out of here before the psycho levels this entire mountain."

Will looked around, suddenly realizing they were missing someone.

"Where's my papaw?" he said.

"*Will, we can't wait!*" Powell shouted, sending a short burst of lead into a wolf skinner's chest. "*We have to go now!*"

Scanning the ruins, Will's eyes locked on their target.

Papaw Jimmy sat amongst the flaming debris, holding Pete's lifeless body.

"Papaw!!"

More skinners jumped at them from the rainy shadows, and more bullets were required to knock them down. Shenandoah blasted them away with her FN SCAR until it ran empty, so she dropped it and grabbed her sidearm. Powell and Curtis fired away at the monsters snapping for their throats.

"Fall back!" Curtis screamed. *"Fall back!"*

Will shoved Casey to the sliding door of the van, pulling Shenandoah along too. "Claude! Skipper! Let's *go!"* Will shouted, pushing Casey inside. "I have to get my papaw!"

"We can't just leave you!" Casey protested, but Will pushed her back.

"You already saved me, kiddo," Will said, touching her cheek. "Now let me save you, okay? Go."

Shenandoah said, "I'm staying with you, Will."

"Powell, come on!!" Jackson shouted.

Claude Powell emptied his final magazine and ran for the van, letting the rifle swing to his side as he pulled out his MK-23. Suddenly, a giant preying mantis-skinner dropped down from the trees in front of him.

With long and powerful raptorial forelimbs, the creature snapped a bone-crunching grip onto the hardened Ranger's arms, lifting him off his feet. Powell wailed in pain and watched as the beast's nightmarish mandibles and palps unfolded, the horrible mouth opening wide and wrapping around his head.

"Powell!!!" Jackson screamed.

With skull-shattering chomps, the mantis tore the top of the corporal's head off, munching away at his brains and blood as his body twitched helplessly. Jackson opened fire, as did Shenandoah and Curtis, ending their friend's suffering and cutting the giant insect down.

Will heaved the sliding door closed and pounded the side of the van.

"Jax, get them out of here! *Go go go!!*" Will ordered. "I'll be right behind you!"

Wasting no time, Jackson shifted into reverse and hit the gas.

"Copper, get to Pete's truck!" Will commanded, running back into the war zone. "I'm going to get my papaw!"

BUDDABUDDABUDDABUDDA!!!

Batshit circled around for another pass, spitting a hailstorm of burning lead into the giant death trap. He sent two more M134 rockets flying.

FWOOM!! KA-THOOOOM!!!

Giant fireballs spun and churned. The once-majestic community theater burned and crumbled. The few remaining skinners trampled over each other to get back to the parking lot, jumping in their vehicles to escape. Batshit Barry swung Katie around and chased after them.

"Citizens and soldiers of New Rome, lift up your hearts!" Batshit recited his favorite speech by Constantine XI. "Though the hordes of the Grand Turk are ranged about our walls in numbers beyond measure, our resolve must not falter in the face of these enemies of God!"

THOOM!! THOOM!!

"The Turk is advancing into Christian lands, and Jerusalem, the city of our Savior, is already occupied by these enemies of God! He calls to you in particular,

because He has given you above all nations, great glory in arms!"

Batshit gleefully continued mowing down the foul beasties.

JIMMY SHAW SAT WITH HIS HEAD HANGING LOW.

He held his old friend Pete in his arms. His tears were masked by the rain. All around him seemed to move in slow motion, an out-of-focus world of muffled screams and the odors of wet gunpowder and burnt dog. A blurry figure came running at him through the wreckage in slow motion. He was saying something, shouting—

"Papaw!" Will screamed. *"Papaw! Come on! We gotta go!"*

The Cherokee Ranger ran up to his grandfather, shaking the old man's shoulders with urgency. Jimmy remained in a daze.

"Papaw, come on!!"

"Someone...has to stay with Pete..." Jimmy muttered.

Will grabbed his grandfather by both sides of the face and looked into his eyes.

"Papaw... Please."

Jimmy blinked and snapped out of it. He gently laid Pete down amongst the muddy debris and let Will pull him away.

"Come on!"

. . .

BATSHIT CHASED THE REMAINING SKINNERS OF THE
Council up the stairs and into the parking lot above the
venue, showering them with automatic fire. One was
reduced to a red splat on the asphalt. Two more made it
to their car, started the engine, and peeled away. Popping
the last bit of his Hot Pocket into his mouth, Batshit
aimed and fired another rocket.

The small missile struck the racing vehicle head-on,
combusting into a massive burst of flames. The two skinners howled in anguish as their flesh roasted and the
vehicle flipped through the air, crashing into a flaming
heap of steel and fiberglass.

Barry swung around and incinerated another while
whistling a chipper tune.

Keonee, Orenda, Lambert, and Teoc made it to their
Ford Expedition.

"*Go! Hurry!*" Keonee shouted, jumping into the
passenger seat.

Lambert got behind the wheel and started the engine
as Orenda and Teoc leapt into the back, slamming the
doors behind them. They raced away toward the exit as
fire and shards of concrete exploded behind them.

Janae reached her bike, bleeding and panting for
breath as she hopped on, kicking the engine into action.
She revved up the black beast and sent it roaring away,
the tires kicking up a spray of water in her wake.
Catching up with her comrades in the other car, they all
retreated as the chopper swooped in from behind.

THOOM!! THOOM!!

Walls of fire kicked up behind them as Batshit Barry sent two more mini-missiles. The shockwaves shook the car and motorcycle, nearly knocking Janae over, but they made it out of the lot and floored it down the dirt road out of there. Batshit accelerated behind them, determined to not let any escape alive, when a dark figure suddenly swooped out of the sky from nowhere.

With black, leathery wings and course hair all over her body, Apu shrieked as she attacked the mechanical bird, slapping into the cockpit window. Her red eyes thirsted for blood as she looked right at the pilot, her jaws lined with needle-sharp teeth. She was expecting to see terror in the man's eyes.

Batshit Barry was mildly annoyed.

"Hm. Crap," he said.

The raging bat skinner clung to the front of the Huey, wrapping her fleshy wings around the windows of the cockpit. Batshit tried to steady the bird, but he was flying blind. Apu smashed the window again and again, fracturing the glass.

"Hang in there, baby," Batshit said, struggling with the stick.

The bat creature reached around and began smashing through the pilot's side window. Batshit flinched as shards of glass exploded in and a monstrous, clawed hand reached through. He leaned away as far as he could, trying to evade the swiping talons of the beast.

Katie swerved and bucked in the storm, the flying machine dangerously close to crashing into the pavement below. Apu continued to smash and thrash, reaching deeper inside the cockpit, straining to rip Batshit's face off.

Pulling out his 1911, Batshit unloaded a magazine, blasting through the front and side windows at the monster until his mag clicked empty. Bullets smashed through the glass, three of them ripping through the creature's wings. But that didn't stop her.

Out of options, Batshit had to think quick.

He looked around. The emergency parachute.

As Apu strained to stick her head through the side window, snapping her jaws at her enemy's face, Batshit snatched up the chute from its side compartment. With hot bat breath on his face and flesh-tearing fangs inches away, he lashed the straps around the creature's neck, then pulled the cords to cinch them tight.

As Apu backed up and struggled with the choking straps around her throat, Batshit gave the rip cord a good, hard tug. The parachute bloomed open and Apu was instantly sucked up into the propellors above.

Apu's shriek of surprise and terror was cut short as the blades chopped her into dog food, sending her blood and chunks of flesh raining down.

Katie's motor choked and seized up as the parachute and dead chunks of bat creature twisted around the propellor blades. The machine began to wheeze and spin out of control as thick white smoke poured from between the clogged gears.

Batshit struggled to hold the stick steady, easing his wounded bird down and hoping not to crash. He remained calm.

"Easy, girl," he said. "We're goin' down."

36

MOMENT OF TRUTH

THE RAIN WAS DYING DOWN. The battle was not.

Shenandoah pushed Pete's F-150 to its limit, racing through the woods and dirt roads behind the Mountainside theater, splashing through mud puddles and ripping through foliage. Jimmy sat in the passenger seat, Will in the back of the cab. He was delighted when he jumped in to find his papaw had brought along his backpack and leather jacket. With the cold, wet wind whipping in through the shattered windows, slipping back into his warm, cozy jacket was a small luxury.

"Hang on!" Shenandoah shouted.

She whipped the wheel to the right, sending the truck bursting through the backroad overgrowth and back out onto Highway 19. The tires spun on the wet asphalt until finally finding their grip and shooting the trio forward. Cyan lightning strobed over the distant mountains behind them as the storm gradually stalked away.

Janae cut out onto the road behind them on her Ducati.

"God damn it!" Shenandoah snapped. "This bitch won't let up!"

Right behind her came the black Expedition, Teoc behind the wheel. Agent Lambert sat up front, with Keonee and Orenda in the back. Teoc floored it, and the two pursuers sped right up behind the pickup truck, trying to run them off the road.

"Faster! Faster!" Will shouted, and began rummaging through his bag for a weapon. He zipped open the top pocket and fished around. Keys, a few pens, a bandana, Leah's medicine bag necklace, a knife, his sunglasses, cell phone charger, loose change... nothing that would fire a bullet. He dug into the larger pocket, rifling through the clean clothes he'd packed for the trip. Tucked deep down, he found his backup Canik SFx Rival and two spare mags.

"Run them down!" Keonee ordered.

Teoc gunned it, speeding up behind the pickup and smashing them. Shenandoah swerved on the two-lane highway and Janae hit the brakes to avoid being crushed against her rear bumper. Together, the SUV and motor-cycle refused to let them go. Teoc rolled down his window and reached out with his Glock 17, steering the car with his right hand.

BLAMBLAMBLAMBLAMBLAM!!!

The bullets punched through the F-150's tailgate and shattered the back window. Will whipped around and took aim, firing back with deadly intent.

BOOMBOOMBOOMBOOMBOOM!!!

The chase plunged forward into the wet, dripping night, moving away from town. Highway 19 was a winding, serpentine road, flanked on the right by rocky cliffs, and on the left by the rushing Oconaluftee River. Shenandoah struggled to keep the vehicle from sliding off the slick surface as the aggressors gave them no room to breathe.

Will and Teoc traded gunfire. Janae sped up on the right, looking like she might try to jump into the bed of the speeding pickup. Shenandoah jerked the wheel to the right, trying to drive the lone rider into the side of the cliff.

Janae hit the brakes and shifted back behind them as the truck smashed into the rocky wall. Molten sparks blazed as metal met stone, and the lady cop fought to keep the vehicle on the road. Will and Jimmy slammed back and forth in their seats as the truck swerved and banked dangerously on the wet surface.

"Daggone women drivers..." Jimmy quipped.

Shenandoah gritted her teeth, doing her best to keep them on the road.

"You want to trade places, old timer?" she growled.

Teoc raced up from behind and smashed them again. And again.

Will popped out his empty mag and smacked in a fresh one. His last one. He popped up from behind the seat and squeezed off a series of shots, peppering the windshield of the SUV. Keonee hissed as one of Will's bullets grazed his left arm, leaving a burning, bloody gash.

"Hnng! Damn it, Teoc! Take them *down!"* he hissed.

Teoc smashed into them repeatedly.

Shenandoah suddenly saw the headlights of another

oncoming vehicle. She screamed and whipped the wheel to the right, missing the oncoming car but once again grinding into the craggy cliff face. The F-150 swerved, knicking the Expedition and nearly causing them to fly off the road.

Tugging the wheel back to the left, Shenandoah fought to keep the truck from smashing through the guard rail and tumbling into the river. Teoc rammed them again, and though she used all her strength, she could not make the turn. She felt the wheels beneath her begin to hydroplane and knew with a sinking feeling that there was nothing she could do.

"Oh shiiiiiit!!!" she screamed as the truck slammed through the divider.

They went airborne. Everything went silent.

The rocky riverbed rushed up to greet them.

Will shouted, *"Hold on!!!"*

The pickup careened nose-first into the boulders and cold, rushing water of the Oconaluftee River. Glass shattered. Metal crumpled. Airbags deployed. Will felt a hard, wet impact, and then everything went black.

THE WORLD SLOWLY CAME BACK INTO FOCUS. LIGHT rain continued to sprinkle.

Will's eyes fluttered open. Everything was buzzing.

Okay, Will thought, *I'm concussed and in shock...*

He slowly lifted his head and looked around. The wreckage of the car lay several feet behind him. He was laying face-down, half submerged in the flowing water, half on one of the many giant boulders scattered throughout the riverbed. His backpack lay on the rock beside him, its contents spilled and splayed all around.

Will had been thrown from the vehicle and landed to its right. He sat up, delirious, and looked around. There directly in front of the vehicle, its headlights still shining on him, was Jimmy. The old man lay face-up in the water, bloody and injured, but still alive. Will could see him grimacing and thrashing in pain.

"P-Papaw..." Will croaked.

"*Nnng!* Leg's broke," Jimmy cursed, holding a badly-shattered right leg. There were two compound fractures, and the sharp edges of broken bones had ripped through the skin and pants. His Indian blood ran into the river.

Will looked into the truck through the passenger door.

Shenandoah was still in the driver's seat, leaning into the airbag like a pillow. Blood streaked her face and her eyes were closed, and Will couldn't tell if she was alive or dead. He sat up, straining to move towards her.

"Copper..." Will called out. "C-Copper?"

He began to pull himself up to check on her, when he heard a familiar sound. Footsteps. Turning to look back up the hill at the road above, he saw five figures in silhouette. The Expedition and the Ducati were parked behind them, the engines still idling, the headlights still on. Keonee and his people were coming. Will grunted and frantically started feeling around, looking for his gun.

Keonee, Orenda, Teoc, Agent Lambert, and Janae made their way down the rocky hill leading to the riverbed. Janae and Lambert closed in on Will, while Teoc sloshed through the rushing water, Glock held at his side. Keonee and Orenda kept their distance, standing up on a boulder and letting their underlings do all the work.

Janae drew her gun. "Time's up, hot stuff."

"Nowhere left to run, Mr. Shaw," Keonee said, stepping forward into the knee-deep water. "This is your last chance to cooperate."

"Don't you tell these sumbitches *nothin'*, boy! Y'hear me?" Jimmy said, cringing at the intense pain shooting through his leg. "You tell that White boy to go to hell!"

"Kasa?" Keonee said.

Hearing her Council name, Lambert knew what to do. She moved in closer and looked into Will's eyes, blood dripping from the four parallel wounds across her cheek. Her pupils swirled with black clouds until they were completely filled like ebony marbles, using her power to compel the truth.

"Where is the child?" she demanded. "Where have you hidden him?"

"God damn it," Will snapped, *"what child?"*

"You can only resist her power so long," Keonee said. "Our Kasa can compel anyone to tell the truth. Even you."

"Where have you hidden the child?" Lambert asked again with her black eyes.

"Fuck you! I don't know what you're talking about!"

"Oh, no?" Keonee asked. "Well then, maybe we should ask my old buddy. Maybe he knows." The husky old man with the ponytail turned to face his old friend Jimmy, who writhed in pain, leaning against the glaring front headlights of the pickup. "What do you say, Jimmy? For old time's sake?"

Teoc lifted his firearm and aimed it point-blank at Jimmy's head.

"For old time's sake?" Jimmy said, leaning forward with a glare of defiance in his Cherokee eyes. "For old time's sake, I say fuck you, *Jack*."

Teoc looked over at his leader. Keonee gave the nod of approval.

Without a moment's hesitation, Teoc pulled the trigger.

There was a flash and a bang, and a bullet tore into Jimmy's skull.

He was killed instantly, his lifeless body slumping back against the twisted front bumper of the pickup truck. Will's eyes bulged and his heart dropped.

"PAPAW!!!"

Weary, bloody, and exhausted, Will jumped up, fueled by rage. He took one running step towards Teoc, ready to tear him to bloody ribbons, when Orenda suddenly commanded, "Weak."

Will lost his strength mid-stride, collapsing back down to the boulder with a bone-crunching thud. He fought against it, but Orenda's power was too strong. Helpless and unable to even crawl, let alone stand or run, Will broke down into tears.

"You fucking bastards..." Will sobbed. "God damn sons of bitches!"

Janae stood before him, watching him wail in grief.

A sinking sadness began to come over her, and she tried her best to stuff it back down inside herself. Against her better judgment, she had sympathy for the dark one, the deceiver. Doubt began to creep back into her mind.

"Let's try this again," Keonee said as Will Shaw wept.

Lambert bent down and grabbed his chin, forcing him to look up at her.

"Where is the child?" she said, her eyes black like a shark's.

Papaw Jimmy... Oh God, no...

Will could do nothing but cry.

"Where is the child?" she repeated angrily.

"I don't know... what you're... talking about..." Will said, collapsing back down, his belongings strewn around him. Lambert stood back up and turned to Keonee.

"He doesn't know," she said. "He'd have told me by now."

Keonee sighed and looked over at Orenda.

"Well," Keonee said, wading in closer to Will. "I guess we're going to have to do it the hard way. "If the child's father doesn't know where he is..." Keonee glanced over to his side and looked Janae in the eye, "... then surely his *mother* does."

A shiver ran up Janae's spine and her whole body tightened.

"W-What...?" she said, looking from Keonee to Orenda.

"Do you think we're stupid, Janae?" Orenda said.

"I-I don't know what you're talking about..." Janae began to back up.

"I was hoping it wouldn't have to come to this, my daughter," Keonee said, holding his hands out. "I really was. I raised you since you were a child, but now you leave me no choice. You love the deceiver... You have betrayed your father."

Will's mind raced as they began to close in around Janae.

Wait a second, what is going on here?

"Please don't do this," Janae said as they moved in. She pointed her gun, trying in vain to hold them off. "Stay back! Please, don't come any—"

"Weak," Orenda said.

Janae dropped the gun into the river and fell to her knees. Almost all of her strength drained, she lifted her weary head and found Will Shaw staring at her. She looked back at him. Suddenly, he understood.

Oh my God, Will thought. *No way... It can't be...*

Lambert grabbed Janae by the collar and shook her hard, using her black eyes to bore into her thoughts.

"Where is your baby, Janae?" Lambert asked.

"Please..." Janae began to cry. "Don't do this..."

"Where is your baby, Janae?"

"I don't know, please..."

"Where is your baby, Janae?"

"I don't know!"

Lambert turned and looked back at Keonee. "She doesn't know."

"If she doesn't know where the baby is," he said, "perhaps she will know who the baby is *with?* You gave him to a friend, didn't you? Someone you trusted to hide him? Hide him from us? Who is it, Janae?"

Janae wept, "P-Please... no..."

"Who has the baby, Janae?" Lambert demanded.

"No... Please... I can't..."

"Who has the baby, Janae?"

The federal agent's eyes probed Janae's mind, her

voice breaking through her willpower. Janae fought with everything she had, but the wall she'd built up in her mind was crumbling down, and she was helpless to resist.

Finally, she broke down and said, "Sharice... Sharice McKee."

Janae's head dropped in shame.

"And where might we find this Sharice McKee?"

"New York... New York City..."

Keonee and his cohorts shared a smile.

"Well, I'm sure this McKee is hiding somewhere," Lambert said. "But now we know where to start. We'll find them. We'll get you that boy."

"Please," Janae begged, "what are you gonna do with him?"

"Very good," Keonee ignored Janae's question, and said to Lambert, "Charter a private jet to New York, right away."

She nodded, took out her phone, and made the call.

"I suppose we don't need you anymore, then," Keonee said to Janae regretfully, then turned his gaze over to Will. "And we certainly don't need *you* anymore, Will Shaw."

Teoc lifted his pistol and pressed it against Will's head, a sadistic smile on his face. "Your ass is *mine*," he said, beginning to squeeze the trigger.

"No, my son," Keonee smiled. "I've promised him to someone else, a friend of mine. I believe you two have already met. Right, Will?" Keonee turned and called out to the darkness, rubbing the pendant hanging from his neck. "Come on out, my friend! Time to collect your reward!"

Will and Janae looked around, scanning the shadows.

At first, there was nothing. But then, a haunting hum. A strange chattering, clicking laughter. The shadows began to move and contort. Descending over the river, the oily, black pieces swirled and came together.

Oh, you scumbag, Will thought.

The raven mocker materialized before their eyes.

"Son of a bitch," Will growled.

"Oh my God," Janae muttered. "Keonee, you... *you?*"

Keonee smiled and laughed as the sinister wraith undulated between this world and another, floating over the water to make its grand entrance. Orenda and Lambert grinned in approval. Confused, Teoc just stood there obediently, watching the creature slither through the air toward Will.

"Father, please... no!" Janae begged.

"Watch closely and enjoy the show, my child," Keonee said. "After this, it's your turn. So go ahead and say goodbye to your little loverboy."

"Bastard," Will seethed, watching helplessly as the swirling mass of black membranes and tentacles approached, rattling its evil laugh. It unfolded its barbed appendages and flashed its circular rows of teeth. It closed the distance, ready to tear him to pieces.

FAITH

BLOOD!　　***HATE!***　　***REVENGE!***　　***HEART POUNDING!***

　CLAWS SHREDDING FLESH! MURDER! BLOOD!

　LET ME OUT!!!

WILL SHAW WAS ON HIS KNEES.

His body was a collection of bruises and lacerations. Sprawled on a large boulder, with his feet hanging into the running water, and blood and muck covering every inch of him, he was a defeated man. He looked up at all present: Keonee and Orenda, Agent Lambert, Teoc, and Janae. She looked back at him, her eyes begging forgiveness.

The raven mocker floated in close, ready to have its way with the already-tenderized victim. Its nightmarish jaws unraveled, its barbs and prongs ready to strike. Will glanced over at the crashed truck. Papaw Jimmy. Murdered in cold blood.

No way. Can't quit, Will thought. *Get up, Shaw! Get up!*

Will pushed with everything he had, wobbling to his feet. He looked up at his black-cloaked executioner, defiant. The creature laughed at him as he put up his fists, lurching forward.

"Come on, you son of a bitch! Let's go!" Will raged, throwing a looping, weak punch at the demon. The raven mocker didn't even bother to dodge it. Will threw another and another, both sliding through the fabric of the beast's DNA, leaving it unfazed. Will launched two more, slipped and dribbled back to his knees.

Keonee and his gang laughed as the raven mocker circled him.

"Stop it, Father! Please!" Janae begged, tears rolling down her face. She tried to move, to charge forward, to somehow stop them. But Orenda's power was too strong, and she didn't have the strength to even stand.

Will grunted in pain and pushed himself back up, fighting Orenda's spell with trademark Cherokee stubbornness. He charged at the monster, swinging punches feebly. It slid around him and lashed out with a whipping tendril, slicing open his left cheek, then knocking the wind out of him.

Will fell to his hands and knees. He gasped for air, looking down at the boulder he knelt on. Everything that was in his backpack had spilled around him. The pens, the sunglasses, the dog-tags.

With herculean effort, Will forced himself back to his

rubbery feet. He lobbed out one punch after another, his arms feeling like he was holding fifty-pound dumbbells. The old witch was making him weak and there was nothing he could do. He swung again and again, but the creature unleashed a flurry of quick, stinging blows, slicing him open and knocking him back down.

"So, so weak," Orenda said with a cruel smile. "Look at you."

"*Stop it!*" Janae pleaded.

Will found himself face down on the rock. His whole body ached and stung. All he knew was pain. *Looks like this is how it ends. This is how I die. On a rock, in a river, and in my hometown. Okay, you shit stain from Hell, go ahead and get it over with.* Will let his body go limp, not fighting it anymore. It was time.

Then he noticed the medicine bag Leah had given him. It had fallen out of his jacket pocket and lay on the ground a few feet from his Army dog-tags. Just a trinket, a necklace—it had no deeper meaning and served no other function. Still, if he was going to die, he wanted to die with his tags.

Will reached out his bloodied hand and picked them up. He looked at the aluminum plates, reading his name stamped into them.

Will Shaw. United States Army... that's me. This is who I am. I am an Army Ranger, an elite operator. The best of the best... these tags are special, just like Papaw Jimmy said...

Will's heart began to beat faster.

The raven mocker floated in, preparing to deliver its death blow.

Will looked back down at the medicine bag and picked it up.

And this... it's a symbol of my people. Papaw tried to tell me, Leah tried to tell me... this is also who I am! I am a Cherokee warrior. These things, they're not just trinkets! They hold power... and the power is inside of me, always has been!

Will placed the Army tags and medicine bag in his hand.

He clenched his fist tight, squeezing the sacred talismans together.

A jolt of power rushed through his battered body.

Will looked up, his eyes blazing.

He got his feet back under him and stood up.

"Weak," Orenda said again, but this time her words had no effect.

"My name is Will Shaw," he said, wrapping the chain and leather lanyard of the two pendants tightly around his fist. "I will never quit. I will never break." He stepped closer to the raven mocker, unafraid. "I am a Cherokee. I am a soldier. I am a jaguar. You hold no power over me. I've never given a shit about your stupid Council, never wanted to destroy it... if you just left me alone, you never would have had this problem. You'd get to keep your little club and I'd go on not caring. But *now*?" Will stepped closer and the vile black beast actually backed up. "Now, I am absolutely going to burn every one of you fuckers to the ground. I *am* going to destroy the Spirit Council and I'm starting with you motherfuckers right now!"

"Weak!" Orenda said, but Will kept coming.

"Kill him!" Keonee commanded the beast and it struck out at him.

Will dodged the whipping tendril, pulled back the fist holding the Army tags and medicine bag, and launched the hardest punch he could at the slithering fiend. Speeding through the air, powered by a strength deep in his soul, light warped and bent around his fist. The fist became a black claw.

The claw did not pass harmlessly through the etherial beast.

It connected.

WHACK!!

The raven mocker experienced something new. Pain. It swerved in the air, looking back at its opponent in shock. Standing before it was the jaguar. Thick muscles flexed beneath a black coat criss-crossed with fresh wounds. Fiery eyes blazed hotter than the sun. Will snarled, baring his deadly fangs.

The creature spun around, shrieked its awful cry and shot forward at the black cat in a rage. Its swirling masses lashed out at him, whipping his hide, trying to grab and strangle him. Will broke its grip and fought back. His claws slashed through the creature repeatedly, but it was still a creature not fully tethered to this world.

Will didn't care. He kept fighting, swinging and swinging until he caught it with another slashing blow. Hooked claws tore through the black fabric of the evil beast and it released a hellish scream. It backed up and the cat pushed forward through sheer will. He tore through it again and again. The raven mocker wrapped an oily tentacle around Will's throat, choking him in its vice grip.

Will bit into the appendage, lashing his head back and forth until he ripped it off. The raven mocker screamed as the severed tendril fell to the rocks below and fizzled into a stinking, black residue.

"That's impossible," Keonee hissed, panic in his eyes.

Orenda held her hands out, as if that would somehow amplify her psychic gift. She strained, summoning all her strength and focused it on Will. "Weak! You are weak!"

Will sagged, nearly dropping to his knees.

No. Get back up! Fight this!

Catching himself, he stood back up, resisting the debilitating effects of Orenda's spell. He lashed out again with two more swipes. The first passed through the slimy, gaseous mass. The second connected. The evil specter screamed and fell into the rushing water. Its tentacles and membranes swirled as it floated back up, raging at the black cat. But Will slashed it down yet again.

As Will's strength grew, the creature's faded.

No sooner than the raven mocker's vaporous wounds began to melt back together, than Will ripped them apart again. Pieces of the beast fell to the rocks and rushing water, fizzling and bubbling away as the panther whittled it down to nothing.

Keonee watched in shock. He grabbed Janae and yanked her to her feet, pulling a .38 special from his jacket and holding the barrel against her head. Exhausted, Orenda gave up trying to drain Will's strength. Lambert and Teoc stood by, guns at the ready, as Will tore their monster down.

The foul beast staggered, shredded into ribbons. It tried to regenerate and recover, to retreat and vanish into the shadows where it could heal and be safe. Will was having none of that. He grabbed its flailing tendrils, whipped the creature over his head and pounded it down into the rocks. Again. Again. It turned to look up at him, screaming in shrill defiance for the final time.

Will shot a fist into its hideous maw and dug his arm deep into the beast's throat. He issued his mighty roar, driving his claw into the raven mocker's gullet until his arm was elbow-deep. The black jaguar ripped the vile creature's black heart out through its mouth.

The raven mocker finally collapsed, its body bubbling and smoking as it sizzled away. Its heart melted until nothing was left but black goo in Will's hand.

The black jaguar roared triumphantly.

Keonee cocked the hammer on his .38. Janae winced.

"Very impressive, Mr. Shaw," Keonee hissed, furious. "But it changes nothing."

Teoc had his pistol aimed at Will, as did Agent Lambert. Janae struggled in Keonee's grip, tears brimming in her eyes as he pressed the gun to her head.

"Will..." Janae begged.

Will snarled, "Let her go." His eyes burned and his claws flexed.

"You want her?" Keonee suddenly shoved Janae forward. "Take her!"

The black cat caught her in his arms. She looked into his eyes.

Then the sound of three gunshots echoed in the riverbed.

CRACK! CRACK! CRACK!

Janae's eyes went wide in shock as the bullets tore into her back and burned into her vital organs. She gripped Will's arms and began to sag as the pain set in.

"*NO!!*" Will screamed, catching her.

Keonee stood with the smoking gun in his hand.

Will fell to his knees, clutching Janae as she coughed up blood, her body spasming. The black cat's roar morphed into a scream as the beast dissolved back into the ether, and the man came back into the earthly dimension. He could do nothing but hold her and touch her face tenderly.

"Isn't this romantic?" Orenda smirked. "Now you get to die together."

Lambert and Teoc raised their weapons and aimed at Will.

Keonee sneered, "Goodbye, Will Shaw."

"*Goodbye, motherfucker!*" Shenandoah screamed.

The lady cop jumped out of the car, a pistol in each hand.

BOOM! BOOM! BOOM! BOOM! BOOM!!

Everyone turned in shock as Shenandoah opened fire. She was weary and concussed, with dried blood gluing her left eye closed, but she was on fire. She snarled in determination, most of her shots going wild.

Will held Janae tight and ducked down out of the way.

Teoc and Lambert returned fire, but Shenandoah took cover behind the wrecked truck. Keonee and Orenda retreated as bullets criss-crossed through the air. One clipped Teoc's arm, forcing him to drop his gun and flee. Lambert emptied her magazine and furiously began to reload.

Shenandoah shot back, missing Lambert but striking Orenda.

The old witch gasped in pain as the round tore into her chest, toppling to the rocky shore. Keonee immediately rushed to her aid, but she was fading fast. "No!" he screamed, trying to pull Orenda to her feet.

Lambert fired back, her hollow-points punching holes in the crashed pickup truck. One shot ripped through and pierced Shenandoah's side, and another grazed her shoulder. She hissed at the burning pain and took cover, reloaded , and jumped back into the fight.

BOOM! BOOM! BOOM! BOOM! BOOM!!

Shenandoah's rounds peppered the riverbed and surrounding woods, driving them back further. Lambert ran out of ammo, and pulled at Keonee's jacket as he clutched hopelessly to Orenda.

"Come on! We have to go!" Lambert shouted.

Tears ran down Keonee's face. "Orenda... my darling..."

She was dying in his arms.

"*Come on!!*" Lambert pulled at him with all her might.

With Teoc's help, they finally pried Keonee away as Shenandoah continued to fire. Her shots kicked up spouts of water and mud all around them as they retreated back up the hill to their black SUV.

Will watched as Shenandoah limped out from behind Pete's pickup, running after the villains and emptying another magazine. She spat it out, punched in a fresh one, and continued firing. Bullets kicked up muddy soil on the hillside and punched through into the side of the vehicle. Lambert jumped behind the wheel while Teoc threw Keonee into the back, and they tore off down the highway with a wet skid.

Shenandoah stopped, panting for breath.

She turned to face Will. He sat in the river, holding Janae as she struggled to breathe, her right lung filling with blood. Will looked up at the copper, pain in his eyes. No words needed to be said. A gurgling sound came from her left, and Shenandoah went to investigate.

Orenda lay half in the water, half on the shore, bleeding out from the wound in her chest. Shenandoah looked down at her with zero compassion. Orenda grimaced, her eyes full of hate as blood bubbled from her mouth. In one final attempt, she reached out with a trembling hand, aiming her spell at Shenandoah.

"W-We...wea..." she gurgled.

Shenandoah lifted her gun and fired. *BOOM!*

She blasted one round into Orenda's brain, ending her instantly.

"Weak," Shenandoah said, then turned back to Will.

Janae was dying and Will was helpless to do anything.

"W-Will..." Janae gasped. "Will... I'm s-sorry..."

"Shhh, don't speak."

"Please... you have to stop... them..." she struggled to get the words out. "Can't... can't let them get... Adam..."

"Adam?" Will asked.

"Our... our son."

AIRBORNE

THE NIGHT WAS SUDDENLY STILL and silent.

Even though the river flowed and remnants of the passing storm dripped from the trees, time seemed to be frozen. Will knelt in the water with Janae in his arms, watching helplessly as she clung to life. Shenandoah stood by, saying nothing. She spent a minute wiping the dried blood out of her eye, and was relieved to learn that she wasn't blinded. The wounds in her abdomen and arm also seemed to be superficial. She looked down at the man she loved tenderly cradling his ex who had just tried to kill him a few minutes earlier.

"Stay with me, okay?" Will said. "I'm gonna get you out of here."

Shenandoah doubted that. After the wake of chaos and destruction they'd left behind in town, all police and emergency personnel were either dead or having the busiest night of their lives. Nobody was coming to help them.

"Copper, call someone!" Will said. "Call for help!"

Shenandoah felt in her pocket, but her phone wasn't there. She looked wearily around the wreckage of Pete's truck, realizing that it must have been lost in the crash.

"My phone..." she said, looking for it in vain.

"Shit!" Will said. "Don't worry Janae, you're gonna be okay."

"Shhh, j-just... find Adam," she said. "He needs you..."

Adam. My son. I have a son.

"I'm so sorry," Janae whispered. "Couldn't... tell you."

Will growled, gripping her tight, wanting to kiss her and strangle her at the same time. Even caked in blood and dirt and bruises, her face was still a thing of beauty. Perfectly polished, curved surfaces. Rich, dark brown skin. Her eyes, her lips... Will could feel her energy fading. He glanced over at his Papaw Jimmy, slumped over against the mangled front bumper of Pete's pickup.

Janae... Papaw... I'm going to lose them both tonight...

Will pulled Janae close and quietly sobbed on her shoulder.

Janae's eyes ticked over to the unfamiliar blonde standing behind Will.

The two shared a look and understood each other immediately.

Time passed. Whether it was seconds or hours, Will couldn't tell. But gradually, he became aware of a change in the wind and heard a faint and distant chopping sound. Shenandoah heard it too. The wind intensified. The noise became deafening and soon a bright light shone down on them from the sky as Batshit Barry piloted a crippled Katie over highway 19.

The Huey turned on its axis, slowly descending and landing on one of the larger boulders in the rushing river. The windows were smashed, bullet holes pocked the hull, and the engine was coughing out black smoke. Will, Janae, and Shenandoah squinted as the mechanical bird's intense breath kicked them in the face. A moment later, Batshit cut the engine and hopped out to greet them.

"Yeahp, looks like I missed this party," Batshit said.

He looked like a knight from the crusades on vacation in Daytona Beach. Despite everything else Shenandoah had seen that day, the sight of a bearded old man in a Hawaiian shirt and Roman centurion armor still left an impression. Barry stepped over a few smaller boulders to get over to them. Will chortled and shook his head.

"Evenin', Captain," Will said.

"Sergeant," Batshit nodded, and acknowledged the ladies as well. Janae struggled to keep her eyes open and had random spasms of sharp pain. "She don't look so good. We better get her to the hospital."

"Right," Will said and began hurriedly lifting Janae up. "Come on now, Janae. Nice and slow..."

Janae grimaced and shook her head. "No... stop it! Leave me here..."

"Are you crazy? You need a doctor!"

"It's too late... for that now..." Janae whispered. "Go help Adam, Will... You have to stop... Keonee."

"Look, there is no way I'm just leaving you here to die!" Will snapped. "Now, come on! Copper, can you give me a hand?"

Janae grabbed Will by the collar and yanked him forward, pressing her forehead into his, her intense eyes boring into his. "*Will!* ... Save the baby! They're on their way to New York *right now!* They chartered a plane... You can still stop him... *Go!*"

Will knew she was right.

"If you wanted to charter a private plane to New York," Batshit said, "closest airport is Asheville Regional. I don't know if Katie can make it that far. I just spent the last half hour untangling bat-monster guts from her prop gears and gettin' her up and runnin' again. She's barely holdin' together."

"How long would it take them to drive there?" Shenandoah asked.

Batshit thought a second, then said, "It's about an hour and a half by car."

"And by bird?" Will asked.

"Eh, thirty minutes or so. That's *if* baby can make it."

"Please," Janae said. "Please try..."

Will wrestled with the decision. "I can't just leave you here alone," he said.

Shenandoah sighed and stepped up. "I'll stay with her."

Janae smiled at the petite blonde, then looked back at Will. "Go... go."

He hung his head low, knowing she was right. She was out of time and he didn't want to be there to see the light dim in her eyes. Begrudgingly, Will stood up, laying Janae gently down on the smooth, flat boulder. He stopped. There was one more thing he needed to do.

Will went over to his Papaw Jimmy. He knelt down

beside the old man, and tenderly stroked his white hair. He was covered in blood, his spirit gone. Will dutifully pulled him from his slumped position onto the shore, straightening his legs. He unwrapped the chain of his dog-tags and the leather lanyard of his medicine bag, and put them into Jimmy's hand, closing the chubby-old fingers around them.

Will said a silent prayer, then went to join Batshit at the Huey.

Shenandoah went to Janae's side, sat next to her, and held her hand. Will stopped and looked back at them both. No words were spoken. He turned again and stalked across the rocks and running water to meet his old friend. They shared a firm handshake.

"Let's go to work," Will said.

"To all who vow to undertake this holy pilgrimage, we grant the remission of sins and the glorious reward of Paradise!" Batshit orated, and ran back to his baby, jumping in. "Soldiers of this world, become warriors of Christ, for God wills it!" Will shook his head as the old coot fired up the outdated machine and pulled back on the stick.

Janae and Shenandoah watched as the wounded bird lurched into the sky, spouting black smoke. Katie rumbled and roared, and banked east towards Asheville, fading into the gray smudge of the night horizon.

There was silence. The two women sat in the dark together, Shenandoah holding Janae's bloody hand. She shook her head and chuckled.

"Bitch," she said.

Janae started to laugh but it hurt too much. She

squeezed Shenandoah's hand hard as the pain spiked through her core. She took a few seconds to calm herself, and said, "Ho."

Shenandoah smiled and tried to be comforting to the dying woman. She knew there was nothing else she could do or say, but to not let her die alone. But suddenly, Shenandoah did not feel alone. Someone was there with them.

"Hello?" Copper looked all around. All she saw was shadows and trees. Moonlight cutting through the clouds. She heard only the flow of the river, and a few crickets singing old hymns. But still, she knew someone else was there. Janae felt the presence too, and her weary eyes scanned the darkness. There came a sound, the soft thump of footsteps. Shadows darted behind trees. "Who's there? Please, we need help!"

Whoever it was, there were many of them and they were coming closer, approaching through the woods on the west side of the riverbank. Shenandoah leaned forward and squinted for a better look as they began to step into the light. Her jaw dropped and her eyes flapped open in astonishment as they finally revealed themselves.

"Ho-ly shit..."

ASHEVILLE REGIONAL AIRPORT, ASHEVILLE, NC

A Lear 60 private jet was parked on the main runway of the small airfield, its two pilots and flight attendant waiting outside for their passengers to arrive. Lights flashed inside the one-story terminal, and ground crew workers guided the small aircrafts with their glow wands.

A bullet-riddled, black Expedition skidded onto the runway and zipped across the wet tarmac, headed for the small jet. The flight crew flinched as the beat-up vehicle screeched to a halt beside them, its passengers jumping out immediately. The pilots gasped when they saw the bloodied, beat-up condition of Keonee, Teoc, and Agent Lambert.

"Okay, let's go! C'mon!" Keonee said with urgency, brushing away strands of white hair hanging over his eyes as he stormed to the plane.

Lambert marched up to the flight crew and whipped out her badge.

"Agent Lambert, FBI. Thanks for being ready on such short notice."

"Jesus, are you guys *okay?*" the pilot asked her, eyeing the four bloody, parallel wounds across her cheek.

"Yes, but we need to hurry," she said.

Teoc held his wounded arm, blood dripping from his fingertips. The pilots and flight attendant shared an uneasy look.

"Uh, I'm sorry, b-but this is a private jet," the flight attendant said with her practiced customer service charm. "We can't get blood all over the cabin. Can we call a med-evac chopper to come take you all to a hospital—?"

Lambert drew her pistol and pointed it at them.

"I'm going to have to insist."

· · ·

Katie limped through the sky as fast as she could.

Nearly out of oil and fuel, the old Huey spat a jagged line of black smoke from its engine. Batshit held onto the shaking control stick the best he could, but the bird was fading fast. Up ahead, he saw the lights of the airport.

"There it is," he said.

Will could think of only one thing. Revenge.

"Faster!" Will said.

"I'm 'fraid this is about as fast she goes right now, buddy," Batshit said. "It's all I can do to just keep her in the air."

Will saw the specs of light on the runways growing closer. Then he saw it, a black SUV parked beside a small jet. Will's eyes lit up and he shook Batshit's shoulder.

"There they are!" he said, his pulse racing. "Get me right on top of them!"

"Uh huh. And do you have some kind of plan, or...?"

"Yeah. I jump on top of the plane."

Batshit digested that last statement, then smiled. "I like it!"

Teoc plunked into a seat on the private plane, pressing a towel against his gunshot wound. He looked through the window and saw a familiar military UH1D Huey on their tail. He bolted upright, furious.

"It's them!" Teoc shouted, pointing. "Look!"

Keonee and Lambert spun to peer through the window. Brimming with anger, Keonee rushed to the cabin, where the already-terrified pilots were starting the engines, running their checklists and getting their instruments ready.

"Get this plane in the air now!" Keonee commanded.

"B-But we're not cleared for take-off," the co-pilot said. "We haven't even—"

Keonee drew his .38 and pressed the cold steel against the man's temple.

"Now!! Do it!!"

Fearing for their lives, the pilots did as they were told and started the engines. Slowly, the aircraft began to roll forward and the flight attendant was forced to slam the outer door closed. Lambert grabbed her by the wrist and threw her into a seat, then sat down and buckled her safety belt. Teoc buckled up, keeping his eyes on the approaching chopper.

"They're getting close!" Teoc shouted.

"Move it!" Keonee snarled. *"Get us off the ground!"*

BATSHIT PUSHED HIS OLD GIRL HARDER, COMING UP fast behind the jet. A wicked smile broke his lips and he began to shout, as if addressing a thousand troops, "If the Almighty has ordained that our beloved city should fall, let no man say that it was for lack of courage!" Will would have laughed at the old coot if his mind wasn't so focused on inflicting horrible pain and death on his enemies.

The plane began to speed down the runway.

Batshit got right up behind it, but his controls were shaking badly.

"Push it, Barry!" Will shouted.

"I can't, damn it!" Batshit snarled, fighting his control stick. "We're caught in the jet blasts! Have to get above them! Here! By the seat! Take it! It's my standby!"

Will saw a standard-issue 1911 in a holster mounted to the seat.

"No thanks, I won't be needing that," he said, going to the back and whipping open the side door to let the night air rush in. The tarmac blurred by below them.

"Well then, what the hell are you gonna use, harsh language?" Batshit balked.

"Not exactly."

There was a strange shifting of light behind the pilot's seat, and Batshit suddenly felt a change in weight distribution, as if a heavy load had been dropped in Katie's belly. He turned to look back and caught the tail-end of Will's transition from man to beast. The black jaguar opened his eyes and looked at his old friend. The beast flashed his favorite hang-loose hand sign.

Batshit turned back around. "Well... Alrighty then. Hoorah."

The cat crouched at the open doorway, cold wind whipping through his short, black coat. It felt good. He prepared to pounce, seeing the plane's tail directly below. The plane was picking up speed, but the chopper was fading.

"Push it, Barry!! Stay right over them!"

"If you jump right over them, you'll get sucked back and miss 'em completely! I gotta get out in front of them if you're gonna have any chance!"

Batshit pressed all his weight into the controls, speeding up at the risk of his engine blowing out. Metal groaned. Rivets shook. The wounded helicopter barely hung on as Batshit pushed it to the limit, moving out in front and above the jet.

The plane's nose tilted up. It took to the air.

"Do it!" Batshit shouted. *"Go! Go! Go!"*

Will did not hesitate. His coiled haunches sprang him forward through the air, a black cat outstretched like an arrow, being sucked back and flying at its target. At first, there was nothing but cold wind and silence.

Then he collided into the roof of the jet.

The cat snarled as he quickly slid over the side, his claws scraping across the surface before catching in a riveted side panel. The plane ascended high into the sky, a black jaguar skinwalker clinging to it, refusing to let go.

Batshit Barry pulled back and slowed down before losing control.

He eased the helicopter down as gently as he could, watching the plane vanish into the cloudy night. Katie's frame groaned and creaked as her landing struts smashed down onto the tarmac. He cut the engine and let out a sigh of relief as he listened to the sad mechanical wheeze of it fading away.

"Godspeed, Will Shaw," Batshit said, saluting him. He sat there in his cockpit, catching his breath. Racing towards him from the main airport terminal were several police and security vehicles. He began to laugh. "Ahhh, it's going to be fun explaining this one..."

WILL DUG HIS CLAWS INTO THE SIDE OF THE JET, refusing to let go. He slapped against the icy, steel fuselage as the aircraft climbed ever higher into the heavens. Wounded and physically exhausted, he stubbornly held on.

"*Shake him off!!*" Keonee ordered the pilots with his gun to their backs.

"Oh, please God... please..." The pilot prayed, trembling.

"*Do it!!*"

The pilot obeyed his demands, yanking the wheel left and right, up and down, making the aircraft twist and swerve and dive in the air. Will hung on for his life as the jet soared higher over the Blue Ridge mountains. Higher. The air was frigid and wet and all he could hear was a low drone, like being caught in a vacuum cleaner.

So cold, so tired, Will thought. *Body getting numb... air getting thin... no! They can't get away! Hang on, Will!! Just... hang...*

Will passed out. His grip finally broke.

The black cat toppled through the void.

He fell like a rock, plummeting to the earth from thousands of feet up. His limp body dropped through rain clouds high above the Earth. Faster and faster, he reached terminal velocity. The ground was racing up to meet him. Only seconds remained. Will's amber eyes fluttered open. He saw nothing but darkness, felt nothing but cold and penetrating wind. He knew right then that he had failed.

Sorry, Papaw... I tried.

Will closed his eyes and surrendered, ready to die.

The high-pitched scream of a raptor sliced through the stratosphere like a steam whistle. Gold and brown feathers. Massive talons. Like a bullet, the bird of prey shot straight down through the clouds, racing to catch up with the falling cat.

Redhawk swooped out of the sky and caught Will.

Just as the black panther expected to crash into the ground, he felt a sudden pull upwards and back into the sky instead, a surreal experience, as the birdman's overpowering grip scooped him up and they soared away. Redhawk was hurt, his feathers dirty, bloody, and singed, but he powered on, using his last reserves of strength to lift the black beast. Will looked around and watched in shock as Redhawk carried him over the wooded, mountainous terrain.

Seeing a rocky perch up ahead, Redhawk veered that way, changing his angle and beating his mighty, brown wings harder. Exhausted, the raptor touched down on the craggy cliff, gently releasing Will first. He landed and folded his wings, exhausted. Will looked up at his former enemy and Redhawk met his gaze.

With a flickering of light and shadows, reality warped around the birdman, until the feathers and beak and talons were gone, and all that remained was a man. The tall, young Indian sat down on a rock, bloodied and burned, and began to catch his breath. Will relaxed as well, letting the black cat dissolve away back into the ether.

Both men sat in silence and looked at each other.

Finally, Will said, "Why... why did you...?"

"I had seen enough," Redhawk said, hanging his head in shame. "Keonee is the true deceiver."

Will looked around at the sprawling nighttime vista

around him. Fraser firs and red spruce trees reached for the sky. Rolling mountains. Stars sparkling from behind the rolling clouds. Off in the distance, flying into the east, were the lights of the small private jet, carrying Keonee and his team to New York. Will put his head in his hands.

"Keonee won" he said. "It's all over..."

"No, it's not," Redhawk said.

"He's on his way to New York right now to find the baby of this prophecy... To find *my* son! And when he does, he'll..."

"Adam is not in New York," Redhawk said. "Not anymore."

"How... how do you know?"

"Janae and I grew up together. We've always been close. When she was pregnant, she confided in me. She left him with her friend Sharice in New York, but told her to take the baby far away and to tell no one, not even her."

"Great. So nobody knows where they are?"

"I know." Redhawk smiled. "They're in Brazil."

Will sat up, baffled.

"What the... how the hell do you know?"

Redhawk's smile widened. "I'm pretty good at surveillance."

Will sat back and let that sink in. He began to laugh, a small chuckle at first, then a howling bellow. Redhawk joined in. When the laughter faded, Will looked at the other man in a new light.

"Thanks," Will said.

"You're welcome."

They sat in silence for another few moments.

"Don't think this means we're best friends now, or anything," Will said.

Redhawk laughed again. The two men sat on the mountaintop together, bruised and bloody and broken, but alive. Will gazed out at the grandeur of Mother Nature all around him, the unsurpassable beauty of it all. So much love, so much joy, so much good... and so much evil. Will Shaw's smile faded.

There was still so much work to be done.

ART GALLERY

Teoc

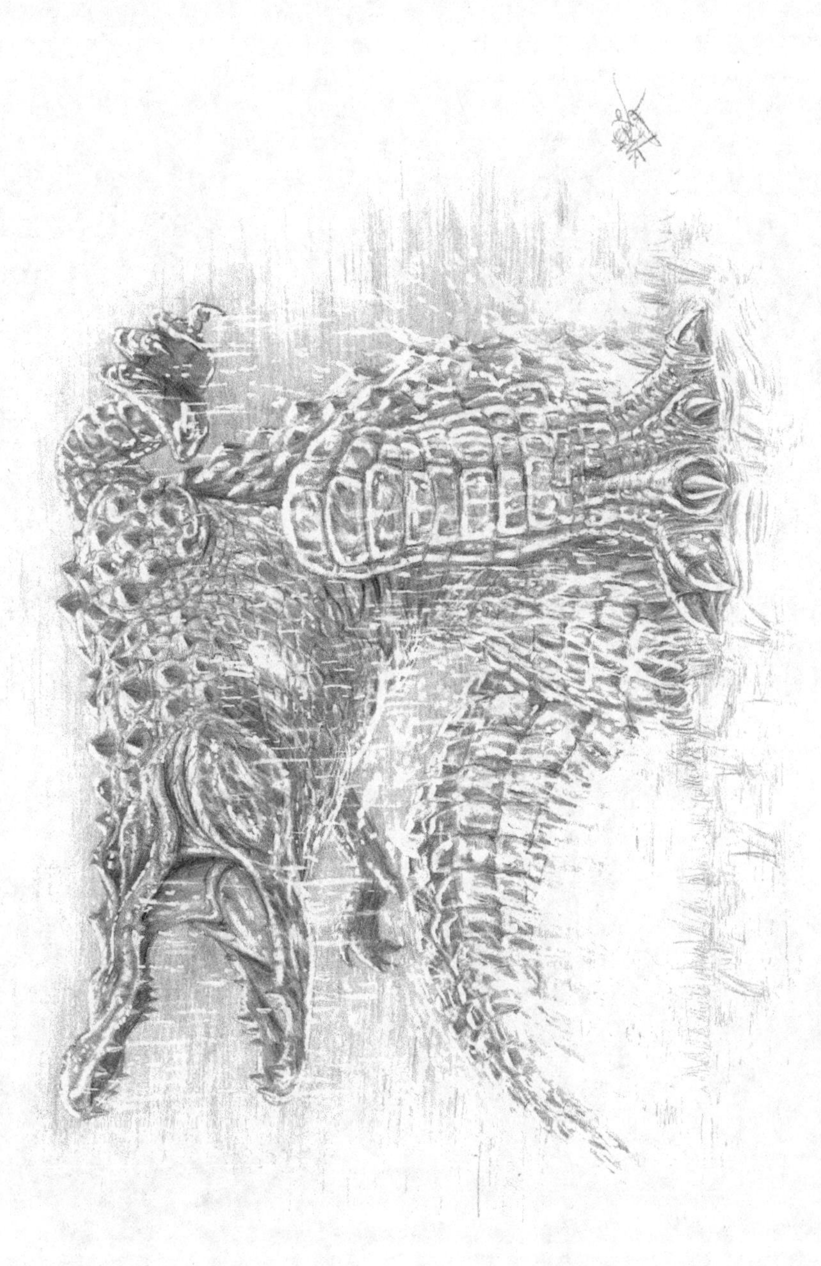

WILL SHAW RETURNS IN
THE JUNGLE
PRIEST
THE SKINNER SAGA
PART 3

Killer Queen
A *CASEY MADISON* SHORT STORY

CHATTANOOGA, *Tennessee*

BRI MADISON'S SUSPICIONS BEGAN ALMOST AS SOON as her daughter had come home from her weekend trip to Paradise Park. The scrapes and bruises on Casey's face, her anxious demeanor, her avoidance of eye contact. It wasn't like her. She explained that she'd fallen down some stairs while running to get in line for her favorite ride, and face-planted pretty hard on the pavement. She explained that she'd lost her phone and that's why she was not able to return her mother's calls or texts. Bri asked questions and Casey gave her answers. She had an answer for everything.

Still, those injuries. That evasive attitude. The Instagram photos that looked somehow fishy to the concerned mother, though she couldn't put her finger on it. The girl had also taken to wearing long-sleeve shirts in the house, which she almost never did, but on the second morning after her return, Bri caught a glimpse of Casey walking into the bathroom wearing a t-shirt. There were two large bruises on her arm.

"How did that happen?" Bri asked.

"Oh, from when I fell at the park."

403

A strange feeling began to churn in Bri Madison's stomach. A subtle nausea laced with pins and needles. Her mama-sense was tingling. Something was up, she knew it. Could taste it, smell it, that all-too familiar smell. Lies. Deception.

What is this little diva hiding? Bri thought.

With little recourse she turned back to the vacation photos, determined to figure out why they were bothering her. On her lunch break at the hospital she scrolled through Casey's posts on Instagram. Once again, something about them just didn't seem right, but it was so hard to see clearly on the small screen of her phone, even when zooming in. She turned to the comments. Most, including her own, were the usual expected well-wishes and exclamations.

"That looks like so much fun—OMG you guys are so cute—Have a great time" and others cheerfully added to the comments section. But then there were some other comments that stood out. *"Weak Photoshop skillz yo—Faaaaaake AF lol—Are these pictures AI?"* Bri felt her ire percolating along with a simultaneous sense of relief that no, it wasn't just her. She wasn't crazy. Bri processed this new information the rest of the day at work, chewing on it like a stale pizza crust. She glided through the hours, somehow finishing her tasks on auto-pilot, with only one thought in mind: get home, get to the computer.

The desktop iMac at home had a twenty-inch screen, so as soon as she was home from work and knew Casey was in her room, she went back to Instagram. Now, looking at her daughter's photos on the big screen, the artifice was evident. Each picture featured Casey and

Ieshia in a close or medium framing. Their clothes were different from shot to shot, but the lighting was always the same. While the directionality of the light changed in the images of the fun park behind them, the girls themselves were always lit from directly overhead.

Bri suddenly realized that she was grinding her teeth.

There was only one thing to do, and the phone was already in her hand before she finished the thought. She dialed the number for the one person she knew would give it to her straight, pacing around as the phone rang.

"Hey, Bri," Ieshia's mother answered cheerfully.

"Hi, Nicole. How's it going?"

"Girl, I am exhausted," the woman on the other end chuckled. "Long day. How you doing? What's going on?"

"Oh, I'm good, I just..." Bri searched for the words. "Y'know, just... I'm good. Uh, so... y'all have a good time at Paradise Park?"

"Oh yeah, it was a blast! Still recovering a bit, honestly."

"Yeah, I can imagine," Bri said, clearing her throat. "I, uh... I hope Casey didn't give you any trouble?"

Casey Madison was sprawled across her bed and watching UFC and Bellator highlight reels on her phone when her bedroom door flew open. Casey jolted to attention as her mother stormed inside, an iPad in her hand and fire in her eyes.

"Jesus, Mom! Don't you knock?"

"Oh, I'm sorry," Bri said, tapping her foot, "were you doing something secretive that I shouldn't know about?"

Casey sat up, assuming a defensive posture.

Oh no, she thought. *What is this now?*

"N-No. I was just playing on my phone..."

"Mm. Something secretive *on your phone* that I shouldn't know about," Bri said and swiped the device out of Casey's hand.

"Hey!" Casey said in protest, trying to grab it back. But Bri pulled away, casually beginning to scroll and search through the phone's files. "What are you doing?"

"I just want to look at more of your pics from last weekend," the young mother said. "It looks like you guys had so much fun! I just want to know more about it, that's all. You kind of glossed over it, didn't tell me all the details."

Oh God, no. Oh, shit shit shit shit. She knows. Oh God, she knows!

"It...It was great," Casey said, a weak offering.

"Go on."

"W-We went on a lot of rides... I had a hot dog. A-And ice cream. Mint chocolate-cranberry swirl. It was really good..."

"Mm. Sounds delicious."

"A-And we watched a movie in the hotel. And Ieshia's mom let us stay up late. And then the next day, that's when I fell and dropped my phone. And, uh... yeah."

"That sounds like quite a weekend! Ieshia's mom let ya'll stay up late?"

"Y-Yeah."

"That's interesting," Bri said, flexing the muscles in her jaw and slipping Casey's phone into her own pocket.

"Because I talked to Ieshia's mom a little while ago and she says you weren't with them at all last weekend."

Oh. My. God.

Casey's heart sank.

"I—I... uh, what? I mean... she what?"

"I know, pretty weird, right?" Bri said. She pulled up a chair and sat down, sliding forward until she and her trembling daughter were almost nose to nose. "Now, why don't we start again, and this time just tell me the truth?"

"M-Mom, really. I don't know what you're talking about. Of course I went with them to Paradise Park! Ieshia's mom is trippin' or something. C-Can I have my phone back pl—"

Bri slapped her hand onto the chair's armrest with force.

"Baby," Bri said, holding back a wellspring of anger with great difficulty, "I am trying here. Okay? I love you no matter what. But you gotta talk to me, Case."

"Mom, I swear!"

Bri suppressed a growl.

"Here, you see this?" she said, holding up her iPad.

"Your tablet?" Casey asked, not following.

Bri nodded and opened up the tablet, scrolling through the various programs and applications. Finding what she was looking for, she tapped on the icon and the app began to run.

"I have a lot of cool stuff on this thing," Bri said. "All my music, my contacts, video games, banking... Y'know, everything. Well, as a security measure, I installed this app called Device Tracker Plus. It's basically a GPS locator. Using this thing, I can find my cell phone or yours in about two seconds. See?" She held up the screen and Casey saw a digital illustration depicting her every movement over the weekend. "Pretty nifty, especially for a single mother with a beautiful, young teenage daughter. Don't you think?"

"M-Mom, I..." Casey was all out of excuses.

Bri slid in even closer.

"Now," she said, stern and authoritative. "Why don't we start *again*. This time tell me the *truth*. I want to hear all about your time in Cherokee, North Carolina. And please, don't leave out a single detail."

AFTER ONLY THE FIRST WEEK OF BEING GROUNDED for life, Casey was ready to burst. It wasn't just being on lockdown, not being allowed to go anywhere but school. It wasn't just the confiscation of her devices, like her computer or the TV in her room. No MMA classes, no hanging with any friends—Ieshia had also been grounded thanks to her—no form of communication or entertainment whatsoever. What stung the worst was the look in her mother's eyes. The coldness. The distrust.

Bars had been installed on every window in the house and a coded lock on both doors. She was a prisoner. The one person she could always turn to had turned against her. There were no hugs, no smiles. Now when Bri looked at her daughter, she saw only a stranger and a liar. The stories she'd told when put on the spot, those clunky, stuttering excuses did nothing but add insult to injury.

At first, Casey had insisted that the GPS program

was wrong before stumbling into a fabrication that involved one of her friends being abducted by an abusive stepfather and taken to Cherokee, and Casey secretly went to help. Bri wasn't buying it. Casey then reluctantly threw in the name Will Shaw, to add some verisimilitude to the tall tale. It was in fact Will who needed her help.

"Help with what?" her mother had asked.

That was were the excuses and explanations came to a grinding halt. Casey contemplated fabricating some whole story involving Will that would somehow seem plausible and justified to the outraged mother of a teenage girl. But there was nothing. Her mom wasn't stupid. And she couldn't hear the truth either. To be told her little girl was a shapeshifting monster, she would just laugh. And to see the proof with her own eyes, she would scream in horror.

"I-I'm sorry, Mom. I can't tell you any more."

"*What does a grown man need help with from a fourteen year-old girl?*"

"Mom, please. I can't, I—"

"Did he *touch* you? Did he... did he...?"

"No, Mom! I can't, okay? I'm sorry, I just ca—"

"You better start talkin' *right now*, young lady!" Bri suddenly caught herself, pulling that fire back in and trying a different approach. With tears brimming in her eyes, she stepped forward and reached out, tenderly touching her little girl's shoulders. "Casey Jade. You know you can tell me anything, right? *Anything*. I am your biggest fan, your number-one supporter. I love you more than my own life, baby. Whatever happened, whatever you did, I am on *your side*. Okay? Whatever this is, we can get through it together. You have nothing to be ashamed of. But you have to tell me, baby. You have to let me in..."

"Mom, no." Casey began to squirm from her mother's grip.

"You just need to..." Bri insisted, holding on.

"Mom, stop it!" Casey broke free and stepped back.

"God damn it!!"

Bri hadn't consciously wanted to hit the candle-stick, but then there was a sharp pain across her knuckles and the candle and its pewter base flew against the wall with a startling crash. Casey recoiled at the eruption, suddenly realizing she'd never seen her mother this furious. Before the tears could form, Casey bolted away to her room, slamming the door behind her.

Bri just stood there steaming. Crying. Heart breaking. She looked down at her hand and saw a small bead of blood leaking from her knuckle.

"Shit," she said and went to treat her injury.

During third period Algebra, Casey began to feel it again.

That strange and familiar tingling, that slight vibration. It could only mean one thing. She was having one of her 'episodes' as she liked to say, though her new term of choice that seemed to fit the experience better was 'glimpses.' She liked that one, as these visions of hers were often poetic and esoteric, never clear. She only got a glimpse. These experiences were intense, sometimes terrifying, and completely inconsiderate in their timing. *Damn it, not now!* she thought.

Casey gritted her teeth and gripped the edges of her desk tightly. She controlled her breathing as the feeling intensified, doing her best to appear calm and relaxed, letting neither her teacher nor her classmates have any idea of the amount of fireworks exploding in her head. She held on for the ride, her eyes seeing past the confines of her classroom and into a dark realm.

Underground tunnels. Concrete and filth.

Spider webs. Dripping water. Flies.

Her mother came around a corner, her face taut with confusion and fear. She looked left and right, lost. Casey ran to her side, but the girl was invisible to her.

"Mom!" Casey cried out, but Bri continued to stumble in the darkness.

A centipede slithered across the woman's bare toes and she recoiled with a yelp. Flies began to circle her like vultures. Bri plunged on through the dank hallways, her daughter chasing behind.

"Casey!" Bri called out as she swatted at the flies.

"Mom, I'm here! Mom!"

Her mother could not see her.

More flies and centipedes. Spiders and scorpions and earwigs.

Bri screamed and thrashed as the shadows came alive around her, thousands of tiny legs scuttling up onto her exposed flesh. With each swat and terrified shriek, their numbers doubled. Soon, she was completely covered with pincers and stingers and mandibles, her terrified screams muted by the crawling masses invading into the warm cavity of her mouth and throat. Bri fell to her knees as the legions of insects and arachnids swarmed over her.

"MOM!" CASEY SCREAMED OUT LOUD IN CLASS.

All eyes turned to the fourteen year-old. She was gasping for air, beads of cold sweat sprinkled across her face. Her teacher was aghast. Ieshia looked annoyed. Casey glanced around at their judgmental faces, some confused, others worried, others amused. None of them could ever understand.

Casey grabbed her bag and bolted for the door before her teacher could even finish asking if she was okay. Faces in the hallways were a blur. Before she knew it she was outside on the streets, sneakers pounding the pavement. She found her bus pass in her hand and put it to use.

It was the longest bus ride home of her life.

Her first thought was of course to call her mother, but she had no cell phone anymore. *What would I tell her anyway? 'Careful Mom, I had a dream where you were covered with insects. Just making sure you're okay.' Yeah, real good, Case.*

She tapped her feet nervously and gripped the handle beside her seat as the driver steered the electric bus leisurely through downtown Chattanooga. Her mom was working second shift that day, so she should still be home. *And she'll be fine. Everything will be fine.*

Once the bus stopped and its doors lurched open,

Casey flew out into the chilly fall air and hot-footed it down Market Street. With each racing step her heartbeat accelerated, her anticipation turning to dread. She had to get home before—no, she couldn't even think it. By the time she reached her front porch, Casey was gasping for air, her hands shaking as she pulled out her house keys.

"*Mom?*" Casey shouted as she hurried through the front door.

Bri's head immediately popped out from around the corner in the kitchen. She was on the phone, and a look of surprise and annoyance came across her face.

"*There* you are," Bri said, shaking her head, then returned to her call. "She's here. I'll call you back."

Casey came into the kitchen, noting that her mother looked perfectly fine, aside from not having her good wig on yet.

"Mom, are you okay?"

"I just got off the phone with Ms. Santos. Y'know, your guidance counselor? She said you started screaming and ran out in the middle of class." Bri stood with her arms folded, awaiting an explanation.

"I just... I had to make sure you were okay, that's all."

"Casey baby, what does that even *mean*? Why wouldn't I be okay?"

Mom, I'm not who you think I am. I've changed, and I'm part of something now, something I can't just get out of. I want to tell you, but I just can't. You could never understand, and if you knew the truth, you'd just think I'm a monster. You'd be afraid of me. And I don't want to lose you. You're all I got. I love you so much.

"I guess I just got scared," Casey finally said sheepishly.

Bri wasn't buying it.

"I'm about to go to work and *you* are going back to school," she said and pointed her finger. "And tomorrow you and I are going to sit down with Ms. Santos, and we're going to have a nice little talk."

The meeting was to take place during study hall the following day. Casey squirmed and fidgeted through her first few classes, unable to focus on the pedestrian knowledge her teachers peddled in vain. But unlike all the other disaffected teenagers not paying attention, her eyes were not dull and lifeless—they were on fire. They were the eyes of a young woman searching for answers.

I can't go to this stupid meeting, I just can't. Can't be in therapy talking about this shit! Come on! I can't ever answer Mama's questions, I just can't... And she'll never stop asking. She won't just give up. So what do I do, run away? Shit!

The decision was made quickly.

Instead of heading to the counselor's office after the bell, Casey snuck out the back door. It was a foolproof plan. *Run back home, pack a bag, leave Mom a note, go somewhere and hide a few days until I figure something out.*

She raced home, not even bothering to catch the electric bus. *Damn thing is slow AF anyway.* Her feet flew over the pavement as she dodged around pedestrians and took every shortcut she could find. She took the alley behind the old Choo-Choo museum and trotted the rest of the way into the residential area. Another few blocks and she would be home.

Casey's heart pounded and her eyes brimmed with tears. Once she left with a few belongings, she had no idea when she'd see her home again, or her mother. Her first thought was to call Will, but she still hadn't heard from him after the insanity at the Cherokee reservation. Her next thought was Shenandoah, and despite knowing for certain that the cop lady was on her side, she was also a strict mother herself. She wouldn't let Casey just hide out in her house while her own mother was worried sick.

Casey had no answers yet, but she was compelled to leave just the same.

She rounded the corner onto her block and saw her house. The driveway was empty, as expected. Her mother would be at the school now, probably just about to learn that Casey wasn't there. She didn't have long. She took out her keys as she trotted up the front pathway to her house.

Casey opened the front door and charged in.

Her mother sat at the kitchen table with another woman.

They were drinking coffee.

Casey's heart jumped up into her throat.

"I-I...uh...um..." Casey blubbered.

"Oh, there you are," Bri said calmly. "Ms. Santos and I have been waiting for you."

"Hello, Casey," the other woman said.

"Y-You're not Ms. Santos," Casey said.

The real Ms. Santos was young, chubby and sweet, never without a warm smile. This woman appeared to be in her mid-fifties and of South American origin. A wiry physique was accentuated by a form-fitting black suit. Her hair was black. Her face was pretty, yet severe. Her fingernails were black and pointed. The polite smile across her thin lips was measured, and her demure eyes betrayed no warmth. But there was something else about her, something Casey didn't notice at first. Suddenly, her heart dropped back down from her throat and fell into her stomach.

The woman was a skinner.

"Y-You're..." Casey suddenly found it hard to breathe.

"Baby, what are you talking about?" Bri asked. "What do you mean this isn't Ms. Santos?"

The woman in black stood up, her prim smile unwavering. Her skinner aura was dark and oily, with a shape Casey couldn't quite make out, though it was definitely insectoid. *Oh no, the glimpse!* Casey backed up, terrified. The woman followed her.

"Baby, what's going on?" Bri demanded, a feeling of confusion and dread filling her being. She watched as the unknown woman began talking to her teenage daughter, her posture suddenly threatening.

"We figured you'd bail on the meeting at school, Casey," the stranger said. "So we just waited here for you. Glad you showed up. I've been wanting to talk to you. I hope you'll be willing to cooperate."

"Wait, are you not Ms. Santos?" Bri asked. "Who are you? What the hell is going on? Hello, excuse me!"

"Please," Casey held her hands up, pleading. "Please, don't hurt my mother."

"I don't want to hurt anybody," said the woman as she circled the kitchen table and began to corner the girl. "Just tell me what I want to know and I'll be happy to leave... Where is Will Shaw, Casey?"

"Hey!" Bri said, crossing in front of the woman and getting right in her face. "You don't come in my house and threaten my daughter! Who the *fuck* do you think you are?"

"Mama, please..."

"You better start talking, bitch! Who the fuck are you?" Bri screamed.

"Do you want to tell her?" the woman said, a bemused smile curling her lips.

"P-Please stop it..."

"Where's Will, Casey?"

"Please, I don't know. I have no idea," Casey begged, her legs trembling.

Bri looked to her daughter for answers. "Baby, what is she talking about?"

"Tell her, Casey," the woman said, stalking forward. "Tell your mother what's going on. Tell her what you *are*."

"That's enough!" Bri said, accentuating her demand with a forceful shove.

Her hands barely made contact with the woman's shoulders when she felt an icy grip around her wrists and a violent snap that sent her reeling across the living room. Casey screamed as her mother sailed over the couch and crashed into the coffee table, finally colliding with the book shelf and being pummeled by the falling books, dvds, and framed family photos.

"Tell your mother everything, Casey," the woman said with venom in her breath. She stepped forward, towering over the shocked Bri Madison. The confused young mother watched in horror as the intruder's shape began to warp and fluctuate. "Tell her about you and Will Shaw," the woman continued, her harsh features melting away into something far more sinister. "Tell her about the child, about the prophecy. Tell her about all my friends that you *killed*."

Reality shifted around the menacing woman, replacing her soft, human form with something hard, black, and cold. Long, segmented legs unfolded, and huge pincers snapped where hands once were. Convex, black eyes bulged from the armored head, and whiskered-mandibles twitched and squirmed like sickly fingers to guide food into its horrible mouth. Raising high overhead, a segmented tail curved up like a menacing question mark, its deadly stinger aimed like a spear at the helpless young mother. The scorpion lurched forward.

Bri screamed in horror as the fiend loomed over her.

"*No!*" Casey charged ahead without thinking.

An armored leg sprouting with coarse hairs punched into the girl's chest and pinned her against a wall. A picture frame shattered behind Casey's head as she struggled to break free. But the beast was far too strong, easily holding her in place.

"Where is he?" the creature asked.

"P-Please! I don't know! He disappeared! I haven't heard from—"

The words were yanked from Casey's mouth as she felt herself flying across the room and crashing into the television. The wooden counter fractured and glass shattered. Casey yelped in pain as she crumpled into the corner, covered with debris. A trickle of blood ran down her forehead and pain was etched across her face.

With a demon from hell in her living room and the fabric of reality crumbling down around her, the only thing Bri Madison could see was her little girl in pain. In danger. As the black scorpion closed in on the child, the young mother didn't need to think before acting. She just jumped up and grabbed a chair.

"Get away from my baby!!"

Smashhh!! The chair splintered on the creature's back.

Whirling around in anger, the monster dropped Casey and centered its soulless eyes on her mother. Casey slid to the floor, the wind knocked out of her. She watched helplessly as the beast closed in on its new target.

Bri clutched the broken leg of what was left of her chair, waving it desperately in the face of the approaching devil. Tears streamed down her face as she made her futile stand, defiantly remaining on her feet despite her nervous system sending shockwaves through her legs and reducing them to gelatin.

"Our father... who art in Heaven..." Bri began.

The scorpion did not let her finish. It shot out a powerful claw and clamped the deadly pincer around Bri Madison's wrist. She screamed in agony and dropped her weapon as the bones in her wrist shattered like breadsticks. Her legs gave out and her body sagged, but the monster held its grip on the ruined hand, holding her up.

It leered down at her, eyes glassy and black.

It lifted its horrible tail up high, ready to spear the helpless prey.

"Deliver... us... from evil..." Bri closed her eyes.

The stinger shot down into Bri's chest, pumping its sizzling neurotoxin into her. Hot torture shot through her veins as the venom spread quickly, burning and swelling the soft tissues before leaving them numb and paralyzed. The scorpion released its prey, letting her crumple to the floor and convulse.

"Don't worry," it said, closing in on Bri, mandibles dripping. "You'll be numb when I start eating your face off. You'll barely even feel it..."

Bri gasped and tried to scream as the horrible mouth unfolded.

"*NOOO!!!*"

The scorpion lurched off balance as another creature blurred across the room and leapt on its back. The beast had a spotted coat the color of corn in the sun, long teeth and claws, a lashing tail, and furious, amber eyes. Casey dug her claws into the gaps in the scorpion's shell and tried ripping into the vital organs beneath.

The destruction of the Madison home began.

With a scream like the buzzing of a hornet's nest, the scorpion skinner thrashed wildly as the young cheetah fought to hang on. Picture frames, furniture, lamps, windows and walls, the battling creatures smashed through it everything. Casey dodged the lethal stinger as it jutted forward, stabbing violently at her. The cat lost her grip and slid, and the scorpion snatched her up in its claws.

Like a pitcher throwing a fastball, the monster whipped Casey through the air and sent her crashing into the refrigerator, denting the stainless steel doors. It pounced after her, lashing pincers and stinger at the cat as she dodged each strike. Dishes, glasses, pots and pans, everything was flying around and crashing in the cacophony of aggression. Casey tried to kick and scratch, but her short claws were no match for that armor. Instead, she found the large cast-iron skillet laying amongst the mess and gripped it like a hammer.

The cheetah launched her own attack, slashing wildly with the heavy weapon. The impact from the blows drove the fiend back, and Casey continued on the offensive, doing her best to crack through that hard, black shell. Back and forth they danced, striking and dodging, biting and clawing. Casey fought valiantly, but the black arachnid was too big and strong. It swatted the iron skillet away and knocked the cat into the staircase. Casey snarled in pain, refusing the give up.

Bri watched the whole thing.

She lay there on her back in a pile of rubble, blood dribbling from her mouth, cold paralysis spreading through her body. There before her eyes were two monsters, an armored, black demon from hell... and a cat. The feline was like nothing she'd ever seen; neither cat nor human, but the extraordinary spirit of both merged as one. The cheetah glanced over at Bri for a split second and their eyes met.

All of Bri Madison's questions were answered in that moment.

She watched her daughter, somehow transformed into this majestic beast, battling the menacing, oily arachnid. Pincers slashed at the golden coat of the cat, and blood flowed. Drywall smashed and crumbled. A fire began to flicker in the kitchen. The world was crumbling down around her as the numbness began to run through her shoulders and into her arms.

"Where is Will Shaw, bitch?"

"Fuck you!"

The scorpion swatted Casey away and the young cat crumpled to the floor, defeated. All eight legs scuttled over the ruins of the Madison house, propelling the monster back into the living room where Bri lay fighting for her life.

"You won't tell me? Maybe you'll tell mommy!"

A black claw reached for Bri to yank her up, but Casey was up in a flash, bloodied and bruised and exhausted. She exploded her feet down and shot herself forward like a bullet riding a bolt of lightning.

As long as my heart is beating. As long as there is air in my lungs.

You will not touch my mother again.

Casey collided into the massive scorpion before it could deliver its next strike. The cat roared ferociously, clawing at the black eyes, but the monster swatted her back and they continued to exchange blows as the fire consumed the kitchen and began spreading into the house.

The scorpion flung Casey into the kitchen island.

She hissed as the room burned around her. Scrambling back to her feet in a pile of rubbish and ruin, she saw a large carving knife and scooped it up. With a roar of fury, she charged in again at the enemy, wielding the knife. A cheetah's claws are not long and sharp like a jaguar's or a leopard's; they're short and don't retract. More designed for running than slicing and dicing.

Focusing herself and using her speed, Casey lunged at the monster with the knife. It dodged and struck back, but Casey dodged as well, remembering to use proper footwork and head movement. Suddenly she was back on the mats, having a nice sparring session with Will, going through the motions.

The scorpion slashed out with a claw, and Casey ducked under.

She shot forward, getting up close, and whipped the knife up into the scorpion's bulging, black eye. The creature shrieked and violently lurched as its eyeball popped, and a clear goo began oozing out. Casey stumbled back and dropped the knife as the angry beast thrashed around in agony, blinded and pissed off.

Now injured and choking on smoke, the scorpion woman decided she'd had enough, and leapt for the front windows. In a blur of motion and a shattering of wood and glass and iron, the monster smashed through the front wall and windows, ripping through the newly installed security bars like they were nothing, staggering off outside and disappearing from sight.

I need to act fast.

She ran through the smoke and flames to her mother's side. Bri looked up at the young cheetah in awe and wonder. Casey delicately crouched down beside her mother, scooping her up into her lap. Bri's head rested in the cat's large, padded paw. She looked up into the deep, amber eyes of her daughter and tears rolled down her cheeks. With her arms going numb, she struggled to raise her hand to touch Casey's face.

Her trembling fingers caressed the cat's cheek, running through whiskers and soft, golden fur. She smiled. This was no strange creature, no monster. This was her baby girl. Bri opened her mouth and fought to speak.

"You're... so... beautiful."

Casey cried as her mother stroked her face.

The house was blooming with angry flames and black smoke. This was no time to weep, she knew she had to move.

Scooping her mother up into her arms, the cheetah kicked the sofa and a pile of burning rubble aside. She ran for the gaping hole in the front wall and in a moment they were outside on the front lawn. Fresh air, broad daylight. The neighbors were all still at work at this hour, so no one was on the streets yet, though the sounds of sirens in the distance were fast approaching.

Casey sagged down onto her knees once she'd reached the edge of the lawn, away from the roaring inferno. The cause of this misery was nowhere in sight and seemed to have fled for the time being. But for now, all she could think of was her mother. She closed her eyes and relaxed, let herself slip away into that relaxing void.

Light and shadows warped around the cat until there was nothing left but a teenage girl holding her mother.

Casey opened her eyes and looked down. Bri's eyes were closed. She didn't appear to be breathing.

"Mom? Mama?... *Mama?*"

She shook her mother's shoulders and called out for her again and again. It was no use. She was gone. Casey screamed. And screamed. She screamed as onlookers came to watch and she screamed as the fire trucks arrived and she screamed as they took her mother away.

Her world was shattered. Casey didn't know anything anymore. She didn't know where she would stay or what would happen. But as first responders began to lead her away, her fists balled up tightly, her eyes burned with rage, and she knew with perfect clarity what she must do. Somewhere in the world was a woman with one eye, and it was now Casey's job to find her and kill her.

Your ass is mine, bitch.

Jesse D'Angelo is an author and illustrator, born in New York, raised in California, and currently residing in Tennessee with his wife and son. He is a veteran of the film and television industries and has also worked with law enforcement as a sketch artist on multiple criminal investigations.

When not writing books about horrible monsters and brutal serial killers, he spends his time changing diapers, scooping cat litter, and trying to avoid other human beings to the best of his ability.